Curse of

Darkness

A DARK COURT RISING NOVEL

BEC MCMASTER

Curse of Darkness
ISBN: 978-1-925491-77-7

Cover: Gene Mollica
Editing: Hot Tree Edits and Olivia Ventura
Proofread: Julie K

To obtain permission to excerpt portions of the
text, please contact the author at
www.becmcmaster.com

✣ Created with Vellum

MAP OF

ARCAEDIA

DARK COURT
RISING
SERIES

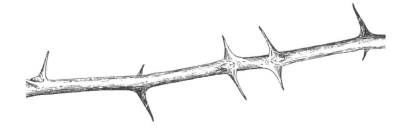

I would wait for you in the Darkness...

would wait for you in the Darkness."

"I   I stare at the enormous pyre waiting to be lit, and suddenly I can't move.

My heart doesn't skip a beat. There is no lump in my throat, threatening to choke me. I am simply dead inside, my chest scooped out and empty, waiting to be filled.

"Your Majesty," says Maia's high priestess.

It sounds like it comes from miles away.

All I can see is the empty pyre where my husband's body *should* lie.

There is nothing to burn.

When we were forced to flee from the Black Keep—and the newly risen Horned One—Thiago was already dead. I see him falling again and again—I see it every night in my nightmares. And I hear the sound his head made as it struck the slate floors. A sharp crack he wouldn't have even felt because he was already *gone*, and yet it splintered my heart and cleaved it open.

I'll never feel him in my arms again.

I'll never wake to see his smile.

I will never—

"Mama?" whispers a little voice and then a hand slips inside my own.

There's the fist to the solar plexus. There's the knife to the heart. Suddenly, it's beating again, all for her. Amaya is the only thing tethering me to this mortal plane at the moment. Her hand is warm, so warm. Warm where his is cold.

I reel out of the nightmare, realizing thousands of faces watch us.

This grassy knoll overlooking the city is where the people of Evernight honor their dead. I never expected to be here staring at Thiago's funeral pyre, even though his body doesn't lie upon it.

It burned to ash in the implosion of the Horned One's Hallow.

I'd like to think the entire city turned out to honor their

prince, but though thousands of them crowd around the base of the hill, not all of them welcomed him as their ruler. Some of them say he slew their rightful queen and over-threw her sons, and I want to scream the truth to the skies —that he was Queen Araya's last-born son and he honored his mother to the very end.

But that was not my secret to reveal.

As much as I want to draw the curtains that shroud his mother's portrait so the people can *see* the truth—that Thiago was their rightful prince and worthy of their respect —I will not spit upon his final wishes.

"It's fine, Amaya. I'm fine," I whisper, squeezing my daughter's hand. A part of me didn't want her to be here for this—I want to protect her from every danger and ounce of pain I can—but again, it isn't my choice to make.

She's nearly nine years old, and I've only known of her existence for a week.

I will not lock her away from the world.

I will not shroud her in secrets and lies.

She will never know what it feels like to peer through closed windows at the world, wondering what she did wrong.

And when I asked if she wished to be here for this cere-mony, she gave a solemn little nod and said, "Yes."

"*I never knew him,*" she whispered, "*but I would like to say goodbye.*"

Her choice. Always her choice.

"Your Majesty, if you would light the pyre?" the high priestess says, and it sounds like she's repeating herself.

"My queen." Finn offers me the torch, and in his eyes I

3

see an echo of the pain that clutches my heart in its falcon claws.

I don't need it.

I could set the pyre alight with a thought, and yet, this is symbolic.

Baylor bows.

Eris nods grimly to me, one hand resting on the hilt of her sword as she kneels. They're all here—the circle of friends that stood at Thiago's side during life and who stand here now, ready to guard my daughter and me.

And then the entire city goes to its knees.

All except Thalia, who awaits me at the bonfire, gowned in black.

She holds her hands out for Amaya, giving her a tremulous smile. "He would have been so very proud of you, my darling," she whispers, drawing my daughter into her arms.

I'm not the only one grieving. As his cousin, she knew him best, after all.

I steel myself, staring out over the crowd. "We come here today to honor our prince, who gave his life so his daughter could live. We come here today to send him swift flight on the winds. We come here today to sing him into the... the...."

I can't say it.

"I would wait for you in the Darkness" come his words again, for he knew his soul was not bound for the Bright Lands.

"To sing him into the Bright Lands," Thalia says, taking my hand and squeezing it. "We come here today to share our love of him and praise the honor of his deeds in life."

The priestess of Maia starts chanting, and the crowd joins in.

"*Praise Maia. Bless this soul and sing him into the Bright Lands....*"

All I have to do is set the pyre alight.

I lower the torch, and a flicker of flame licks at the dry tinder. It spreads hungrily, but it's not enough.

I want it to *burn*.

Flames lick at the oak. It leaps from log to log and an inferno suddenly roars. Heat scorches the tears from my face as I stare blankly into the flames.

"*Child?*" It's a whisper stirring through my scattered thoughts, a tug from the leyline beneath the castle. "*Can you hear me?*"

An ancient mind turns toward mine, trying to connect with me through my link to the Hallow in the castle.

It's not the first time the Mother of Night has tried to contact me this week.

"*Leave me alone,*" I tell her, ripping my thoughts away from the leyline. "*I want nothing more to do with you.*"

* * *

"Once upon a time there was a wicked prince," I whisper, turning the pages of the book for Amaya. It's the only time I've been able to escape the indescribable crush of emotion. "And he was very—"

A knock raps at the door.

My fingers pause on the page. I've barely set foot outside these chambers in days. Nobody would dare disturb us for any simple reason. Not in our grief. I want to

5

ignore it. I'm not ready to face the outside world. I just want to stay here with Amaya and pretend the world will forget me.

"My queen?" Finn's voice calls through the door. He hesitates. "A rider arrived twenty minutes ago at the gates insisting he needs to see you."

I close the book with a snap. "Is it someone from the war camps?"

"No. I—"

"Is it urgent? Is it a matter of life and death?"

Another hesitation. "He won't speak to me. He won't speak to any of us. He just says he needs to talk to you."

"Then take care of it," I snap.

"I think you'll want to see him too."

I don't want to see *anyone*. Can I not have just one more day of peace?

It's a selfish thought. I'm the queen of Evernight now and we're at war with my mother's kingdom. I can't let Thiago down. I can't let his people down.

You don't have the luxury of grief.

But the intrusion feels like a knife dragging through the ragged remains of my chest.

"Will you be all right?"

Amaya looks at me, and I see *his* eyes in her heart-shaped face. "I'll stay here," she says, "and play with Grimsby."

I know the grimalkin watches over her from the shadows, but he's been scarce since the ordeal at Black Keep. He lied to me. He said he couldn't see past that moment in time when I would hold my daughter in my arms but he *knew* that one of us would fall. He knew the Horned One would be unleashed upon the world, and only the sacrifice of a powerful fae could destroy the bindings that trapped the Horned One within his prison world.

I'd expected it to be me.

But Grimm had admitted he saw my husband fall.

The grimalkin's bound to Amaya as her familiar. I can't stop him from appearing when I'm not around. Indeed, as much as I want to wring his furry little neck, there's a part of me that knows he's the best companion she could ever have—he would give his life to save her, and grimalkin are powerful foes.

Nothing can enter this room and hurt her without going through Grimm.

"I'll be back," I promise, "and we'll finish the story later."

The second I open the door, it's like being splashed in the face with a bucket of ice water. Our rooms are my refuge, but out here it feels like the whole world is rushing at me, and right now, I don't have the heart to deal with it.

"Who is it?"

Its only when Finn flinches that I realize how sharp my voice is.

"It's your stepbrother." Finn blows out a breath. "I never thought I'd say this, but I think you need to talk to him. He's in the audience chamber. Eris is standing guard."

Edain.

I was wrong. I do still have a heart.

Because it plummets toward my feet.

"You let him *inside* the castle?" I take off toward the audience chamber at a run. I've told them how dangerous he is. He's both my mother's lover and her assassin.

7

"Eris won't let him out of her sight!" Finn yells behind me.

As dangerous as Eris is, I don't truly know the extent of Edain's powers.

Or what he wants.

The only reason he could be here is if my mother has heard of Thiago's death and wants to destroy what is left of Evernight. Isn't it?

* * *

I burst through the audience chamber doors, slamming them open so hard they crash against the walls.

Finn brushes past me, one hand on his sword hilt. "Let me go first!"

But every inch of rage within me dies when I see the male kneeling by the dais.

We stare at each other, and I'm not so lost in grief that I don't see the change in Edain's demeanor. Once he was a pet leopard, leashed at my mother's feet. Once he wore silk robes that revealed a healthy slice of his chest, with glittering rings on his fingers and a curved dagger at his hip. To look at him was to see sex and sin and all manner of wicked vices.

None of that remains.

Instead, a stranger tilts his head back, his shirt ripped and stained and his black hair raked back off his face. There's a sheath at his hip, but no knife, and claw marks leave dried blood on the back of his hands.

Old blood.

My steps slow. "What do you want?"

If he mentions Thiago's death, I swear I'll kill him.

Instead he tips his chin up, wincing a little in the light. "I have nowhere else to go. Your mother's cast me out—"

"And you thought you would be welcome *here*?"

Silence settles over the room like a mantle.

The stiffness leaches out of Edain's shoulders. "No. I did not think I would find welcome. I wouldn't have come if I weren't desperate." There's a hint of his old bite in his voice as he meets my gaze once more. "You didn't ask why your mother cast me out."

I should have. I'm not thinking as clearly as I once did.

Edain is my mother's pet.

A toy, in her eyes. Her dearest weapon.

My mother would never discard such a weapon when he was so useful. She would forgive him murder. She would forgive him any lie. She would forgive him almost any betrayal except for the one I once taunted him with.

"Where's Andraste?" I whisper, ice settling in my heart, in my soul, in the room. It suddenly sheets across the audience chamber floors, plunging the temperature of the room to arctic levels. "Where is my sister?"

"Vi!" Finn skids on the ice.

It's everywhere.

I've been able to shield the world from my burgeoning powers, but I can't control this. I can't control the rage that ignites my magic. Where once there was heat and flame, now there's only ice.

Because ice doesn't hurt.

Ice has no heart.

"Your sister is gone," Edain says, pushing to his feet and shifting warily as hoarfrost creeps up the walls. "Your

9

mother discovered Andraste had a hand in stealing her crown and giving it to you. She wanted to punish her—"

"What did Mother *do*?" I would know if my sister was dead. I would know. Wouldn't I?

"Your mother sent her north to the goblin clans." Finally, I know why his eyes look so fucking wretched. "She's to be the bride of the goblin king. And I can't rescue her by myself."

Chapter Two

Iskvien

"**B**ride?" Dubiousness fills Finn's voice as we all gather in the council chamber Thiago used to brief his circle of confidantes. "It's been a long time since the goblins came looking for brides within the alliance."

I wrap my arms around myself as I stand by the window staring out over Ceres. I know what Finn's not saying. The goblin clans haunt the mountains north of Evernight, though they keep to themselves. They struck an ancient treaty with our people citing peace, and while they despise both the seelie and unseelie, to break the peace means to spit in the eyes of their ancestors.

It doesn't mean there haven't been incursions.

The goblin clans are wild and unruly. They were once ruled by a long line of stern kings, but the last king was murdered, and the clans tore themselves apart, with his heirs proclaiming themselves "kings" left and right.

It's been over fifty years since the last king died. Edain said Andraste was to be the bride of the goblin king, but which one?

How many of these false kings remain?

And does this mean war with the north too?

"Your mother said she didn't care what they did to Andraste," Edain says, heat flaring in his blue eyes, "as long as they claimed she was legally wed. She knows Andraste is popular within her court and wants to make a fuss about the great 'sacrifice' your sister is making for her people."

"My mother wants to trap Evernight between the goblins and her own armies." I push away from the windows. If she's used this to make a truce with the horde, we're as good as dead. The goblins outnumber us five-to-one.

The only reason the Seelie Alliance was able to push them back was because we worked together, and with the alliance between the five southern kingdoms as good as shattered, there's nothing to stop the goblins from striking south. Nothing more than an ancient treaty with a long-dead king.

What is Mother *thinking*?

If one of these potential kings can capture a fae bride and destroy a fae kingdom, then thousands of goblins will flock to his cause. They're hungry for conquest, and while many of them will respect our treaty, others will yearn for war and plunder. Whoever this king is, he's effectively taking the ancient crown of the goblins and settling it firmly on his head.

But to keep it there....

To keep his stolen crown....

It won't stop at Evernight. It can't. He must offer them more. More war. More plunder. He has to promise them victory. Asturia is the next kingdom beyond us, and if Mother thinks this king will restrict himself to waging war upon my people, then she's truly lost her mind.

"Which king was she promised to?" Eris demands.

"Urach of the Black Hand."

Her dark skin goes ashen. The sight of it makes my stomach drop. *Eris* is afraid. Eris—who makes entire armies sweat in fear when they know they're facing her—actually *pales*.

"What's wrong?" I demand.

Eris rubs the knuckles of one hand into the palm of her other. "Urach's been gaining followers for years. He bears only a drop of the royal bloodlines, but with the true heir in exile, there's no one to deny him. Thalia's been keeping an eye on him. He's ruthless. Cruel. Ambitious." She meets my gaze. "If Urach decides to crush Evernight then we don't have the might to face him. The only thing that has kept him off our back has been the presence of the true heir. Urach hasn't dared attack us when Raith and his followers

13

are out there somewhere at his back." She closes her eyes. "And he didn't dare face Thiago."

But Thiago is gone.

And now I'm the only thing standing between the goblins and complete annihilation.

An untried queen.

A grieving queen.

One who can barely control her magic.

I turn back to the map of Unseelie, sucking in a sharp breath as I eye the unconquerable mountains that loom to the north of Evernight. There's a knot in my chest—a heavy weight that threatens to drown me—but I can't let them see it. I have to be strong in this moment. I have to make sure they can't see my panic. My doubt....

What in the Darkness's name am I going to do?

"If he comes, then we will face him. We have a queen," Finn says quietly, "one who is bound to the lands and the Hallow."

I stare at that fucking map. All those little red and gold figures that represent my mother's armies, marching upon the Firenze river—the natural barrier between our lands. There are no little figures in the mountains. Until now, we haven't needed to add them, but with the goblins in play, I guess we'll have to find the set that represents them.

And then there's Blaedwyn's banners beyond them—the unseelie queen I tricked and stole from.

Queen Maren of Aska to the southwest. No friend of mine.

Lucere of Ravenal beyond my mother—the princess who once thought to marry my husband before I "took" him from her, even though she never truly had him.

old arrogance rising. "I'm not here to play games, Vi. I'm finally free of that bitch—"

"I find it difficult to believe my mother simply cast you aside." Without a tether, he's a dangerous weapon.

"She didn't simply set me free. But...."

"What?"

A muscle in his jaw ticks. "She gave me one last twisted little gift. Besides, there's more I haven't told you." He takes a deep breath and looks at me. "Are you ready?"

Ready for what?

What more could my mother do to me?

"I'm almost afraid to ask," I admit.

Edain squares his shoulders like he's facing an onrush of cavalry from an opposing force all by himself. "Apparently your mother kept some secrets even from me, although I believe your sister was aware of this one." His lips press thinly together. "I don't like you. We've never been friends but believe me when I say that this... this was wrong."

This coming from my mother's assassin?

"Tell me."

Little thorns creep across the floor, circling him. It's not quite a threat, but if he dares make a move, I'll kill him.

"During one of the years when your mother stole your memories, you birthed a child," he grates out. "She'd be a little girl of about eight or nine now...."

I can't breathe. *Amaya.*

Instantly, there's a knife at his throat. Eris bares her teeth. "Who did you send? Vi, this has to be a decoy. Finn?"

"On it!" Finn bolts toward the door.

For all that I've never been fond of my stepbrother, I

have to concede he's brave enough to look her in the eye as if she doesn't hold his life in her hands. "What's going on?"

I raise my hand, and the doors slam in Finn's face.

Something's not right here.

And if anyone is stealing into Amaya's rooms, they're going to be very surprised to meet Grimm.

"Who else is here in the castle? Who did my mother send?" I stalk toward him as my thorns circle his boots, curling up his calves. "If you lie to me, I promise I will make this so slow you'll beg for my mother's mercy."

They circle his throat, and Edain finally breaks a sweat as he lifts his chin and stares at me wild-eyed. "There's no one else in the castle. I came alone. Mother of Night, Vi. What the fuck is going on?" His gaze darts between us, and then his eyes narrow. "I just told you that you have a daughter.... But you.... You *know* you have a daughter?"

One of my thorns strokes across his lips and he freezes.

"My mother stole my memories, but they've been returning. Yes, I know."

"And you just left her there?" he explodes.

Wait. Andraste claimed she swapped the babies at birth and sent my daughter to live with Old Mother Hibbert in secret. But he wouldn't know that. Which means... "My mother has a little girl with her, doesn't she?"

He nods, pushing a curious bramble aside. "Can you fucking call them off?"

It's not a threat against Amaya.

I wave my thorns to retreat and they skitter back to the crevices they've made in the stone floors.

"Eris."

Eris slowly lowers the blade and arches a brow at me.

18

Everything happened so quickly. We discovered the truth about Amaya and set off to rescue her, but I've been so shrouded in grief ever since that I haven't thought through the repercussions.

My mother has a little girl at her side who she thinks is her granddaughter.

An innocent orphan who was switched with my child.

Oh, fuck.

The doors to the room suddenly open.

I swing toward them, then freeze when Amaya steps inside the room, hugging Grimm under the shoulders so his body drapes toward the floor. He looks about as pleased at this as I can imagine he'd be, but he suffers it.

"Amaya." What is she doing here?

I shoot a sharp look at Grimm.

"*This was not my idea,*" he replies, his voice imprinting itself in my mind.

"*Clearly.*" This is a catastrophe. "Amaya, you're not supposed to leave our rooms—"

"Amaya?" Edain barks, staring at her.

"I know, Mama," she says, her eyes locking on Edain. "But she told me I needed to be here. I had to meet him."

"*She?*"

Amaya bites her lip. "The woman in the hood."

Breathlessness punches through me. Thousands of fae wear hoods, but I know exactly who she's talking about. I've been blocking the Mother of Night from my thoughts, and she dared contact my daughter instead.

That bitch. That fucking bitch.

I turn toward the Hallow, but Finn grabs my wrist. "Later," he urges.

19

And he's right.

I need to deal with this here and now.

Because Edain gapes at my daughter as if she's a two-headed puppy.

"She said you'd be angry," Amaya says, stroking Grimm's fur. "but he needed to know. He's going to help us."

Edain staggers back against the table. "Who is this? *What* is this? Is this a trick?"

"It's not a trick." What is the Mother of Night thinking? "This is my daughter, Amaya. And if you dare breathe a word of this...."

"He won't," Eris says confidently. "I can ensure he never so much as speaks her name."

Finn cracks his knuckles. "Dungeons?"

"Dungeons," Eris confirms.

"This is what she meant," Edain says breathlessly. "Andraste's last words to me were to protect May. She said she was innocent. Andraste knew. She knew there were two of them." He blinks in horror. "How are there two of them?"

Can I trust him?

The Edain I know is the watchful leopard who stalks my mother's court. He plays the whore, but there's no mistaking there's a sharp mind behind those vicious blue eyes.

"Andraste switched the babies at birth. I begged her to protect my daughter, and so she found a way to ensure my mother never got her hands on Amaya. The other child is a changeling. An orphan she found days after Amaya was born."

Mother would never have killed Amaya—she has too much potential to cause me damage in Mother's eyes—but I know what my daughter would have suffered through if she was raised in my mother's care.

She promised she would raise Amaya to despise her father and know him for the monster she calls him.

She promised she would turn Amaya against everything my husband and I stood for.

She would poison the girl's thoughts, poison her magic, her soul....

She would turn her into a weapon to be used against us.

Edain closes his eyes and breathes out. "Sometimes I wonder if I knew your sister at all. All these years and she's been working against the queen."

It's a feeling I've known too. Once upon a time I loved my sister, but she made it clear she sided with my mother when I first fell in love with Thiago. I'd thought her the enemy too, only to discover she's been twisting my mother's thoughts and actions for years.

"The perfect daughter," I whisper.

His eyes meet mine. "The perfect façade. But she stretched too far. She lost control of the game. Your mother found out everything. And now she will pay."

Unless we can get her back.

"She had a message for you," Amaya says, cocking her head as she considers Edain. "She made me repeat it several times so I'd remember."

"She?" He looks toward me, still a little wild-eyed.

"The Mother of Night."

"Well, fuck," he whispers, sinking into a chair at the table and sliding his hands down his face.

21

"Language," Eris growls.

Edain peers between his fingers at Amaya. "My apologies, Princess." Steeling himself, he asks softly, "What did she want you to tell me?"

"To truly know love, you must first lose it," Amaya repeats carefully. "To truly know hope you must walk in darkness. To finally find peace you must look in the most unexpected place. Your curse will never be broken. This is your payment due. But you will find re...re...." She suddenly winces and mouths a few words. "I get a little confused here. Remption?"

"Redemption?" Finn asks.

"Yes!" Amaya beams at him. "You will find redemption if you choose to walk this path, and with it, a second chance. Does that make sense?"

The color bleeds from Edain's olive skin. "It makes perfect sense."

"She cursed you?" Of course Mother cursed him. She would never have let him live through this betrayal if she couldn't somehow twist the knife. "What did she curse you with?"

His blue eyes turn flat and hard. "That is one thing I will keep to myself, if you don't mind."

It's the one thing that makes me realize he's speaking the truth and can be trusted.

She cursed him.

She cast him aside, and she cursed him—and whatever she did to him, she knows it is worse than death, because my mother doesn't believe in mercy.

"This is a nightmare. Right now, Mother thinks she has

my daughter. She'll"—I shoot a glance toward Amaya—"Not be happy if she realizes the truth."

"And everyone saw Amaya at the rites," Thalia says quietly. "Somewhere in this city, Adaia will have a spy or two. We can't hide this."

"She has her spies," Edain confirms.

If I don't do something then a little girl might die.

A little girl who is innocent of all of this.

"Vi." Eris slowly shakes her head as if she can see exactly where my thoughts lead. "We can't attack Hawthorne Castle. Without him...."

Without Thiago, nobody is powerful enough to defeat my mother.

"The castle's locked up tighter than a vault," Edain says. "You can't get in. I don't think even I can get in." And he looks away, shielding himself from my stare. "And if we don't rescue your sister.... Adaia gave Urach her permission to do whatever he wanted with her."

I want to be sick.

I don't have time to give into my feelings, however.

"The rites were this morning. She won't have received word about Amaya yet." *Would she?* "But Mother will expect an attack the second we receive word of... May's existence. If we don't make some sort of move...."

I pinch the bridge of my nose. She won't know what's happening at first. She'll wonder, who is the child at my side? Is it a trick, meant to distract her? Am I playing games? Which child is the real child?

But she's not a fool, and she knows my sister betrayed her.

23

She'll put the orphan child—this *May*—through one of her little tests.

The heat fades from my face. No child should have to suffer through that. If the girl has a little magic, she might pass.

But if she doesn't....

I have to rescue May.

I can't attack Hawthorne Castle. I don't have the strength; I'm barely functioning myself—

And then it hits me.

The one person who might be able to get into Hawthorne Castle unscathed. He bragged about it after all.

I turn toward Eris. "Send for the Prince of Shadows."

Chapter Three

Iskvien

"You want me to do *what*?"

The Prince of Shadows kneels on one knee before the dais, looking as though his obeisance is a matter of choice and not merely respect. Theron's long, silky-dark hair falls down his spine like a spill of black water, two thin strands gathered back from his face and braided at the back—just enough to keep it out of his face.

A hint of stubble roughens his jaw, and he wears a white silk shirt and tight leather breeches, with boots that hit his knees. Golden rings glitter on his fingers. A gleaming ruby is stabbed through his ear.

He's the very picture of a rich, somewhat spoiled merchant prince.

But the black tattoos that crawl up his throat belong to no merchant, and for a second, a blood moon appears in the writhing mass of thorns and wolves, so that it almost looks like the wolves on his throat howl at it.

The blood moon is a mark of the assassin guild in the city.

The Prince of Shadows helped us once. For a price. But as I stare into Theron's eyes, I realize I might be asking more than he will give.

Thiago held him in check, but I'm merely a grieving queen—and from the assassin's point of view, probably a liability if he ties his fate to mine.

"I want you to steal inside Hawthorne Castle and rescue a little girl for me," I repeat loudly and clearly, my spine straightening as I sit on the throne. It's something Mother taught me.

It doesn't matter if your heart is trembling or tears seek to overwhelm you. It doesn't matter if there's a knife to your throat, or one buried in your heart.

You don't let your weaknesses show.

"A little girl?" Theron looks incredulous, pushing to his feet and taking a step toward me—a move which is abruptly aborted as Eris puts her sword to his throat.

"Go ahead," she tells him, her spine and demeanor like

the steel I so desperately need to emulate. "I would enjoy it."

"And I would enjoy watching it," Finn adds from where he stands at my side, one hand resting on the hilt of his own sword. The enormous hunter is usually quick with a smile, but there's no hint of it now. His blue eyes are icier than I've ever seen them.

Eris's antagonistic stance I can understand. Theron's been flirting with her for years.

I'm not quite sure where Finn's comes from.

Theron's mouth twists, but he merely pushes the sword away from his carotid with a single finger and gracefully steps back before his attention returns to me. "For what reason? What is this child to you?"

Suddenly, there's an ache stabbing behind my eyes. I choke it down ruthlessly. "I know your spies would have been among those who watched me set fire to my husband's memorial pyre. I know you're aware of my daughter's presence."

"I'm aware." Theron purses his lips, his voice comes out gruffly. "And I'm sorry to hear of everything that happened in the past week. I know you loved him."

I wave the words away. They will not touch me. So far, I've been managing to hold the crushing wave at bay. "My mother is unaware that Amaya is safely at my side. She thinks the child she is currently raising is mine. She calls her May, and May is a little girl who has found herself—through no fault of her own—on the wrong side of a war." I meet his eyes. "If my mother realizes May is not my daughter, she may hurt the girl. I don't want her to suffer for the consequences of my actions."

Theron scrubs at his mouth. "I don't *rescue* princesses. I... remove them. This is not within my area of expertise."

"You once told me you could get inside any locked door in the south."

He winces. "Technically, yes."

"My mother has Hawthorne Castle locked up tighter than a vault. She will expect retaliation. She will have May hidden away so thoroughly that she probably can't even see the sun. None of my people can rescue her. But you can. You will be aptly compensated—"

Theron shakes his head. "It's not about the money—"

"Then, what?" I push to my feet. "She is *nine* years old. An orphan who was exchanged with Amaya at birth. A decoy I never knew about. And my mother will kill her the second she realizes she's not my daughter."

"Politically, this makes no sense," he points out. "You can't save them all, Your Highness."

His words ring true.

One child, when hundreds may be starving. One child, when many go missing every year in the forests of Arcaedia, snatched by the monsters that lurk there. One child, when my mother has caused torment to so many others.

One child, when I have a war to plan; two opposing forces threatening to crash down on Evernight's unprotected flanks; a missing sister; a murderous mother; and a stepbrother who may or may not be here to kill me.

To ask this of him will cost me.

It makes no sense.

And yet, somehow, it makes all the sense in the world.

I couldn't save *him*. For all the power within me, the ability to tap the leylines and rouse the Hallows, there was nothing I could do as Angharad drove that knife through my husband's heart.

I didn't get to burn his body.

I didn't get to say goodbye.

I didn't get to tell him I loved him one last time....

I couldn't control any of it.

I can control this. I can *try*. May's just a little girl, forced into a murderous game between two rival kingdoms. My mother took my daughter from my arms when she was born and stole my memories of her. I never had a chance to rock Amaya to sleep or hold her when she was upset.

But I can stop this.

I can rescue May.

The little girl who saved my daughter's life.

"Please," I whisper, and that single word nearly breaks me.

Queens do not beg.

Theron's expression hardens. "I want access to the royal treasury. If I'm going to take this risk then I intend to be suitably rewarded."

"You may have anything you may carry with both hands on a single visit," I reply, even as the exhale of relief sends me sinking back onto the throne.

He will do it. He will rescue her.

This one thing I can do right.

The silence stretches out.

Dark lashes flicker over his eyes. "I expected you to ask for your mother's head. But you're not going to ask for that, are you?"

"I wouldn't throw your life away on a reckless gamble."

"You never know... I might be able to kill her."

"No." The word comes quietly. "No, you wouldn't be able to kill her. My mother has spent her entire life seeing threats in shadows. She expects an assassin. She's made... provisions for one. You would be able to get close enough. You would see a path open for you—but what you would not realize is that she allows such openings, because she *wants* someone to play their hand. And then you would die painfully, because my mother is vicious and merciless. No. All I ask is that you rescue May and bring her here, where she may be safe."

Theron laughs under his breath. "I keep misreading you. The queens I have known would not shed a single tear for a little girl who's merely a pawn. They would think you weak for this moment of mercy."

"Let them think it." I'm too fucking tired to care.

"When the prince brought you here the first time, I saw you from a distance. I thought it was your beauty that had caught his eye. I thought him a fool for taking such a risk when there are beautiful females in every city. But he saw more than your face. He saw your *heart*. He saw what I see here today." Theron tilts his face toward me, his expression impenetrable. "I don't think with my heart, my queen. I don't take risks I deem unacceptable. I don't accept jobs where death seems a more likely outcome than reward. I can't even believe I just accepted *this* task.

"And so I say this: The other queens would think you weak, but it is not weakness you show me. It is not weakness that inspires me to risk my life for a child I don't even know."

Theron steps forward. Finn stiffens, but the assassin

merely takes my hand and presses a kiss to the ring I wear on my finger. The ring Thiago gave me to close our vows.

"If you are allowed the chance to grow into your rule, then I think you will be the greatest queen of all," he says before he nods at Finn and turns away from the dais.

He stops right in front of Eris.

She stares through him.

"I asked for the wrong reward," he finally says. "I should have asked for a single meal with your stern-faced warlord instead of the finest gifts in your treasury."

Finn tenses at my side—enough to capture my attention.

"But then... I have not beaten her yet." Theron smiles a little dangerously.

Eris challenged the world many years ago when she said she would only ever give her heart to the male who could beat her in battle. Since then, hundreds of fae lords have come to try their hand at fate.

All have failed.

"Ever," Eris says coldly, and their eyes meet.

There's heat in Theron's face—a promise unspoken.

But my friend remains as merciless as a killing frost.

Theron winks. "You never know."

"Oh, I know," Eris replies with the soft malice of a knife drawing across a throat. "You will never beat me, Theron. And I will never yield. You may as well give up this foolishness before it costs you your life."

The assassin steps back, his arms open as he grins at her. "Clearly you don't know me. I've never met a challenge I can't surmount. Eventually."

"The problem is," Finn mutters at my side, low enough

31

for me alone to hear him, "she's not just a fucking challenge to be won."

Eris's head whips toward him, her brows drawing together as if she didn't quite hear what he said.

"Rescue the little girl," she suddenly says, her attention returning to Theron. "And then I will give you a chance. Bring May back here safely, and we will cross swords, the two of us. Then we will see where fate leaves us."

"Consider it done," Theron purrs as he backs toward the double doors.

* * *

Surprisingly, it's in the dungeon where I find some respite from my grief.

Lysander paces beyond the bars, an enormous creature of rippling sinew, fur, and fury. His golden eyes watch me like a caged wolf just waiting for its prey to get close enough for it to snatch.

Banes are monstrous, magic-twisted creatures lost to hunger and rage. My mother cursed him when she found him sniffing around Clydain—where she was keeping May hidden safely away from court so I wouldn't remember the daughter I gave birth to.

It's not impossible to break a curse, but this one is proving hard to shift.

We even bargained with Theron for the use of one of his hexbreakers, and while she's been here three times, Lysander is still caged in fur and sinew. He's not as angry as he once was. Nor as determined to murder me—another lovely little twist of my mother's "gift"—but he can't seem to shatter the bonds that tether him to the beast form.

"How is he?"

"He's getting better," Baylor murmurs from where he sits against the wall, polishing a knife with slow, steady strokes. The *rasp-rasp-rasp* gets on my nerves, but I know it gives his hands something to do.

The enormous warlord has spent every spare waking hour with his twin brother since Lysander was returned to us.

I feel his grief. It matches mine. We've both lost the person we loved most in the world, and there's some comfort in that. Baylor doesn't push me. He never speaks of what happened, he never insists I need to pull myself together. He understands that I just want to be left alone to pretend I have some sort of semblance of life still beating in my chest.

Does the same crushing weight fill him too?

"He spoke this morning," he continues. "He's beginning to put sentences together."

Sentences are good. Sentences are proof there's a rational mind locked within that creature.

"What did he say?"

The knife pauses. "He... wanted to know who the girl was. The one who was crying in the yard the other day."

The words lock me in place.

It hasn't been easy bringing Amaya into my life.

She's my daughter, but she's still a stranger in so many ways. I'm not the one who sang to her or taught her how to hunt. I'm not the one who dried her eyes, or patched her bleeding knees. I'm not the one who kissed her goodnight as I drew the covers over her every night.

No. That was Old Mother Hibbert, and now she's dead.

Because of me.

Because she took my child off an old stone altar in the forest and raised her as her own.

Because she loved her when I couldn't.

The hardest moment of this entire ordeal was telling Amaya that Old Mother Hibbert had been killed by the creatures who kidnapped her. I think some part of her had known, but to wonder about it is different than hearing it stated. Those words nailed any of her last hopes in a coffin and buried them. She'd wiped her gleaming eyes, her lip quivering, but she'd nodded abruptly.

And then she'd said, "I want to be alone."

"What did you tell him?"

"The truth." Baylor's golden eyes meet mine. The twins aren't fae, even though the form they wear is. I don't know exactly what they are. Shapeshifters of some description, wearing faces that look like mine, with the same slightly tapered ears. But while you might mistake them for fae, there's... something that makes your blood run cold when you look at them.

It's like being trapped in a cage with a pair of wolves.

Handsome wolves.

There's always a hint of their former heritage in their eyes. A wildness. A hunger. The howling of an ancient moon.... Once upon a time Baylor was one of the hounds who served the Grimm One, and I can still see it in the vicious glint in his savage eyes. "I told him that we'd managed to rescue Amaya. We managed to fulfil his final mission."

A snarl comes from the cage, and a muscle in Baylor's jaw twitches as his gaze cuts that way. "I told him that his prince sacrificed his life in order to save her...."

"How did he take it?"

Baylor's face closes down. "As expected."

As expected. I momentarily close my eyes. *Badly, then.*

Lysander paces, his lip curling as those hot amber eyes lock upon me like he'd spring at me if there weren't a row of bars between us.

It breaks my heart that my mother did this to him.

Ever since the Mother of Night broke the curse that kept my memories locked away, they've been coming back to me.

Lysander was my friend once.

And then my mother took him, and she warped him with her magic, and every day she killed him even as she wore my visage and taunted him with my intention to betray Thiago. Every night, when he arose from death, he had to face the promise that I was sent to lead Thiago to his doom.

"I" killed him, again and again.

And "I" taunted him with the lie that I only ever married Thiago in order to worm my way into his court.

It broke him.

Every time he looks at me, he sees a liar. A murderer. A manipulative bitch who was sent to destroy the prince he loved and served. The trauma to both his body and mind twisted him.

Lysander knows the truth. Baylor tells him what truly

happened every morning when he wakes, but the fury and rage of the bane makes it difficult for him to see through the lies imprinted on his soul.

That fury lurks within me too, a seed of anger buried so deep its roots threaten to twine through my soul when I think of my mother.

She killed him.

She ruined my friend.

She is responsible for all of this.

For Amaya. My lack of memories. My husband's death.

For a moment I can't breathe again—I'm lost in the sound Thiago's head makes as it slams against the floor. I can feel that fleshy *thud* seeping through my ribs, forcing them wide open. It hurts. It hurts to breathe. It hurts to remember.

And then a warm hand steals over mine.

Baylor. Not looking at me. Not asking. Just there. There in a way I need so desperately.

It blurts from my lips. "Edain arrived this morning. My mother realized Andraste stole the Crown of Shadows and gave it to me. She cursed him and cast him out, and she sent my sister north to the goblin clans in order to cement an alliance there." I can barely breathe again. "There's movement on the borders—my mother's troops jostling into position as if she's preparing to make a strike against us. If the goblins spill down from the mountains, they'll either force us against my mother's warriors like a meatgrinder or we'll be fighting a war on two fronts. Eris has been arguing for me to allow her to ride for the border and hold our armies against Asturia, but I need her here."

I think of everything Thalia's been telling me. "The

Finn's part Sylvaren. Nothing can get past him. The Fetch's kidnapped you once. We can't risk it again."

"Then I just leave Andraste to the goblin king's mercy?" It hurts to even think the words. "She's my *sister*. She risked everything to give us the crown. She kept my daughter safe. She *saved* Amaya. I can't just let Edain go after her alone. I can't just... abandon her."

And I cannot do it myself.

"If Andraste is in goblin territory, then no army in the world is good enough to get her back," he warns.

"A small party, perhaps—"

"Two, maybe three...." But he's shaking his head. "They would have to be the best trackers in the world."

It's a suicide mission.

I grind the heels of my palms into my eyes. They won't stop leaking.

A gruff snarl echoes from behind the bars. "Sssend me...."

It cuts through the tears.

"What?" I lower my hands.

Lysander grabs the bars and flinches as the iron burns him. Something shudders through him. "Sssend me."

We both turn to him as he growls and rests his forehead against the bars. Something's happening. Something... monumental. Fur twitches along Lysander's spine.

Baylor's eyes burn with intent. "It's breaking. The curse is breaking."

It is...? "But how?"

My mother's curses are powerful and vicious.

"There's always a way to break a curse," Baylor growls.

Some loophole, some trick that inverts the magic.

"But we've tried everything," I whisper.

His gaze focuses sharply on my face.

It's like the dawn clears. He knows. He knows what it is....

"We haven't tried this." Baylor reaches for me and swipes the wetness from my cheeks. Striding across the room, he paints my tears across Lysander's face.

Lysander howls, collapsing to his knees. Fur ripples and recedes down his spine, his back bowing and tendons standing out in stark relief. A hand appears, fingers digging into the floor.

I gasp, hurrying to Baylor's side. "Xander!"

"His fury and hatred for you kept him tied to the beast-form," Baylor says incredulously. "It's your tears. The tears of an enemy he's been trained to hate. The one thing that can cut through his rage: His love for you. It's breaking the curse."

Magic bursts from Lysander in a wave, golden light pulsating through the dungeon. He howls again, wracked with pain as his spine arches, and as the howl extends it somehow becomes more fae.

A scream.

A male screaming.

I grab the bars, desperate to see what's happening, but Baylor hauls me back a step, wary even now. My hands tingle; a mild burn from the iron in those bars.

"Xander?" he rasps.

The light fades. A fae warrior shudders and gasps, forcing his way to his hands and knees. Ragged silvery hair falls over his face and shoulder, his body nude and dirty.

But it's the feral look in his eyes that catches my breath.

The curse broke.

Finally.

But there's still murder and fury in his amber eyes, and something not quite fae.

"Let *me* go," Lysander rasps, looking up at me. Hatred flickers over his expression, but he reins it in, looking away with a curled lip. "Let me go... after your sister." His fingers dig into the floor. "It's still... inside me. The curse is still there. It can hear you breathing. Smell you. I can't stay here. I can't. Not with you here." Our eyes meet, and I see the horror in his. "I want to kill you, even now. And I won't kill you. I *won't*. I won't betray my... my prince. Let me do this one thing for you," he begs. "Let me bring your sister home to you."

The bubble of hope bursts in my chest. "Xander...."

"Go." Baylor pushes me toward the stairs. "I can't let him out of the cage until I know he's not a threat to you."

I swallow hard, tears still slipping down my cheeks. I'd hoped that once the curse broke, Lysander would return to the way he once was.

But the barbs of my mother's curses always leave something behind.

I know that truth only too well.

I nod and head for the stairs, wiping my tears away. "Let me discuss it with Edain."

Chapter Four

"**Y**ou want me to ride north with *him*?" Edain
asks in horror.

Lysander rubs at his wrists. Baylor was
forced to put him in chains—just in case he made one last
attempt at me—but the second he entered the audience
chamber, I was forgotten. The two males went still as they
eyed each other.

One clad in merciless black leather—Thalia must have
found something for Edain to wear—and the other in a

white silk shirt that does nothing to hide the gaunt slash of his ribs or soften the rage in his eyes.

"*You*," Lysander rasps, and for a second I think there's actually someone he hates more than me.

Edain's left foot steps back into a defensive stance. "We meet again," he mocks, cutting me a look, "and here's me without my knife. This is a *bad* idea."

It's Lysander who makes the first move. He sneers. "What's wrong, pet? Think I'll rip out your throat in your sleep?"

Edain cuts him a dangerous smile, hands splaying wide as if to say "you can try."

Lysander's eyes narrow. "I've had a lot of time to think about all the ways I could kill you. That's what kept me anchored to myself. The idea of how I'd tear out your throat. Kill your queen. Kill—"

And then he seems to remember who the next person on his list is.

Me.

Baylor steps between us.

And Lysander shudders. "I'm not going to *do it*."

"Even if you could." Edain snorts.

That earns him another hateful glare.

"Stop it! That's enough! Both of you." I pause in front of Edain. "Lysander is one of our best trackers, and thanks to my mother he can't stay here. What is she worth to you? What is my sister's life worth to you? Your pride?"

"It's not my pride that threatens this fucking idea."

"Why don't you tell her the truth, then?" Lysander growls. "About what you did to me?"

"What he did to you?" Baylor's head swivels toward Edain.

But neither of them hear him. *No.* It's as if the rest of us no longer exist.

The heat drains from my face.

Andraste said Mother wore my face as she killed Lysander every day.

But she didn't say that my mother held the knife herself.

No. That's what she had Edain for. He was Mother's shadow, her assassin, her knife in the dark. If someone needed to die, then he was the one who made sure it happened.

For the first time in my life, Edain lowers his gaze. "The queen made me do many things I didn't... particularly wish to do. I can't take the past back, but I can... make amends."

"You didn't seem to fight real fucking hard."

Edain looks up, his hot, insolent glare finding Lysander again. "You know *nothing* of fighting."

"*Enough.*" Is this the best I can offer my sister? A bane who begged to be sent because he can't stand to be in the same room with me? A stepbrother who spent his entire life killing at my mother's request? "If the two of you cannot bury your enmity then I will have to find someone else—"

"No." Edain goes to one knee before me. "No. I will get her back. I swear. I will do anything to get her back."

I turn to Lysander.

He closes his eyes, but not before I see the feral gleam within them. "I will pay him back, one day. I won't forget any of it. I promise once. I promise twice. I promise thrice... I will have my vengeance upon him. One day. But for now..." He presses his lips thinly together and bows his head toward me. "I will serve my queen."

"Good," Thalia says, sweeping out of the shadows to hug him. "I'm so glad to see you back, Xander."

He captures her in his arms, pressing his face into her hair. The way he clings to her makes my heart feel heavy again; it's like he needed this so desperately. Needed to be embraced by a friend.

Thalia's eyes are wet when she draws back, but she's smiling. "You know, this whole week has been one long, monstrously shitty experience. It's about time we got some good news." Then she turns on me and I see her humor melt away.

Not good news.

"You need to pack," Baylor tells Lysander, clapping a hand on his shoulder. He always reads the room so well, and right now, it's telling him Thalia needs to talk to me alone. "A good meal, and then we'll saddle the horses."

It has to hurt—sending his brother away the second he returns—but there's no sign of it on Baylor's face.

I don't deserve such loyal friends.

"Edain will need supplies too," I tell them. "They can leave in the morning."

Baylor doesn't so much as twitch a brow. He's faced enough difficult decisions in his time that he doesn't let his emotions hold sway. "I'll organize it." He tips his head to me. "I'll organize it all, Vi. You just focus on the rest."

And then they're gone, leaving me alone with Thalia.

Both of us grief-stained and stretched thin with duty.

I can't fail them. No matter how much I want to hide

myself in my rooms with Amaya and let the world exist without me.

"What's the next order of business?" I sink onto the throne I never wanted to sit on.

Thalia claps her hands, and a hovering cloud of demi-fae appear, carrying a platter between them. "You need to eat."

I stare at the papers on the table. "I'm not hungry."

"You missed breakfast."

I blink, trying to think back. Breakfast was a whirl. All I'd been able to think about was the fires....

"You had three mouthfuls of soup last night for dinner. Maybe a bite of bread with it," Thalia continues, directing the demi-fae to set the food out in front of me.

I press my finger tips to my temples. "I've had a lot on my mind, T."

She slides a plate in front of me, her voice strangely gentle. "He'd never forgive me if I let you waste away."

He.

Suddenly I feel sick, tears pricking at the corners of my eyes.

It hits me at odd moments. I've been trying to keep busy, trying not to think of him, trying not to *hear* that moment his head struck the stone—

"Amaya is worried about you," Thalia says softly, offering me a grape. "I'm worried about you. We're all worried. If you faint in front of the court, your mother's going to think she's won—"

Grief sloughs away, replaced by a hot, vicious anger so bright it burns. "I hope she does think I am weakened. I hope she dares to make a move toward me."

I will kill her.

I will ruin her for everything she has ever dared do to me.

She can't stop me. Not now I have the crown. I will burn her fucking castle to the ground and finish what we started the night we stole it from her—

"Vi." Thalia captures my wrists, tearing my hands away from the edges of the throne.

Two smoking handprints linger in the polished wood.

And just like that, the anger is gone, leaving me with the image of a burning forest and a castle wreathed in smoke. Of fae screaming as they flee from the town that surrounds Hawthorne Castle.

I shove the grape in my mouth and barely taste it. I've been keeping the images at bay, but this one slipped beneath my conscious thought before I knew what was happening.

That's not my thought.

I would never burn my mother's castle down.

I would never hurt the people I was raised to protect.

That fucking crown....

The squeezing cage in my chest grows a little tighter. It's too much. I can't fight this. Not without him.

I have to.

I have to hold myself together.

For Amaya. For all of them.

"What's going on?" Thalia whispers, squeezing my wrists.

"Nothing."

There's no fooling her. She gives me a pointed look, her right brow lifting. "You nearly set the throne on fire."

I gesture at the thorns rustling against the walls. "And

the entire city is overgrown with thorns. I'll learn to control it, I swear. But I just need... a moment's respite."

"Eat," Thalia says, crossing her arms over her chest, "or else I won't tell you what news I bring."

One grape after the other. And then a slice of peach, even though I barely taste it. I chew my way through the cheese and dry biscuits, suddenly ravenous.

Thalia purses her lips, rifling through her papers as I chew each mouthful. She pauses as she finds the one she's clearly looking for. "The Queen of Ravenal is here to see you. I've been putting her off, but her retinue arrived through the Hallow—*without warning*—an hour ago. Luckily, Captain Naira was on duty and was able to differentiate between a threat that ought to be subdued and a threat that needed to be escorted to the audience chambers and offered sustenance."

"Queen?" The last time I saw Lucere, she was crown princess, fighting for her right to be crowned queen in the wake of her grandmother's death.

"Matters have changed in Ravenal."

But not within the Queen of Ravenal's heart. Lucere hates me for "stealing" Thiago from her all those years ago.

And to arrive like this is a bloody insult.

"What does she want?"

"For the first time in my life, I have to admit I don't know, Vi." Every inch of her hates making this statement. "She also insists the two of you are to be alone for the meeting. She's being obnoxiously insistent."

Alone?

Lucere's no friend of mine, but I doubt she'd have some intention to attack me. This is my kingdom, my home. And

I am bound to the lands here, which gives me the edge in terms of power. If she tries to hurt me, then I could skewer her with my thorns.

As if they sense I'm thinking of them, I feel those brambles whispering as they rustle within the walls of the castle. They started winding their way through the stones six days ago. So far I've been holding them at bay—I don't even know how I conjured them—but they're there.

Little suckers attaching themselves to walls. Dormant. Waiting. Whispering.

Whispering like that fucking crown in my dreams....

I curl my fingers into a fist, the sting of my fingernails digging into my palms. I know it bothers the others to see them—thorns are my mother's favorite weapon, after all, and I can't help thinking that she was the last person who wore the Crown of Shadows.

Were the thorns her weapon of choice?

Or is it something that comes with the crown?

Or something to do with my own growing power?

I don't know.

I don't fucking *know*.

"Send wine and food," I whisper. "I'll meet her there."

Ravenal is the knife at my throat—Lucere refused to join with us against my mother, but to my knowledge she hasn't yet sided with Asturia. She intended to remain neutral in the coming conflict, and I need to ensure she stays that way.

But as Thalia bows her head and turns for the door, I can't help wondering...

Why would Lucere want to talk to me alone?

Chapter Five

Iskvien

I slip inside the audience chambers, taking a moment to examine Queen Lucere. Raven-black hair is wound into a flawless knot atop her head and surrounded by a small jeweled gold crown. Her back remains stiff as she examines a painting of Roswen, a former queen of Evernight, and her gown is a scarlet brocade cut in clean lines, with elegant form. It's considerably more formal than the sheath of dark violet that Thalia forced me into this morning.

She's lovely.

Hair black as a raven's wing; lips red as blood; skin pale as snow; and her heart as merciless as her smile....

I can't help hearing Nanny Redwyne's voice in my head, an echo of a story she told me a thousand times as a child.

"I hear my condolences are in order," Lucere says, never taking her eyes off the portrait. Her head slowly bows as if she's considering something, and then she turns, and I cannot help squaring my shoulders.

"Thank you." Somehow my voice remains smooth. "It's a long way to come to send your condolences. I don't know whether to be thankful for the kindness—or whether I ought to be on guard."

She circles the enormous round table in the center of the room, her dark eyes gliding over every feature. Including the thorns circling several chair legs. "One would be a fool indeed, to attack a queen in her own lands."

"And yet"—there's a hint of acid in my voice—"that's precisely what you claimed of me, when we visited Ravenal. What do you want?"

I can almost sense Thalia clapping a hand over her face with a sigh.

I tried.

But Lucere and I have never been friends, and my ability to play games these days is wearing thin.

"I envied you once," Lucere says, twitching her skirts

out of the way of a bramble as she continues her smooth glide. Somehow, we're both circling the table like predators eyeing each other. "My grandmother promised I would marry him. It should have been me. It would have been me if you had not caught his—"

"It would *never* have been you."

Lucere reacts as if slapped, then visibly swallows. Breathing out a bitter laugh, she turns to the sideboard where she pours herself a goblet of wine. Since I'm clearly not going to offer her one. "You're right. Of course. Thiago never looked at me twice, no matter what dreams I conjured." Throwing half the glass back, she lowers it, and then stares down into its depths. "I wanted it to be true. I wanted to... escape. Thiago was going to whisk me away from Ravenal, from my grandmother, from all my wretched cousins.... I was so excited the night of that long-ago Lammastide that I could barely breathe. And then he laid eyes upon you, and I knew that moment was gone. I saw it happen, right before me. You were dancing, and he turned and saw you, and... the look on his face. It was happening exactly as I'd always imagined, only... it was happening to someone else. He gathered you up. He took you away from your mother. He loved you. You were living my dream, and I hated you so much for it. For taking what I thought was mine."

"What do you want?"

Even I can hear the pain in my voice.

Lucere startles out of her reverie. The rigid line of her shoulder slumps. "You were right. When you came to Ravenal and told me your mother could not to be trusted, you were right. She took Imerys as handmaiden to her court. A kindness, she said. A favor for her dearest friends of Ravenal for their loyalty. I tried to argue, but she... she took my *sister,* and I was not strong enough to prevent it. If I'd fought...." A hint of tears gleams in her eyes. "I know how to play these games. I know who wins between your mother and me. My magic is not strong enough to stop her. I had to let Imerys go. I had to smile and pretend it was an honor. And she will keep my sister locked away in her castle like a knife to my throat. If I make any move to stop Adaia's war or betray her, then my sister will suffer. If I smile and curtsy and thank Adaia for her kindness, then she will tie Ravenal in knots for years as a vassal, and not as a fellow kingdom. I have just traded servitude to another queen in order to protect my sister, and I know it. I have just given your mother my kingdom on a gilded platter, and though it will take years for her to slowly absorb us, eventually we will barely remember we held our own right to power."

There's nothing to say.

I warned her.

"And you came all this way to tell me this?"

"Officially? I came to pay Ravenal's respects. Unofficially? Because your mother wants me to spy upon you. She's heard reports there is a child at your side, a child you claim is your own. She wants to know if the girl is a decoy."

That was quick.

"She will believe me"—Lucere shoots my rustling thorns a wary glance—"if I tell her the girl is a lie. A changeling. Adaia has no reason not to trust me." Another bitter smile. "She thinks she owns me."

The thorns subside.

"Why would you do that?"

"Because Ravenal will abstain from this war. We will not stand at Evernight's side. I cannot, or I will cost my sister her life." Lucere takes a deep breath. "So I must play a deeper game. I must find a means to remove this threat from our throats, and I must do it so obliquely that no one will ever suspect I am playing both sides of this field."

My heart starts beating again. Is she offering assistance?

"How?"

"They tell me you have bound yourself to the land and it has accepted you as queen. They say you have stolen your mother's crown—"

"They?"

She gives a little shrug. "My brother's ravens are everywhere. I know this is not news to you, because your warlord has put a bounty on the head of every raven in Evernight, but there are still ways to glean information if one is careful enough." Another breath. "You pushed Adaia back at the Queensmoot. You burned the oak that bound her to Asturia. Do you have the power to confront her?"

It's the question I've asked myself a thousand times.

But I owe her the truth if we're to form any sort of alliance.

"I don't know."

Silence fills the room.

"I can't control... my magic right now. You've seen the thorns. It's not conscious." Turning toward the sideboard, I pour myself some wine too. "And my mother is vicious and invulnerable—"

"Adaia's not invulnerable." Lucere prowls toward me

54

slowly. "I think you dealt her a blow when you burned her sacred oak. She's cut thin as glass, and is twice as savage as usual, but one can see the dark circles beneath her eyes and the ragged edges of her fingernails."

"A rabid wolf backed into a corner is twice as dangerous as a pack on the run."

"Agreed." Lucere's eyes narrow. "Though I have to concede you look half rabid yourself."

"It's been a bad week."

Lucere looks away. "A queen cannot allow herself to love. My grandmother told me that, but I never believed it until this moment." Her lips twist ruefully. "Love is a thorn, festering in the heart. To lose it is to rip that thorn right out until one bleeds pale."

Maybe that's exactly how I feel.

Like something has been torn from me.

But even so...

"I don't regret it," I whisper. "I don't regret it one bit. Even if I live a thousand long, empty years, I will remember him and what we had."

I swear there's sympathy in her expression.

She turns away with a swish, but this time, it's as if she's pacing.

My eyes narrow. "You didn't just come all this way to warn me that my mother is planning something or to mock me for loving him."

"No. I came to strike a deal."

"Correction. You came to test me. You came to see if I could handle this little problem you have set for yourself. If I kill my mother, then Imerys will be returned to you. Ravenal will be freed of her influence, and you will be queen. But if I don't succeed and Adaia wins, then you have managed to keep Ravenal's hands clean. She will not suspect you. So what does Evernight get out of this exchange? We face all the threat, and you will not grant me even a single warrior?"

"You're right," she points out, crossing to the table. "But I can give you something far more valuable than my entire army."

My gaze drops to a package I hadn't even realized was sitting there.

"Ravenal has never been a military strength, but we have our own means of protection. Information is a greater currency than gold itself, and when my grand-mother first broached the subject of my potential betrothal to Thiago, she put a half-burned book into my hands and told me I needed to know everything I could about him."

Lucere slides the package across the table toward me. "I know what Thiago's tattoos meant. I know who his father is. I know what his powers were. I know how he came about them. And I know that your daughter will bear them too."

"She's too young. Her magic hasn't come in yet. We don't know—"

"She will bear his power," Lucere tells me. And then she tears the simple paper wrap from the package, revealing a book. The way she strokes it before pushing it toward me... like she's finally conceding a long-lost battle. "I was honest when I said I envied you, but there's a little part of me that feels it may have been a blessing. Did you know your husband was bred from the Darkyn?"

Only what Thiago told me. "I... am aware of certain facts, yes."

"But not all of them?" she pushes.

"He didn't like to talk about it, but he said he could control it."

"He may not have known the entire truth himself." She sighs. "Thousands of years ago, Queen Maia fought Queen Sylvian at Charun and ascended to godhood. Maia was the first of the fae on this new world to be prayed to. But she was not the last. Selena followed suit not long after her, ascending to godhood and lifting the veil of night that lingered over the northern half of the continent. But there is one other god we do not speak of very often. Kato. God of Death. God of Mercy and Justice. He who rules the Underworld and guards those gates against the monstrous creatures that seek to break forth from the Darkness."

"The Darkness?" It's what Thiago called his darker half.

"The primordial Darkness," Lucere explains, flipping the book open. "Kato was a fae prince who was challenged with the role of containing it. And the creatures it spawned."

The image on the page is of a warrior prince lifting his shining sword against an all-consuming cloud of shadow.

"This is Darkness. This is Death," she whispers, tracing her finger over the shadow. "A creature who stalked the night and sucked the life from the lungs of all who passed it by. Nobody saw its face or form, though there is rumor it could walk as both shadow and fae. And when it did, Death was beautiful. Smoldering. Entrancing. Vicious and violent and as savage as the merciless chill that lingers in the north of Unseelie. It yearned for blood and drank it directly from the vein. And they say it plucked the hearts from fae chests, for its own did not beat."

Lucere takes a deep breath. "And as its heart did not beat, Death could not be killed. It could not be hunted, for it turned into a swarm of shadow when confronted. One glimpse of its eyes struck a fae frozen. Mortal steel passed right through it. The only thing that could strike it a blow was a shaft cut from the mighty ash tree, and the only thing it feared was sunlight, for even Death is no match for the might of day.

"Kato and his warriors were tasked with slaying it, but they found it impossible. They set out with a hundred warriors to bring it down—the best of the best. And one by one, Death slew them until only thirteen remained.

"Knowing it hunted them, they lured it into a trap and tore it into thirteen pieces of shadow. His warriors used its blood to tattoo a ward into their forearms in order to contain its power within them. They swallowed a piece of the Darkness they'd cut from it. And then they made a pact that they could never be together again. They each took a horse and rode to different ends of the world so the creature could not bind itself together again. Kato alone remained behind to shield the gates, and he alone is remembered and prayed to. Thus he ascended to godhood."

Her voice lowers. "They called themselves the Dark Kin, and over the centuries that became Darkyn. If one fell, that wisp of Death's soul would return to the primordial Darkness where it would be trapped, but to bring all thirteen together again? Impossible. Or so they thought. But they found Death had its own methods of striking back. Within them was a piece of its soul. A piece that hungered to be reunited with its other selves. Centuries passed. One by one they were driven mad, overwhelmed by the creature within them. The first to fall to Death's will set about hunting the others. His name was Malakhai, and he consumed the Darkness within his fellow, until the first two pieces of Death's soul were reunited within him. He became stronger. More powerful. Dangerous. And he yearned for more.

"The only thing that thwarted him was the fact that some of those Darkyn had bred children. And within each of those children were fragments of the creature within them. Its soul bled down. Wisps of its power scattered like grains of barley on the winds. After centuries, there were hundreds of them. And so, he set about hunting each and every single one of them until only five others remain."

The breath explodes out of me. "Thiago. And Amaya."

"Correct. Kato and two others," she murmurs, "according to my brother's ravens."

"Who are they?"

"I don't know. Not on this continent, Corvin assures me." Lucere takes a deep breath, even as her words leave me reeling. She snaps the book closed and then places it on the table in front of me. "Your daughter will contain a seed of this power within her. And she will be hunted for it. I don't know if those other Darkyn know of her yet, but I do know that Malakhai does, and he's the only one that matters. He was under Queen Angharad's control for several centuries, though he disappeared from her court at some stage during the last two hundred years. Nobody knows where he is. None of my brother's ravens have seen him. But at last count, he'd claimed nearly two hundred Darkyn souls. One wonders if he's controlling Death, or if Death is controlling him? My grandmother considered him a threat that needed to be subdued at some stage, but very few have the power to confront him, and so far, he's remained content to stay in the north." She pauses. "She considered your husband to be the only weapon we had against him, should Malakhai complete his transformation into Death."

"But now that Thiago is gone... surely Malakhai can't complete the transformation?"

I would wait for you in the Darkness....

He's gone. Lost to this world. Safe from his father.

Isn't he?

Kato would never let Malakhai past the gates to the Underworld.

"Malakhai is but four pieces of the puzzle away from becoming Deathless. Can even Kato stop him if he consumes your daughter and the other two?" Lucere's lips thin as if she's keeping one last secret. "I don't know how your husband died. Was he killed by another Darkyn?"

"No." I see him falling again, with Angharad's knife driven through his chest. That wretched lump is in my throat again. "She killed him. Angharad killed him with the knife she was using for her ritual."

Grim lines form around Lucere's mouth, and she twists one of the rings on her finger. "I cannot give you hope. Know that. But... it is said that the Darkyn cannot truly *die*. Your husband's soul will have returned to the primordial Darkness. He cannot cross the threshold of the Underworld, not with Kato guarding it. But I do know that his soul will remain there. Forever. He will not pass on to the Bright Lands."

A slow breath escapes me. "What are you trying to say?"

"There's a chance he's not entirely lost to you forever, Your Highness. But know this: He may not be the same as he once was. The male you knew is gone. But the Darkness within him? The darker half of his soul? It's still there. Beyond the Gates of the Underworld."

Chapter Six

Iskvien

"Do I need to kill her?" Thalia asks as I stare at nothing, long after Lucere has gone.

I blink. I hadn't even realized she was in the room.

"No." I draw the book toward me, not daring to close it. The pictures haunt me. Shadows. Ancient warriors fighting an all-consuming darkness. And there, an elegant sketch of a creature with enormous black wings, turned away from the viewer. It could almost be Thiago. "Lucere wasn't here to hurt us."

Thalia arches a brow.

Hope. It's a supernova burning within me, and I think I hate Lucere a little bit for doing this to me. I saw him die. My hand closed around his ashes before magic swept them away. But if he cannot truly die, then maybe I could see him? Maybe I could talk to him? Say goodbye. *Something.* The need is so strong it makes me want to choke.

I would wait for you in the Darkness.

I breathe out slowly, exhaling all the emotions slicing through me. "What if there was a chance we could see Thiago again?"

Thalia rears back. "What?"

The words spill from my lips, everything Lucere just told me.

But the look on her face—it's not what I want to see.

"I know what you have lost. I miss him too." Our eyes meet. "This darkness inside him.... Vi, there was a reason he kept it carefully leashed. If it survived him.... It won't be him, Vi. It won't be the prince you loved. It will be everything he hated and feared about himself."

And yet he barely even mentioned it to *me.*

I don't want to be angry at him, but I can't help feeling as though so much of our love was built upon a platform of lies.

He wanted to be my lover, my husband, my prince, but he never gave me the chance to love him for every part of him. All I ever got to see was the surface.

A shiver runs through me as Thalia squeezes my hand.

"I need to know more—for Amaya's sake, if nothing else." I squeeze her hand back. "But I trust you. More than I trust anyone else in this world." She's been there for me at every step of the way, backing me even when she didn't entirely trust me. "If I find something... if I find him... then I will take no step you haven't approved."

Thalia presses a kiss to my cheek. "I'll set my demi-fey to hunting any word of this. If there's a threat to Amaya... well, we'll be ready for it. Now, come. It's time for dinner."

I push my wretched thoughts aside. "*Thalia.*"

"Three slices of peach and half a dozen grapes is not enough to face your mother. Go and fetch Amaya. I'll make sure dinner is served."

* * *

As I climb the tallest tower in the castle, stepping onto the parapet, I realize this is the first time I've seen the sun in days. The clouds are finally clearing.

Amaya sits on the parapet, staring toward the north with her knees drawn up to her chest. Grimm nods at me from where he's watching her from a distance. He doesn't hold my gaze long, lowering his face to lick his paw.

Traitor.

The first time I found Amaya up here, my heart was in my throat the whole time. The courtyard seemed miles below us, and all I could think of was how close she sat to certain death.

This child of mine is wild and fae. She was raised in the north, in a house full of changeling children who were left on stone altars in the woods by their parents, left to either die or be raised by Old Mother Hibbert. I cannot even imagine what she's known, though little comments she's made have given me a hint of her life.

She was a hunter, one of the children who went into the forests in search of prey to bring down in order to feed all those hungry mouths.

There's a fierceness to her that's hard to penetrate, an ancient look in her eyes.

The more I pushed at her to be careful in those first few days, the more she would square her shoulders in defiance.

And as Finn said to me three days ago, she has her father's gifts.

"She yearns for the wind, Vi," he murmured to me as Amaya fled inside with a slam of her bedroom door. "She cannot shift shape yet. Or at least, I don't think she can. But it's inside her. That longing. This is where she feels safe."

Those words do nothing to settle the jagged fist lodged right up under my ribs, but I've given up on trying to rein her in.

I have to build a relationship with her first.

"Hey," I murmur. "Have you eaten?"

"Finn brought me a tray," she says, though her nose wrinkles. The palace fare is like nothing she's known, and we're still trying to discover what she will eat. She prefers soups and stews and thick crusty bread with warmed butter. Pudding, if we have it.

At least she's inherited one thing from me.

I sit myself on the edge of the parapet beside her, though I face the other way. I have not her—and her father's—lack of fear for heights. "Why didn't you tell me the Mother of Night was coming to you in your dreams?"

Amaya rests her chin on her knees. "She told me you weren't ready to hear it."

Of course she did. "You cannot trust her. She's not our ally—"

"She's been *my* ally ever since I can remember," Amaya cuts back.

What? "How long has she been coming to you?"

"All my life," Amaya replies. She shrugs. "I hear her voice sometimes. At first it was when I was in danger and didn't know it. I'd hear this voice, warning me to run. I didn't know who it belonged to until this last year, when she started visiting my dreams."

The shock of it leaves me breathless. I don't even know where to start with this revelation—that my daughter has been in danger so many times that she can speak of it with merely a shrug, or that the Mother of Night has been watching over her all these years.

What in Maia's name does that *mean*?

The Mother told me I was the *leanabh an dan*, but there was another one out there if I refused to heed her call.

If that fucking bitch thinks she's going to use my—

"And she sings to me." Amaya stares into the distance. "She used to sing me to sleep at night sometimes. When I was sad." She closes her eyes. "She's been singing me to sleep all week. If you would let yourself hear her, she'd sing to you too."

"Amaya." I force my voice to be calm and steady. "She's not a friend. She wants to use me. She wants to—"

"She wants to be free," she tells me firmly, those green eyes staring right through me. "I know. She wants to protect her people and—"

"The Old Ones are powerful and capricious. The last time they were freed they allied themselves with the unseelie, and marched south. We *barely* won."

"She said the seelie killed her people and drove them from their lands, from their forests." Amaya wears a mulish look. "And then you locked them all away in their prison worlds."

You.

"I wasn't even born yet."

"Does it matter?" She slips off the parapet, and I recognize signs of an imminent retreat. "When you accept someone else's truth, then you become an active participant in covering their crimes."

That sounds infinitely wiser than a nine-year-old ought to be. "Did she say that to you?"

Color heats Amaya's cheeks. *Guilty.* "Would it be so bad to set her free?" she whispers. "She's always been there for me. She said she could be there for you too."

A shudder runs through me. It's not only Grimm who bears my fury. The Mother of Night knew one of us was going to die when we broke into the Black Keep.

She knew *exactly* who was going to die.

Not me. Not her precious key to escape. She threw herself at me to protect me from the Horned One's power before she vanished.

She could have done the same for him.

I won't have her use my daughter to get what she wants.

It's time to deal with the Mother of Night once and for all.

But first—

I reach out a hand. I want Amaya to know me. I want

her trust. Only then can I protect her. "Thalia's sent for dinner. It's been a long day. Why don't you join us?"

"What is it?"

"Roast venison. Your favorite."

"How do you know I like it?"

"You asked for a third helping three nights ago."

Amaya rolls a tongue over her teeth and then nods. But she takes my hand. "Okay."

* * *

After I've tucked Amaya in bed, I set foot within the Hallow that's housed high in one of the towers in the castle, clasping the Crown of Shadows in both hands.

"Are you there?" I call.

There's no answer; nothing but the sensation of a dark awareness turning in my direction.

It's getting far too easy to step between worlds. My bare feet barely land on the solid stone floor of the Hallow, and between one blink and the next, I'm plunged into darkness.

Another world.

A prison.

And a hooded figure waiting for me by the lake within her cave, staring out over the dark waters as though she hasn't heard me.

I know she's aware of me.

In a way, she's won. She's brought me back here, even after I swore I would never see her again.

My hands curl around the crown.

"You've been ignoring me," she whispers as I stride down the shale-lined path toward her.

"I have what you want. I brought you the crown. And with this, our pact is done. You have no further claim upon my daughter."

The Mother of Night turns, her hood slipping back from her face.

And I can't stop a gasp.

She was always beautiful, with flawless skin and dark infinite eyes. Patient eyes. But now the right side of her face is blackened and charred, though little embers seem to eat away at the smooth edges where skin meets scab. It's like the fire still burns within her.

"What... happened?" The words fall away, because I *know* what happened to her.

When the Horned One was unleashed from his prison world, he threw a blast of raw magic toward me, and she stepped between us, shielding me from the explosion.

I'd thought.... She was always reputed to be the only Old One with the power to stand against the Horned One.

"You know what happened," she says, touching her cheek with a slight wince. She takes a limping step toward me. "I warned you that you were not strong enough to face him head-on. No one is. No one ever was. The Horned One was once the protector of my kind, but when the fae came, he tapped into the raw current of *ala*—the power that fuels the world—and he drank of it. It darkened his heart and turned him away from all that we were. All that we were reborn to do. It is forbidden for a reason."

I catch her arm, and her weight staggers against me.

There's nothing left of my anger.

Only shock.

"Here. Sit." I ease her onto a rock and hesitate. It's been

69

over eight days since the Horned One was set free. "Do you need healing?"

It's the one small gift I was always able to access, though my skills with it are rudimentary.

The Mother shakes her head. "Nothing will heal this damage, Iskvien."

"What about this?"

I offer her the crown.

It's powerful enough that one of the fae can channel the power of the leylines—tapping directly into the magic that belonged exclusively to the Old Ones.

"Use it." I curl her fingers around the golden prongs. "It's yours now. I have fulfilled my promise to you: The crown in your hands in exchange for my daughter's life."

Her hands cup the crown, and she looks at it for a long moment, before she sighs and hands it back to me. "Your debt is forgiven. But you misunderstood me, Iskvien. I never meant to use the crown myself. It was always meant for you."

The cave falls away from me.

Some of my confusion must show in my eyes. "But I can't—"

"Come," she says, taking my arm. "Take me to the waters of remembrance."

I lead her slowly toward the shallow well where she showed me the truth about her people.

Fog fills the small well, little lights twinkling within it.

"Come," she whispers, drawing me down into the fog.

I take a deep breath as icy-cold water laps at my knees, at my hips, higher—

And then she shoves my head under, and we both step through into another world.

Music erupts. Creatures spin to life in a forest, breathing joy into pipes and dancing around a fire. They're not fae. Little horns peer through their hair. Some of them bear wings. Other sport the legs of a deer, or the eyes of a goat.

Otherkin.

The creatures who ruled this world before the fae arrived.

The ones who lay with fae before the wars, birthing the unseelie into the world. I can't stop looking at one of the otherkin sitting in a tree. He has wings as black as a raven's, made of long elegant feathers. Horns peep through his hair, and his eyes bear the savage golden gleam of a hawk's.

Thiago was Darkyn, but I can't help looking at the otherkin's wings and wondering.

"I've seen the past," I whisper.

"This isn't the past. This is now. These are my people," she whispers, gesturing to the otherkin around us. "Or what is left of them. They pray to me still from the secret nooks and lairs of their forests. They beg for mercy. They beg for protection." Anger clouds her face. "And I cannot help them. Not from here." She turns to me. "I cannot break free, Iskvien, because I am trapped here, and the locks to my prison are in *your* world. To be freed, one would need to either use one of the great keys—the Sword of Mourning, the Crown of Shadows—and break the locks on the Hallows. Or sacrifice someone of a royal bloodline. Someone powerful enough to shatter those wards. And I would need *you* to do it."

The same way I broke the Erlking free.

"Please," she whispers. "War is coming. My people will die if we are not there to protect them. The Horned One will slaughter them."

"Are they not his people too?"

She turns the ruined side of her face toward me. "He has forgotten who he is and where he came from. He has formed new alliances now and gained the power and prayers of Angharad and her unseelie. He will crush my kind in his quest for vengeance against the seelie and barely even notice. We want the same things, Vi. Peace. Freedom. And the Horned One dead."

"How can I trust you?" I whisper. "When you lied to me? When you've been whispering in my daughter's fucking head?"

"I never lied to you."

"'If you go to the Black Keep'"—I throw her words right back at her—"'a part of you won't return.' You knew. You knew he would die. Why should I trust you? How do I forgive you? What if this is another trick? Another lie? Another manipulation?"

"Because you have never understood me." Anger darkens her face. "There was a choice to be made. If you walked into the Black Keep, then one of you would die. You. Amaya. Thiago. It was inevitable. So I gave fate a little nudge. I could see it all play out in my waters. No matter what I did, the Horned One *would* rise. One of you would die. And so I did the one thing I could do to thwart him. I saved you. *You*, Vi. You're the key to everything."

"What in the Darkness does that *mean*? I am nothing. And he—"

He was my everything.

Her face grows cold. "I offered him the choice. I could save one of you. And he chose you."

That's even worse. Tears stream down my face. I knew he went too easily.

"You haven't been listening," she whispers, grabbing my shoulders. "You haven't been listening to me. You haven't been listening to Lucere—"

"Lucere?" I look up sharply, dashing the tears from my eyes. "What does she have to do with this?"

"*Everything.*"

She hauls me toward her, and we vanish back into the fog. I gasp as she drags me from the well, its frigid waters sluicing off me.

The Mother of Night follows, limping slightly. A single flick of her fingers, and water drains from her hair and clothes, leaving her dry. A shiver runs over my skin as she bestows the same gift upon me.

"Look out into the lake."

I do, and as she lifts a hand, the earth beneath our feet begins to tremble.

Pale rocks appear, rising to the surface of the lake. They form a pathway out to where bubbles hiss to the surface.

Something large is surfacing.

Something pale.

It takes my eyes a moment to realize what I'm looking at.

There's a body on the large flat rock, still and lifeless.

Black wings are splayed wide; the exact same way they lay when he fell.

Thiago.

73

No. *No.* Grabbing my skirts, I wade into the water, climbing aboard the first rock and nearly slipping. This cannot be happening. He was gone. He vanished, leaving nothing more than ash behind in his wake.

I leap from rock to rock, careless of the lights surging toward me through the water as if they sense prey.

"When we were in the Black Keep and your husband was struck down, I told you I had this one last gift for you," the Mother of Night calls. "I used the last of my power that day to remove your husband's body from the world and keep it safe here. For you."

"Thiago." I clamber onto the last rock, staring across the water toward him, but the distance is too great. I can't leap it. I'd need to swim, and there are shapes rising in the water, clawed hands reaching for me. I eye the distance again, heat swimming in my eyes. Maybe it would be worth it—

"You cannot go to him," the Mother of Night says. "Not yet."

Sinking onto my knees, I stare at him, tears streaming down my face. "Is this some twisted game? You want me to free you and you'll what? Give me his body back?"

There's *always* another bargaining point to press.

A shimmer forms in the air, and then she's standing right in front of me, her hand sliding through my hair. "Child, you mistake me. You have always mistaken me. I am the mother of all my people. Even those who think themselves fae."

My heart makes a jagged leap in my chest, and I gape up at her.

"I do not wish for freedom for my sake," she continues,

74

once again touching the scorched mark on her cheek. "I am *dying*, Iskvien. I can slow the spread of this strike, but I cannot stop it. The Horned One's magic will consume me from within as I have always seen."

"What?" I push to my feet.

"I am dying," she repeats, her palm cupping my cheek. "But I have a little time left to set my final pieces into play."

We're going to lose.

Without her, the Horned One is free to wreak as much damage as he can. And then both fae and otherkin alike are going to be destroyed as the Horned One rampages across both seelie and unseelie alike.

"There was one ray of hope in all my nightmares. *One.* A queen is coming, Iskvien. A queen with the power to straddle both worlds. A queen with the weapons at hand to defeat the Horned One himself. She has marked the Sword of Mourning, she has claimed the Crown of Shadows, and now all she needs is Death riding at her side."

I gape at her.

"All I ask is this." She grabs my hand, surprisingly strong. "When I am gone, you will protect our people. You will find them in the forests and you will offer them sanctuary. You will rescind the laws that call for their heads. You will welcome them into your lands and forbid their deaths, their persecution. You will protect them. And you will force the other queens to abide by these rules."

"But I have no sway over the southern alliance," I whisper. My mother would never accept such a deal, nor Queen Maren. Lucere, maybe....

Her face hardens. "Then you will find a way, Vi. Bring

75

those southern queens to their knees and free my people. Promise me once. Promise me twice. Promise me thrice."

I stare at Thiago's body.

"I promise once," I whisper. "I promise twice. I promise thrice. If I am still standing at the end of this, then I will use whatever power I have to welcome your people."

"Our people," she insists. "There is one final thing you will need. Lucere gave you the key to it. And I have kept the vessel." Reaching behind her neck, she undoes a small chain, tugging an amulet forth from her dress. There's a glass moon charm hanging from the end of it.

The key? What the fuck did Lucere say to me?

"Thiago's soul has not crossed on to the Bright Lands. It cannot cross."

Thiago's voice whispers in my memories. *"I would wait for you in the Darkness."*

The primordial Darkness that existed before this world was even formed.

The Darkness that lies trapped in the Underworld, which Kato—the god of Death—guards.

Everything inside me shrivels into a small, hard knot.

I can barely breathe.

"I have your husband's body," the Mother of Night says gently, offering me the amulet. "Kato has his soul. This is a soul-trap. If you venture into the Underworld, you may be able to trap Thiago's soul within it, long enough to bring it back to his body. Open it in his presence and it will trap his soul inside. If you combine the two of them and then wield the power of this Hallow, you may be able to restore him to you. Resurrect Thiago, kill his father and reap the fragments of Death's soul from within him. Your husband will rise as Death. You only have one chance to kill the Horned One, Vi. You are the *leanabh an dan*, the Daughter of Destiny. Your mere presence twists fate." And then she leans closer. "So yes, I knew Thiago would die, Vi. But I also knew there was a possibility you could bring him back."

Chapter Seven

Iskvien

B leak silence rings through the council chamber as I tell the others what the Mother of Night said. The amulet hangs around my neck, strangely cool against my skin.

Eris is the first to speak, slamming her hands on the table. "No. *No.* You do not understand what you're suggesting. He would not want this. Thiago would not want this."

I run a tired hand over my brow. "Then what do I do,

Eris? Do I let the Horned One overrun the world? Do I go to him by myself and try to... to kill him?"

The idea's so fucking ludicrous, a tired little laugh escapes me.

"And you don't think that bitch is playing with your mind again?" she demands. "She wants to be *freed*, Iskvien. She's an Old One. She's the enemy, the one who—"

"Threw herself between me and the Horned One," I point out, "at great cost to herself. I know what she is. I know what the stories say." The whole world feels like it settles on my shoulders. "She said he's my only hope to defeat the Horned One."

Silence falls across the council chambers, shattering in its stillness.

"You would have to find the Gates to the Underworld," Thalia says softly. "And manage to either steal past Kato or beg him to allow Thiago's soul to be freed."

Then Finn rocks forward, setting all four legs of his chair on the ground. "I've been to the Gates of the Underworld. I can take you."

Incredulousness steals through me.

One by one, the little pieces are falling into place.

"*Are you doing this?*" I send the thought to the Mother of Night.

There is no reply.

"When did *you* go to the mouth of the Underworld?" Eris demands.

There's enough tension between them for his gaze to be cool as it meets hers. "That's none of your business. Suffice it to say I've been there." He blows out a breath as he turns to me. "I'll take you, Vi. I can take you as far as the opening."

"What about Amaya?" He's been at her side night and day, protecting her.

"I can stay with Amaya," Thalia says quickly. "Between Grimm and me, she'll be safe Vi. And if you don't go, and the Horned One comes south for us then it's not as though we have the strength to fight him. Not without Thiago. As much as this is a risk, we have to take it. Before it's too late." She bites her lip and meets my eyes. "Because, while Lucere seems to think there were two other Darkyn out there, my sources lost them over a year ago. Conveniently, around the same time Malakhai went missing from view for several months."

I get what she's telling me: Maybe there are only two Darkyn walking this world now.

Malakhai.

And Amaya.

I cannot describe the chill that runs through me.

A chair scrapes across the floor.

Eris's jaw locks as she slowly pushes to her feet. "I can't. I can't say yes to this. Have you heard what you're suggesting?"

"We break into the Underworld," Finn says, "and demand our prince's soul back."

"And what if he doesn't come back the way he was?" she demands. A furious glare rakes the table. "You all know what he was like... before Vi arrived."

An awkward silence falls.

"What he was like?"

Thalia looks troubled. "He was beginning to lose hope

he'd ever find you, Vi. And while he didn't like to admit it, the Darkyn inside him was beginning to strain against the edges of its cage."

"Strain?" Eris barks. "He was struggling to control it at all."

"True." Thalia meets her friend's gaze. "But he did control it. And then he found Vi, and it was like there was light in his heart again. If she can resurrect him, there's nothing to say he won't be the same male he's always been."

"There's nothing to say he will be, either. His wards will be shattered," Eris argues.

"And the Darkyn souls he'd consumed are gone," Thalia counters.

"Baylor?" Eris looks helplessly at the enormous warlord.

Baylor sits back in his chair, staring through the table. It's as if he hasn't heard a word we've said. Until he slowly lifts his gaze to her face. "When I was bound to serve the Grimm," he says quietly, "I came face-to-face with the Horned One. I saw his madness, Eris. His yearning to crush the world. Now he's been freed from his prison, his fury will only be stronger, and this time, he won't fall for our seelie tricks. It's going to take everything we have to destroy him." He hesitates. "And maybe what we need right now is not our prince. Maybe what we need is the Darkness inside him. If anyone can wield Death—and not the other way around—it's Thiago."

Eris's shoulders slump. "I want no part of this."

"We all have our parts to play, E," Baylor tells her gently. "Even you."

But Eris shakes her head. "No part of this."

Thalia reaches for her. "E—"

"Let her go," Finn says coldly as Eris turns for the door. "She's not going to listen to reason right now. And we have to take this chance. We have to get him back."

There's a quiver inside me: Hope. It feels like I've been in the dark for so long and now, I can finally see light ahead of me. "What do we need?"

Finn grimaces. "Your warmest clothing. The crown—"

"I'm not taking the crown," I say quickly. As if it senses me thinking about it, I feel its touch like cool fingernails trailing down my spine. Instantly, there are images in my mind: The God of Death cowering before me. Tearing the gates to the Underworld open with my bare hands. Sitting on a throne that's not mine— "It would be safer here. After everything we went through to get it back... it would be safer here."

"As you wish, Vi." Finn arches a brow. "Cursed shame you left the Sword of Mourning driven into the slate floors of the Hallow at Malagath. If we're going to be facing Kato, it would have been nice to have something like that on our side."

Neither fae nor immortal can stand against the Sword of Mourning.

It's invincible.

Would go nicely with me, chuckles the dark voice in my head. *Nothing would stop us.*

Shut up, I tell it.

"Yes, well. Somehow I don't think the Erlking would appreciate us stealing into his territory and taking back the sword that was his downfall."

Finn shrugs. "Maybe we don't have to steal it? He owes you two boons, does he not?"

A breathless laugh threatens to escape me, but then I still and glance down at the pair of golden antlers stamped onto the inside of my wrist. "The Erlking owes me two boons...."

Suddenly my mind is racing.

I stare at the map table in front of us.

The armies rising from the south and north. The goblins threatening to crash down upon my country like a wave breaking. And Malagath sitting to the north of the goblin lands like a dagger at its spine. My mother wants to play this game? Well, why the fuck not play it back?

"Why do I feel like you're not just repeating everything I say?" Finn asks.

A smile breaks over my lips. "Because I've finally realized how we're going to ruin my mother's plans."

* * *

Amaya's room is dark and silent when I slip inside to make sure her blankets cover her. Grimm's eyes blink open, and he stares at me from his nest on the pillow beside her.

This time, he doesn't disappear.

Setting the candle holder on the mantel by the fireplace, I cross to the bed. Amaya's dark hair spreads across the pillow and she's kicked her feet free of the blankets. I lift them carefully and tuck them over her toes, taking care not to wake her.

This has become my favorite ritual of the day.

Sometimes I simply sit here and stare at her while she sleeps. It's a moment of silence. A place of peace. When I'm here, I know she's safe, and an incredible surge of love fills me.

I'd do anything to protect this child of mine.

Anything.

"I'm not asleep," she whispers into the dark.

With a sigh, I ease onto the side of the bed and stroke her hair. "You should be."

"You're leaving."

Curse it. There's a lump in my throat. "I'm not going away forever. There's a chance I can bring your father back—"

She rolls over to face me. "You're leaving. I overheard you talking. Your friends said it's dangerous. Finn said the Guardian of the Underworld demands a heavy due for those who dare barter with him." Every inch of her face tightens, but it's the silvery gleam of not-quite-shed tears across her eyes that buries a knife in my heart. "You said you'd always be here for me."

I promised her that the first night we arrived. I dragged her into my arms and breathed in the scent of her air, my heart still ravaged with loss as I promised her she would never know fear again. That she was safe. That I would protect her.

"It's not that simple—"

"You *lied.*"

"*Child.*" Grimm flicks her with his tail. "*Do you remember when I said I had to go away and that it would be scary, but it was the only way I could make things right?*"

Amaya bites her lip and drags him into her arms. But she nods.

"*And it* was *scary,*" Grimm says gently, butting his head

84

against her chin, "*but I came back for you. I made things right. Just like I promised.*"

Another nod.

"*And now your mother has to make things right.*"

A tear spills over the edge of her cheek.

"I don't want to go. I'm scared too. I've only just found you. I want to stay right here with you, but... The Mother of Night wants me to bring your father back. I need him at my side if I'm going to kill the Horned One."

Amaya sneaks her hand into mine. It's forgiveness of a sort. "Okay," she whispers. "But stay with me tonight."

There are a million things to do. I have to pack. I have to plot war. I have to deal with Eris. But right now, none of them matter. Tugging aside the blankets, I slip beneath them and snuggle against her.

"Tell us a story," she begs Grimm.

I'm used to being the one who tells the stories. When I was a young girl, the library was my only retreat. I could lose myself in other worlds, where I could be the daughter of a mother who loved her. I could be a warrior, brave and true. I could be the hero who struck the fell blow against a monster and saved her people.

I could be brave and defiant and powerful and true; all the things I wasn't.

And a part of me loves the fact that she adores stories too.

Grimm blinks, looking pleased with himself. "*Who is Death?*"

"It was a creature who stalked this world long before the fae arrived. A god."

85

"*Perhaps,*" he murmurs, resting his chin on his paws as he stares at me, "*you should ask yourself 'what is Death?'*"

What is Death? Everything inside me goes still.

He is older than time immortal....

Been here even before the fae arrived.

"*The Shadow Sinister,*" Grimm says, conjuring a ball of shadow on the walls with a twist of his claw. He twirls his paw, and the shadow spins itself out into a hooded figure atop a nightmare horse. "*The Ancient Chill. The Hungry One. The Inevitable. A creature who struck terror into the heart of every mortal alike, and that fear gave him strength and power, for what is fear if not belief?*"

Death.

Death was an Old One. They were forged of prayer and belief, gaining strength over the centuries from the otherkin who made their sacrifices to the Hallows, until they finally became gods.

My jaw drops open. That's impossible. "Death is... forged of the primordial Darkness."

"*What is the Darkness? The Old Ones wield* ala, *the power of the leylines, the power of the earth beneath their feet, the power of creation. But there are other power currents to tap into.*" Grimm smirks as I gape at him. "*The Lord of Death rode these lands on a vicious black steed; carved of shadows and midnight. He carried a scythe as his weapon of choice and cast a shroud of shadow across the lands behind him.*" It almost sounds as if Grimm is quoting something he once read. "*And there were only three things he feared: Love. Light. And the Lord of Life.*"

Lord of Life? "Who?"

Grimm blinks smugly, watching me as if he's waiting

for me to make the connections. "*Sing to the darkness. Kick up thy heels as night falls. Bring mead and wine and dancing to distract him. Bar thy door. For the Erlking is coming....*"

There's a rock sitting heavy in my chest.

The Erlking.

The *Erlking*.

Savage and merciless and as capricious as the west wind.

There's a smile on the grimalkin's face as our eyes meet and his voice drops into a mocking whisper. "*Only the Erlking was a match for Death.*"

I try one more time before we leave.

"Eris?" I call, knocking on the door to her rooms. "E?"

There's no answer.

But I can feel her inside, listening.

"You said you would always be there for me," I whisper, letting my palm lie flat against the door. "That we'd do this together."

Nothing.

I bow my head against the door. "We're leaving in half an hour. Finn's taking me north. We'll be back... well, soon, hopefully."

Again nothing.

"Goodbye," I whisper.

I retreat to the yard, my heart heavy and all my nerves screaming at me that this is wrong. That I need Eris at my side.

But Finn will have to do.

"Packs are ready," the enormous fae warrior says, dumping a heavy-looking canvas bag next to another. "Enough supplies to make it through the north and back again. Did you talk to her?"

"She won't answer the door."

He grunts under his breath. "I don't know what's going on with her. This isn't Eris. I thought she'd be the first to volunteer to bring him back."

"Bring who back?"

Finn straightens. It's amazing how easily he can slip his skin. One moment he's laughing. Smiling. Threatening to dump me in the horse trough. And in the next moment, something lethal gleams in those cold blue eyes. None of the charismatic, charming joker remains. Instead, it's like finding a predator in your midst.

I spin around, following his line of sight.

"Relax," Edain drawls, once again clean-shaven and groomed as he steps into the courtyard. His dark hair has been slicked back, revealing cheekbones that could cut like a knife, and if Finn's the monster in the undergrowth, then Edain's a sleek, lethal panther. "If I wanted Vi dead, she'd be dead."

"Where's Baylor?" Finn growls. No doubt the two of them have concocted some plan to ensure Edain isn't given a single moment alone to stir trouble.

Edain rolls his eyes. "Breathing down the back of my neck. As always."

Two seconds later, I catch a glimpse of pale, silvery hair as Baylor and Lysander follow him. Both of them carry heavy saddlebags.

"Here," Baylor says, tossing the one in his arms at Edain.

Edain staggers back as he catches it, gritting his teeth faintly. "Thanks."

"Horses are there," Baylor continues, gesturing to where a pair of stable boys lead several horses out.

"And my knives?" Edain asks.

"You'll get your knives"—Baylor cuts him a look— "when I'm ready to give them back to you."

Arguing with Baylor is like arguing with a wall.

The look Edain gives me is almost enough to make me smile.

Almost.

"There you are, baby girl," Lysander murmurs, stroking the gray muzzle of his favorite mare. He offers her a sugar cube, talking sweet nothings to her that would make half the males at court jealous. "Did you miss me?"

Edain eyes the murderous-looking black gelding pacing fractiously beside Lysander's mare. "I'll assume that black bastard kicks."

"Bites too," Baylor replies, baring his teeth in a smile. "Has a habit of bucking when he thinks your attention has strayed. And watch out for low-hanging branches, because he'll scrape you off any chance he gets. But he'll outrun anything with legs."

Lysander snickers. "Including you if he dumps you on your ass."

"Duly noted." Edain runs a gloved hand over the gelding's smooth neck, removing it swiftly when the horse bares its teeth at him. "A little petty though."

"What are you talking about?" Lysander asks, slinging

his saddlebags over the back of his horse. "That black prick belongs to Baylor. He just gave you his best mount. It's not his fault they share a personality."

"And if you don't bring him back in one piece, then you and I will be having words." Baylor gives his horse a pat.

Edain carefully takes up the reins and swings up into the saddle. The gelding flicks an ear back and whickers.

"Be good," Baylor tells him, capturing the bridle with both hands and bringing his face close to the gelding's. "No biting the goblins. They taste like shit, and you might catch something."

"But I guess I'm fair game?" Edain mutters.

Baylor shrugs. "You've been warned."

Edain finally seems to notice my attire. "And where are *you* going?"

"None of your business," Finn growls out.

Edain's eye skips over the leather breeches I wear when I spar, the thick dark green doublet, and the black fur cloak that ripples over my shoulder. And then his gaze returns to my boots, which are lined with fur. "Somewhere where you can expect to be cold," he finally says. "North." His eyes glitter. "Into Unseelie."

It's a reasonable assumption.

If I'm not going north to the goblins, then I have to be travelling farther than that.

I rest one hand on Edain's stirrup. He doesn't know exactly where my mother's warriors will have taken Andraste, so they're going to have to follow their tracks. All he's been able to discover is that they took the Hallow to Mistmere, and from there went on foot.

"Find her," I whisper. "And bring her back to me."

Lysander pauses at my side, reining in his horse. "We'll find her, Vi. Or die trying."

Edain glances beneath his lashes at my friend.

"If you come back without Lysander," I point out, "then I am going to be most displeased with you."

"He can't die," Edain returns, arching a crisp brow. "So unless I chain him to the bottom of a mine and bury the bloody thing with rubble, he's going to be haunting my fucking steps anyway."

"That sounds remarkably well thought out."

A slight hint of a smile. "When you can't kill someone, Vi, you have to come up with alternatives. If there's one thing your mother taught me, it's to have a plan to kill everyone in the room."

"Even Adaia?"

He stills, gathering the reins in his hands. "Especially Adaia."

I think of everything she's done to me. "You might have to stand in line."

Edain actually winks at me. "Maybe, once this is all said and done, we can both hold the knife?"

Chapter Eight

Iskvien

"So this is your plan," Finn says, whistling under his breath as he examines the landscape.

The ancient seat of Malagath looms over the forest like a watchful vulture, the broken ridges of its walls crumbling into the forest. A single tower stands tall, and there's a beacon of light in the window there. A shadow moves behind the glass as if someone watches.

The last time I was here was my first visit into Unseelie. Blaedwyn—the queen of these lands—captured Thiago and the others, and in order to free them, Eris and I stole the Sword of Mourning and set the Erlking free from his prison world.

In return, he granted me two boons and took the keep from Blaedwyn. From what Thalia has managed to glean from her network of demi-fae spies, the queen herself is tucked away in that tower as a prisoner within her own court.

Suffice it to say, I'm no doubt head of the list of fae she'd like to see dead.

"It's time to call in an old debt," I mutter, staring up at that window.

She's definitely watching us.

"Seems cozy," Finn mutters. "I like the changes the Erlking's made to the place."

"Changes?" I tear my gaze away.

"No mistletoe in the trees," he points out. "It's been cut down."

Because mistletoe is dangerous to the Erlking.

"The stables have been repaired." He points to a low thatched roof as we cross the drawbridge. "Some of the vines encircling the castle have been cut away. Lines of sight have been cleared."

We share a look.

"Cozy," I repeat.

Finn suddenly moves, slamming an arm in front of me.

"Halt." An enormous troll steps out from behind the guard gate, one hand coming to rest on the hilt of the ax strapped to its hip. "Who goes there?"

Here goes nothing. I lower my hood, trying not to gag on the stench of the creature. "I am Queen Iskvien of

Evernight. And I am here to see the Erlking. He owes me a debt or two."

The troll stares at me, its brow wrinkling as if he's trying to work his way through those sentences.

"For fuck's sake." Finn pushes forward. "Take us to the Erlking. Now. Or risk his temper."

That does the trick.

The troll steps out of the way, gesturing us inside. As far as he's concerned, two strangers aren't much of a danger when there's an entire keep of warriors inside.

"Ready?" Finn whispers.

"For anything," I mutter, one hand falling to rest on my sword hilt.

The Erlking rests on Blaedwyn's throne, one knee slung over the massive arm.

The banners that hung from the walls the last time we were here—the snarling white wolf that heralded Blaedwyn—are gone. Instead, boughs of holly thicken the lintels, and fat candles weep globules of wax. Enormous trestle tables line the hall, and numerous hobgoblins and sorrows and unseelie caper about, watching as Finn and I stride toward the dais with curious eyes.

"Queen of Evernight," the Erlking muses as the fiddler draws pause in order to gawk at us. "Welcome to my halls."

A crown made of antlers sits atop his head. Golden beads wink in the mess of plaits that sweep his long tangle of hair back from his face. But it's the predatory slope of his cheekbones and the hawkish look in his dark eyes that draws attention.

A brute of a male.

Powerful. Carnal. Dangerous in all the ways that matter.

Even standing before him makes me feel like prey.

"And does this welcome include guest-right?" I ask politely, in the manner of the old ways between seelie and unseelie courts.

"On my word, so be it." He gestures toward Finn. "Put up thy weapons, hunter. Speak no lie, nor conceit. Break bread with me and drink my wine, and come morning I shall see thee safely on thy way."

I bow my head. "Let no blood be spilled between us and no song be silenced. We come in peace and seek only the answering of a debt between us."

The Erlking leans forward, resting both elbows on his knees. "Ah, yes. I promised you a debt in exchange for freeing me from the Hallow. Speak wisely, little one."

"You promised two," I point out, turning my wrist to reveal two sets of golden antlers imprinted into my skin.

"That I did."

The tone of his voice is not inspiring.

It says: *Be careful what you ask for.*

"Bring wine," he calls, snapping his fingers. "And platters."

A half dozen servants spring into action.

I turn to accept a goblet from the servant, and my hand nearly knocks it over when I catch sight of his cat-slit golden eyes and the blunt horns half hidden by his tangled hair.

Not fae. Not troll or hobgoblin or sorrow or cast of the unseelie courts at all.

Otherkin.

They were the race of creatures that walked this world long before the fae fought their way through the portal they rode from another world. They prayed to the Hallows and made their sacrifices there. They danced to the equinoxes and sang to the solstices. Their ruins dot the forests, and there are even ancient walls in Ceres that bear the mark of their chiseled runes.

He's gone before I can do anything more than stare at him.

"Well, Daughter of Evernight?" muses the Erlking as I accept the wine. "Shall we drink and dance the night away? Or have you come to presume immediately upon your favor?"

I sip the elderberry wine carefully in order to give no insult. "I have come because times are desperate and the Mother of Night has granted me a quest. Else I would stay to dance the night with you."

The cup of wine pauses at his lips.

The Mother of Night is one of the most powerful Old Ones in existence, and though she's trapped within her prison world still, it's interesting to note that her name gives even the Erlking pause.

"Ah." He seems amused. "The Horned One stirs in the north, and of course, Imrhien wishes to involve herself."

"You do not fear him?"

"He and I have danced the dance of war before. I owe him my respect, but I do not fear him. My brother will not come here. Not while I'm in residence. And the world is big enough for the two of us."

What about the rest of us?

I grit my teeth.

"So speak," he compels me. "Tell me how I may assist you."

"Is Queen Blaedwyn still in residence?"

The Erlking's smile fades.

They were lovers once.

"Aye," he says. "Though I am uncertain as to how she serves any purpose in this debt of ours?"

"May I speak with her?"

He leans forward. "Is this the debt you wish to slake?"

"No." I force a smile. "Mere courtesy instead. She owes me the answer to a certain question. It has been vexing me."

He's a long time in replying. The musicians watch with bated breath, and every set of lungs in the room seems to arrest.

Finally he smiles, snapping his fingers. The fiddlers jolt into action as the Erlking pushes to his feet. "Call me curious, but I shall allow it. Come."

* * *

The Erlking pauses before the door to Blaedwyn's tower chambers, the enormous breadth of his shoulders blotting it from sight. He doesn't bother to knock.

The door slams open the second his palm hits it, but he doesn't progress into the tower room.

Instead, he steps aside, gesturing me forward.

"As you requested," he purrs.

Inside, the room is filled with debris. The tower's long been neglected, and little sparrows flit around the room, nesting in the trunk of the age-thickened vine that's grown through the walls. A broken spindle sits in the corner, but it's the set of chairs in the middle of the room that captures my attention.

And the silent figure that stares out through a hole in the wall as if surveying the kingdom she has lost.

"Two visitors," Blaedwyn says, turning around slowly. "And one of them a thief."

Tangled, matted hair lies swept back from her face. She's bound it with silk thread in bunches that almost touch her hips. A circlet of gold sits on her brow. The elegant kohl she once wore is smudged around her eyes, and her pale skin is almost ashen. A plain dark red gown clings to her lean figure, the neckline cut square and edged with fur. It looks like something a maid may have cast off, and I have to wonder who brought her the clothes.

Does it amuse the Erlking to see her in such rags?

Or is this some sort of game between them?

Her gaze drops to my side, searching hungrily for something that isn't there. "Although, you appear not to wield that which you stole."

"I'm not a thief. The sword is still here," I tell her. "I returned it to the Hallow and there it stands, driven deep into the stone there. Though I do intend to claim it this time."

"A *thief*," she hisses, her eyes bleeding blue with fury and her knuckles clenching. "That sword is mine."

"Better a thief than a liar." Surprisingly, the Erlking comes to my rescue. "The sword belongs to the one who has claimed it." Their eyes meet. "Though perhaps I have the most right to it, since you buried it in my heart."

Blaedwyn cuts him a look. "Alas, I did not leave it there."

Stillness seeps through my veins. I've been promised safe passage here today, but even I'm not tempted to step between their incinerating glares.

This is the problem with near-immortals falling into bed together. I don't know the truth behind their story, but I do know it ended with Blaedwyn betraying him and burying the Sword of Mourning in his heart in order to trap him inside the prison world bound to the Hallow.

Five hundred years is an excellent space of time in which to nurture a grudge.

And I guess there wasn't much else to do in his prison.

The Erlking's hate is polished like steel.

"What do you want?" Blaedwyn turns to me.

"A moment of your time. I wished to speak to you."

I wasn't sure what I expected to find. The last time I saw Blaedwyn, she was a queen in the full flight of her power. Her glossy black hair hung down her spine in smooth folds, and she'd worn armor woven from braided leather and painted black. Snarling silver wolf heads were pressed into the leather to hold a black silk cape to her shoulders, and she'd worn some sort of elaborate jeweled gauntlet on each hand.

But it had been her merciless blue eyes—darkened with kohl—that caught my attention then.

Even as they stab through me now.

"Then do come in," she replies, those upswept eyes turning to him with a predatory intent.

The Erlking merely smiles. "If I step over this doorway, you'll have me trapped in here." He glances at the spider-webs that circle the room, the pattern of the webs strangely hypnotic. "Your spellcraft is exquisite."

"But you're so powerful," she whispers, biting her lip. "Surely you don't imagine I can vanquish you."

The humor in his eyes dies. "Vanquish me? No. But I have no intention of killing you just yet. And if I cross this threshold, then I will have to."

I set a hand on his arm. "Can I enter the tower without becoming trapped?"

He doesn't like it. But he nods. Guest-right is a powerful thing. The moment I stepped over his threshold and asked for it was the moment I placed my life in his hands. To see a guest die when you have promised them safety is anathema to an Old One—even the fae keep to the old traditions. "You may enter. A spider bit me and wove my blood into the strands of her spellcraft. The trap is meant for me alone."

"But may I leave?" Wordplay can be so important.

His smile is a dangerous thing. "You may enter and leave. But if you enter, you are at the mercy of her whims, and while she is no longer a queen bound to her lands, she is still dangerous."

Warning then. His offer of protection extends only so far.

I consider Blaedwyn. I can sense the Hallow pulsing from the distance now, where I was never able to do so before. One tug and I could access its powers. But still.... "I have a proposition for you. And you would be a fool not to hear me out."

"Then I will hear you out." Her eyes glitter.

This time, my words are for the Erlking. "Alone. I wish to speak to her alone. Please."

Stillness slides through his enormous frame.

But it seems I have said the magic word.

"As you wish," he says. And then he laughs. "But beware of betraying me. I've had a taste of it once, and I will not suffer it again."

* * *

The first step over the threshold ignites a tingle in my veins. It shivers over my skin like water, and then it's gone. The door shuts behind me, and both of us stare at each other as we listen to the Erlking's footsteps retreat.

"You have me intrigued." Blaedwyn's lip curls. "But I'll warn you that my curiosity has limits. What do you want, little queen?"

This might be the most dangerous gambit of all.

But with Evernight surrounded on all fronts, I have no choice. Blaedwyn's territories abut the horde lands from behind. She's made her peace with the goblins—a wary one if anything—but she's still the only knife at their back.

And I am done playing nicely.

There is nothing I won't do to get Thiago back. Nothing I won't risk in order to save those I love.

Now I have a goal, a direction, it's like all that weight has sloughed off.

I am playing the game now.

And that game leads directly to my mother.

Blaedwyn is just the first piece of the puzzle.

Sweeping out the long spill of my cloak, I take a seat opposite her, summoning every last hint of arrogance I can muster. The only way to deal with a starving wolf is to become a wolf yourself. "I want you to swear allegiance to me for the terms of a year and a day."

Blaedwyn's eyes pop wide. "*What?*" But she's swift to recover. "And why would I do such a foolish thing as offer my fealty to another queen?"

"Because"—I point out, pouring each of us a glass of wine—"I'm the only one who can set you free from the Erlking and reinstate your crown. He owes me a boon. What is a year and a day of fealty to a near-immortal?"

Those cattish eyes narrow. And then she smiles and accepts the wine as she purrs, "I'm listening."

* * *

The hall is full of revelry when I return.

"You owe me a boon," I tell the Erlking. "And now I have come to claim it."

The music fades. The dancing stops. Heads whip toward me. Breaths catch in chests. And the Erlking's tapping fingers still on the edge of his throne.

"So I do," he murmurs.

I step aside, and the former Queen of Malagath strides into the hall.

She refused to come down until she'd put herself back together, and now she wears a capelet of black and dark green feathers bound at her throat with a heavy gold necklace. Black feathers have been glued to the skin around her kohled eyes so that she looks like she wears a mask, and gold glitter glints on the bridge of her nose and across her upswept cheekbones.

There is no crown—the Erlking claimed it when he captured her. But in this moment, Blaedwyn needs no crown.

It's clear that she is a queen, and as she stalks toward us, her eyes locked hotly upon him, no one can be left in any doubt that she rules this room.

I need to work on my walk if I'm to ever have an ounce of her self-possession.

The Erlking sits forward, half prepared to launch himself toward her before he stills. Maybe some ancient sense of preservation warns him. His gaze cuts toward me, and he's no doubt thinking this is the first time Blaedwyn's left the protection of her tower since he escaped the Hallow. A hint of threat dances across his expression: If we've concocted some sort of plot between us, then we'd best beware.

"Come to dance?" he asks, his eyes glittering as he sinks back on her throne.

"I've come to claim something of mine." Blaedwyn's voice rings through the throne room.

"Do tell."

"You're sitting on it."

Correction: I need to channel some of her arrogance. It's barely been a minute since she walked in here, and she's already making demands of the most dangerous creature I know.

If I have any chance of savoring this moment, I need to speak now. "You promised me two boons, oh Erlking, in exchange for setting you free from the Hallow."

103

He stills.

"For my first favor, I have this to ask: I want you to release the Queen of Malagath from her imprisonment. You will see her reinstated as queen of this court, and you will serve her for a year and a day, unless she asks of you a desire to hurt me and mine."

Shock ripples through the court.

Setting his second boot on the floor, the Erlking leans forward, the ruthless smile slipping from his face as if it never existed. "You want me to release the unseelie queen?"

"Blaedwyn," I say. "And yes, I wish you to release her—and serve her, unless she makes the slightest move against me and the seelie kingdoms. Then you are free to do as you wish with her."

Blaedwyn glances at me from beneath her lashes.

Did you really think I was going to be foolish enough to leave a loophole?

"She may not harm you either," I point out, even as he gives me an incredulous look that seems to say, *as if she even could.* I hold up my hand, revealing the bloodied slash across my palm. "She has sworn thrice that she will not harm you, imprison you, or order another to cause you injury. She will treat you as her trusted vassal for a year and a day, provided you make no attempt on her life."

They've both given their word to obey—and the price of breaking such an oath is total and utter disgrace in this world.

"Done," the Erlking says softly.

Pain sears through my wrist: One set of golden antlers is gone.

Payment for the debt has been rendered.

"You have one boon left," he continues, pushing to his feet and towering over the pair of us. "Mind you use it wisely."

Blaedwyn stalks onto the dais, her shoulder slamming against his as she takes her seat on the recently vacated throne. Her fingers caress the arms as if she's luxuriating in the sensation of it again. She'd best not get too comfortable and start considering how to remove the yoke I've quite neatly placed around her throat.

"War is coming," I tell her. "My mother conspires with the goblin horde to break their treaty with Evernight and rise upon us from the north. As my vassal, you will keep them off my back."

Her brow arches. "We're hunting goblins now, are we?"

For the first time she seems to realize what vassalage for a year and a day to me will include.

I smile. It's not my fault she saw an untried queen and an opportunity to slake her vengeance upon the Erlking. No doubt I'll pay for this year once it's over, but by then either the threat of the Horned One will be vanquished— or I won't have to worry about the debts I've earned ever again.

"To begin with, yes," I say. "But don't forget to keep an eye on the north. The Horned One is turning his gaze south, with all the unseelie forces Angharad and Morwenna can muster between them. When they come, I will expect your host to ride against them." As she pales, my smile extends. "Perhaps you would be wise not to antagonize the Erlking in the near future, as it seems only he may give the Horned One pause."

The two of them share another look.

And then Blaedwyn laughs.

"Well, well," she whispers as her laughter fades. "The little queen of Evernight is learning to play the game." A nod toward me. "Very well, you have my word. For the next year and a day, Malagath will stand with Evernight. Not a day less. Not a day more. You have my word." She raises her voice so all in her hall can hear. "Prepare yourself my birds and blades! We have goblins to hunt and a war to prepare for."

Chapter Nine

"I swear I nearly shat my pants when you told the Erlking what you wanted of him," Finn says as we walk toward the Hallow where the Sword of Mourning stands, driven deep into the heart of the slate circle. "I was expecting you to ask him to come north with us."

"I have you to protect me. I do *not* need a capricious old

god at my side trying to find loopholes to slip through to renege upon his debt."

"Oh, I don't think you need to worry about that," he said, his brows high. "I'm fairly certain he's going to be focused on trying not to kill Blaedwyn for the next year. After that, however, I think you're going to have to watch your back. Why didn't you let him kill the goblins?"

"Again, because he's capricious and untrustworthy. And I don't want them dead. I just want them distracted. This way, both the Erlking and Blaedwyn are going to be focusing on each other."

Mist surrounds the Hallow.

Our voices lower, almost in conspiracy.

It's colder here. And it almost feels as though there are eyes watching us.

I stare at the sword plunged right into the center of the Hallow.

Whosoever wields it shall never fall in battle. Its swing shall never miss. And it can slice through the strongest of metals in a single blow.

Even as it sings a song of tyranny in your ear.

The last time I held it, I wasn't ready for the power, the seduction.... I'm still not ready, truth be told. And with the Crown of Shadows already whispering in my ear, I don't know if I dare bring it into my court.

I close my eyes, picturing the sword in hand.

With the crown and the sword, I'd be unstoppable. Empires would rise and fall before me. Foes would be crushed beneath my heel. Even my mother would fail. I can practically see the look of shock and horror on her face as I swing the sword, and take her head from her shoulders.

Which is why I can never wield both.

Because I know myself well enough to know that that thought was not mine.

I turn to Finn. "The first time I saw this sword, I thought it was meant for Eris's hand."

But Eris hosts her own demons, and she too, cannot afford to become unstoppable.

Circling the sword, I listen to the hum vibrating off it. It knows I'm here. Featherlight strokes brush against my psychic senses.

Only my hand can draw the sword.

That doesn't mean it has to stay there.

Taking a deep breath, I close my hand around the hilt. The shock of it shears through me. Light obliterates the fog, tearing it to pieces, and my hair blows back in the sudden wind as I draw it from the stone.

"Vi?"

The weight of it nearly drives me to my knees. It's so much more than mere steel. But as I take a deep breath and focus upon it, I managed to lift the point.

Yes, whispers a voice in my head. *Let us remake the world.*

I turn to Finn.

"Kneel," I tell him.

A knowing look lights those blue eyes. "You had better not be planning something reckless."

"Please."

It's the "please" that does it. With a sigh, Finn goes to one knee.

I rest the tip of the blade on his right shoulder. "You were bred for war," I whisper. "You have spent your entire

109

life turning away from it. I know the fight you fight, each and every day. And I know what this sword represents to you." I shift the sword to his left shoulder. "You have stood at my side, strong and unyielding. You have been there for me at every step of the way, shouldering my burdens when I didn't understand them, protecting me from harm when I could barely remember you. You are loyal, you are brave, and you are true. And now your queen asks this burden of you. Wield the Sword of Mourning against my enemies. Use it to protect my daughter, my family, my court. Lift it on the field of war against those who will come. If there is any hand that should take this sword, it should be yours."

Finn's face pales. "Vi—"

"Promise me," I tell him harshly. "Promise me you'll wield it until this is done. And then you will return it. Stand as my knight and ride at my will."

There's horror in his eyes as his gaze slides to the length of steel. "Vi—"

"I hear that fucking crown whispering in my head every night." My voice comes in a rush. "I feel it now, urging me to not pass this over. To take up both sword and crown. Sometimes I think things—see a future I would never imagine in a thousand years—where I sit on a throne at the head of an empire that rules the world. So don't tell me I don't know what I'm asking of you." I take an unsteady breath. "I know what temptation whispers. I know the fight. Just as I know that if there is one hand that can stay temptation, it is yours. You, Finn. One of my husband's most loyal warriors."

His jaw stiffens, his eyes downcast.

And then he slowly looks up and holds out his hand.

This is the moment in which we test the truth: Few can wield the Sword of Mourning.

But as Finn's hand curls around the hilt, our gazes meet, and then there's another shock of cataclysmic ringing in my ears. The sword seems to vibrate. My fingers fight the urge to curl around the hilt and rip it back from him, but it's too late—

He has the sword.

"As my queen commands," he rasps, pushing to his feet and lifting the cursed steel.

Chapter Ten

Iskvien

North again. Our passage through the Hallow is effortless and leaves us standing in a world kissed with snow.

The Hallow is shielded by the curve of the valley. There's no wind down here, and it's a little eerie. It feels like we're standing on the edge of the world—the farthest Hallow north, and one where visitors rarely return from.

"These are the Shadowfall ranges," Finn mutters, breathing into his cupped hands as he takes a few careful steps through the Hallow stones. "They stand at the very edge of the world. No one has gone beyond them—or at least, no one has ever returned. They say if the cold doesn't get you, then the monsters that lurk here will."

I press my hand against one of the enormous standing stones that circle the Hallow. The top of it is sheared off and might explain the odd buzzing sound I heard when we finally arrived. The Hallow didn't fight us, but there was definitely a moment where the magic pulsed and I wondered if it was going to spit us out into the middle of nowhere.

"What sort of monsters should we expect?" It's so fucking cold I can't stop shivering. Easing out a breath, I still my mind and then reach for the dark flame within me. It's getting easier to access my fae magics the more I use them, as if the curse my mother laid upon me is finally disintegrating. I forge heat into my cloak and clothes—just enough to still the seeping cold.

And then I grab Finn's cloak and do the same for him.

"Thanks," he mutters, though he doesn't take his eyes off the surrounding forest. "And I'd really prefer not to find out. I only ever came this far north once, and *something* was hunting us, but I didn't stick around to find out what."

"Us?"

He passes between the stones. "Long story, Vi. An old story."

And one he clearly doesn't want to speak of. I follow him, boots sinking into the snow. It's nearly a foot deep,

113

and so soft and pristine that it's clear we're the only ones
who've been here for a while.

Maybe even years.

"There was an Old One tied to this Hallow," I murmur,
"from what I saw in Imerys's book about the old myths."

Finn surges ahead. "Do I really want to know?"

"A figure dressed in ragged furs. Wolfbrother, they
called him. A child left out in the snows who was found by
a pack of wolves and raised by them. He became their
master—their alpha—and his howl used to echo through
these mountain ranges." I chance a glance beneath the
nearest snow-clad fir. "He was unlike the rest of the Old
Ones. The only ones who prayed to him were the wolves
and local fae who offered him and his pack animal sacrifices
so they'd leave them alone. The book said he slipped from
memory, from this world long ago. He became more wolf
than otherkin, and they say eventually he learned the gift of
slipping skins until he truly ran on all fours. Nobody's seen
him in over five hundred years, but the wolves in the north
here hunt in the dozens together."

"A skinshifter. Curse it. I knew we should have brought
Baylor."

"Have you ever seen him shift shape?"

Baylor and Lysander were born somewhere in Unseelie
thousands of years ago—they're the oldest among us. They
were bound to serve the Grimm, the Old One who rides
with a pack of hounds, though I seem to recall a drunken
night, long ago, where Lysander let slip that they'd been
enemies of the Grimm. He turned them into hounds and
they were forced to ride at his will for thousands of years,

until they became more beast than fae. I don't know how they escaped him, but when I mentioned that I was destined to break open the prison worlds and restore the Old Ones to the world, Baylor grew a little pale.

"Yes," Finn says. "He becomes an enormous silver wolf-like creature, and let's just say I would rather stick my hand in a fire than be hunted by either of them. They have teeth the size of my index finger."

"I'm fairly certain they'd never hunt you."

"Baylor's not so certain," he finally admits. "I think you scared him, Vi, when you said the Mother of Night wants you to free the rest of her kin. He escaped the Grimm once, but if he's free again, then they'll hear his call. It's a siren song, Lysander once admitted when he was deep in his cups. When the Grimm forged them into his hounds, he laid his mark on them, and they'll never truly escape it."

The same way Thalia fears the Father of Storms if I free him. She has just enough blood from her saltkissed father to wonder if she's going to be bound to the Father of Storms's will.

I'm not going to free them.

The words die on the tip of my tongue.

I wasn't going to offer the Mother of Night the crown either.

I didn't want anything to do with any of this.

But now the Horned One is free. My mother is making feints at our borders. And Angharad is rousing an army for the Horned One.

Everything the Mother of Night predicted is coming true, and like it or not, I feel like I'm slowly circling the maelstrom, heading toward the whirlpool in the center, no matter how hard I try to swim against the current.

The Mother of Night couldn't stop the Horned One.

How am I meant to do it?

"But don't take that to heart," Finn throws over his shoulder, as if he can sense my sudden consternation. His blue eyes lock on me, serious for once. "Don't let your doubt or your guilt stop you from doing what you need to do. If you have to smash open the Hallows and the Grimm rises up and puts a leash on Baylor and Lysander again, then we'll hunt him down and I'll put this sword through his heart. If the Father of Storms rises, then we'll steal a ship—preferably one of Prince Kyrian's—and ram the figurehead on the front of it right through him. Thalia, Baylor and Lysander—they all understand that. We're family, Vi. Now you need to understand that."

My heart feels so fucking heavy in my chest. "I know."

Finn falls back to clap a hand on my shoulder. "You're not alone, Vi. I just want you to know that. And the weight on your shoulders isn't your burden to carry alone."

Hot tears threaten to spill down my cheeks. There's a part of me—the little girl who watched as her sister was hauled away from her, doors slamming in her face—that feels like she's always alone.

"Thanks," I whisper, bumping my shoulder against his.

Giving my shoulder one last squeeze, Finn slips ahead. "The entrance to the Underworld isn't far. It's on an island in the middle of a lake. That's where we'll find him. That's where we'll find Kato."

"What should I expect?"

"Nobody knows," he says quietly. "Nobody's ever come back from the Underworld that I know of."

"There's always a first time."

Finn suddenly freezes, his hand coming to rest upon the hilt of the sword.

He holds his other hand up.

"What is it?" I whisper.

He suddenly shoves me behind him, drawing the sword in one smooth glide. The ringing in my ears is back, the power of the sword emanating from it in a teeth-gritting buzz.

I string my bow and put an arrow to it, searching the darkness of the forest.

Something moves. Just to the left.

And then Eris bursts out of the forest, a drawn bow in her hands.

"Run!" she yells.

And at the look on her face, I don't bother to argue.

"What the fuck are you doing here?" Finn bellows at her as he shoves me ahead of him.

Neither of us missed the glimpse of sleek pale shapes darting through the snow behind her.

"Can we argue about this later?" she snaps, twisting and sending an arrow arching through the trees. "There's an entire pack of ice wolves on your ass."

A yelp sounds.

"Ice wolves?" I hadn't seen a thing.

"They've been downwind," she calls. "Hunting you from the second you left the Hallow."

We slip and slide down the slate-covered path toward the lake. Tundra grasses mark the edges of the trail and patches of snow lie in clumps here and there.

But it's the sound of a howl that sets my teeth on edge.

"There!" Finn points at a jagged stone sticking out of the ground ahead of us. A rune is carved into the flat surface of it. "If we make it past that point, they won't follow!"

My legs stretch into a ground-eating run. Finn stands a head taller than me, but it's clear he's setting a pace I can match, and Eris shields my rear.

"Three on the left!" Eris yells. She shoves me in the back, "Keep moving!"

An arrow twangs.

Another ice wolf yelps.

The blood hammers through my veins, pulsing in my ears. My bow's strung across my back, along with my pack, but I don't have time to nock an arrow to it.

I reach for the dark flame within me, the one that whispers through my veins.

"Eris!" I yell, turning and waving a hand.

She sprints toward me, barely one yard in front of a pair of wolves focusing on her hamstrings.

"Down!" I scream.

Eris hits the ground, and I throw my hand forward, a wash of heat and flame bursting from my fingertips. It sizzles over her skin, smashing into the pair of wolves. White fur erupts into fire. Howls of pain echo. And then they're rolling in a patch of snow, yelping as they flee into the woods.

I hold my hands out as the alpha draws to a halt, his lip curling back off his enormous teeth. "Go ahead," I yell at him. "Eris! Move!"

She scrambles across the ground toward me, finally pushing to her feet.

Huge shapes slink out of the trees as we back toward the pillar of stone.

Eris wrenches me after her just as the entire pack bursts forth from the fir. Dozens of them snap and snarl, forming an arrowhead of attack.

"Run!" Finn yells, and an arrow flashes past me, burrowing in the heart of the silvery wolf to the right of the alpha. "You're nearly there!"

Another hiss.

Another yelp as a second wolf goes down.

We burst past the pillar, and it's like we run straight through an invisible barrier—one that feels like a shock of lightning. It disorients me enough that my feet go out from under me as we hit loose shale. Slamming against the ground, I start sliding down the hill, sharp rocks stabbing at my legs and ass. The ground whooshes past, and then the edge of the cliff comes up fast.

Below it, a glittering lake glimmers, the surface reflecting back the endless gray skies.

I flip to the side, reaching desperately for something—anything—to grab onto before I go over the edge, and Eris snags my hand.

She's on her back, sliding with me, but the second our fingers lock together, she digs her heels in.

Suddenly there's nothing beneath me. A scream tears free of my throat as I lash out wildly and catch her wrist right before I go over the edge of the cliff. Eris slams to a halt, heels driving into a runnel in the stone. My body swings and then slams back into the granite face of the cliff.

"Got you!" Eris grinds her teeth as she tries to haul me back up. "Don't look down!"

"Curse it, Eris!" I close my eyes, my pulse a thundering waterfall. "That's the worst thing you can ever say to someone who's hanging over the edge of a cliff!"

Every ounce of my being wants to look down.

I catch a glimpse of dark water nearly fifty feet below me. The surface of the lake is so smooth it looks like a black mirror, and there's something ominous about that thought.

I suck in a sharp gasp, my fingers instinctively curling around hers.

Gravel rains over me as Finn skids to a halt beside us, reaching down. "Got you!"

Together they haul me back over the edge, Finn curling his fist in my pack and yanking me higher.

I collapse on the ground, my entire body shaking.

"Wolves," I gasp.

Finn sits back, breathing hard. "Fuck. I thought you were gone for a second." He rubs his mouth and casts a dark look back up the hill. "They won't come any farther. We passed the marker."

The alpha growls above us, prowling back and forth on the top of a rock as if he'd love to come and play, but this stone plinth marks the edge of his territory.

Eris pushes to her feet, resting her hands on her knees as she gasps for breath. "Are you okay, Vi?"

Now that the thrill of the moment is over, everything is starting to hurt.

"You're bleeding," Finn mutters, flipping up the edge of my shirt.

"Gravel rash." I wince and cup my arm across my body. The skin on my elbow is a distant memory, and every inch of my right side feels like it just made love to sandpaper. "I'm fine."

"You're not fine," Finn snaps.

I grab his hand. "Fine, Finn. Maybe not up to dancing a jig right now, but it's not going to affect me."

Finn mutters something unintelligible as he tugs a small pot of something from his pack and then dabs a clear gel on the worst of my wounds. My gifts of healing don't extend to myself, and the others have no such magic.

"Ouch!"

Unscrewing the top of a water canteen, Finn offers it to me. I drink deeply, then climb to my feet and pass it to Eris.

"Do I even want to know why those wolves stopped?" Or what might scare them enough to make them forsake the thought of three easy meals?

"This is the Lake of Silence," Finn says. "The rune on that stone belongs to Kato. Nothing will cross the barrier. Not even a bird. Didn't you feel it?"

It felt like a static shock at the time, but now, as I look around, I realize it was more of an... absence.

Nothing moves around us. Not even the wind.

There's no sound. No birds. Not even the drift of the wolves howling. It's like this world exists within a bubble and nothing can penetrate it.

"We made the lake." The oppressive *absence* highlights the quietness of my voice. *We made the lake, which means the island's not far ahead.* When we set out from Ceres, I

121

was so focused on getting Thiago's soul back that I didn't comprehend what that would mean.

We're here.

We're so close.

And now I have to bargain with the God of the Dead; the Guardian to the gates of the Underworld.

* * *

There's a boat waiting at the edge of the lake, tied to a rickety old dock.

"Can we trust it?" I murmur.

Finn checks the boat out. "He knows we're coming." Steeling himself, he glances across the water toward the island. It's half a mile out. "Whether he chooses to dump us in the lake or not, well, I guess we'll find out."

I shiver. "I'd rather not."

"I'm an excellent swimmer."

"So am I," I reply, "but that doesn't mean I want to take a dip in these frigid climes."

Finn's smile fades as he lifts his gaze to Eris. "Get in," he tells her, hauling the boat off the beach.

Eris paces at the edge of the lake. "I cannot continue with you."

Finn's halfway into the water with the boat. He looks up. "What?"

Eris grits her teeth. "I can't go any farther."

"Why not?"

"Death isn't the only thing the primordial Darkness spawned," she says. "And if I get in that boat, then I can almost guarantee it's going to tip over. There are spells carved into the timber. They won't want *me* anywhere near that island."

"Then why the fuck did you even bother to follow us?"

Her cheeks burn dark, but it's to me that her attention turns. "Because I didn't want you doing this alone. You were right. Even if I don't like this, I still have a duty to my prince to see you carry this plan out."

Finn looks like he's going to argue, but I hold up a hand. Eris wouldn't be making this choice if she didn't deem it necessary. "Then wait for us here. Hold this side of the lake for us—just in case we need to leave in a hurry."

She nods.

Impulsively, I wrap my arms around her.

Eris returns the hug. "You know I would come with you if I could," she whispers, too low for Finn to hear.

I squeeze her back. "You've been with me at every step of this journey." I draw back. "I know, Eris. I know you would."

"I didn't mean what I said at home."

"I know." Grief affects us all differently. "If we're not back in three days, then I want you to return to Ceres. Without me, Amaya's the only one with the power to break the Hallows open. The Mother of Night will seek to use her. Protect her, Eris. Protect her from them all."

Maybe the Mother of Night is an ally, but she won't care that she's setting Amaya straight into the sights of a dozen power-hungry queens and a ruthless old god.

"With my life," she promises.

Relief fills me, and I turn to where Finn is waiting. I don't know why, but I'm not afraid anymore. Grief has hollowed me dry.

I have done what I can to protect those I love.

The world has become very simple. I don't have to worry about the Horned One or my mother, or any number of ruthless queens.

All I have to do is convince the Guardian of the Underworld to relinquish my husband's soul.

Chapter Eleven

Iskvien

W e row across the lake, the island looming through the mists.

"It seems a little easy, doesn't it?" Finn mutters, putting his back into the oars.

"Stop tempting the gods," I try to joke, but a shiver runs down my spine. If Kato protects the Underworld from spilling forth into the world, then wouldn't there be more... guards?

"I like the ambiance," Finn notes as he hauls us to shore. The second the boat beaches itself on the sand, he offers me a hand. "Why is it that all these places decorate themselves with moss and gloom? You'd think the gateway to the Underworld would be a little grander."

"I think it manages that aura of 'keep away' quite well," I murmur as he assists me onto the sand. "I also think that's precisely the effect Kato was going for."

There's a hill in the center of the island, though the thick fir trees hide the sides of it.

"Stairs," Finn says, pointing toward a set of ancient, chiseled sandstone stairs.

"Are you ready?"

Finn secures our packs under a pile of rocks, leaving us with only the necessities. "Always, Vi."

Pulling my hood over my face, I ignore my racing heart and start along the small path toward the steps.

The forest swallows us whole.

Each step is taking me closer to Thiago.

I have to remember that as the oppressive silence falls heavily over us.

We start up the steps, and it takes me several minutes to realize that what was once rough-hewn sandstone has now become smooth, polished alabaster. A terrace appears. Another. I pause at the next landing, taking note of the marble sentries that linger on the edges. There are thirteen of them in all: six females and seven males.

All of them have been carved to wear what appears to

be braided leather armor. Hints of scale mail drape over their shoulders, but it's the wings that catch my attention.

The detailing on the feathers is so lifelike that if they weren't carved of alabaster, I'd be a little unnerved at the thought they might simply step off the ledge and turn upon me with drawn swords.

"Darkyn," Finn murmurs.

Until Lucere told me, I knew little to nothing about the race of creatures that spawned my husband. "You knew what he was?"

"It's not something he ever spoke of. I wasn't even aware until.... Well, Eris was the one who revealed it. There was a period during our third century together when she became well-nigh unbearable. She would snap at everyone and everything. She was drinking down in the city, alone. Always off by herself. It was starting to worry Thalia, and so I followed Eris into the Old City one night and spent the night drinking with her." He shrugs. "I thought it was something to do with her past, and in a way it was. Just... not as I expected."

He pauses in front of a lethal-looking female who crouches low with a spear in her hand. Cracks spear through the alabaster here, and half her face has crumbled to the ground, but there's nothing but ferocity lingering in the single eye that remains. "Thiago was in a bad state. We all knew it, though none of us understood it. It started when word came of a creature stirring trouble in the north. Malakhai."

His father.

"There was some disagreement between the Unseelie

queens, with Angharad and Blaedwyn at each other's throats, and at that time, Malakhai rode at Angharad's whims. His warband attacked Blaedwyn's forces, and Thalia was beside herself trying to keep track of him, because all her sources had identified him as a threat. She keeps track of the major players in all the lands, but this Malakhai had appeared from seemingly nowhere. We were discussing whether we'd need to shore up our northern borders. Arguing about fortifications. Our alliance with the goblins. None of us noticed how withdrawn Thiago became until he placed one hand flat on the map table and all the little figures that represented Malakhai's warriors fell flat. 'I'll handle it,' he said, and then he walked out."

Finn holds his hands wide. "There was something about the way he said it. His voice was so cold. I swear his eyes were black. And Eris stared after him, her skin turning ashen before she went after him."

I pause in fascination.

"After that, Eris insisted she'd handle him. But while Thiago seemed to shrug off the incident, Eris didn't. We were about three flagons down when she finally admitted that several years after she joined our court, Thiago had asked her to kill him."

"*What?*"

Finn looks about as pleased as I do with this pronouncement. "Eris was the only one perhaps capable of doing the task. He told her that if the Darkness ever overcame him, then she was to set him free—before he could hurt anyone. She would know it for the black of his eyes, the coldness of his voice, the violence of his choices. He finally admitted Malakhai had sired him, and that he could feel him out there, like calling to like. A threat coming

128

closer and closer, like two magnetic forces drawn to each other. If Malakhai learned of him, then he would come for Thiago's soul. And the part of Thiago that he fought to repress would surface. He'd no longer be the prince he was. He'd be forced to a lethal edge, given over to the predatory nature of his primal self. Eris was finally facing the consequences of the bargain she'd made."

She loved my husband—he'd saved her from almost certain death, and for the first time in her life, Eris learned what trust looked like.

To suddenly face the inevitable.... For it to be her own hand that dealt the killing blow, and for him to ask such a thing of her....

He must have been desperate.

He knew how much it would hurt her.

And here I am, asking her to accept the fact that the soul I bring back may not be the Thiago we all knew.

"He needed that failsafe," he says quietly, "but he'll never know how much it cost her to agree to it."

"*Oh.*" Suddenly, all her recent actions make sense.

"And now I think I need to apologize to her." Finn grimaces. "I hate it when I realize I'm being an asshole."

"This is why I like you so much though. Because you *can* actually realize it."

He sighs and walks along the gallery, examining the statues. "That and my insanely good looks."

"Alas, I'm quite partial to guys with dark hair."

"Ouch." He mimics taking an arrow to the chest. "From all angles."

"Someone's got to keep that sense of arrogance at bay."

"I'm gorgeous and I know it," he snorts. "What's wrong with that?"

I can't stop myself from bumping shoulders with him. I know what he's doing, of course. Making me smile. Taking the tension out of the situation, so I'm not thinking about what lies ahead. It's part of Finn's charm.

"Granted. Though I think you're getting some competition from the marble here."

Finn pauses in front of a shirtless marble statue, and then imitates it's flexing pose. "Who holds a spear like that?"

"You. You definitely hold a spear like that. Mostly when there are females visiting the training yards."

"My ancestors would curse me to a thousand frozen eternities if I ever struck a pose like that."

I take a step toward the next statue, and then I slam to a halt, my laughter trickling off.

Because it looks like Thiago.

Overlapping scales plate his armor, and his cloak is caught at his throat with what is presumably some sort of jewel. His wild hair blows back in a long-ago breeze, but it's the look in his eyes that freezes me. It feels like he's staring right through me, and not kindly.

Not Thiago. It takes a second for my eyes to note the differences, even if my rampaging heartbeat doesn't quite catch that message as swiftly.

Malakhai of the Black Reaches. Malakhai of Malagaddon.

My husband's father.

It's like a punch to the throat. One second, I've almost summoned the strength to smile, and the next....

130

I see it all over again.

I hear him fall.

My fingers clench the way they did when I tried to capture his ashes.

"Scary-looking prick, isn't he?" Finn muses.

The tightness in my chest is almost unbearable, and I can't help leaning into him as he squeezes my shoulder in silent recognition.

"I'm not quite sure the artist quite captured his nature." Finn leaps up on the rail, digging around in his pack for something. Two seconds later, he reaches up and draws a curl on the statue's face.

"*Finn!*"

"Hush, now." He traces his piece of charcoal carefully over the marble. "There's no rushing good art."

By the time he climbs down, Malakhai is sporting a rather ridiculous mustache.

It eases some of the tension in my chest. "Kato is going to kill you if he sees what you've done to his statuary."

Finn winks at me. "I don't know. He might think I've improved it. Why don't we find out?"

* * *

The entrance to the Underworld stands atop the island's peak. It's a long winding staircase carved of the same marble as the statuary. Deep within it beats the heart of a Hallow, I'd swear it. It's like an ancient pulse buried deep beneath the earth's core, one that sucks at me, rather than offering succor.

I've never felt anything like it.

The Gates to the Underworld.
The Gates to Darkness.

I've been focusing so much on getting Thiago back that I haven't truly considered what I'm facing.

"Climbing out of here is going to be a bitch," Finn says, stalking into the darkness ahead of me. "My thighs are protesting at the mere thought of it."

I don't know what's more unnerving: That the gateway to the primordial Darkness lies ahead of us, or that with every level we descend, torches flicker to life on the walls as if someone is fully aware we're coming.

The temperature plunges a degree with every curve of the stairs.

Soon my breath is fogging the air and I can't stop myself from shivering.

I'm a daughter of a summer queen. Summer is in my blood. This is a bad sign.

"I'm fairly certain my balls just tucked tail and ran," Finn says, his exhale misting the air as he rubs his arms. "Indeed, my toes might join them."

Summoning my magic, I set warming spells into his cloak and boots, and then mine.

"It's not going to catch fire, is it?" he asks.

"That only happened one time."

"Memorable though, Vi. It's not the sort of thing you forget. I had to throw myself into a water trough."

"I can remove the spell," I tell him sweetly.

He runs his tongue over his teeth. "I trust you."

"Good. Keep walking."

We pass an ice-blue statue as we descend. It's a fae male

sitting with his back to the wall, his knees drawn up to his chest.

Not a statue.

Finn holds his sword on the stranger as we circle past it, and with every step I swear he's going to look up and attack us.

But we pass by without incident, every level taking us down into a cold that's starting to hurt the lungs.

"Vi." Finn breathes the word into the frost-tinged world.

"We keep going." I surge ahead, thighs burning on the never-ending stairs.

Nothing is going to stop me. Not now I have my husband's soul in my sights.

* * *

I can barely feel my fingers and toes by the time we make our way down to the bottom of the pit. My blood slides through my veins like viscous honey, and it's difficult to breathe, even with my warming spells.

The only thing keeping me going is that hypnotic drumbeat pulsing through me in time to my heartbeat, as if the Hallow can sense me. It's a smoky song of allure, a curiosity. If I didn't know any better, I'd almost say it feels *alive*.

But the second I catch a glimpse of the cavern ahead of us, all my bodily concerns vanish.

We're here.

Silent sentries guard the enormous gates that lead into a throne room beyond, wearing black cloaks and helmets that disguise their entire faces. They're so still I'm not entirely certain they're alive until two of them step forward, crossing spears to bar our way.

The gates themselves though.... I can't stop my gaze from lifting, tracing over the writhing wyrm carved into the lintel. Gold flecks the edge of its scales, and its eye is a blank circle of gold. Dragons vanished from this world eons ago, they say, but I can't help feeling as though that circle is watching me.

"Who goes this way?" The guardian demands.

Beyond them, a dark figure lounges on a throne.

To his right stands an archway, and within it, swirls of inky shadow, much like the ones my husband could summon.

The Gate to the Underworld.

Straightening my spine, I summon all my courage, all my bravery. *Be like Blaedwyn*. "My name is Iskvien, and I am the Queen of Evernight, come to seek an audience with your master."

"Denied," says the one on the left.

The word echoes through the chamber like a slap.

"May I ask why?"

"None living may enter this world," says the other. "Our king has turned his face from the mortal plane, and lives only to serve as Keeper of the Darkness. He has no concern with your mortal cares."

I step forward, ignoring the way the figures tense. I *have* to speak to Kato. "Does he know what is happening in the world above?"

"Mortals fight. Mortals fall. He does not care."

"The Horned One is risen," I call, my fingers curling

into fists. "He seeks to subjugate the world. Perhaps your king will care when the Horned One comes for him."

"The Horned One may come." This time, I swear there's a hint of smirk to the guardian's voice. "And he will be turned back, just as you are. Go now, mortal. Before the cold steals away the last of your breath."

This is not happening.

I want to scream. To come so close and to be denied like this.... It's more than I can bear.

Hatefully, it's my mother's voice I hear in my head, and I see her anew, reaching across the *fari* board to take out three of my pieces. "*Never cringe, Iskvien, even if your heart races, never let them see it. Power respects power. Claim your power. Make them respect you.*"

In the silence, I hear the Hallow's pulse beat.

It's in my veins, echoing through my heart.

I am not going back. Not without him.

"Vi?" Finn asks.

This time, there's no need to summon my inner Blaedwyn.

I open myself up to the Hallow, even as another doorway suddenly opens in my mind.

"*You must not claim this Hallow, Iskvien,*" whispers the Mother of Night's voice in my head. "*It is forbidden.*"

"*Kato doesn't need to know that,*" I respond.

I just need him to think I will.

She subsides into wary silence.

I pluck on the strings of the Hallow, feeling some sort of unearthly presence sit up and take notice. Its power cascades over my skin as if it's tasting me. It's like nothing I've ever known before. It's almost... sentient.

135

I grasp the reins of the Hallow and force it to my whims.

Boom. Boom. Boom.

The sound echoes through the throne room before it falls away into silence. Gravel rains from the ceiling.

Knock, knock, bitch.

Movement shifts. The King of the Underworld sitting forward as if I've finally caught his attention.

"I came here for an audience with the King of the Underworld." I force Kato to look at me. "I can amend the nature of my intentions in an instant if you do not deign to hear me out."

"Vi." Finn groans under his breath, and I can practically feel his hand shifting to the hilt of his sword. "Don't be rash, remember? He's a god."

I thought Maia was a goddess too, until I learned the truth.

Maia was merely a fae queen who learned how the Old Ones leashed the powers of the Hallows. She bound herself to the Hallow in Charun and ascended, using its power to "reveal" her godhood.

The cavern shivers, rocks skittering to the polished stone floors. Kato grips the arms of his throne as the floor ripples like an enormous leviathan slides below it. The gate to the Underworld shifts, and light winks through an enormous ruby mounted above it that's only just been revealed.

Not a ruby.

An eye.

An eye opening as if to see what is causing all this ruckus.

There's something back there, hugging the curves of the walls and wrapped around the gate.

Something... not fae.

I meet the king's pale eyes. I've passed beyond fear somehow. There is only the gate. There is only the Underworld.

There is only my husband.

"Let her pass," calls the Guardian of Death.

I step forward, ignoring the crossed spears in front of me until they're slowly—grudgingly—withdrawn.

Each step takes me closer to the black throne and the figure upon it. The King of the Underworld's wings sit folded behind him, his dark hair raked back off his face. A skull mask covers half of his face, bound across his forehead by a strip of leather carved with ancient knots and whorls. It's not a fae skull. There's a tooth on the end of it, something sharp and feline.

And his eyes are such a pale gray, they're almost filmy.

For some reason, I expected Kato to be Darkyn, but he's fae.

Enormous. Powerful. Dangerous.

But still only fae.

Even if he's been siphoning off the Hallow for years.

"Didn't your mother ever tell you that it's rude to demand entrance once you've already been denied?" The slightest hint of a snarl echoes in his voice.

I stalk right toward his dais, resting one hand on the hilt of my sword. "My mother told me that if someone tried to slam the door in my face then I was to kick it down."

Kato's fingers curl around the arms of his throne. "I am

a god, little girl. I am marked by Death itself. You will respect me."

I stare at him for long moments.

And then I graciously lower my eyes.

"My apologies for the brash entrance, my Lord of Death." I give the faintest of curtsies before I straighten. "I ask only for the same respect."

"Speak your piece then."

"I am here on behalf of the Mother of Night." I force strength into my voice. "I am here because the Horned One has been freed from his prison, and she has told me I might be able to kill him, once and for all, but I will need Death at my side if I am to have any hope of defeating him."

Kato's lips quirk. "That does not explain what you are doing here."

Tugging the amulet from within my neckline, I show it to him. "She gave me this soul-trap. With it, I can return my husband's soul to his body and resurrect him."

"Your husband is gone, vanished into the Darkness." Kato gestures to his guards with a pair of fingers. "Remove her."

"Wait!" I push forward two steps. "Please. Just listen to me. He's not gone. I *know* he's not gone. He said he would wait for me in the Darkness. And I need him. The Mother of Night said I would need him to slay the Horned One."

The enormous figure on the throne leans forward, pale gray eyes gleaming behind his mask. "The Mother of Night is trapped in a prison world. She has no power here."

"She has the power to meddle in this world. Through me. And Thiago is the only one who can reap the Horned

138

One's soul. Would you condemn the world to darkness? True darkness?"

Kato pushes to his feet, vibrating with anger. "You dare come here and demand such of me? I spent the lives of everyone I know just to tear that creature apart. I gave up an eternity of freedom merely to guard this domain, to *protect* the fae of this world. The Shadow Sinister cannot be resurrected. It *must* not be resurrected."

"Then you're too late," I cry. "Malakhai of the Black Reaches is a mere handful of souls away from resurrecting Death. If he comes for my daughter, he will have them *all*. No one will be able to stop him."

Kato stills. "There are two others."

"There were. Word has reached us from foreign shores of a pair of murders in the night. Coincidentally, around the same time Malakhai vanished for a year or two."

If anything, Kato appears to pale. He glances to the side, and one of the guards beside his throne cocks their head.

They slowly nod.

"My daughter, Amaya, holds the last known vestige of Death's soul. What you fear is already close to coming to pass. If left free...." I swallow. "I cannot stop this Malakhai. My fellow queen, Lucere, is of the belief that there are none left alive who may stop him. Only Thiago had the strength. This is our only hope."

"No. A thousand times no."

The guard beside him clears his throat.

Kato's nostrils flare as he cuts them a hard look.

They seem to silently commune, before Kato eases back onto his throne. "I will allow you through the gates on one condition. Once your husband has all the pieces of Death's soul, you will bring them to me. And I will banish them to the Darkness, once and for all."

All the pieces....

Amaya.

I can't help taking a half step back. "But my daughter.... How do we....?"

"There is a means to cleave Death's soul from your own," he says coldly. "The dark flame can be taken from her without harming her."

"How?"

"Death must will it. He must be willing to leave behind a living host and re-enter the Darkness. He must willingly give himself over."

"Has anyone ever done it before?" I whisper.

Kato's smile is chilling. "No, little queen. Death takes all he resides within. Eventually."

I stare down at the small amulet in front of me, swallowing hard. Time. This buys us time. And it's not the first attempt we've had dancing with impossible odds. "So shall I swear, so shall it be done."

"On a blood oath," he says, drawing a knife. "The second the Horned One is dead, you will bring me Death and bring him whole, and in return, I will allow you eternity in your husband's arms."

My fingers tremble as I accept the dagger. Carved from bone, with tiny little knots worked into it, it still holds an edge akin to none. I can't help recalling the paintings of Kato and the knife he used to carve Death's soul into pieces. This knife. It's the work of a second to draw blood from my fingertip, and a shiver runs through me as if the knife can taste my blood. "I promise once. I promise twice. I promise thrice."

Kato accepts the knife, licking my blood from the edge of it. "Done," he whispers.

Stillness falls over the cavern.

"Now," he says coldly. "Venture into the Darkness and call for your husband. Prove his love for you is stronger than his desire to kill you. Prove he can contain the creature inside him. And I will return him to you."

* * *

The Darkness.

A realm made of shadows.

I stare at the obsidian plane within the arch. The Underworld lies beyond it. The primeval Darkness. A realm of monstrous souls and creatures so horrific the world has no name for them.

I never expected I'd have to walk within it. I thought Kato would be able to bring him to me.

"Does your courage fail?" Kato purrs.

"Vi." Finn. Rough-edged with nervousness. "Vi, don't do this. Don't take this risk. It's not worth it."

His words do what nothing else could have done: Steel my nerves.

"Thiago spent thirteen years wooing me, again and again, in the face of my mother's curse. He died for *me*. For Amaya. There is nothing he would not have risked for me." I stare into the Darkness, clutching the small amulet the Mother of Night gave me. "I can do no less."

141

"Nobody's ever returned from the Darkness," Finn argues. "This is a trap. This prick knows it too."

Maybe that was what his guard suggested.

Agree to her terms. Send her into the Darkness.

Let the monsters deal with her rudeness.

If so, then he has sorely misjudged my determination.

"A trap." My gaze falls on the bone knife I just used to pledge myself. "Then grant me your blade. It is said even the creatures of the Darkness fear it."

Kato flips it in his fingers, smiling faintly as I take it. "Some may fear it, brash fae queen. But is it long enough to penetrate their hides?"

It's the guard beside Kato that steps between me and the gate.

"Here" comes a very female voice from within her helmet. Tearing it free, she reveals a spill of honey-brown hair bound in a braid, and blue eyes. But it's the shock of bright light gleaming around her throat that she reaches for. An amulet with what seems the heart of a star within it. "Take this with you. It contains a single drop of sunshine. It will light your way in even the truest dark and guide you to your heart's desire."

The sudden shock of kindness makes me suspicious. "Thank you...."

"My name is Orlagh. I hunt the Darkness when needed." Tugging the rough leather thong over her head, she offers it to me. "Beware the guardian beyond the gate. He's an ancient wyrm who hungers for those foolish enough to walk through it."

The amulet falls into place beside the one the Mother of

Night gave me. I'm not entirely certain if Orlagh's words are a warning, or a threat.

"True love," she tells Kato, with a slightly mocking tone as she turns back to him. "Some of us have not forgotten what that means."

If anything, his eyes narrow further.

"Let me go with her," Finn argues.

"Only one may pass through," Kato replies. "Your choice, little queen. Will you sacrifice your brave knight for yourself?"

Finn's eyes shine with courage. He'd do this for me. He'd do this for his prince. Never was a truer heart ever known.

But the choice was made long ago. "If I don't return, then protect Amaya for me. Tell her.... Tell her I loved her more than anything. And so I must take this risk in order to protect her."

And then, before my courage fails me, I plunge through the gate.

* * *

The darkness is so absolute it chokes me.

But it's the cold that gets to me. A cold that penetrates instantly, even though I'd thought myself numb to such feelings after entering Kato's throne room.

I stagger forward, trying to find my feet with the loss of such a major sense such as sight. This is the hungry emptiness, the expanse that awaits beyond death.

All I can hear is my heart, beating so fast it sounds like a bell chiming.

And a rasp of scales slithering through the Darkness. Something large moving toward me.

The wyrm.

I clutch the knife, heart pounding. Dare I risk the light? It will lead the creature right toward me, but then, if it's stalking me—which I think it might be—it already knows I'm here.

And if all it has known is this darkness, then its other senses will be incredibly attuned to me.

Maybe light doesn't have to be a weakness.

Maybe it can be a weapon.

I stagger to the left as the *shush-shush* sound comes inexorably toward me, reaching inside my collar—

A single drop of sunshine, Orlagh said.

But the sun may as well rise as I lift the amulet out. Even prepared as I am—face turned away—the searing light obliterates my vision for a good three seconds.

An enormous shape rears away from me with a hiss. Armless. Legless. A pale body seemingly segmented into forever, the battle-hardened scales covering it scarred and ravaged. Its eyes are a pale, milky blue.

And beyond it....

A world within a void.

The Darkness beyond the stars.

And a city.

Or something that was once a city.

Spires soar into the velvety dark, and elegant arches form the barrier wall that circles the buildings. Empty windows gape within the towers of a castle, and the path leading toward the castle runs along the back of a ridge.

Pennants hang from the tallest towers. But they don't move, for there is no wind.

Everything is still.

So still.

Except for the slithering coil of scales beneath the ledge I stand upon.

"*Thiago!*" I throw the psychic thought into the Darkness. He said he would be here. That he would wait for me.

But as the wyrm recovers, I don't have the time to hover. I need cover.

Scrambling over the stones, I sprint along the spine of the broken wall, conjuring every scrap of focus Finn has ever taught me.

A gaping hole in the wall appears—possibly where the wyrm crashed through it eons ago—and I don't hesitate. I launch myself over the gap, arms wind milling through space before landing right on the other edge. The lip of rock crumbles beneath my foot and I catapult forward, slamming into hard stone.

Light flashes from the amulet as I haul myself up.

I barely have a chance to catch my breath before the wyrm rears over me.

Fuck.

Its endless black eyes lock upon me, its lips drawing back from its vicious teeth in a serpentine smile. "Such a ssmall, tasty morsssel. I can practically tashte your warmth."

Summoning my magic, I whip a lash of fire toward it as it goes to swallow me whole. "Taste this then, asshole."

"Fire!" it shrieks, rearing back.

Darting forward, I clap my hands over my ears as it's scream makes my head throb.

145

The wyrm darts ahead of me, blisteringly fast. It lunges again, and I spin a rope of pure flame above my head.

Snap. Clash.

Its teeth crash together dangerously close to my body, but the fire seems to be holding it off.

And then I see it.

The pale, milky underskin of its throat. The scales there that are almost translucent.

Everything has a weakness.

The wyrm cuts in front of me and the only chance I have is now.

I sprint toward it, launching off the wall and jamming the bone knife into its vulnerable throat.

The wyrm screams, thrashing instantly.

Gravity does the rest. Plunging down its throat, I tear a seam all the way down before I crash into stone. My ankle gives out, a shock of pain lancing through me, but I can't hesitate.

If I hesitate, I'm dead.

I stagger toward a gaping arch, plunging inside one of the buildings and pressing my back flat against the wall as I gasp with adrenaline. *Fuck.* My ankle is on fire.

But I still have the knife.

Silence falls. Did I kill it? Or wound it?

I chance a look through the arch—

"Can sssmell you," hisses the wyrm, its blunt nose hammering toward me so fast I scream.

The wall trembles as it slams against it, but the arch keeps it out.

"Little, filthy lightbringer." It's maw jams at the arch to

my right. "I will crunch your bones and chew your screams. Come out, little wretch. There issh... no escape."

"*Thiago?*"

There is no answer. And my mind can't help conjuring images of the wyrm outside, and those teeth. *What if—*

No.

No. I won't go there.

Helplessly, I look around.

It's a hall of some sort, the glass shattered and strewn across the slate floors.

But above us....

I glimpsed a broken tower as we entered. Enormous stone blocks that had taken a previous battering.

Staying here means ending up dead.

Yanking the amulet over my head, I drive the knife into the mortar and hang it there.

The wyrm keeps slamming the wall, trying to break through the arches as I back away.

My ankle hurts, but the initial shock of pain is subsiding. I can limp on it. Maybe even stagger.

But can I climb?

There's only one way to find out.

Hauling myself up the back wall, crevice by crevice, I find the gallery, and then slip out one of the broken windows onto the roofline.

I was wrong.

It's not true darkness outside.

There's a hint of violet to the sky above us, a smattering of stars, though they're very, very distant. If the wyrm wasn't besieging the wall below me, I'd almost think it peaceful.

One thing at a time. Gauging the tower, I lean over the roof and check the wyrm's position. It's still drawn to the light. And the wall won't hold. One or two more blows, and I'm fairly certain the entire thing will cave in.

The tower shivers.

I give it a kick with my good foot, just as the wyrm slams against the wall again.

Rocks slide. They're stacked precariously now, the mortar long-gone. Driving my shoulder against the wall, I shove with my magic, though force is not truly one of my gifts.

A stone tumbles free.

I catch a glimpse of the wyrm's face tilting up and slam my fists against the tower, infusing the blow with all my power.

"Wretch!" It rears up just as the tower topples. The entire thing smashes into its face, crushing its body back down.

The problem is, the tower takes half the roof with it.

"Help!" I scream as I plunge through the opening.

At the very last second, I summon a cushion of force beneath me. Slamming into it steals my breath, but it breaks my fall somewhat. Until a piece of stone slams into my ribs, leaving me breathless and winded on the floor.

Silence falls.

Dust begins to settle.

Every inch of me hurts.

But nothing... seems broken?

Shoving a flagstone off my side with a groan, I push myself upright. The pain in my ribs is so sharp it's obliterating everything else, though I suspect my knee took a nasty knock too. I breathe through the pain, trying to consider my options.

Can't run.

Can't fly.

Kato's bone knife is no longer with me.

"Filthy wretch," comes a hiss. A nose nudges the rubble aside, hunting for me.

Surprisingly, the thin portion of wall where the amulet still glows remains intact, the glowing light mocking me with its close ness.

A wince steals through me as I crawl to my knees. *Fire. It's afraid of my fire.*

But how long can my magic last?

Fae magic isn't like draining power from the Hallows. It comes from within. I've been flexing and training those muscles, building my strength and my reserves, but I'm still barely mastering myself.

"Where are you?" The wyrm screams, battering its way closer.

Rocks and debris scatter like toys. I manage to crawl two steps before an enormous rock slams into me. I can't stop a cry.

And the delighted squeal of air behind me tells me it heard me.

The wyrm snakes toward me.

I throw an arm over my face and—

Nothing.

Barely breathing, I risk a look.

The wyrm is frozen in place, black blood dripping down its pale face and violence in its glittering eyes as it rises over me.

But it bares its teeth, clearly hesitant to strike, its gaze settled on something behind me.

And that's when I hear the first footstep.

Boots crunching over shattered glass. The wisp of a cloak trailing through the dust.

We're no longer alone.

"Hello, my lady of summer," whispers a familiar voice. A shadow falls over me, wings draped behind it.

Thiago.

I spin around and there he is, stalking toward us with unhurried steps. Tall, lean, viciously elegant. I've seen him move like this in company, in the courts. It's like he slips into another skin and becomes the savage Prince of Evernight, but the Thiago I loved is a different male. He's kinder. Softer. Prone to dangerous smiles that steal my breath.

My gaze leaps to his face—to those eyes.

They're black.

This is not my husband. Not the charmer. Not the rogue who pins me to the bed and laughs against my throat.

This is the Prince of Evernight.

The Master of Darkness.

My heart cursed near bursts in my chest, a strangled sob choking in my throat. *He's back. He's here.* I can't stop myself from raking my gaze over his face. I've tasted those hard lips and felt them soften beneath mine.

I know every inch of my husband.

But the power spilling from within him....

It's thick enough in the air to choke me. A banked threat. A whispered malice. And the glitter in his eyes as he stares at the wyrm sends a shiver all the way through me....

Thiago slowly smiles as he plucks at the buttons on his wrist, and carefully rolls his sleeve back, like a gentleman preparing for a ball. "Would you care to dance again, Great Enryathan?"

"My territory," the wyrm hisses. It bares its teeth, its forked tongue flickering between them.

Thiago's face remains cold and expressionless. "My wife."

The words ring through the silence.

They're a claim.

But they sound... wrong.

"*Mine*," he says again, this time softly. It's no less dangerous. He takes another step closer, returning his attention to the wyrm. "You dared strike a blow against my wife?"

Enryathan writhes, fighting the urge to pounce upon me while I'm injured, but desperately wary of the threat slowly stalking him.

"It was mine!" he shrieks. "My tithe! They gave it me! As is my right! They make their sacrificesss every year!"

No wonder Kato had a little smirk on his face as I entered the gate.

That asshole.

Thiago spreads his wings.

They're not wings.

They're shadows, looming wide. The vial with its drop of sunlight casts light across everything here, but it's as though the light can't quite touch his face.

"She bears my psychic scent," he croons, taking another step. "You could smell it on her. And yet, you still attacked."

151

The wyrm twists this way and that, retreating mere feet. "No, Great One! No!"

"Yes...." Thiago lifts his hands, summoning the shadows from around us. They twist like ribbons, curling around his fingers like curious cats.

"No." The wyrm cringes as it undulates backward. "No, my prince. I beg forgiveness. In my rage, in my hunger, I did not ssssense the truth. She smells like the mortal landsss. She smellsss like light and heat. She burned me! She ssstabbed me!"

Shadows crawl toward it, slinking up its carapace.

"So I see," Thiago says as his shadows slip inside the bloody gash running down its throat.

He gives a sharp jerk with his hands and the shadows tear the wound open.

"Sstop!" the wyrm shrieks. "Stop! Pleassse! Mercy, my prince! Mercy!"

A gurgle erupts, inky blood spilling in great, weeping spurts.

I would have killed it myself, but I'm not sure I can stand to watch this. Not with it cringing and begging for mercy.

I grab Thiago's boot. "Please. Don't."

Thiago stares at the creature as if he doesn't hear me. His lashes flicker down, shielding his eyes. And then he cocks his head. "Remember this moment, Enryathan. Remember my wife's sense of mercy. Now, begone. Before I forget mine."

And he finally, finally reaches a hand down toward me as the wyrm slithers in retreat.

The shadows stream back toward us, swirling around us

in ribbons as he gently eases me to my feet. My ankle gives way and I collapse against him. My hands won't stop running over his chest. *Real. He's real.* Yet there's a certain sense of coldness emanating. And I don't know what's wrong with me, but it feels like some invisible layer stands between us. I can feel the pressure of his body. But I can't feel the roughness of his cloak. Or the slick glide of his leather scaled body armor.

"You're hurt." A finger brushes against my lips. And healing magic sweeps through me.

The pain eases. My aches vanish. I gasp against him. The strength of his body is so familiar that tears wet my eyes. "You're back. I found you."

"Did you?"

Something about the way he says it warns me.

Capturing my chin, he twists my face this way and that.

"Did you find me, Iskvien? Did my dreams finally come true?" There's a dangerous twist to his smile, something mocking. "Or is this another honey-baited trap?"

"*What?*" I whisper.

Thiago's hard gaze rakes the landscape. "This wouldn't be the first time you've walked my dreams." His voice roughens. "It wouldn't be the first time I've seen your face beckoning me toward danger."

"I'm *real.*" Capturing his face in both hands, I stroke his cheeks. "Look at me, Thiago. Look me in the eyes. I came here for you. I came to bring you back."

Our eyes meet, and for the first time, I feel the shock of connection between us.

Light and heat shivers through me, bridging the gap between us. It spills through my fingertips, leaving little

153

glowing marks on his skin. The rasp of his stubble plays under my fingertips.

Thiago gasps, clapping a hand to his face. Covering mine as if he can't bear for me to stop touching him.

"You said you would wait in the Darkness for me." I tug my chin out of his grasp. "I am real. *This* is real!"

Dark lashes flutter over his eyes. A desperate yearning fills them. "Prove it."

"How do I...?" He's never questioned our love before.

His lips curl in a mocking smile. "First misstep, my *love*. You're supposed to tell me something only you would know." His fist brushes against his temple. "But we both know you're in my head. We both know I can't trust the answers to anything I ask. You're not the first shapeshifter I've dealt with."

I draw back, studying him. There are so many layers to Thiago. So many masks he wears. I shouldn't take offense. This one is the shield. The one that guards his heart. Because if you strip them all away, deep inside there's a young man staring up at a gilded castle, wondering why his mother abandoned him. Wondering if maybe there was something wrong with him, something unlovable.

He knows I love him.

But I'm not sure he believes he's worthy of it.

My mother's curse was merely another knife in the heart, because every time she would return me to him, I would stare at him as if he were a stranger.

"Then maybe I should tell you something you don't know. Would you like to know a secret?" I whisper, caressing the back of my knuckles against his leather breast-plate. "I loved you from the moment you took me away from my mother. I loved you the night you married me, the night you first made love to me. But I never said it. Because it was new love, a wary love, the love of someone who did not love herself enough to truly give herself over to it. Do you remember the night I first told you I loved you? That I felt it? And knew it? And owned it?"

His dark eyes smolder. "Of course I do. It was the night before I was forced to send you back that first time." His smile has edges. "Try again, my love."

"You're wrong."

Shock brings some of the empathy back into his expression. "I—*what*?"

"That wasn't the first time I told you I loved you. The first time was the night of our first argument." I can't help swallowing. "There'd been an attack by the border. Banes. An entire village of our people had been slaughtered, and your face— You were so furious you could barely breathe. You knew it was my mother. She had taken the insult of our marriage and retaliated in the most brutal way she could. The most hurtful way she could. She slaughtered innocents, and yet, we could not prove it.

"I wanted to come with you to visit the village, and we argued about it. You didn't want me to see such a thing, but I'd spent so long hidden away in my mother's court, my voice silenced and my presence shunned. I wanted to be your queen, your partner. I didn't want to be protected or smothered. So you said, 'Fine, then. Don't say I didn't warn you.'" I shudder at the memory. "It was horrible. I watched you dig the graves with your power, and suddenly our argument didn't matter. You were so cold as you organized the entire affair. A stranger in some ways. And I realized that

155

you did it to protect yourself. Because if nobody could see your pain, then nobody could hurt you. But you *did* feel pain. You felt guilty those deaths were on your head. Because you had dared to love me, to take something for yourself, in a world where you felt as though you didn't deserve such happiness.

"When you came to me that night, you apologized. You finally let me see you. The real you. The one who aches for his people. The one who bleeds so his people do not. The one who wanted to protect me, because you are no stranger to pain. I could see it in your eyes—that vow you silently made me. You would go on hurting, if only so I never knew an ounce of pain.

"But I didn't want that. I wanted a partnership. A marriage of equals. I wanted to shoulder your burdens too. And so you bent knee and agreed. You promised you would not spare me from your pain and your burdens. You promised you would share them. It's the first time in my life that someone had truly granted me their heart. I was no longer a caged bird, but this... what you offered me.... It was true freedom.

"We made love and afterward, as I was lying in your arms, the strangest urge overcame me. I loved you, you see. I loved that you let me argue with you, that you didn't quash my voice. I loved that you could apologize when you were wrong. That your love for me never wavered, even when we were yelling at each other. You didn't care if I wasn't perfect. You loved *me*, truly loved me, flaws and all. And there you were, asleep on the pillow beside me. And I was still such a coward. I couldn't say it to your face. Not yet. But I had to say it. I had to whisper it in the dark while you were sleeping, before I lost this feeling. This bravery. But that is the first moment I loved you. Truly loved you. The first moment you let me see you."

He clenches his eyes shut, physically shaking against the pain of restraint. He won't believe me. He *can't*.

Because he has never truly dared show me all of him.

All the darkness. All the savagery. All the scars on his soul.

And I want them all. I want to kiss them and lick them and soothe them away. Because I'm not perfect either.

"You're lying," he whispers. "You have to be lying."

"You know I'm not."

Our eyes meet, his holding a certain sort of challenge.

The air thickens between us.

There is only one way to truly prove it's me.

Lifting on my toes, I brush my hands down his chest.

"A kiss," he breathes, his eyes lighting with predatory intensity. "How original."

"Well," I growl. "I could just set your britches on fire. Instead of the bed. That's a fairly signature move."

Thiago rears back. This time, the look in his eyes is considering.

And there's something else on his face too. Something tremulous and guarded. Something heartbreaking.

Hope.

"*Vi*?" he whispers.

"In the flesh."

Gripping my shoulders, he unleashes a powerful breath. "Vi, you *can't* be here. This is the Darkness. It was never meant for mortals."

"Wherever you are, I will go too."

157

This time the look in his eyes slays me.

Rising on my toes, I kiss him, but it's not simply a kiss. It's breathing him in, Inhaling him. Digging my fingernails into the hard planes of muscle that line his shoulders. *He's back.* A choked sound echoes in my throat, and as if he feels it too, he growls back, his hands sliding down my spine and digging into my ass.

The grind of his hard, warrior's body is a shock.

I can feel him now. There are no more barriers between us. Only little fingerprints of light glowing on his skin where I touch him as if some of the heat in my veins is slowly bringing him back to life.

I would give him *everything* of me, if I could only bring him back.

His hand slides up the length of my spine, burying itself in a fistful of hair at my nape. I'm no longer kissing him, I'm being consumed. It's not so much hunger as it's desperation. The lash of his tongue. The press of his body. The feel of his hands, driving away the nightmares wrapped around my heart.

Mine.

He's mine once more.

Hauling me up, he wraps my thighs around his hips and then drives me back against the wall of the ruins. Winding my fists into his short, dark hair, I clutch the silky strands, marveling at the sensation of it. He breaks for breath, kissing my throat, and I moan as I feel that touch ravage me deep inside, leaving me slick and aching.

My lover.

My husband.

My *everything*.

All the tears, all the rage, all the pain.... None of it means anything anymore. Not now I'm in his arms. Not now I'm home.

"Vi." He punctuates the word with a short, rough kiss. "Vi, you shouldn't have come."

"I came to bring you home."

Thiago freezes, his hands capturing my face between them. "There is no going back. Not for me."

Reaching inside my collar, I grasp the amulet the Mother of Night gave me. *Open it*, she said. *Open it in his presence and it will trap his soul inside.*

"I don't know what this will feel like," I whisper. "But just remember.... I will protect you. I will bring you back to me. We'll be together. *Forever*."

"Vi, no!" Thiago hisses, reaching for me, with shadows streaming from his fingers—

He shrinks and vanishes inside the soul-trap, the light inside it gleaming before I snap it shut. I slide down the wall, landing on my ass in the rubble, my body on fire, even as the sensation of his touch vanishes.

The amulet burns cold in my hands.

And the light of his soul boils in rage.

I can't stop myself collapsing back against the wall, gasping for breath, a single tear streaming down my face.

I convinced him.

I know I convinced him.

But he didn't sound happy at the end.

Sound echoes in the distance; a clatter of rocks falling somewhere in the ruined city.

It's a stark reminder. I don't have time for the maelstrom of emotions tearing through me. I need to get back through the gate, and get Thiago's soul home to Ceres.

Before some other predator realizes my protector is no longer here.

Dashing my tears from my face, I wrench the bone knife and the sunlight amulet from the wall.

I can deal with Thiago later.

I need to get to the gate.

Chapter Twelve

The gates spill me back inside the throne room.

Guards turn, hands going to swords as I stagger through. And Finn, who's been resting with his knees drawn to his chest against the far wall, looks up sharply.

"Vi?" Incredulousness stains his face as he shoves to his feet. "Vi, you've got him?"

"Got him." I can't help grinning at him as I display the amulet. "Now we just have to get home."

Hauling me into his arms, he squeezes me tight, then steps back and looks at me. "What happened to you? You look awful."

There's inky blood on my boots and shirt, and my hair is a ragged mess. I don't care. My heart blazes with hope. "I feel amazing though."

Finn's smile etches into an actual grin as if my happiness is contagious.

"We need to get going then." His smile vanishes, his tone careful. His stare burns through me, but I can almost sense him trying to warn me about the roomful of guardians around us.

I tuck the amulet away and then remove the vial of sunlight. "Thank you." I offer it to Orlagh. "I would be dead without it."

The tall blonde gives a wry smile, her hand curling around the vial and swallowing the light.

Kato reclines on his throne like some ancient warrior god. "So you have returned triumphant."

Tugging the bone knife from my belt, I hurl it at his feet where it sticks, the shaft quivering.

Instantly, a half dozen spears are pointed at me.

"You pay a tithe to Enryathan every year?" There's acid in my voice. "And you just forgot to mention he'd be waiting on the other side of the gate? Waiting for a snack?"

Kato holds up a hand and the spears vanish. "You should have asked more questions about what was on the other side."

This is what I get for dealing with one that was once fae, and for being so distracted with Thiago's death.

"And it's once a month," he says coldly. "Not once a year."

"Once a *month*?" But Enryathan said—

"Vi, you've been gone for days," Finn says, rubbing my arms. "And you're freezing. Tell me it's not colder in there than it is in here."

"Colder," I admit, reeling at the time difference. It felt like hours at most. And if this has been days.... My stomach drops into freefall. How long has it been for Thiago? Six months? A year? Has it felt like a year trapped in the Darkness all alone? No wonder he didn't trust me.

"Come on then." Finn wrenches a heavier cloak out of his pack and wraps it around my body. "Time to head for the surface then. Before we both freeze to death."

"Wait." Kato stirs.

I tug the cloak tighter. "You swore an oath."

"As did you," he says coldly. "You have a month, at most, to bring me the rest of Death's soul."

"When the Horned One is vanquished," I snap at him. "Not a day more. Not a day less."

"Best hurry," Orlagh suggests. "It looks like there's a storm coming on the surface."

I don't know how to interpret the look Kato gives her —exasperation, maybe—but I take the warning on board.

"Thank you," I tell her again, clasping hands with her. "If you are ever in the south, you are always welcome at Ceres."

She laughs, crossing toward the throne and sinking onto the arm of it as if she belongs there. "Pray tell I never have need to venture south." Caressing Kato's sleeve, she shares a look with him. "Because the only time I will ever come south is if my lord sends me there."

Another warning.

If we don't return with Death's soul, she will come to claim it.

I shiver and meet Finn's eyes.

Past time to get out of here.

"Vi?"

"I don't want to talk about it," I snap as I hurry toward the surface. Thunderous skies greet us and the world is bathed in fog. Here, at the tip of the island's peak, it feels like we're floating in the clouds.

"How the fuck do we manage to get Death to leave Thiago and Amaya?"

We have to convince Death to leave.... But why would it do that? Why would it give up everything it wants to return to a world where not even the wind stirs? "I don't know."

Yet.

"What the fuck is that sound?" he asks, as he follows me down the stairs.

I can't hear a cursed thing as I stride along the terrace where the statues stand. "What?"

Finn frowns, turning one way and then the other. Lightning flickers in distant clouds, but nothing moves.

Even so, he sets his hand to rest on the hilt of his sword. "Something's wrong."

Orlagh said there was a storm up here. Once again, she was warning me. "What?"

He prowls through the fog carefully, tilting his head this way and that. I follow, placing careful footsteps exactly where he placed his.

He freezes. "Vi, how many statues were here earlier?"

I think about it, my heartbeat starting to race as my memories provide an alternate answer to the reality. "*Thirteen.*"

There are fifteen still forms lingering along the rail.

One of them laughs. "Well spotted, half breed."

Finn whips the Sword of Mourning from its scabbard, the steely whine of its passage cutting through the air as the figure leaps for him.

Their blades meet and his shears straight through the other. Without pausing, glowing steel cuts right through the shadowy figure.

It folds in on itself and as it hits the floor, the cape collapsing into nothing more than material.

"Behind you!" I scream as a second figure launches itself off the railing, a spear held high.

With its cowl and cloak, all I see is a flash of vicious teeth and glowing eyes before Finn stabs back under his arm and buries the sword in its gut. It curls over his shoulder, but he shrugs it off, feet dancing as he whirls the sword into a defensive position.

The flame tattoo on his forehead is glowing.

I've never seen it do that before.

The second the body hits the ground, it bursts apart in clumps that shudder and writhe across the ground.

"What the fuck?" Finn whispers, nudging one with his

boot.

Instantly, it bursts into a raven. Dozens of them shake off a black ichor and leap into the sky, cawing as they vanish into the clouds.

"What was that?"

"Go!" Finn yells, shoving me in the back. There's a gold ring around his blue irises, the flame between his eyes burning like a brand. "We need to get to the beach now!"

"What in the Darkness were they?" Did Kato send them?

"Trouble."

Distant howls echo in the storm as we skid onto the beach, looking for our boat. I stare into the murky clouds but can't see a thing.

"Come on!" Finn grabs my arm and hauls me into the frigid shallows. "Get in the boat!"

There's no sign of the creatures making that howling noise.

"But what about—?"

Finn picks me up around the waist and dumps in the front end of the boat. Grabbing hold of the edges, I curse under my breath as he leaps in behind me.

"Can't you hear that?"

"Hear *what*?" Even as I say the words a shiver trembles over my skin. There's a hint of drums somewhere in the distance. Not the ones that march you to war, but the sound of something on the hunt.

Grabbing the oars, Finn set himself to rowing. "I knew that fucking bitch couldn't be trusted." A snarl curls his lip. "It's a trap. The entire fucking thing is a trap."

"By who?"

"Lucere!" he snarls.

"You think Lucere set this?"

"I think she was the only one—outside of the five of us—who knew where we were going."

"Blaedwyn might have sent someone to follow—"

"She wouldn't have had time to set this up."

He still hasn't said what we're facing. "Set *what* up?"

"The first thing you hear are the drums," he says grimly. "The second thing you know is a shadowy figure stretching over you. You hear their shrieks in your ears. You feel your breath catching in your lungs as if it's freezing, until your veins will barely pump blood through your veins. They're hunting. Hunting us."

"Mother of Darkness, Finn! *Who?*"

"The *sluagh na marbh* in the old tongue. The host of the dead."

The hairs down my arms rise.

The host of the dead.

Ruled over by Malakhai of the Black Reaches.

Souls torn from the dead and forged into monstrous beings. They're the sort of tale you don't hear about in Seelie.

But everyone in Unseelie knows that when the host of the dead is hunting you, then there's no point running.

"But why would he be here...?" It hits me then and my hand curls protectively around the locket with Thiago's soul trapped within. No. *No.*

"Death searches for a way to combine all the pieces of its fragmented soul," Finn says grimly. "And Malakhai wants power. With Thiago trapped within the Darkness, there was no means to get at him."

But now, with his soul nestled safely in the locket, we just gave him the means.

A heated flush fills my cheeks. "If that son of a bitch dares try and harm him, I'll fry him on the spot."

Our eyes meet.

We're a long way from the Hallow.

A long way from Evernight.

My power is weak, and these aren't my lands.

"Can you row?" Finn demands, stringing his bow with swift fingers.

"I've got a better idea," I tell him, shoving the oars toward him. "You row. I'll shoot."

"You won't be able to nock my bow—"

"I won't need to," I tell him grimly, shifting onto my knees on the bench and summoning a bow made of pure fire.

It's something Thiago insisted I work on in those brief few months where we had a chance to be together in Ceres.

The mist parts, and I catch a glimpse of a dark shadow flying overhead as Finn puts his back into the oars.

I can almost feel Thiago's arms around me as he helps me forge an arrow of pure flame. Together, we nock it to the bow, and as I draw the string back, the memory of him whispers against my cheek. "*Hold the flame, Vi.*"

Hold the flame.

The second it leaves the bow is the moment I need to concentrate. My gifts with fae magic are small. The further the arrow flies, the harder it is to hold the heat together. It's a constant battle with the wind threatening to snuff the flame.

"Where did it go?" Finn demands, setting his back into

the oars. We surge forward, forcing me to recalibrate my aim as I scan the skies.

There. Right there.

I loose the arrow.

It vanishes with a hiss into the mist, and then a scream echoes through the air.

Something dark tumbles from the sky and slams into the lake surface barely twenty feet away.

There is no splash. Somehow, that's eerier than anything else I've seen today.

"One down," Finn says grimly. "It will be a lead scout."

Storm clouds rumble in the sky. Within the darkness, lightning lances, highlighting dozens of dark shapes. They stretch as far as the eye can see.

"There are... hundreds of them." My bow lowers involuntarily. We'll never escape them. Not like this. My pulse kicks. I've failed. I managed to get so close to my dream and yet—

"Just got to make it to the Hallow," Finn says grimly, his thighs and shoulders surging as he forces us through the water. "Keep them off our backs, Vi."

I've spent enough time training with him to know what he's asking of me. *Focus.* One sluagh hunter at a time.

A shadow plunges toward us, wings stretched out wide. I catch a glimpse of a pale face and black, merciless eyes, and then I put another fire arrow right between those eyes. It hits the lake, plunging beneath the oily waters.

Again and again, until the reek of burning feathers fills my nostrils.

They're divebombing in waves. I can barely keep up, my fingers burned and blistering.

And then the bottom of the boat scrapes over the sandy lakebed, making me stagger.

"Hold on, Vi!"

Leaping out of the boat, Finn hauls it ashore. Scrambling over the bench, I grab his hand and launch myself toward the edge of the lake, but Finn glances up at the last moment and—

Hands snatch at my shoulders, and a vicious laugh echoes in my ears.

"Vi!"

I scream as my feet are lifted off the ground. The bow vanishes as my concentration breaks. Finn catches my ankle, his jaw grim as he hauls on me with all his strength. Talons dig into my shoulders, pain slicing through me. But it's the rotting reek of damp flesh that makes me gag.

"Knife, Vi!" he yells.

Snatching my knife from my hip, I slash at the unseen hands gripping me. A scream vibrates through the air, and then I'm falling, falling....

I land on Finn, both of us smashing to the ground.

Above us, a shadowy figure rushes past, deprived of its prey.

But as I look up, I see hundreds of them circling us, mouths agape in vicious, cackling smiles.

Hundreds.

I've barely killed a handful.

The heat drains from my face. There's no way we can escape them all. There are simply too many.

"We just have to make it to the Hallow. Up." Finn whips me to my feet and starts yanking me toward the path leading to the Hallow. "Curse it. Where the fuck is Eris?"

The forest whips past, bleached trees reaching toward the sky with skeletal branches. Something enormous crashes through the forest toward us.

"What in the Darkness is that?" I scream, a branch catching me across the face as I leap over a rock.

"I'd really rather not find out!" A hand shoves me in the middle of the back. "Faster!"

He doesn't have to tell me twice.

My lungs heave for breath. My heart races. I can feel it in my chest. Hear it in my head. The Hallow. My heart echoes with the pulsing beat of its magic.

My thighs burn as we both sprint up the hill.

A loud crash echoes behind me.

I shoot a quick glance over my shoulder as Finn hauls one of the sluagh to the ground, cutting its throat.

"Run!" he yells at me, then his eyes shift over my shoulder and he lifts his arm and throws his knife directly at me.

I fling my arms up, but the knife hisses past my ear.

And then a shadow falls just in front of me.

I leap over it, not daring to look back.

The Hallow looms ahead, pulsing like it's calling to me in distress.

I'm here, I whisper to it. *I'm coming.*

The stones start to glow, all the runes chiseled into their surface lighting up as if they can sense me.

"Eris!" Finn yells, and his sword clashes with another behind me.

Ripples of light paint over the rocky hill as he fights for his life. I can't just leave him here. I can't— But he's wielding the Sword of Mourning. With it, he can't fall.

Can he? Not even to the host of the dead?

If they get their hands on you and Thiago's soul, then it's all over....

I hate this decision, but I have to think as a queen now. My feet fly over the stone, my desperate gaze locking on the Hallow...

And an enormous shadow ripples over me.

No. No. *No.* I sprint up the rocky path, gravel flying behind me as I risk a glance.

There's a winged figure above me, his pale skin marked with hundreds of sprawling tattoos.

The locket burns hot against my throat.

And then something slams between my shoulder blades —like a boot.

I stagger forward, trying to right my feet, but it's to no avail. My palms graze along the gravel, a hot sting searing my skin as I crash face-first into the path and skid along the shale.

Terror sweeps through me. *The locket.* Its familiar weight fills my palm as I grab it and roll, my magic bunched within me—

There's nothing there.

Nothing to attack.

Nothing but light gleaming below me as Finn backs between six ghostly pale figures who encircle him. Our gazes meet, and his nostrils flare as he attacks the closest figure, desperate to get to me.

Then an eddy of mist sweeps between us, and all I can hear is the grunt of his breath and the ringing echo of his steel.

"Finn!" I yell, crouching low.

"Don't stop! Go!"

Go? Every inch of my soul rebels against that command.

Footsteps crunch over gravel.

A figure stalks through the mist toward me.

An enormous figure with thick dark hair sweeping over his broad shoulders, where the hint of wings linger.

It's like watching every nightmare I've ever had step forth from my dreams. For a second my heart leaps—*it's Thiago, he's back*—but then my eye starts to notice the small details I missed at first glance.

He's taller than my husband by an inch, and where Thiago moves with the lithe grace of a predator, this bastard *stalks*. His long black hair blows around a pale face which is marked with black tattoos.

And his eyes are black.

Black as soulless night. Black as the Darkness I stared into when I begged my husband to return. Black as the frigid depths of the lake.

Black as ice.

Everything inside me goes cold.

"Well, you little bitch," Malakhai sneers. "You might finally be good for something."

Sauntering toward me, he slowly draws his sword. It's the same color of his eyes, as if darkness merely coalesced into a blade. Shadows stream off it, and I stare at it in horror, knowing that if it touches my skin, it won't be mere death that greets me.

No. This is a sword of oblivion.

I forge my bow again, but my singed fingers flinch, and the magic flickers and dies as I hiss. Pain throbs through them.

"Pathetic." Malakhai steps over a fallen log. "How did that wretched little wyrm ever look at you and see something worthy of him?"

My knife. I have one knife left.

I whip it toward him. "Don't you dare speak of him. Don't you *dare*. Your tongue isn't worthy to even breathe his name."

He feints to the left with the sword and I dance out of the way—right into a fist.

The shock of it reverberates through me, but I haven't spent all these months training with Finn for nothing. I turn with the impact, sweeping low and spinning so that I dive right below his reach, my knife scoring across the back of his thigh.

As I stagger to face him again, he bares his teeth at me, reaching down to wipe at the slash cut across his trousers.

Blood. Black blood.

Rage ignites in those eyes.

And then the sword swings toward me, enormous sweeping blows I can barely dodge. I barely parry one with the knife, altering the sword's course just enough that it scores through the upper slope of my shoulder.

White fire rakes through me. I scream and spin away, staggering over a rock. I can't feel my arm. My fingers tingle, but there's a creeping dread within me....

Malakhai lifts the sword again, lightning flickering in the sky behind him—

"Get away from her," says a cold voice behind us.

A voice I know.

A voice I never ever dreamed I'd hear again.

"Eris," I sob, as I dart aside.

Chapter Thirteen

Iskvien

Eris stands between the lintel stones that shield the Hallow, her chest heaving as if she's been running and blood slick on her dark skin. "Get up, Vi," she says, but she doesn't dare take her eyes off Malakhai.

"You." Malakhai flashes her a hungry smile as he turns toward her.

"Sorry," she says to me. "Something drove the ice wolves away, and I was trying to see what it was."

"You're here now." That's all that matters.

Their swords meet.

It's like watching lightning dancing, but even I can see that Eris is being driven back. Malakhai forces her sword low, then punches her in the face.

"Eris!"

"E!" Finn launches off a rock, the Sword of Mourning whining as it cuts through the air.

Malakhai glances behind him, taking in Finn with an almost bored expression. His smile lights up as he spins to meet the Sword of Mourning. Far from being unnerved to find himself between two of the south's best warriors, he actually looks like this is going to be enjoyable for him.

The two swords clash.

Light versus dark.

The shock of their impact slaps like a roll of thunder, and I clap my hands over my ears and sink to my knees as the impact slams into me. It's like being in the middle of a lightning detonation.

When the world finally falls still and silent again, Finn's on his knees, looking shocked as he scrambles to find his sword in the gravel.

"This blade was crafted by Death's hand itself," Malakhai says, flipping his sword from hand to hand as he circles him. "Not even Blaedwyn's steel can match it."

It's impossible.

Nothing can stand against the Sword of Mourning.

Nothing can—

But those stories are seelie stories.

"You think you can stand against me?" Malakhai's smirk turns dark. "*Me?* What a fucking insult."

Finn pushes to his feet. Blood drips down his thigh, and he's limping. He's hurt.

"Eris," Finn says, locking desperate eyes with her. "Get her out of here!"

And then he steps into Malakhai's path, sword held low in both hands.

I know what he's saying.

Leave him there. Leave him there to die....

And I can't do it.

"Come on." Eris grabs my arm, shoving me back toward the Hallow.

"No! No." I wrestle with her. "Eris, *no!*"

Not this. Not Finn.

"Someone has to look after Amaya. He'll come for her, Vi. He'll come for her next. We always knew...." Her voice breaks. "Finn's going to give us time."

There's a crushing weight in my chest.

I am powerless. Without a sword. No match for a creature like this.

And I want to scream with rage at the thought.

I can't protect them. I can't help them.

Because a queen's purpose is not merely to rule; it's to protect those who are loyal to her.

Nothing can stop Malakhai. Finn can't. Eris can't. I can't.

Nothing on this earth can stop Death itself....

Nothing *of* this earth.

My breath catches.

Grimm. That furry little prick. He was warning me. He

177

saw this.

"I've got a better idea. Slow Malakhai down," I whisper to her.

I just need to reach the center of the Hallow.

Bolting through the stones, I scramble for the heart of the polished slate.

Malakhai laughs as steel clashes again and again. "Such a queen. Fleeing on her knees. Is this what you give your worthless life for?"

Skidding across the slate on my knees until I reach the heart of the Hallow, I whip my knife across the palm of my hand and look up.

Hesitation strikes like an arrow.

Finn's down. On his knees as Eris guards the entrance to the Hallow.

Malakhai grabs a fistful of his hair and wrenches his head back so that I can see my most faithful warrior. Our eyes meet. His flare wide with desperation. It's like Finn's trying to tell me something.

"Look at her, little wyrm. Look at her trying to escape me." Malakhai throws back his head and laughs as he sets the knife to Finn's throat. He raises his voice. "Flee, little queen. Scuttle back to Ceres like the maggot you are. Nothing can stop me from coming for you. Nothing."

Finn gasps as the knife rips across his throat.

Arterial blood sprays.

My heart breaks.

"*No!*"

But even as my tears obliterate the sight of his face, my resolve firms. *You bastard. You prick.*

"I summon thee." I slam my bloody palm flat on the

Hallow's stone heart. "I summon thee forth, my lord. A second deed offered freely and thus I claim it. Come forth, my lord. Come forth and fight our foes."

Malakhai's laughter chokes off as he realizes I'm not going anywhere.

Letting go of Finn, he takes a step toward me.

"Finn!" Eris screams, sliding to her knees as Finn falls forward, clutching at his ruined throat. She captures him in her arms.

"You're a fool," Malakhai sneers, stepping over the brass line that circles the Hallow. "You should have run when you had the chance."

Slowly, I push myself to my feet, my bloody fingers clenching around the locket.

"Why run? When I'm not the one who's going to die."

A quiver runs through the stone beneath our feet.

Gravel skitters over the slate. The entire hilltop seems to be shaking.

Malakhai pauses.

"Flee," I tell him fiercely. "Flee into the skies like the skulking wraith you are. Fly as fast as you can, and you just might be able to escape." And then I lift my voice and quote the famous poem. "For even Death is no match for the Erlking."

Lightning strikes as the Hallow powers up.

And when the light dies down, I feel a shadowy presence behind me, as if the Erlking just stepped into flesh.

179

Chapter Fourteen

Iskvien

"A second boon dealt and a second requested. What would you have of me, Queen of Evernight?" The Erlking's hand comes to rest on my shoulder.

My eyes lock with Malakhai's. There's something highly enjoyable about watching the color drain from his savage face.

"Kill him," I say. "Kill Malakhai of the Black Reaches and bring me his head."

Malakhai bares his teeth at me, then takes a step back. "You will pay for this, you bitch. I'm coming for you."

And then his wings drive out and he thrusts himself into the sky.

"Hunt him to farthest corners of the world," I tell the Erlking fiercely. "Give him no quarter. Grant him no mercy. Kill him for me."

A faint smile plays about his lips. "You're growing far more bloodthirsty than I ever expected."

He turns to take a step, and Finn gasps.

"Wait!"

The Erlking's head tilts toward me.

"Can you heal him? Can you heal my warrior?"

Dark eyes lock upon Finn where he lies gasping for breath, choking on blood. Eris's palms encircle his throat as if she's trying to hold the tide back.

"I may not," he says finally. Something almost like pity floods his eyes. "The answer is within you, Queen of Evernight."

"I don't know how!" Healing's a paltry gift of mine. It may run in the veins of the summer queens of Asturia, but I was never taught to master the art. Only the base rudiments.

If nothing else, I could kill my mother for that alone.

I hate her for leaving me defenseless. For stealing my magic, my memories, and any hope I ever had of mastering myself. Was I that much of a threat to her that she couldn't even allow me to learn this?

And now Finn is going to die because of it.

Another faint smile, this time a mocking one. "I wasn't referring to your fae gifts. The answer is inside you, Vi. You

are more than fae. And now your warrior has made a sacrifice in the heart of the Hallow. You alone have the ability to
reap the power of his sacrifice. Drag him within its stones.
Bind him to you."

And then he's gone, bursting into a flock of ravens.

They flap and caw, wheeling to follow where Malakhai
disappeared.

Bind him to me. I clench my fists. That's not an answer
at all.

But I have to try.

Sliding to my knees beside him, I try to see the damage.
"We have to get him inside the Hallow."

Eris looks up, her dark hands slick with blood where she
holds his throat. "If I let go, he'll die."

"Then I'll do it."

I grab his cloak and use it to haul him over the gravel
toward the Hallow, as Eris presses down grimly on his
wound.

"Don't you die," she whispers fiercely. "Don't you dare
die on me, you bastard."

Finn's Sylvaren. He's harder to kill than we are. And he
heals faster than we do.

There has to be something I can do.

"Here." I ease him into my lap, my heart breaking as
Eris reaches for me. "Let me see... if I do this. Finn?"

I reach for the power of the Hallow, letting it tremble
through me.

And then I reach for Finn.

"I accept your sacrifice," I whisper, pressing my
bloodied palm on his chest.

There is no answer. Power bubbles within me, like the

inside of a volcano threatening to explode. But there's nothing... there. Nothing to grab. Nothing to tie him to me.

I force healing weaves through him, my fae magic trying to staunch the spill of torn arteries.

The breath leaves him in one long exhale.

One last exhale.

Everything inside me stops. Those gossamer glimmers of his soul vanish through my fingers like I'm trying to hold moonlight in my hands. No. *No!* It's too late. He's gone.

"Finn?" Eris grabs his shoulders, shaking him. "*Finn!*"

I sit back in horror as he flops bonelessly.

"Come back," she whispers. "Come back, please come back. Don't you do this to me!" Desperate eyes lock on me. "Do *something*."

There's nothing I can do.

No breath in his lungs.

No heartbeat in his chest.

As if to spite me, the curse that choked my memories unravels, as if his death has finally pulled a knot in the pattern of it.

Images of us hammer through me.

"Come on, princess," he says to me, reaching down to offer me a hand up after Eris dumped me on my ass in the training yard. "I'll show you how to beat her."

Another memory.

"Open my present first, Vi," he chortles as he shoves a box toward me. Inside the box is a book. One I've been looking for for years. "Happy not-birthday," he says, because my birthday falls in the months when I'm returned to Asturia, and so we celebrate this date now.

And another.

183

"I've got her, Vi," he whispers as we step through the Hallow, arriving back in Ceres after the shock of the Black Keep. I can barely breathe through the gaping wound in my chest, and he's carrying Amaya in his arms even as he supports me.

Tears wet my eyes. A single tear slides down my cheek and lands on his forehead, flaring gold before his skin absorbs it.

Beneath his skin, the light blooms, travelling through his veins. It hits a branch in the capillaries beneath his cheek and separates. And again. And again. It's a network of light spearing through him. I've never seen anything like it.

"*Vi*," Eris whispers.

It hits his heart, and a sudden pulse of power throbs within him.

His chest rises and falls.

The wound across his throat seals.

And Finn's eyes go wide as he sits up, his lungs heaving for air—and finding none.

"I accept your sacrifice." I don't even know where the words come from. But I can feel the heat of that single tear spearing through his body. It's like there's a part of me inside him. Neurons fire. Muscles clench. Blood pumps. And I'm inside every single cell of him. "*Mine*." My fingers dig into his shoulders. "My knight. Bound to me until the breath leaves my body. Step forth and live, my knight."

Power and heat gushes through me.

Finn clutches at his throat, his lungs making that horrible sucking sound.

Eris collapses over him, sobbing against his chest as she hugs him.

"You're alive," she whispers. "*Alive.*"

I can't hold myself up anymore. Healing him—binding him to me—took everything I had left in me.

The last thing I see is Finn rolling onto his knees, one hand clasped around his throat and his eyes wild as he seeks me out and finds me.

I need to get us back home.

I need to get us to safety.

Reaching through the Hallow, I pluck at the thread that sings to me. Home. Evernight. *Ceres.*

A hum vibrates through the Hallow as the portal activates.

And then the slate floor rushes up to meet me.

* * *

"What's wrong with her?"

Thalia?

Somehow I blink my eyes, and there are familiar walls around me. Light. Shadows.

Someone's arms holding me.

"She's fine," Finn says, though I've never heard his voice sound like this before. Rasping. Thick as molasses. Virtually a growl. "She's overextended herself."

Finn. Finn is carrying me. His heart beats in time with mine, but the second I reach for it, brushing featherlight strands of my self against that... bond between us, the dark threatens to roll me under again.

"Do we need a healer? Do we need a magi?" Thalia blurts. A palm cups my forehead.

"I'm... furnn..." I swear I say it.

185

"Mama?" someone says in a very small voice.

Amaya.

I try to turn toward her, but she's vanishing, the sound of her voice calling my name chasing me down a long, dark tunnel.

And then it's warm and dark and someone's easing me onto something soft.

A bed. My bed.

I blink, and the three of them hover over me.

Thalia, her olive skin pale and ashen.

Eris, watching from over her shoulder with a grim look on her face.

And Finn, easing the covers over me.

"'maya." Where is she? She was right there....

"She's asleep," Thalia murmurs. "You've just come from the infirmary. Mariana was most put out with you. You nearly killed yourself, Vi."

"And now you need rest." Finn sees me watching him, and his jawline tenses. His voice was always velvet over gravel, but now there's more gravel to it. "Sleep, my queen. You've done enough. You've done more than enough."

The weight at my throat is gone. My heartbeat races. I can't *feel* the little soul-trap that Kato gave me.... "Thiago?"

"I have him," Eris promises, lifting the amulet from around her throat to show me. "I'll keep him safe for you."

"Lie back down." Thalia pushes on my shoulders. "Go to sleep." She shudders as a wave of warmth floods through me. "You need to rest, Vi. Rest and let us all take care of you."

Chapter Fifteen

Iskvien

Light cracks through my eyelids, and I groan as the door creaks open.

"Mama?"

"Amaya," I murmur, rolling onto my side. Every inch of me feels like I was run down by a carriage.

A blur darts toward me, and then Amaya throws herself on the bed and into my arms, sobbing against my shoulder. I wrap my arms around her, burrowing my face into her hair. "I'm okay."

"I know." She squeezes me tight. "Grimm told me you were alright. But...."

I know.

I know.

I squeeze her back.

"*The doubt you people cast upon me,*" says an arrogant purr as a weight lands on the bed. "*Don't listen to Grimm. It's not as though he can see through the Shadows. Have I ever been wrong?*"

Amaya lifts her head, her eyes red-rimmed. "No," she says. "But sometimes you don't tell me everything."

He blinks. "*When have I ever—?*"

"Old Mother Hibbert."

Grimm stills.

"Elodie."

His tail flicks.

I have the distinct impression he wants to slink off the bed.

"And then there was—"

"*Fine,*" he cuts in. "*Occasionally I don't see certain consequences.*"

Grimm settles at our feet, a huge furry weight.

The gush of emotion threatens to choke me. He knew what would happen with Malakhai. Once again, he knew. "Thank you," I whisper.

Grimm settles his chin on his paws and subsides with a sigh. "*At least someone appreciates me.*"

The door opens again and Thalia strides inside, followed by a half dozen maids. Eris is right behind them, long legs clad in leather and her hand resting on her hip.

"What are you—?"

"There," Thalia says, directing two of the maids to lay something out on the bed. "Supper on the table. Water for the queen's bath. And then leave us in privacy."

A fluttering demi-fey hovers over her shoulder. The second the maid places a platter on the table by the window, it flies down, driving a tiny little spear through a fat grape before it retreats to the windowsill with its bounty. Another flies after it, and they set to squabbling over the grape.

Grimm starts to slip into shadows, his golden eyes locking upon the unsuspecting demi-fey and his tail twitching.

"Don't you even dare," Thalia tells him, thwacking him on the butt with a rolled-up newspaper. "The Court of Milk and Honey is under my protection, and I have promised them safe passage within these walls. If you harm a single one of them, then I shall be forced to go to war against you."

Grimm solidifies, sniffing disdainfully. *You are no warrior. And I am He Who Stalks The Shadows.*

Thalia snaps her fingers, and every single demi-fey in the room falls into formation behind her, tiny spears at the ready. "I am She Who Runs This Bloody Castle. If we go to war, O Mighty Shadow Spawn, then there will be vinegar in the milk, pretty bows to tie around your neck... oh, and baths. Daily. Baths." A diabolical look sweeps across her expression. "Actually, Cook has a nephew who likes to knit. He creates these lovely little coats for my demi-fey. Would you like a new outfit, O Claws Like Knives? I can get you a matching little hat too, with a pom-pom on the top. And a ruff of frills around the neck of your coat." Her face lights up. "Pink. Definitely pink. I feel it's your color—"

"*Try it and die.*" Grimm growls under his breath.

"Who's a pretty little kitty," Thalia coos, scratching under his chin.

Amaya giggles.

With that, Grimm is gone. I see a tail lash beneath the armchair, and wary eyes peer out.

"I think Thalia won the opening rout," Eris mutters.

I can't stop a smile as I push out of bed.

And then I feel guilty for letting myself dare, when my husband is still gone.

"Amaya, do you think you could go pick some oils for your mother's bath?" Thalia asks her sweetly.

Amaya's gaze shifts between us and then she sighs. "I am nine, Aunt Thalia. I am not a fool. If you want to talk privately, just tell me to go."

Thalia eyes her for a long time. "I need to say something to your mother, and I think it needs to be private. Adult talk."

Amaya sighs. "Come on, Grimsby." She turns toward the wash chambers. "We get to do something really exciting and choose bath oils. Yay."

"Smart mouth," Thalia mutters.

"She's going to eavesdrop anyway," Eris says.

"No, she's not," Thalia replies, then swirls a finger.

I can't see a thing, but I know she warded the room. Thalia's gifts run toward vocal, auditory, and wards. Before she lost the power of her saltkissed voice, she could sing the sea into submission. Now her gifts are a shadow of their former self, but when it comes to information, she's an absolute master.

"What do we need to talk about?"

Thalia eases me into a chair, gathering handfuls of my hair and drawing it behind me. "Stop doing that," she clucks.

"What?"

"You're allowed to smile. You're allowed to *live*, Vi. Thiago wouldn't have wanted this for you. He would have wanted you to be happy, no matter what. And if this... this thing today doesn't work, then that's what you're going to do. You're going to *live*."

"You don't think I'm taking a foolish risk just to see him again?"

Eris sprawls on my bed. "Fairly certain we're beyond that point."

I *know*. But the pressure boils up inside me, a veritable storm hammering within my chest. We're so close. Today's the day I make that bargain with the Mother of Night and get him back, and....

What if it goes wrong?

What if it doesn't work?

"Hush, you." Thalia threatens Eris with the brush, then strokes it through my hair. "If there was even the slightest chance I could get him back, then I'd risk anything. I'd even challenge Prince Kyrian to a duel, and we both know how that would end."

I think about the Prince of Stormlight and the way the two of them faced off against each other the last time they met.

"Naked?" I suggest. "Rolling around in a bed together?"

"You're supposed to be on my side."

"He looks at you like he'd like to eat you all up," Eris drawls.

"For dessert," I point out.

Thalia tugs a bunch of my hair in retort, then begins braiding it. "I'm going to ignore that. I'm going to pretend you are both my dearest friends and would never even plant that suggestion in my head."

"We are your dearest friends," Eris points out. "And I'm fairly certain that suggestion was planted long ago."

Thalia groans. "It's those fucking leather breeches he wears. I swear you could bounce a copper off his ass."

"Or sink your teeth into it." The words feel hollow. It's like I'm trying to play at our old sense of camaraderie; but that's all it is. An attempt at normal.

"I can't even remember what that feels like," she says with a sigh.

"I'm fairly certain you had several males dancing with you the night the city celebrated me as queen."

"Yes," she says. "But then a Fetch kidnapped you, and the last thing I was thinking of was how handsome my current dance partner was."

"Sorry."

She sighs. "It has been an eventful few months, hasn't it?"

Eventful doesn't even come close to describing it. I just want to crawl into my bed and never get out. I want to close my eyes and *not* see him falling for just one night.

"It's all right not to be all right, Vi," she whispers, as if she can see where my thoughts went.

The steady methodical movement of her hands is soothing. She doesn't have to do this—I have maids, after

192

all—but I know what she's doing. Thalia feeds us when she's upset. It gives her something to do with her hands when I know her heart is full of grief too.

I shake it off with a deep breath. I don't have time to grieve.

I have my husband's soul to resurrect.

A country to protect.

A war to win.

"Speaking of Prince Kyrian, do we know where he stands in regards to this war?" I hate to bring it up, but he didn't come to the burning of the pyre, and Thiago was his closest friend.

I can't help feeling as though Kyrian's long-ago words were a prophecy that came true.

"*You will be his ruin,*" he once told me. "*His death.*"

And with Ravenal abstaining from war, we need Stormlight at my mother's back in order to keep her away from our throats—for just long enough for me to beg the Mother of Night for Thiago's body.

"Leave Kyrian to me," Thalia sniffs.

"We need him as ally," Eris says, no longer looking like a sleek panther reclining on the bed. Tension marks her frame.

Thalia sets the brush aside, a dangerous gleam highlighting her uptilted green eyes. "If I have to haul that smug pirate to his knees and force him to side with us, then I will. Stormlight will grant us the warriors we need. And Eris is going to make an appearance at the border today so that your mother's attention is focused there."

"And Finn? How's Finn?"

The second I think of him, he's there in my mind. Steel

flashes. A sword weaving through familiar patterns. The point of it pauses, as if he senses me thinking of him, and then he flows into another sweeping lunge toward an imaginary opponent.

Thalia and Eris share a look.

"He's in the training yard," Eris mutters. "He's been there since daybreak."

"What's wrong?"

"Nothing's wrong," Thalia says swiftly.

Eris arches a brow. "He won't tell us. But he's clearly bottling some sort of emotion."

"Is he—?"

"You just focus on Thiago," Thalia chides. "Finn needs a little bit of time alone. He needs to hit the punching bags, slay a few imaginary foes, perhaps even trade a few *actual* blows if our dearest Eris would get off her ass and go down there and offer to hit him a few times."

"Subtle," Eris grumbles.

"Something I've never been accused of. Work it out of him, E. That's an official order." Leaning down, Thalia rests her chin on my shoulder as our gazes meet in the mirror. "As for you, you look beautiful, Vi. But you smell. Now go and take your bath. Bring our prince home, and don't worry about the rest. Finn, Baylor, Eris and I have it covered."

I screw up my nose. "When did she ever get this bossy?"

"I thought your memories were nearly all returned?" Eris arches a brow. "She's always been this bossy."

"Someone has to keep you all on your toes," Thalia replies briskly. On edge, and trying to control everyone and everything around her in order to contain it.

I kiss her cheek as I stand, and she blinks in surprise. "Thank you. For everything."

"Here." Eris reaches behind her neck, unclasping the locket that contains Thiago's soul.

It spills into my cupped palms. The wisps of silvery soul within the glass stir restlessly.

"I'm going to bring him back," I tell them, looking up fiercely as I drape the chain around my neck and tuck the locket safely against my skin. "I'm going to bring Thiago back. I promise."

"We know." Then Thalia blinks and seems to realize Eris is still standing there. She claps her hands sharply. "Off you go. Make Finn sweat."

Chapter Sixteen

Iskvien

The Mother of Night waits for me.

All the remaining torches have been lit along the shore as I arrive deep in the heart of her cavern and land upon the island in the middle of the underground lake. I'm getting better at this sidestep into another world. No more slamming into the lake with its creepy carnivorous ghostfish.

The torches flicker. There are fewer of them than I remember.

It gives the impression the island is slowly dying.

"It is," the Mother of Night murmurs, cradling her arms across her chest as she steps out of the darkness. She looks weary today. As if she's carrying the weight of the world on her shoulders. And the dark cloak she wears seems to cling to a skeletal frame.

"Are you all right?"

She waves a hand as if it doesn't matter.

But it does.

I've seen her power, seen her strength. I've fought her with every inch of my soul. And yet here, now, with those fine lines around her eyes and the gauntness of her cheeks as if she's using her own power to prevent this slow collapse, I can't help feeling the bite of guilt.

I don't understand her. I never have.

"Why is this Hallow dying?" Angharad resurrected the Hallow stones of Mistmark in the real world and made the appropriate sacrifices. This shouldn't be happening.

"What do you know of the Hallows?" she murmurs.

"They're ancient stone monoliths set in place to capture and wield the power of the leylines where they cross. They were places of worship for the otherkin, and places the Old Ones claimed as their own. This one—Mistmark—was yours. Then the... the fae used it to turn your magic back upon you and trapped you here."

She smiles weakly. "The stones are merely stones, Iskvien. They're sentinels meant to focus the power of the wells. The Hallow itself is a well of power, a means to channel the leylines. And the leylines themselves are merely conduits of power meant to connect each Hallow. It's a network that circles the entire world. If one Hallow begins to ebb, then it may draw power from the others. It's an infinite balance, and now that balance is off." She sighs. "When Thiago's death released the Horned One at the Black Keep, it sent shockwaves rippling through the network. The Horned One was weakened by his captivity, and he knows how to draw upon *ala*—the energy that each well of power draws from the lands. To build his strength, he's been siphoning power from other Hallows. But the cost of that...."

She staggers and I catch her by the arm, surprised by how thin she is.

I can't say I understand it all, but... "You've been restoring the balance across the networks, haven't you?"

"The balance *must* be restored, Iskvien. He's already drained three Hallows dry in Unseelie. They're dead now, and the impact of that will threaten the world. The energy that runs along those leylines will simply vanish into those empty wells, spilling through the core the world. It will build and grow, making the earth volatile. Eventually they'll erupt. You'll feel the tremors in the lands as they tear themselves apart. Castles will fall. Houses will topple. It will kill thousands if he is allowed to continue."

"How do we stop him?"

She looks at me. Just looks. "A queen will rise, Vi. I have always foreseen it."

I am not that queen. "A queen may rise, but will she fall?"

Blankness smooths her face. "That is not set in stone."

A bitter, breathless laugh escapes me. "I knew it. I *knew* it. All along you've been leading me toward this. You want me to set you free. You want me to kill an ancient fucking god. But you haven't said a word about how I'm to accomplish any of that—or even if I'll survive."

She captures my fingers as I turn away. "Because I do not *know*. I don't see the future, Iskvien. I see *possibilities*. And with every choice made, ripples of consequences spread out, changing all those possibilities. There are a thousand futures where the Horned One kills us all. And dozens where we cast him down. But there is always a cost in those mere dozen."

"Do I survive in any of them?"

She hesitates. "Yes."

"And if I bring Thiago back, does *he* survive?" Because I don't think I can face that again.

A long silence brews. "There is only one future in which I see him survive."

One future. One shot.

"You must both accept your destinies," she says sadly. "It is your only hope."

"I'm not ready." There's been too much to confront. Thiago's death. The shock of Amaya's appearance. My mother. Andraste. Edain. Lysander. All of it. I haven't had a chance to unpack any of it, and it keeps coming at me.

"No," she says quietly, "you're not ready. But you are all we have, and we don't have time to make you ready. He will not stop, Iskvien. The Horned One will not stop until he has wrought his vengeance upon those who locked him away. And your mother invites it because she thinks she can control him. She thinks she can stop him if she regains the Crown of Shadows."

I've faced impossible odds before.

And for the first time, I stare at the destiny in front of me.

A child whose birth was orchestrated by the old gods. A child who straddles both worlds. A queen who will break apart Unseelie.

The saithe oracle promised it too. She demanded that I seek out the prophecy that spoke of my coming and read the entire thing. Maybe that's what I'll do if we survive this and get the chance.

"The written remnants of the prophecy are no longer whole," the Mother says.

"That's incredibly creepy, you know?" I rub my tired face. "If it's not whole, then how do I read it?"

"What is a prophecy?"

"A vision of the future, granted to a prophet."

"How?"

"Through visions or dreams...." The second I say it, I know how it came about. "A dream. It was gifted in a dream, wasn't it?"

Maybe we're so closely linked I'm picking up her thoughts too.

"It was granted in a dream, yes."

And there's only one repository of dreams on this entire cursed continent. "Darkness's black breath. Queen *Maren* has a copy of the prophecy at her court?"

I've seen the fabled Tower of Dreams, where Maren's dreamthieves and spies spin dreams into glass globes so that others may consume them at a later date.

The Mother smiles.

Maren's court is practically impenetrable.

"You can't simply tell me what it says?"

"I don't know what it says. I'm not omnipotent. But first things first, Vi...."

Squaring my shoulders, I shove that little snippet about the prophecy to the back of my mind. "If I free you, will you protect Amaya? Even if I fall? Even if Thiago falls? I want you to promise you will protect her with your life."

Sadness blinks through her eyes. "I will protect Amaya with what is left of my life if you free me." She repeats the statement. Once. Twice. Thrice.

The deal is done.

Swallowing down the pain and fear inside me—something I am so very good at doing—I reach behind my neck and unlock the chain around my throat. "I have his soul. How do we bring him back?"

"Take me to the water's edge," she whispers.

Curling the amulet in the palm of my hand, I gently lead her down to the water. The Mother of Night kneels and places her palm flat on the surface of the lake.

Golden light reflects across that dark mirror, chasing away the vicious phosphorescent glow of those hungry lights. It gleams like a rising sun, warming the water, warming the air....

Water surges.

Thiago's body lifts to the surface on an enormous flat rock, individual stepping stones appearing in the still, dark waters of that lake.

I can't stop my breath from catching.

He's so pale.

So still.

I hate seeing him like this.

"Help me across," she says.

201

Step by step, we cross toward him. My heart breaks when we finally reach him, and I go to my knees, my hand skating over his freezing cold skin. "Thiago?"

There's nothing there.

Nothing but the vessel he left behind. Tearing off my cloak, I place it over him, trying to warm him. Hot tears slip down my cheeks.

"Break the glass," the Mother says, "and bring it to his lips."

I crack the ampoule against the rock, somewhat like cracking an egg. Wisps of silvery soul stream through the fracture lines, but it's not until I lift it to his mouth that they pause, as if they sense where they should be going.

I break the glass apart and hold it to his lips.

His soul gushes toward his mouth, and then vanishes inside him.

Thiago's chest rattles as if he sucks it in.

And then it falls.

I place a hand on his shoulder, the pressure in my chest increasing as I search for a single sign of life....

His eyelashes don't flutter.

The muscle in his jaw doesn't flex.

Nothing happens.

He's cold and pale, and *nothing* happens.

"*Please.* I don't want to do this alone." Hot tears escape me. "Please come back to me. Come back to me."

I slam my fists down on his chest, and try to force the heat and hurt building within me through him. My tears splash on his chest, but they don't gleam golden. They don't sink inside his skin, nor stir through his veins.

I can't bring him back, and it nearly ruins me.

The Hallow's magic slips through my fingers.

"Think of the network, Vi. In the past, to wield the Hallow's magic, those without the gift of the gods would use a kingly sacrifice or a relic of power. Neither is necessary. Not for you. You can sense the leylines; you can pluck their strings and drink their power. Now you must learn to refill the well. Here." The Mother of Night places her hand over mine. "Close your eyes. Let yourself *feel.*"

Taking a shuddering breath, I release everything that's bottled up inside me and reach for the song of the Hallows.

At first it's distant.

Faint pulsing magic. I can feel this Hallow. The echo of Mistmere.

"Reach out," she whispers. "Pluck the strings."

Five Hallows are linked to Mistmere. If I concentrate, I can just feel the distant buzz. They sing back to me.

"There," she breathes. "Wells full of power. Bring it to you, Vi."

The trickle of magic runs over my senses. Then it becomes a flood.

"Not too much," she warns. "Just enough to fill Mistmere's glutted pool of magic."

Heat lights through my veins. Energy. All the hairs on my body stand on end. I try and channel it through him.

"It's not working." After everything we've been through.... "He's not breathing."

"This one last gift I give you," the Mother says, kneeling and placing her palm over mine on his chest. Golden heat flows around her hand, and then it pulses through me, through him. "Breathe. Return to life, o dark one."

The shudder of her power echoes through the cavern,

and dust and gravel rain down from above. Where I can play the Hallows, she's a maestro. She makes the magic sing, makes that inferno of golden heat dance to her tune.

All of it centered on Thiago.

The water of the lake remains deathly still, as if even the luminescent creatures who lurk beneath its surface don't dare draw attention right now.

But it's the incandescent gleam of her hands that I can't look away from.

"Breathe," she tells him, and another shudder of power kicks through his chest.

Please. Please don't leave me here alone.

Thiago's spine arches.

And then he starts screaming.

"Go," the Mother of Night says, collapsing back onto her hands. She looks desperately tired. "Take him from this world and go."

"Thank you." I sob, cradling him close and tearing us from her prison world.

* * *

The Hallow pulses, and we slam back into being, landing flat on the floor of the tower. Thiago fights me, but I throw my arms around him and try to rein him in.

"Thiago! T! It's me!"

Harsh sobs rack through him.

I rock against him, barely daring to breathe, to hope. He's back. He's back.

Cold hands capture my wrists. His breath shudders

through him. But the harsh sobbing finally slows down. It's as though he finally knows where he is.

"*Vi?*" My name. On his tongue. A whisper of pain and hope and longing.

"I've got you," I whisper, curling my arms around him.

I'm never letting go again.

Chapter Seventeen

Iskvien

He's so cold. Like ice.

Thiago lowers his shaking hands, and slowly lifts his head, my cloak draped around his nudity. The shock of his eyes—no longer the heated green of a jungle cat's but black as midnight—takes me by surprise. "I saw you," he rasps. "I saw you. *There*. You came for me."

I go to my knees beside him, "Always."

"What did you do?" he rasps.

I run my fingers through his hair, breathless with the sensation of it. There's so much to talk about. So much to see to.

And I don't give a damn about any of it.

I just want him. I need him. *This.* The taste of his mouth, the sensation of his hands on my skin. And maybe he feels it too. This need binding us together. Because his eyes darken, and his hands capture my forearms, the cloak sliding from his naked shoulder.

"You're back," I whisper, leaning toward him. "You're home. You're safe."

Our mouths crash against each other.

It's a kiss forged of desperation and fury. Raw. Possessive. A blistering firestorm of emotion that makes the one we shared in the Darkness a mere facsimile. His tongue drives inside my mouth, desperate to claim me, and I let him, my body undulating against every hard inch of him. There's nothing elegant about the way we eat of each other, but maybe that's exactly what we need right now.

Raking my fingernails over the hardened flesh of his upper arms, I can't stop a half sob from escaping me. *It's real. He's real.* In my arms. In my bed. In my heart.... But for how long? Can we fight off Malakhai? Defy Kato? Kill the Horned One?

The desperation rising within me threatens to overwhelm. I would give anything to keep him here forever. *Anything.*

"Vi." His mouth breaks from mine and there's a hot-eyed look on his face that tells me he knows exactly what's going through my mind. He whispers as if through a throat raw from screaming. "Vi, what did you do? Who did you bargain with? What does this cost?"

"I made a deal with Kato," I tell him everything, still trying to touch him. "Once we kill the Horned One, then we have to return to the Gates of the Underworld. We have to cast Death from inside you."

Thiago's eyes flare a vicious emerald. "*Vi*. I've tried to get rid of this thing inside me. It's impossible."

"Nothing is impossible. I brought you back, did I not?"

"You brought me back." He gasps, staring at his hands.

"I had to." I capture his face between my palms.

"You don't understand." The muscle in his jaw flexes as he turns away from me, every inch of him tight with tension. "You have no idea what you've just done."

"Saved you." I push to my knees again. "I saved you." A sob catches in my throat. "You spent thirteen years trying to remind me of our love. I couldn't just... let you die."

Thiago closes his eyes, tilting his face toward the ceiling. "Vi." A shudder escapes him as he finally meets my eyes. "When I died, I wasn't the only soul set free. Those five Darkyn souls trapped within me? They were tethered with my soul, contained by the magic of my wards.... Wards that shattered the second I died."

"Does that mean they're... alive again?"

Thiago shakes his head grimly. "Not alive, no. But free. And even the wraiths of their past selves are powerful and dangerous." His dark lashes fall, obscuring his eyes. "And hungry for revenge."

Upon him.

"My father will be searching for them in order to consume them if he hasn't done so already." Thiago shudders. "But they're not the only ones he'll come for." Resting his hands on his knees, he gives me a look full of hungry intent. "When I was trapped in the Darkness, Death was thwarted its endgame. It couldn't be whole without me—or the other pieces of its soul."

And now that's all changed, because I brought him back.

"Malakhai is the least of our problems," he growls. "Death is still there. Taunting me. When I was trapped in the Darkness, I was free of the threat of him for the first time in my life. Because he could never reunite with himself."

"Then we fight him. Together." My gaze runs over his bare chest. "We fight all of them together. If there's one thing I've learned it's that you and I are unstoppable together. If Death wants to take you, then I'll rip him apart. If Malakhai comes for you, you'll take his head." I capture his face again. "And if Kato takes exception with anything, then I'll claim the Hallow that throbs beneath his court, and I'll bring that fucking island down on his head."

A strange light blazes to life in his eyes. "When did you become so fierce?"

"When you died," I whisper, caressing his cheek. "Nothing else mattered. You always said I was your light in the Darkness, but you were the seed of hope that made me gleam. Without you, the world was filled with cold and ashes. Or maybe that was my heart. When you died, so did my fears. And my doubts. For the first time in years, I knew what was important. You. And me. That's all that matters. And if anything tries to take you from me again, then I will destroy them."

My words seem to ignite the inferno within him. Turning his face, he kisses my palm, his dark lashes fluttering over his eyes. When they flutter open, the searing intense need in those depths burns me. "I need to feel your skin on mine. I need you beneath me, Vi."

"Do it. Take what you want from me." He doesn't know how much I need this too.

"You shouldn't say such things." He turns his face away, rubbing his cheek along my jaw and breathing me in. His hand cups my ass, grinding me against him. "I don't know that I have the restraint to be gentle with you tonight."

Capturing his face, I lick at his mouth. "When have I ever wanted gentle?"

A shudder runs through him as he palms my breasts, burying his face against my throat. "Last warning, Vi."

"Fuck me," I breathe into his hair. "Hard. Remind me what it feels like to be loved."

Molten eyes lock on mine. "Remind me what it feels like to live."

I gift him with a dangerous smile. "Done."

This time, I don't know who reaches for who first.

Our mouths come together in a raging inferno of need. Shoving at my shirt, he tears half the buttons off as he wrenches the sleeve back over my shoulder. Breasts straining over the edge of my corset, I crawl into his lap, grinding against the hard ridge of his erection. My cloak is gone, and all I can feel beneath me is skin. Sleek skin, his muscled thighs thick with hair, and the straining drive of his cock pushing into my belly.

Everything inside me goes molten, the wet heat between my thighs throbbing.

"Gods, I've missed you," he breathes, one fist curling into my hair as he stares at my breasts. "Every night I dreamed of you. Every day I begged for the chance to see your face one last time. I had nothing of you. No locket. No strand of hair. Nothing but my memories. It wasn't enough. I've been *starving for you*, Vi. Desperate to taste you again, to kiss you, to hold you in my arms...."

Reaching between us, I find his cock, the taut head slick with seed. "Trousers. Off," I gasp.

Lifting me up, he wraps my thighs around his hips and then he lowers me back onto the floor with a roughened laugh and follows me down. "So eloquent."

"Shut up and kiss me."

He's still laughing as he obliges, his weight settling over me. I dig my thumbs into the hard muscle of his upper arms. Gods, he's so perfect. I want to consume him. The feel of his mouth is raw and unyielding.

And then a hand slides beneath the waistband of my trousers and I nearly die of ecstasy.

"So slick," he breathes, pressing a kiss to my jaw. "So wet. I want to taste you, Vi."

I capture his face in my hands as he withdraws his fingers and sucks them.

Our eyes meet.

And the green in his irises bleeds into darkness.

A little shiver runs through me. "Hello, my prince."

"Hello, my queen," he purrs, his hand sliding down my abdomen again.

Thiago makes short work of my buttons. I spare a brief thought for the maids who are going to find scraps of my clothing strewn around the Hallow as though wild animals tore into each other, but then his hard fingers find me and the thought shatters.

They drive inside me, grinding against the restriction of my leather trousers. "Oh, gods!" I throw my head back, body clenching around him as I arch.

"Scream louder," he commands, crooking those fingers up, just so.

There's no need to fight the order. Everything I've been holding back comes crashing over me as he claims my mouth again, riding me through the firestorm with clever, dancing fingers.

I collapse back on the stone, my nails digging channels in his upper arms. There's nothing but satisfaction in his eyes. He likes it. Likes that I leave my mark there, the same way he's leaving his as he nips his way down my throat.

The hot rasp of his mouth closes over my nipple, and my body clenches again, milking his fingers. A sound echoes in his throat, a growl of need. *More*, it says. *Give me more*. Teeth capture my nipple, his thumb settling directly on my clitoris.

It lights within me like fireflowers shattering in the skies. I explode again, sex pulsing around him as I grind and writhe, desperate for more.

"Get these... gods-cursed trousers... off me!" I gasp as he finally lets me up for air.

Rough laughter rumbles in his chest as he sits back, tugging the slick leather down my sweaty thighs. "So impatient."

I eye the proud jut of his cock and trace my fingers between my slick thighs. It sends a shiver through me, the aftershock of ecstasy. "You're the one denying yourself."

The wicked smile he graces me with makes my heart skip a beat. This time, when he casts my trousers against the wall with a meaty slap, I know we've reached the point of no return.

Rearing above me on his knees, Thiago takes his cock in hand, barely able to close his fingers around it as his wrist works. The chiseled arrow of the groove of his hips flexes as the muscles in his abdomen tighten. He's beautiful. Dangerous. Feral. And his cock, that enormous, brutish weapon, is a thing of glory.

I need it inside me.

"Who's denying themself?" he whispers.

Biting my lip, I drag my fingers up my body, smearing the wetness of my sex around my nipple. His eyes glaze, his jaw locking. The battle cry has been sounded, and I smile a secretive smile as he settles his knuckles beside my head and leans over me.

Slowly, our eyes locked on each other the entire time, he leans down and licks that sleek trail off my skin, tongue circling my nipple.

"Do you want this?" he whispers, brushing the slick head of his cock against my entrance.

Desperately.

"And this?" The weight of him grinds against me.

I want it. I need him inside me.

Now.

Sinking my fingernails into the muscled globes of his ass, I let my thighs fall wide in surrender.

His forearms settle beside my head, the rasp of his thumb gentle against my cheek even as his cock dips inside me. There's reverence in the moment. Hunger bleeding

213

through the darkness of his eyes. I bite his thumb, and our eyes meet again.

A shudder runs through him. "Are you sure?"

"Please," I whisper. "I need you."

Fill me. Take away this emptiness. Make me yours.

Thiago stares into my eyes. "As you wish."

And then he captures my mouth again, tongue lazily stroking mine as he sinks deep within me. Filling me up. Stretching me until the burn deep inside me makes my nerves thrum. For the first time in weeks, I feel whole. Complete.

It's like some missing piece of me is finally returned.

"Gods." A shudder runs through him as he thrusts. "I've missed this."

The next hard thrust drives me into the stone.

Fists curling in his hair, I arch my head back as his mouth claims my throat. Teeth rake down my skin, a hint of danger and possession inherent in the touch. I can sense his intentions, sense the need within him. Tilting my head to the side, I grant him permission.

The shock of his bite sears through me.

It's intense.

A burning, sharp ache spears through my abdomen and steals a soft cry from my lips.

And he knows it.

Thiago's fingers slide between us and then he finds me, wet and molten. Two fingers circle my clit, tracing lazy circles there, and it's enough to tip me over the edge.

I scream as he marks my flesh, his teeth imprinting into the slope of muscle that runs from my throat to my shoulder. It's a ruthless, savage claim. *Mine,* it says. *Mine for now. Mine forever.*

He dominates me completely, fucking his way into me, driving me over that edge, again and again. Lifting my leg, he hooks my knee over his shoulder, the angle deep enough to tear another helpless cry from my throat as his cock fills me to the hilt. The intensity of it obliterates any sense of control I still own.

"You and me, Vi." His fingers slide through mine, pinning both my hands to the floor. "Together. Against anything this world can throw at us."

"Together," I gasp, feeling the tension ratchet within me again. A storm about to burst.

This time, the kiss is desperate and sloppy and *everything*.

Driving into me, he forces me over the edge of that cliff, hurling me straight into the teeth of the storm. Clenching my fingers around his, I writhe and gasp, helpless to control myself as he dominates me so completely I see stars.

And then his thrusts quicken. Short. Hard. Furious.

His mouth breaks from mine and he buries his face against my throat as a moan echoes deep in his chest. Cock pulsing within me, he comes with a harsh exhalation, rocking into me in gentler strokes, his skin slick with sweat, and his entire weight collapsing over me.

"Vi. Gods, *Vi.*"

Hot seed spurts within me.

My knee slides down his arm to his elbow and I can't help moaning a little as stretched muscles soften. Collapsing back on the floor, I gasp for breath. That was intense. Even for him.

Every inch of me feels alive, my skin marked in a hundred different places. Sliding my hand up the curve of his spine, I cup his nape, digging my fingers into his sweaty hair as I close my eyes.

This moment, right here, is the closest I've ever been to peace.

Slowly Thiago lifts his head, pressing the gentlest of kisses to my swollen lips. Easing his weight off me, he pulls free in a gush of wetness. Both of us moan, because he's still hard. And this need, this desperate urge, smolders within us like the banked fires of a hearth.

"If you look at me like that," he whispers, nuzzling against my lips, "then this isn't going to end here."

"Oh, no?" I kiss him back. "What did you have in mind?"

"I want to throw you over my shoulder, haul you upstairs and lock the door for a month."

A husky laugh escapes me. "Thalia will only break the door down."

He groans.

I wince, undulating against the cold stone floor. I swear there's gravel rash on my ass but I have no regrets. "But why don't we revisit the first part of that equation? Hmm? As grateful as I am to have you in my arms again, I'd much prefer the bed."

Thiago laughs, kissing his way down my throat as he hauls me up into his lap. "As you wish, my love. It's also much easier on the knees."

"Whose knees?"

"We can discuss that upstairs," he growls, wrapping the

cloak around me and surging to his feet with me in his arms.

* * *

We collapse into the sheets hours later, sweat-soaked and aching.

Every inch of me is marked with bites and bruises; the kind I demanded of him. I don't want to let him go. I don't want to close my eyes or leave this bed, just in case it all vanishes like a mirage.

The first sob catches me by surprise.

"Vi?" Arms curl around me, hauling me against his chest.

It's been so long since I've lost myself in his arms. Making love to him has always been electric, but *this*.... To know true safety, true happiness.

I don't even know where these tears are coming from.

I bury my face in his throat, unable to stop my shoulders from shaking. "Don't let go."

Don't ever let me go.

I can't go through that ever again.

Thiago's hand strokes through my hair, and then he kisses the slope of my shoulder. "I'm not going anywhere," he whispers. "I promise once. I promise twice. I promise thrice. I'll never leave you again."

My tears burn. "I'm going to hold you to that promise," I tell him, resting my head on his chest. The hypnotic beat of its heart soothes the ragged edges inside me.

And then, for the first time since the Black Keep, blissful, unbroken sleep beckons.

* * *

I wake sometime during the night, reaching for Thiago.

It's a second before I realize that although the sheets on his side of the bed are still warm, he's no longer there.

Panic jerks me to full awareness.

Gone.

No.

Slipping from the bed, I jerk my nightrobe on and hurry from our rooms, my heart racing—

There.

There's a light down the hallway.

The ache in my chest collapses in on itself when I see his familiar silhouette marking the door ahead.

He's caged in his glamor again. Wings vanished. A male formed of shadows and perfection as he leans against the doorjamb at the entrance to Amaya's room, wearing only a black silk robe.

Amaya lies asleep in her bed, golden candlelight washing over her serene face. Beside her, not even bothering to lift his head from the pillow is Grimm, golden-green eyes unblinking as he stares at Thiago.

It's not entirely a friendly look.

Sliding my arms around him, I glance over his shoulder. "She'll be so excited to see you in the morning. It's all been an enormous shock to her."

Thiago turns away, tugging her door closed behind him. There's nothing on his face. Just... emptiness. "Perhaps it's best this way."

I suck in a sharp breath. "What?"

Taking my fingers, he leads me back to our rooms. The

second the door is closed, he kisses me again, but I push my hand against his chest.

"What did you mean by that?"

"It's nothing." He turns away, slipping outside and pausing by the railing.

The lights of Ceres flicker below.

Tugging my robe around me with a shiver, I follow him. "That wasn't nothing."

"Vi, leave it alone."

The forlorn shape of his silhouette tugs at my heartstrings. I've dreamed of reuniting him with his daughter. In all my dreams, he would wrap Amaya in his arms and squeeze her so tightly, promising that he'd never let her go....

I find my voice again. "Together, you said. Together, I pledged. And I meant it, Thiago. Whatever is going through your head right now.... You owe me that. You never told me about the Darkyn and I need to know the truth if I'm going to be able to help our daughter through whatever changes her body may face."

The hard edge of his profile doesn't shift. Instead, the muscle in his jaw locks. "I can always sense my father out there somewhere. It's an itch beneath my skin, a driving need to find him, to take that which belongs to me." Dark eyes flash toward me face. "Or maybe it's not me who feels him. Maybe it's the piece of me that belongs to Death, yearning for the other pieces of itself."

The heat drains from my face as I understand what he's saying.

"It's worse with her here in the castle. I can fucking hear her breathing, Vi. I can sense that dark flame just on the edge of my fingertips, mine for the taking if I only reach out... Reach out and take it."

"You wouldn't."

Thiago clenches his fingers, looking down at them. "I wouldn't. I *couldn't*." But the rawness of his voice shows how much he's bleeding inside. "I wish you hadn't brought me back, Vi. It was safer for her without me here."

Swallowing down the hard lump in my throat, I force myself to look at the facts. He *died* for her. He loves her. And if there's one thing I know for sure, it's that he would never, *ever* hurt her. "You're not a threat to her. I know you. I know you would never harm her."

I trace my fingers down his spine, an act of comfort.

He shudders at my touch. "You don't understand, Vi. Sometimes I don't see Amaya when I look at her. Sometimes... all I see is the shadow within her. The darkness I want to consume." Stark shadows darken his eyes. "My wards are gone. I don't know how much of me... how much *is* me. I was trapped in that Darkness for nearly a year. I did things to survive—things I'm not proud of. Everything I've spent centuries locking away deep inside me I set free, and now, I don't know if I can put the leash back on it."

Stepping forward, I wrap my arms around him from behind, burying my face against his back. "I'm here. I'm here."

The first sob escapes him. Hard arms lock around mine, cradling them against his stomach. He suppresses it, locking it down tight within him, but I feel those rib-shaking heaves of breath.

Finally, eventually, they die down.

"How can you stand here with me?" he whispers.

"Because when I said 'together' I meant it." I look up fiercely. "And because I know we'll... we'll find a means to ward that bastard deep down inside you again until we can excavate it. Kato said there was a way to get it out of you. Death must will it."

He goes so still I half fear he's stopped breathing again. Then the breath explodes out of him. "Vi, he'll never let me go. He wants to stay here in this world. He wants to hunt."

"Then we'll just have to find some sort of motivation to convince him."

Chapter Eighteen

Iskvien

The next morning, Finn looks up moodily from the mug of herbal tea in front of him when I enter the dining room. Thiago wanted a moment alone before he came down, and so I gave it to him, nervous exhilaration running through my veins.

Finn looks like he's hardly slept, and a hint of a blush touches his cheekbones. "We need to work out how to mute this bond."

Oh, gods. I stop in my tracks. It never even occurred to me—

"You... heard us...? Last night?"

He makes a gagging face. "No. Gods, no. I went and drilled with Andyrion for two or three hours, and when you started breaking through again, I got blind, roaringly drunk. As much as I love the two of you, I do *not* need to know what you get up to. It's disgusting."

That's a relief. I pour myself a cup of tea. "You sound jealous, Finn. Long time between drinks?"

Kicking back in his chair, he cups his hands behind his head. "I'll have you know I could... have a drink anytime I wanted to."

Dragging out a chair at the table, I rest my elbows on the table top and sip the soothing taste of peppermint. All is well with the world this morning and I don't care what I have to do, I'm going to keep it that way. "Strange. I was of the opinion that it's been a while since you've had someone in your bed."

"What gives you that opinion?"

"Oh, nothing." I shrug. "Just something Eris said."

Finn's eyes narrow. I can practically see the tip of his tongue pressing against his teeth, trying not to say it—

"What did she say?"

This is almost too easy. "Girl talk. I can't betray her secrets. What's wrong, Finn? You look a little on edge.... Are you sure you're not keeping secrets?"

Finn sits forward. "What is that supposed to mean?"

"I'm in your head, Finn. There has been a stray thought or two slip my way. You can't hide anything from me anymore." I roll my eyes. "You're practically one horse away from demanding she cross swords with you."

Heat darkens his cheeks. "I'm trying to remember why I saved you from a certain treacherous father-in-law. Remind me again...?"

Plucking a bread roll from the basket on the table, I toss it at him.

He snatches it out of the air, scowling at me. And then a smile slips through. "Well, it's good to see you laughing again. Even if it is at my expense."

"Never at your expense." I sigh. Finn's the brother I never had. "You should tell her how you feel."

Finn grimaces into his wine and mutters. "She knows how I feel."

"She does *not* know how you feel," Thalia says as she sails inside the room. "Eris can read every minute quiver of a sword's direction, but when it comes to matters of the heart, she's utterly blind. Tell her how you feel."

"Oh gods, there are two of them. I surrender." Finn holds his hands in the air.

"No, honestly," Thalia continues, "I would love to see—"

"Surrender," he repeats loudly. Clearly. "We're not having this conversation."

I exchange a glance with Thalia. It's not our place to push. And Finn's clearly struggling through the matter.

Thalia kisses him on the top of the head in a message of silent support and then circles the table. She catches the edge of my dress, tugging at the lace there to reveal my throat. One eyebrow arches high at whatever she sees. "Someone had fun last night."

I pop a blueberry in my mouth with a saucy smile. My cheeks ache. I can't quite keep it off my face.

"How is he?" she murmurs.

That steals my smile away. "The same. But also not the same."

Thalia's eyes soften with distress. "What does that mean?"

"I don't know." And I don't. He's locked down tight today, trying to hide the thoughts bothering him.

The shield is up. The mask firmly in place.

"We have to expect he's going to struggle to come to terms with what happened," Finn points out. "I'll take him out for the night and get him drunk. He'll talk."

"Maia's breath." Thalia rolls her eyes. "That is the *worst* idea."

Finn rolls his eyes in return. "Better than yours."

"I haven't even suggested anything yet."

"You're going to smother him," he says. "In love. You're going to hug him and feed him and follow him around the castle until he finally snaps."

Thalia's eyes narrow, and she snatches a grape off the table and throws it at him. Finn catches it with his mouth and chews, winking at her.

Footsteps stride toward the dining room. My heart skips a beat—but then one becomes two, and Baylor and Eris enter.

Finn instantly sits up straighter, cutting the two of us a warning look.

"Maybe you're right," Thalia teases, ruffling his hair. "Maybe I should leave Thiago alone and focus on something else. Something like—"

"I will lock you in a box, naked, and ship you off to Stormlight and Prince Kyrian if you even open your mouth." His glare promises murder.

"What did we miss?" Baylor helps himself to the sideboard.

"Nothing," Finn snaps.

Thalia laughs. "Eris, you're positively glowing today. What's the secret?"

"Didn't stab anyone today," Eris says with a shrug, resting one hip against the table and leaning over to pluck a blueberry from the platter in the middle.

"Do you want a medal?" Finn drawls.

The pair of them share a look.

"Day's still young," Eris points out.

"But you would have to catch me first," he points out, dipping his strip of toast in the yolk of his egg, "and you don't run very fast."

"I don't have reason to run. Nobody worth chasing. Nobody worth running from."

A silent duel takes place across the table, one conveyed in narrowed glances and stiffening shoulders and centuries of tension. The blueberry faces annihilation in Eris's suddenly tense grip.

"Children," Baylor drawls, taking his seat at the table. "The last time we started this, someone nearly lost an eye."

"I think Finn would look rather dashing with an eyepatch," Eris muses, sinking down opposite him.

"You presume you would beat me," Finn replies.

"When have I not?"

Finn gives her a tight smile. "When have I ever truly unleashed myself? I let you win, E, because we're playing. If

226

you and I ever truly go to war, it won't be as easy a victory as you presume."

"If I have to disarm the pair of you," Baylor warns, not even bothering to raise his voice, "then it's going to hurt."

"Big Daddy Baylor," Finn says, pushing to his feet and heading back to the sideboard to fill his plate. "Always threatening to take the enjoyment out of things."

"Who said it wouldn't be fun?" The enormous warrior arches his brow. "I'd enjoy it."

Thalia winks at me. "Are we taking bets?"

"Baylor takes all," I offer.

"Pfft," Thalia shoots back. "Where's your loyalty to the sisterhood? Eris would wipe the floor with the pair of them."

I point a finger at Eris. "Yes, but she likes Baylor, so she won't want to hurt him. Eris surrenders her weapons to Baylor. Then they both take Finn. Therefore, Baylor wins."

"What about me?" Finn protests.

"Annihilated," I insist.

"Someone's in a good mood," he says gruffly, ruffling my hair as he returns to the table. "All that kissing does wonders for your smile."

"Hey!" Thalia blurts. "The maids just spent a half hour making her look like a queen. You are not going to ruin all their good work!"

Finn holds his hands up in surrender.

Hard footsteps echo through the door.

Instantly, smiles die and my heart skips a beat.

The entire table stills.

Thiago slips inside, moving lightly on his feet. I left him to soak in the bath this morning, and his hair's still wet. He walks right into that wall of silence, and only the most minute shift of muscle in his face reveals he feels it.

"Good morning," I say swiftly, extending a hand toward him.

"What's all the noise about?" He lifts a brow in a way that makes me realize just how often he plays a part. It's as natural to him as breathing. "You would think someone let a herd of bawdy cattle into my dining room."

"It was just getting interesting," Thalia says. "Finn was about to bet a hundred horses that he could beat E in the dueling yard."

Thiago blinks.

The room falls still.

Eris's head whips toward her friend. There's an old challenge that Eris once made: She will only ever yield her hand in marriage to the male who manages to defeat her in battle.

If she defeats them, then they will owe her a hundred horses.

I believe the current count is somewhere in the thousands. Eris owns so much horseflesh, she's considered rich in many circles.

If they defeat her... well, marriages have been forged from less in the past.

"Awkward. Silence." Baylor lifts his cup of peppermint tea to his lips and breathes in the sweet-scented fumes.

This time, the smile in Thiago's eyes is real. "Good to see some things haven't changed in my absence."

"Hello, you," Thalia says, pushing to her feet.

Thiago's face softens a hint. "Hello, you."

Thalia simply walks up to him and wraps him in a hug.

Thiago squeezes her tight, his gaze capturing mine. Their relationship is incredibly important to him. He was raised as a bastard, raised as an orphan in Old Mother Hibbert's magical hut, without a single relation in the world. His father tried to kill him. His mother denied him. And he was forced to kill his half-brother in order to save his life.

Thalia is the one fae who's always belonged to him. A cousin. Blood of his blood. The only fae who opened her arms and her love to him when he needed it so desperately.

He'd protect them all, for he loves them, but Thalia is the one he'd die for.

And holding her like this heals some of the pain inside him.

"If you ever do that again," she scolds, closing her eyes and squeezing him tight, "then I will hunt you down in the Darkness, get my demi-fae to tie you down, cover you in honey, and invite a thousand ants to feast on all your tender regions."

"That sounds remarkably well-planned."

"I've had time to think about it." She sniffs, wiping a tear from her eye. "Oh gods, I'm going to cry and ruin my face."

"Didn't have much of a choice at the time," he says softly.

Thalia's grip tightens, and he *oofs* out a soft breath, before he places a kiss to the top of her hair.

"Erlking's hairy balls, T." Finn pushes to his feet. "Give him room to breathe."

The second Thalia lets him go, Finn wraps him in an enormous hug that I swear threatens to crack ribs. "You ever do that again," he says gruffly, "and I'll help her, you know? She won't need her demi-fae. I'll fucking hold you down."

"Good to see you too," Thiago drawls, slapping his shoulder and moving on.

Eris stares at him.

She's not a hugger.

Or at least, she isn't until Thiago hauls her close.

"How's my favorite menace?" he asks.

"On edge. I need to kill something."

He laughs. "Save it for Adaia."

It's such a throwaway line, but the words echo through me. I flash back to my dreams, to the way I gripped my mother's hair as I set a knife to her throat.

"We will water the lands with her blood and make the forests grow," croons the crown.

It's so clear in my head, it may as well be in the room with me.

By the time I blink out of the vision, Thiago claps Baylor's shoulder and smiles. Mine is frozen in place, my heartbeat kicking into a gallop.

Only Finn looks at me, one eyebrow arching.

I let my smile soften again, but he's not fooled. Not at all. So far the bond between us has proven that we share the sensation of emotions, sometimes of touch and vision if we're both closely attuned to each other, but not thoughts.

I want to be sick.

And he, no doubt, can feel it.

"Lysander went north," Thiago concludes, though I told him about Lysander's recovery last night.

Baylor nods. "Lysander went north."

Easing out a breath, Thiago hauls his chair back from the table. "Now," he says. "Vi filled me in on some of it— before she distracted me. But why don't you all tell me just how bad it is."

* * *

"Goblins to the north of us," Thiago muses, brushing a thumb across his dangerously soft mouth. "Adaia to the south. Maren to the south-west. The unseelie to the north. At least the seas to the east appear to be ignoring us."

"Don't tempt fate," Baylor mutters. "The saltkissed are stirring."

"They are?" I look sharply toward Thalia, whose mouth screws up in a grimace.

"Something's set them into a frenzy," she admits. "I don't know what."

Eris suggests that maybe they sense the oncoming war. Finn proffers that maybe my mother has been in contact with them.

But Thiago sits in silence.

It's as if he doesn't see or hear them.

His gaze slides to the door, a preternatural stillness running through him.

Grimm's the first one through the door, sauntering in as if he owns the place. Amaya follows him inside, her shoulders square. She's wearing a plain white shirt and leather breeches in her size, with her black hair braided back tightly. Thalia's starting to despair about ever getting her into a dress.

231

I hurriedly push to my feet and go to greet her. "Good morning, Amaya. Sleep well?"

It was clear in the first two days that she doesn't like to be touched when she's on edge. She doesn't welcome hugs or kisses on the cheek. She'll only seek me out if she's particularly worried.

But for the first time, she slips her hand inside mine, her dark lashes obscuring her green eyes as she glances toward her father.

"I want you to meet someone," I whisper.

Amaya's face drains of color as Thiago stares at her.

"Amaya." It's like he sounds out the word, trying to place what it means to him. And if his face is smooth of emotion, his voice is not.

"You did it," she whispers.

"We did it." I murmur, threading my fingers through hers as I tug her toward the table.

Thiago's chair scrapes back as he stands.

His eyes are all for her.

The daughter he gave his life to protect. The one he risked everything for. My eyes are wet again, but I can barely stop smiling as I reach for his hand too. "Come. Come and meet her."

But for the first time, I realize the look on his face isn't one of eagerness.

Eyes bleeding black, a quiver runs through him.

Thiago wrenches his fingers free from mine, his face hard. "No."

Amaya sucks in a sob, tearing free.

I try to grab his sleeve, giving him a look meant to ask

232

what's going on, but he turns away from me, heading toward the far door.

"Maya!" Thalia calls.

The other doorway is empty.

Only the sound of bare feet slapping on flagstones echoes through it.

Amaya is gone.

Baylor slowly sets his cup of tea on the table. "I'll go after him," he tells me.

And with the wake of everything exploding in my face, I run after my daughter.

Chapter Nineteen

Iskvien

A fter a morning with Amaya, reading through her fairy tales and my book of lore on the Old Ones, I go searching for Thiago. He hasn't returned to the castle, though I know Baylor has. He merely shook his head at me, saying Thiago wanted some space.

Finn knows where Thiago will be, and offers to escort me.

The bridge between being a mother and being a wife has never seemed so difficult. Amaya had to be the priority this morning. She's nine. And afraid. She sobbed in my arms until I could calm her.

But will Thiago take it as rejection?

"I'll stay here," Finn says as he helps me down from my horse. A sigh escapes him. "He needs you more than ever, right now."

"I know," I whisper, starting toward the rusted gates ahead of us.

They were shut many years ago upon the death of Queen Araya—Thiago's mother. I've never been here. No one comes. This place is a silent mausoleum to a long-dead queen.

The gates hang on broken hinges. Once they were carved with a myriad of images; moons, stars, and tangles of roses and thorns woven around the edges. I can't stop my fingers from grazing over those thorns. It feels like a physical embodiment of our marriage, or perhaps a prophetic one. I've never seen the stars and moon of the Evernight banner mingled with the roses and thorns of Asturia on any kind of artwork here in Ceres.

Pushing through the gates, I walk into what was once a garden. Alabaster towers gleam in the distance beneath a golden sun. Every window in the palace has been shattered by time, but if you don't look too closely, you can still see the past glory of it.

I find Thiago standing on one of the terraces in front of the palace, staring into a silent pool of still, black water. He's wearing the long black velvet coat I tend to identify with his 'Prince of Evernight' moods. It comes from an entire separate wardrobe full of clothes for state occasions and visits. All of it black. All of it slightly intimidating.

Thalia truly is a master at creating the right kind of wardrobe for every occasion.

Elegant embroidery adorns the hem and winds around the open collar of his coat; golden peacocks and phoenixes chasing stars through a tangle of knotwork. A small golden chain holds the coat closed at his throat, with two gorgeous gold pins on either side. Little crescent moons.

He chose the coat himself this morning and I can't help wondering if it's some subconscious need to protect himself —to present a picture of aloofness and strength—or because the darker half of him is in ascendancy today.

Either way, he's not okay.

Sliding my arms around his waist, I press my face against his back and breathe him in. "Do you want to talk about it?"

"No."

Stubborn, snarly male. "Okay."

A hand cups mine, squeezing gratefully.

And we stand like that, swaying in the breeze for long minutes, simply listening to the sound of wind whispering through the garden.

"I used to dream of holding our child in my arms," Thiago finally admits. "She would have dark hair like her mother, and green eyes just like me. And she'd smile at me, her little finger curling around mine." A roughened, bitter laugh rumbles through him. "But it was just a dream. Because I knew, in some secret dark part of my soul, that I would never be able to touch her."

Resting my face against his back, I close my eyes and breathe him in. I cannot imagine how it would feel to have yearned for so long for a single hug from his own mother, only to be denied the same with his daughter.

"She's beautiful. She's exactly how I imagined she'd be. Your face. My eyes. Your smile."

"Your soul," I whisper. "She's wild and free, but she will hide with her hurt, never daring to let others see it. I'm slowly working out all her favorite hiding places. They're usually in some place that gives me heart palpitations. Like the highest tower. Finn thinks it's her Darkyn side yearning to fly."

His head half-turns as though this little tidbit of information about her is a lifeline.

"She absolutely refuses to wear a dress." This time I chuckle. "It drives Thalia to her wit's end. Thalia threatened to strap her down and lace her into one the other day and Amaya told her she'd burn it if she tried and walk around naked."

The easy way they've slipped into a relationship—that of aunt and niece—sometimes makes me envious. One would think they'd been arguing for nine years.

The faintest of smiles touches his mouth. "Sounds like she has her mother's sense of stubbornness."

"Hey." I poke him in the ribs. "Don't you pretend to be the innocent one there."

Thiago stares at the pool for long seconds. "If she doesn't want to wear dresses, then she doesn't have to."

"Thalia knows that. She's given up. Now she's working on an entire line of tunics and leggings that a princess can be seen in. And little boots that reach to her knees. I'm so jealous I might steal the idea. Or I would, if I didn't think Thalia would riot."

He breathes out a faint laugh as he turns toward me. "Alas, I think she's already established full command of your wardrobe."

"I'm not the only one." I pluck at the thick belt laced over his coat. "Very dark prince today. I'm not sure if you're planning on seducing me, or slaying your enemies."

"Can't it be both?"

"Preferably not at the same time." Running my hands up his chest, I bite my lip. The tension's easing from his shoulders, which is what I intended. "I'm still a little remiss that you've never brought me here before. It's beautiful."

"This was my mother's favorite place."

And maybe that was why he never brought me.

Because this is more to him than a gorgeous place to view the city. It's pain, wrapped up in heartbreak, with a nicely giftwrapped bow of yearning tied around the entire mess.

He's only spoken once of Queen Araya's summer palace. Araya wintered in the castle overlooking the city, but this sits on the outskirts of Ceres, high above the metropolis. Sharp cliffs plunge toward the old walls of the old town, and from here, the rooves of thousands of houses spread around the bay twinkle in the dreary afternoon sunlight.

It's breathtaking.

Stunning.

Broken and wild.

Roses and thorns choke the courtyard, and fallen tree branches lay overtaken with moss. Fallow fountains remain silent and there's an enormous pool in the center of the courtyard, its still waters reflecting the single golden ray that peaks through the clouds. More pools circle it, though they've been overtaken with frogs and reeds. At night and from the balcony above, it would look exactly like its namesake, if the pools were cleared.

The Palace of Many Moons.

I can only imagine it.

"It's so... peaceful." I can picture summers here, with Amaya running through the grounds and laughing.

"You have that renovating look in your eye," Thiago warns. "How much is this going to cost me?"

"Well," I tell him, "I already have your soul, so not that."

The faintest of smiles touches his mouth.

Reaching out, I capture his fingertips in mine. "Show me the gardens please."

"Don't start planning their overhaul."

"To plan is to envision a future," I reply with a shrug. "And I want this future. You. Me. Amaya. And an entire century of peace, where the hardest decision to make is where to plant the roses."

It's a slow meander through the clifftop gardens. Thiago points out places he remembers, describing their usage to me. He served as a warlord in his mother's armies and was frequently asked to deliver dispatches to her here. There's an undercurrent of awe and bitterness in his voice as he speaks of the lawn games he encountered, the parties, the elderberry wine that flowed in the fountains.

Something he always watched from a distance.

It was the refuge of his mother, a woman who locked herself away here in the palace, safe behind her gates with a smile on her lips, and a hand that never trembled except for the odd moments when her bastard-born son would arrive for a meeting.

"And yet, she kept asking for you to deliver the dispatches. Did you never wonder why?" I muse as we stroll through a courtyard overgrown with flowers.

He's silent for long moments.

"I think she wanted to see you," I add. "Maybe it was all she could bring herself to ask for. Maybe she never spoke of anything other than troop movements or supply lines. But don't dismiss those moments. Maybe they were the brightest spark of her day. Her chance to see the son she couldn't publicly acknowledge."

"Five hundred years," he admits, his voice like roughened gravel. "And it still hurts. But sometimes, you make me see it all in a different light." Our eyes meet. "Thank you, Vi. Now.... Why don't you tell me what the past few weeks have been like for you? Don't think I haven't noticed the way my garden is stalking us."

"Your garden, is it?" Vine tendrils have tracked us over the lawn, one of them daring to curl around my ankle. "It's... a thing that happens now."

"Since you bound yourself to the lands?"

"Yes. Though your loss exacerbated the situation."

"It did?"

I caress a rose bush, feeling the flush of power bubble through my veins. It's becoming as simple as breathing. "I finally discovered what was holding me back from my magic."

"And?"

It's a confession from deep within my soul. We've spent years working on my mental blocks, and while they're crumbling—while I think I'm almost there—this level of soul-searching can be painful. "I've been thinking about my blocks, of late, and I believe it all goes back to the night I set my mother's castle on fire. I remember it now. I remember it all. The look on her face...." The memory conjures itself. Horror. That was horror I saw. That was fear. That was disgust. And in some ways, I internalized all of it.

"We both knew in that moment that the fire that burned within me didn't come from her gifts. Mother could not love the power within me and I could not contain it. She twisted my thoughts, twisted my memories, until the mere remnant of my magic scalded me. I have hated my magic. I have yearned for it. I have fought to control it, to twist it into some semblance of her power... when it was clearly not. And even when you found me—even when you loved me for all the twisted darkness inside me, I... I could not."

I hold my palm up and flames flicker to life mere inches above my hand. My magic has never burned orange. It's gold. Amber. A fluorescent whiteness that burns to look at, and the violence of its light gilds Thiago's dark eyes and illuminates his face, stripping away the soft curve of his cheeks and mouth and replacing them with sinister edges.

"I'm not truly fae." They're words I never thought I'd ever admit out loud. "I am the *leanabh an dàn*. The child of destiny. A melding of two worlds. Fae. And otherkin.

"And when I lost you, I stopped caring what my mother thought of me, and suddenly some of the barriers that had been restricting my magic crumbled. In some secret, stupid part of myself I wanted... to prove myself to her." I caress another deadened husk and this time blood red rose petals burst to life. The entire bush starts to bloom as if my magic runs through the bush's sap, bringing life to wizened old buds. "But those were the fears and desires of a hurt little girl. Now, I have nothing to prove. My magic is mine. And she *should* fear it."

All around us, the garden bursts to life.

Red roses. Pink. White.

Tiny little demi-fey flutter out of the heart of a glowing lily as if to chide me for giving up their hiding spot. Thalia's, no doubt. I shoot them a stern look. She's only watching out for us, but this is our moment.

Shaking off the somber mood, I gesture around us. "And maybe it all fits my grand renovation scheme. If I can cut costs on the garden, then maybe I can convince you to let me give the façade of the palace an overhaul."

Thiago stares at me for long seconds, and then he bursts into laughter.

It's a shock of a sound, perhaps because it's been so long since I've heard it.

Slinging an arm around my waist, he hauls me into his arms. "How do you do this?"

"What?"

"Make me smile when I've been having the worst day I've had in years. Or smile yourself, when you've just finished telling me such a horrible story."

"Magic," I tell him, bopping my finger on his nose.

Thiago captures my finger between his teeth, and everything changes.

Suddenly, I'm aware of how alone we are. And the mood—whilst previously one of confession—shifts, becoming thicker with want, intimate with the knowledge that last night was barely enough to slake the demons between us.

His hands roughen on my hips, his eyes darkening. The ravenous hunger I see reflected there makes my stomach twirl with butterflies, my sex clenching.

It's just a look, but it steals my breath each and every time. "How do you do *this*?"

"Do what?" The silkiness of his voice is merely another weapon in his arsenal.

Two words, rough with longing, and my mind conjures the way he kissed me last night. The sensation of his tongue stroking over mine, and the hot kiss of his breath on my damp skin as he consumed me.

"Make me wet with merely a look. It's the coat," I whisper, brushing my palms against it. "Definitely the coat."

"It's not the coat," he growls.

His lashes flutter against his cheek as he leans down, brushing the faintest of kisses against my mouth. I can't stop my hand from sliding up that sumptuous velvet and fisting in his collar as I yield to his claim.

It makes me want to strip myself bare—or better yet, for him to demand I do so in that soft, dangerous voice.

But not him.

I want him fully dressed, the velvet a slick glide against my heated skin.

I want him to press me against this wall, the cool brickwork imprinting itself on my nakedness while he uses that hard, warrior-born body to take me from behind.

The back of his knuckles brush against my gown, running over the rigid curve of my nipple. "And imagine what I could do with more than a look."

This time, it's not the vine curling up my calf, but the caress of invisible fingers. One of his many gifts.

I lean into him, mouth parting pliantly as he captures it in a heated kiss. His tongue moves in slow curls, stroking against mine. Hands slide over my ass, hauling me against him and crushing my skirts between us.

The unspoken need of his lights a fire in my veins.

"I can feel you," he whispers as I open to him, body and soul. "In here." One hand splays over his heart. "It's the only thing that grounds me."

I can feel it too, fluttering within my chest, binding me to him.

Destiny.

Fate.

All that Maia promised on that long-ago night when she showed him my face.

"I want to feel you"—I breathe into his mouth, brushing my knuckles against the straining leather that guards his cock—"inside me."

Curling a hand up my throat, he captures my chin and pushes me back, back, against the nearest brick wall. The other hand pins my right wrist to the wall, his knee driving between my legs.

And those invisible fingers stroke between my thighs, tracing slick circles over my skin.

Thiago stares into my eyes, daring me to say something about it.

I can't breathe, the tension within me knotting tighter as that touch strokes higher. It's a whisper of a caress. A tease. A possibility. It's torture and pleasure, all entwined with exquisite desperation.

I break first. I always break first. "*Please.*"

"You belong to me," he breathes, the exhalation of his breath casting dampness across my exposed collarbone as he nuzzles into the side of my throat. "Mine, Vi. *Mine*. For all eternity."

"Always." I can't bear it. I have to close my eyes, desperate to give into his touch. The knot between my leg's throbs with need.

There.

A silken lash right between my thighs. Such exquisite control and precision. Sometimes I hate him for that. That he can ruin me in such moments with barely a hint he feels the same chaos. Gooseflesh prickles across my skin, the nerves in that little bundle screaming for more. I can't stop myself from undulating against him.

"I love watching your face," he whispers, painting sharp nips down my throat and lower. "You're so fucking expressive."

"And you, not at all." I fight against the firm hand pinning me to the bricks, until he's forced to grasp my thigh with his other hand, firm fingers splaying me wide with bruising force.

Our eyes meet.

Such wicked, wicked intent in his.

"Do you think me untouched by this?" he challenges.

I grab a fistful of his coat with one hand, clinging for sweet life as that psychic touch traces featherlight circles around my clit. "Gods, you drive me to the edge."

"Only to the edge?" A dark chuckle. "I think we can do more than that."

Something blunt and firm presses at my opening,

gliding through the wetness there. A facsimile of his fingers. Thiago bites his lips, adding another, stretching me. Lost in the wild expression I can't stop myself from revealing as he fucks those invisible fingers inside me.

Gliding his free hand over my abdomen, he tugs my gown to the side, baring my breast. I can't stop a shocked gasp. This place is abandoned, birdsong the only accompaniment to our presence, but anyone could wander inside.

And it does things to me.

Wicked things.

A roughened palm glides over the curve of my breast, followed by his mouth. His tongue sweeps around my nipple in unhurried strokes as those invisible fingers fill me. It's an assault on all my senses, tearing me in two, making me wild with thwarted desire.

"Thiago!" Frantic with need, I jerk against him, shivering on the edge of ecstasy.

He loses his grip on my wrist, capturing my face in both hands as he pins me cruelly to the brickwork and claims my mouth.

One. Last. Touch.

And I am lost.

Pleasure whips its lash down my spine as I kiss him, and eat at his mouth. I come with a soft cry, arching into him, utterly shameless of the noises breaking from my lips, and the way I grind against him. Maybe it's his fist in my hair, but the force of climax nearly ruins me.

"You make the sweetest noises, Vi," he breathes as he lets my skirts fall. "Gods, all the noises."

I can barely catch my own breath.

Reaching down between us, I cup the exquisite bulge of his erection, desperate to taste it.

Capturing my wrist, Thiago shakes his head and backs away, a wicked smile turning his mouth to pure sin. "No."

The sudden shock of coldness—the loss of his body heat—shivers over my ravaged skin like a chill. I'm completely undone. Shivering with aftershock. My breast exposed. My elegant coiffure hanging in dishevelment.

"Why not?" Every inch of me is molten with pleasure, but the ache inside me.... Unfulfillment at its most wretched. "I need you."

"I know," he says, brushing off the shoulder of his coat with a teasing glint in his eyes. "But I'm not going to take you again until you're so desperate you're begging me."

I know this game.

There's nothing sweeter than denial, and he likes to start this game with me when he's in a playful mood.

Pushing away from the wall, I tug my gown up and follow him. "Don't start a war you can't win."

Still wearing that smile, Thiago reaches out, capturing a rose as if he intends to steal it from the bush and place it in my hair.

The second he touches it, the gloriously vibrant red petals wilt and dry until they scatter to the ground in ashen flakes of decay.

"What—?" He draws his hand back sharply, his face absolutely bleak.

It's a discordant, jarring shriek in the middle of an orchestra's exquisite song.

Need dies within me.

An emotionless mask slips into place on his face. One of

many. But as he straightens, I can see how much the act hurt him. "Maybe I'm closer to the edge of losing control than I thought."

"No. Never."

"He rides the night like a merciless hunter," he quotes gently. "And his touch brings ruin."

"The only ruin you've brought was within me. Against that wall." I close my fingers around his hand, letting the power of the lands bubble up within me.

I wasn't imagining it. There's something there in the air between us. The scalding heat of light and power within me meeting the chill decay of death. Push too far one way and the world will be obliterated in a scalding wave of fire. But if we lean too far toward his magic, his power, then the creeping chill of nothingness will silence all kingdoms.

"Vi." The shock and awe in his voice tells me he feels it too.

The power wells inside me, wanting to do *something*. Anything.

It spills from us, golden light tying us in threads. Burning through my veins like dark flames.

"What was that?" Thiago rasps, yanking his hand from mine.

A perfect rose glistens on the bush.

One of crystalline perfection. Translucent, with petals that look like they might shatter at the merest breath of wind, and yet when I reach out to touch them, my nails scrape against living, breathing glass.

"A melding." I can't help staring at my hands, because that power... wasn't wholly mine.

I reach for him again, but as our hands touch, all I can

feel is the physical impressions of it. Whatever just happened, the link is gone. Faded.

"And so the Light sang into the glorious Dark," I whisper, remembering one of my favorite passages from the book Lucere gave to me. "And the Darkness sang back, and together, they fused to create a glorious act of Creation. Something beyond life. Something beyond death." I pluck the rose from the bush, lifting it to my nose. It smells like midnight and sex, like velvet and moonlight, all woven together in a heady mix. "Something beyond forever."

"What does that mean?" Thiago breathes, placing his palm squarely against mine.

"It means that you were made for me, and I for you. And together...." I twirl the rose, still breathless with its beauty, "maybe we can do wondrous things."

Chapter Twenty

T he following three days pass in a blur as my friends help me reorient myself with the world. It's as though I never left. There are endless meetings, arguments about supplies for the warfront, questions about what Adaia is up to. Thalia enforces a strict dinner time in which we all come together.

Me at one end of the table. Amaya at the other.

She won't look at me.

She won't *look* at me.

And maybe it's better this way, because every time we eat, I have to curl my fingers into a fist so tight my nails threaten to break the skin, just to remind myself that I am me.

That I'm not *him*.

Nobody asks about what happened to me. Not even Vi.

It's as though I simply closed my eyes and went to sleep for several weeks, and returned to find mayhem.

Inside, I feel it though.

Every meeting is a means of going through the motions. I can't stop myself from feeling distant as they argue over inconsequential things. Inside, there's a scream trapped deep in my throat. An itch beneath my skin. A knife of pain slicing through my nerves.

"*Do you think you can silence me forever?*" whispers Death, during the middle of one such meeting.

"*Preferably.*"

It surges within me angrily like a sudden lump in my throat. I force it down, focusing on swallowing, on—

Sound bursts out of nowhere like an explosion.

I'm halfway to my feet, heart hammering, shadows slicing around me before I realize what happened.

Thalia freezes, her teaspoon rocking on the table. She must have dropped it on her saucer.

"Thiago?" she asks.

I have to get out of there.

Everyone is looking at me. Finn. Thalia. Baylor.

Eris is at the warfront, thank the gods, and Vi is somewhere with Amaya, but they're all watching me. Gaping. Wondering.

"I need air. Continue... dealing with the supply issues. You don't need me. You know what to do."

Yanking at the door, I practically shove my way through it. It's too tight. This fucking collar is too tight. Tearing at the buttons there brings me some sensation of relief. I press my back against the door and try to breathe, hearing the flurry of whispers through the door.

I can't stay here.

Prowling through the castle, I can't stop myself from reaching for that little beckoning seed of light in my heart.

Vi. Instantly, I'm in her head, seeing through her eyes.

She strokes Amaya's hair off her forehead as our daughter lays in her lap, listening to some sort of story. Gorgeous, gilded images are painted across the pages of a book. Fairy tales, no doubt. Ancient myths. Old legends. They're the books Vi loves the most.

She pauses with her fingers on the pages as if she senses me, and then she's reaching back, linking with me on the psychic plane. "*Thiago?*"

"*Sorry.*" I try to disentangle with her thoughts, but she traps me there, sending me threads of golden light. Threads of warmth and love.

"*Come and find us,*" she whispers down the link. "*Amaya's getting hungry, but she wants another story first.*"

I know what she's doing.

Trying to let me know my daughter through her. Acting as the buffer. Easing us toward a relationship with each other.

"*I can't.*"

I can sense her chewing over that thought. "*You can. You won't hurt her.*"

It's time we both faced the truth. *"She won't want me there. It's... discomforting for both of us."*

Vi gently strokes Amaya's hair again, resuming her reading. *"Perhaps, with frequent exposure, it will become better. But it won't improve unless you both try. Please try. For her. Because you're not the only one staring at your parent and yearning for something from them that they can't give."*

I cut the connection.

She doesn't understand. It's safer this way. I'm not the prince I once was.

Thiago died in the Black Keep.

I am all that remains of him.

But, as if her words conjure the memory, I see my mother seated on her throne, her shoulders square and her face expressionless.

"You're sending me away?" I demand, one hand resting on the hilt of my sword. *"Why?"*

My brother, the Crown Prince Arawn, saunters forward. "Who are you to dare question the queen's commands? She wants your warband to ride for Eidyn and station yourselves there."

"For how long?" I ignore him, searching her face for answers.

There are none.

The queen stares over my head, only the shifting of her fingers on her throne betraying a hint of her doubt.

"Until. You. Are. Recalled," Arawn spits, and I know that if he has his way that moment will never come.

I was an adult male in his prime, a warrior with accolades streaming behind me like a banner.

But I would have given everything within me to have

my mother look my way, stretch out her hand, and beckon me onto the dais beside her.

Not for the power. Not for the position.

But for me.

For us.

And Amaya is only nine.

My vision comes back into focus, and I realize I'm staring at a striking display of roses and lilies, one of the many that seem to be flooding the castle these days. They have to be Vi's flowers.

Staring at it for long moments, I strip my glove off, reaching for the petals of a rose....

And they curl at my touch.

Dropping, one by one, to the floor.

I tug the gloves back on.

But I can't stop myself from hearing Vi's words in my head. A brutal truth, yes, but a truth nonetheless.

I have to try.

Because I don't ever want my daughter to know what it feels like to wonder what you did wrong, when there was never any answer to be had.

Rapping at Amaya's door, I wait for a greeting before I slip inside.

I can tell immediately that Vi has warned her.

Amaya sits up, knees drawn to her chest as she rests on the window seat beside her mother. She's wearing a pair of the boots Vi so envied, her dark hair braided down her back. All I can see over the top of her knees are those enor-

254

mous green eyes.

Wary eyes.

"*Well*," Grimm drawls, "*are you going to just stand there, you overgrown bat, or are you going to come in? The queen was just about to get to the good part. The evisceration.*"

"Remind me why we're keeping him again?" I can't help asking Vi.

"Because someone has to keep the mouse population at bay," Vi replies.

Grimm looks aghast. "*Mice? You think I hunt* mice*? I am the Shadow That Stalks the Night—*"

"Yes, yes," Vi interrupts, opening her book again and patting the window seat on the other side of her unsubtly. "You guard the Shadow Ways and slay the Fetch's who come to steal us away. You make creeping banes shiver with dread, and grown fae tremble."

"He's grown too soft with milk and honey to catch a mouse," Amaya pipes up.

Grimm shoots her an appalled look. "*Soft?*" he sputters. "*How dare you? You little wretch. I have guarded you from the day of your birth and this is how you repay me?*"

Vi lays the book flat, shooting him a look. "From the day of her birth?" she asks in a decidedly neutral voice.

With everyone distracted, I ease across the room, settling on the far side of Vi.

The very far side.

Grimm suddenly looks interested in his paw. "*Oh, look. A furball.*"

And he starts licking at it.

Amaya reaches down and hauls him onto her lap like a

BEC MCMASTER

shield. It's almost laughable, because he's nearly half the size she is, his expression momentarily disgruntled as if—

"*This is so undignified,*" Grimm mutters.

But he settles on her lap.

And turns those knowing eyes toward me.

"The Mother of Night sent him to watch over me," Amaya tells us. "He owed her a debt—"

"*Amaya,*" Grimm warns. "*Not another word.*"

She actually grins. "Something about a wolf. And getting caught in your own trap."

"*That* was no *ordinary wolf,*" Grimm seethes. "*And technically, I killed him once we were stuck in there together. I just couldn't get out again. And of course, that know-it-all goddess just happened to be walking those particular woods at the time.*"

"What is the first rule we abide by, Amaya?" Amaya mocks his proper tones. "We do not make deals with fae creatures."

"Poor little Grimsby," Vi teases. "I can understand why you'd want to keep that one quiet. Your own trap?"

Grimm vanishes, reappearing with a sniff on the bed, where he turns three times and then settles into a little nest he's made himself. "*You're on your own, traitor.*"

Instantly, Amaya tenses.

Moving slowly, I lift one knee, draping my arm over it in a relaxed pose. The itch travels up my spine like icy fingers trailing over the muscles. "What were you reading?"

"It's a fairy tale," Vi admits, her watchful gaze noticing Amaya's sudden tension. "About a beautiful young fae princess whose father sold her hand in marriage to a vicious king. She, er, denied the king her affections, and so he cursed her heart to turn to ice. She would know no love, nor pity, nor happiness. So the new queen promptly used her new powers to freeze the king and set herself free."

Curses. Always wretched curses. "That sounds like an uplifting tale."

"It is," Vi smiles. "No love can touch her. No charm can break the curse. Her entire kingdom is besieged by snow and her loyal guards are transformed into polar bears. Every member of her court is slowly struck with the same curse, their sense of empathy bleeding out of them. Until finally, one of her guards—the same lowly servant who was once her childhood friend—challenges her to a set of tasks in order to break the curse. Each is a good deed done, and inch by inch the Snow Queen's heart melts until she finally realizes what she's done to her kingdom. Her curse is broken, she proclaims her love for the guard, and her abusive father receives his just reward."

"The evisceration?" I ask dubiously.

Vi scowls. "That is Grimm's idea of a happily ever after, not mine. No. He stumbles into a glacier and is frozen himself, body and soul."

"Uplifting," I repeat.

That earns me the Eyebrow of Death. "I think it's uplifting," she sniffs. "True love sets her free."

"Can we *please* finish the story?" Amaya asks in the most aggrieved tone possible.

Vi turns back to her page, her voice settling into a story-telling lilt.

It's somewhat peaceful to watch them together. Sunlight streams through the window, painting highlights of gold in Vi's dark hair. The light softens her high cheekbones and full mouth. Her relationship with Amaya hasn't been an easy one, but I can see the foundations of it strengthening with every word she speaks and every page turned.

Motherhood has changed her, giving her a strength and confidence she previously struggled with. It's a little breathtaking, to be honest.

Vi finishes the story, snapping the book shut. "And thus, they lived happily ever after."

Amaya's fingers stroke the colors on the cover. Vi told me she'd never been taught to read, and the way she holds the book is akin to a priestess cradling a bowl filled with the sacred flame of Maia. "Another one, please!"

"That's the last one in this book," Vi protests.

"*Please.*"

Vi crosses her legs. "Very well then. Another story, though this is one I will have to recall." She clears her throat. "Ever since I made that deal with the Mother of Night, I've been reading stories about her and the otherkin. In the book Princess Imerys gave me, there was something about the primordial Darkness that I thought might interest the pair of you."

Tension slides through me. "Oh?"

Vi's dark eyes slide toward me as if she can feel the stiffness leeching through me. "In the beginning, there was Darkness. The primordial Darkness that spawned the monsters and the otherkin. A Darkness that was shattered by the light of an exploding star when Creation first struck, drawing back the veil of Darkness and forging a world of beauty in its wake. The Darkness was night. It was absence and silence. It was a void, through which the monsters tore screaming."

"*Tell her to stop*," hisses Death.

The world flashes around me: Amaya, finally relaxing on the other side of her mother. And Vi, her voice light and lilting as she launches into her tale.

I freeze. "*Shut up.*"

"It's why the fae feared the night when we first conquered Arcaedia," Vi continues. "To them, night was a forest full of teeth. The breathless panting as you sought to hide or flee from the Wild Hunt. The vicious shadow of the Deathless One riding through a nightscape of predators. It's why we put out the lanterns on Samhain, in order for the hunt to pass us by. It's why we burn the bonfires on Beltane, in order to prove that the sun reigns supreme, and to protect ourselves with the sanctity of the smoke from those fires. The seelie became the Bright Ones. The light and shining. The peoples of the sun. But in the north, those that lay down with the monsters and birthed the unseelie abomination into the world gave themselves over to the Darkness. And it became a spreading plague, a blight that warped the hearts of the righteous fae and stole the light from their souls.

"Books were written—stories of the monsters who lived on this world once, and the brave fae who conquered them. We were always the heroes. The ones who ventured into the dark places and slew the beasts. The ones who rescued princesses when the monsters stole them away. The ones who locked away their old gods in a vicious war between light and dark. But the author of the book was fae and she suggested that much of our literature was formed from the need to cast ourselves as good and true.

"Her name was Keelian, and she sought out the stories of the otherkin in order to write her book on their myths and their gods, and in so doing, she began to understand them." Vi draws her knees up to her chest, turning her face to the sun. "To the otherkin, the night was the realm of the Mother of Night and her kin. It was peace and silence and safety from the invading fae. All the forests and shadows the fae feared were the safe harbors the otherkin fled to. It was the night in which they raised their voices to sing. The moon and the stars they worshipped. To them, the sun was a gaudy thing that flaunted itself. It was a glaring light looking for flaws, gilded in its false sanctity, one that took away their safety, their havens...." She pauses. "And the primordial Darkness was never a place to be feared. It was where the souls of all otherkin who had been birthed into this world would return to. The loving night. A place where the monsters of this world—those who had been feared for so long—could show their faces. A place where they could await their rebirth. The peaceful silence. The enduring eternity. The pitch black of the Underworld, where one could rest before returning to this world in rebirth. Only those that left this life unfinished—those that fought to return—were granted no peace there."

The breath explodes out of me as Death grips my heart in his claws.

We're both right back there.

Lost in the Darkness.

Consumed by the primal need to retreat to our most base selves to survive.

Monsters come at us. I tear their throats out with my claws, but there are so many of them. Dozens. Hundreds. Fueled by the taste of my blood on the wind. Hungry for flesh.

"*Let me rise,*" Death whispered in those moments. "*Let them learn to fear us. Let me save us.*"

I fought for days. Weeks. Months. Wounded and exhausted. Hunted to the highest slopes of the darkest mountains within that silent world until I finally cracked.

I broke.

And I let it happen.

I let Death rise.

Silence fell over me, stillness seeping into my heart. There was no rage, no fear, no grief in those moments. No pain, no suffering, no exhaustion. Merely... nothing.

Nothing but the sounds of screaming as the monsters fought to flee us, and the rippling violence of the ruin that Death cast across the world. The shadows that danced around my fingers turned into scythes of misery.

And with every step I took, the dry, arid terrain crunched beneath my boots as I became the scariest monster of all.

I lost myself in the Darkness.

Coldness seeps through my veins, until my breath comes on a fogged exhale. To survive in that world, I let the Darkness in. I let *Death* in. And when I blinked out of that moment, when all my enemies were fallen, their lifeless bodies splayed at my feet, I realized there was no going back.

Death has been with me ever since, entwined around my soul like a possessive lover.

Vi doesn't notice the faint tremor in my hands.

But Amaya does.

Her heart skips a beat, her gaze sliding toward me.

"*She is so beautiful,*" Death whispers. "*Let me touch her. Let me make us whole.*"

Vi is not finished. "Kato guards the mouth to the Underworld from the kingdoms above, so that those within it cannot escape. Somehow it became a prison of Darkness, but I have walked there. At first I knew fear, for I believed in the stories. But there was a moment—just a moment—where I stood upon that rooftop and the stars there twinkled, all for me. There was no breath in my lungs, but in that moment I knew peace. I was no longer afraid of the silence, nor the darkness. It was a gentle dark. A homecoming. A place that had seen the moment of Creation, and a place that awaits that final hurtling moment of Destruction." Her voice softens. "I knew you were out there, waiting for me, and I just had to find you."

"Vi." The smile on my face feels like a grinning rictus. I can't let them see what is happening inside me, but I need it to stop.

"It is the haven of monsters; those that do not fit the aesthetics of the seelie world. And maybe that's why I felt such affinity with it." She turns her face toward me. "I am the replacement my mother fears, the princess who fell in love with a beast, and the monstrous queen who will end her reign." Her lips quirk. "Maybe one day, in the stories, that is what they will write of me. Maybe they will give me horns and eyes of Darkness. Maybe my lips will be red as sin, and I will whisper torment and ruin into the ears of my victims. My crown will be forged of bones." This time, there's an actual sparkle in her eyes. "What do you think?

Do you think I would make a wonderful monster? Do you like my story?"

I cannot move.

Tension screams through me, a horrific twisting inside. Death fights to rise, to consume, to take over.

All I can see is the Darkness, and the silence, and the glittering stars there. They felt like watchful eyes. "Yes." The word is a lie. My heart beating painfully hard.

I need to get out of here.

"Old Mother Hibbert had a story about the Darkness too," Amaya speaks up, biting her lower lip. "It is the great emptiness that will devour those that are unworthy—"

Exploding to my feet, I try to escape.

Amaya screams, diving behind her mother. Vi blanches, shoving herself between us.

The sudden movement. The look on my face, no doubt. I can see their interpretation of my actions, even as the world comes at me too fast, too sharp.

"I'm not going to hurt her." I blink and my hands are in the air, the words echoing through the room.

I can't remember saying them.

But the look on their faces. The look—

"I need fresh air," I say.

"Thiago." Vi reaches for me, heat and warmth flooding through me. "Why don't we—?"

"I told you!" Amaya screams at her, tears in her eyes. "I told you what he is. I told you I didn't want him in here! But you wouldn't listen!"

And then she's gone, bolting from the room.

Grimm's furry little mouth hangs wide open as if even he didn't sense such a reaction coming.

"Not a word," I warn him.

"I'm so sorry," Vi gasps, torn between both me and Amaya. "I shouldn't have brought it up. But she's been asking questions about the Darkyn, about the Darkness. I thought if we talked about it.... If she wasn't afraid of it, then maybe she wouldn't be afraid of herself—"

"Go," I tell her, locking down the trembling that seems to be soul deep. "Go and see to her. I'm fine."

It is, like all the other times I've said it since I returned, a lie.

Chapter Twenty-One

As always, Amaya is on the parapet.

Grimm shoots me a look of warning as I slowly climb the stairs, and I wrap my arms around myself as I walk toward her. He vanished the second I left her room, but at least he was keeping an eye on her.

I feel like such an idiot.

She's been asking questions about the Darkness all day, no doubt spurred by my recent quest to bring her father back. I'd only meant to discuss it calmly with her. I hadn't even thought of his trauma....

And by the time I realized, it was too late.

"Amaya, I'm so sorry. He wasn't trying to hurt you. He was just... rattled. It's been a trying time for him."

"I'm fine," she says stubbornly.

"*I'm fine*," he said too, lying through his teeth.

Like father, like daughter.

"Why don't you come in for dinner? We'll—"

"I don't want to eat," she says, hopping up on the wall as if to taunt me and walking along it, one foot in front of the other. "I don't want to come in."

She knows I hate it. She knows I just want to grab her down.

A little burr of irritation itches through me. "Yes, well, sometimes we don't get what we want."

"You don't think I know that?" she yells at me. "I don't get *anything* I want!"

Thunder rumbles through the sky in ominous counterpoint.

I try again. "It's going to rain—"

"Let it!"

That's enough. "Amaya. Please climb down from the wall and come inside. Dinner is going to get cold. We're going to get wet. You can tell me what's bothering you while we eat."

"I just want to go *home*. I want to see my friends. I want to be in my own bed. I want to...." A sob escapes her. "I want to see my *mother*."

Old Mother Hibbert.

I swallow down all the feelings those words engender,

266

choking on their jagged edges. *She's young. She's lost everything she's ever known. She's frightened.* "It's not safe for you to go back to the hut where you grew up. And I'm so sorry about what happened to her. Maybe when this is over, we'll be able to visit the other children? This is your home now but maybe—"

"It's not my home," she screams. "I hate you!"

And then she bursts into tears.

I can't do anything. I can't even move as the words hang in the air between us.

A hundred emotions rampage through me.

Anger. Frustration. Hurt.

Failure.

It's that one I think I feel the most.

And I want to scream back at her. *Get inside. Do as you're told. I am trying to protect you!*

Indeed, if I had the breath right now, I probably would be screaming them.

The same way my mother screamed at me.

I won't be like her.

I won't let my anger and hurt rule me.

"Amaya." I curl my fingers into a fist as I start along the wall toward her and take a deep breath. *It's a bad day; she's just having a bad day. I haven't been here for her much this week.... She's scared. I screwed up.* But all I hear are those three horrible words echoing in my ears. "That's not true. I know it's not true. And even... even if you do feel that way, I love *you*. Please come down. Please come to dinner. We can talk about what's going on. And why you feel this way."

She hesitates on the edge of the parapet.

"It's this storm," she whispers, rubbing at her arms. "Can't you feel it?"

"Feel what?"

She presses her fists to her belly, looking at me with wild eyes. "I don't want to go inside. I don't want to be trapped!"

"Trapped?" None of this makes any sense. "Thiago will never hurt you. I promise. We'll be safe inside. Finn's there, if we need a guard. And Thalia has pudding on the menu." I smile at her tentatively. "You like pudding."

She takes a step back, her heel slipping on the edge of the wall.

Come on. I gesture to her desperately, not daring to do anything else in case I distract her. I hate the fact she puts herself at risk like this, but as Finn said, there's enough of her father's background in her to make her long for the skies. Maybe she doesn't have wings yet. Maybe she won't be able to shift. But those clouds still call to her.

"*Come on, child,*" Grimm says, pausing at my side. There's no sign of his usual acerbic wit. Only sympathy in his voice. "*Your mother had me convinced at 'pudding.'*"

"There's a fist in my belly," she moans, curling her fingers and pressing them there. "I don't want to go! If we go, then... then we'll be trapped. We won't be able to run."

Ah. This has something to do with the attack on Old Mother Hibbert's.

Lightning flashes. I don't know why I look up, but there's a sudden lump of dread in my throat. Maybe it's her words, her fear, but....

Those clouds...

They look strange.

It's almost like there are shapes up there. Wraith-shaped shadows circling the clouds above us in the flicker of lightning.

Wraith-shaped shadows.

Ice steals through me.

"Amaya." I start forward, my hand stretched toward her. "Amaya come here. *Now.*"

As if she senses something I don't, she looks up.

I lunge toward her, trying desperately to link with Thiago, "*Thiago! I need you!*"

There is no response. Maybe he's too walled off to hear me.

"Too late, little queen," a disembodied voice laughs.

An enormous black-winged figure plummets from the skies, landing on the parapet right in front of her. Tattoos writhe across his face as if the storm is inside him, and those circling shapes above us suddenly make sense. Sluagh.

"Amaya!"

Amaya gapes at him, but Malakhai merely shoots me a savage smile. "The prodigal princess... finally out in the open. Thank you, Your Highness. You practically gift-wrapped her for me."

His sword of darkness forms in his left hand as Amaya screams.

I throw every inch of my power at him, and thorns erupt through the cobblestones, binding his left arm so tightly he can't move it. Malakhai grits his teeth, his expression furious.

"Get away from her!" I hurl myself at him.

He drops the sword, and it disintegrates into nothing.

Two seconds later, it reforms in his right hand.

269

Malakhai turns to meet my attack and drives the sword right through me.

I grab his wrist and for a second I don't feel it. *There has to be some mistake. There has to be—*

And then the ice hits me. A cold so vicious it burns, radiating out from my abdomen. I look down, and it's buried to the hilt inside me. This is no mortal sword. There's no blood, nothing but a fierce kind of pain and weakness as I clap my hands over the sword where it's buried within my womb.

The shock of it nearly stuns me.

One knee hits the cobbles as I take the sword with me.

Heat bleeds from my face. This cold will not vanish. It's in my bones now. Seeping through my body. Smothering the flame that burns within me.

How long do I have before that creeping chill extinguishes my light?

Somehow, I find the shadows where Grimm lurks, his yellow eyes blinking in horror. "*Get her... out of here.*"

Malakhai grabs a fist of my hair and hauls me close enough to whisper, "Long live the *queen.*"

I slide from the sword as he wrenches it free, and the loss it is almost another blow too. It hurts. It hurts so badly.

"*Mama!*" Amaya's scream cuts through the ringing in my ears.

I hear a baby crying as someone wrenches it from my arms. I scream in desperation for her as she's placed in my mother's hands, and for a second it almost seems as though my baby reaches back....

They took her from me once.

They will not take her from me again.

270

Slamming a palm flat on the cobbled parapet, I reach for my heart, for my lands. The heat within me is dying, but there's warmth there. Far below me. I just have to find it.

"*This way!*" Grimm tries to herd Amaya toward the tower. "*Come on!*"

A pulse shivers through the tower.

The Hallow's magic swims like a leviathan beneath the surface of the lands. It vibrates through me, promising everything.

"You're learning, little queen. You just haven't quite figured out how to wield the gifts he gave you." Malakhai laughs as he advances.

He?

"And that will be your undoing," he says.

Scrambling backward, I lash out again with my thorns, reaching desperately for Finn. "*Get Thiago up here now!*"

Malakhai swipes them aside with his sword, advancing upon me grimly. "Yes, call him out. Bring him to me."

I let him come, my brambles cutting bloody ruins into his legs as he strides through them. The hollow ache inside me seems to be growing. The world grows fuzzy. I just have to hold on.... Just long enough for Amaya to escape.

A shadow darts out of nowhere, launching itself upon Malakhai's back as Amaya tries to drive a knife into his throat. "Mama!"

"Amaya! Run!"

Malakhai reaches over his shoulder for her and hauls her forward. I throw myself at him, grabbing hold of his sword arm and trying not to scream as the movement forces more of that dread chill through my veins.

"Run!" I scream at her, tearing his fingers from her shirt. "Go and find your father. Grimm!"

He grabs Amaya by the wrist, sinking his teeth into her skin. Amaya yells, but as she staggers back, she dissolves into shadows, into nothing....

Gone.

Gone with Grimm into the shadows.

Not safe. Not yet. But hidden for the moment.

"Fuck you," I spit in Malakhai's face.

Hard fingers lock around my throat. "Oh, I'd love to take my time and play with you, little queen... but I've got a granddaughter to kill and her soul to reap."

No! I scratch and claw at his arms, but ice steals out from his fingers as he lifts me out over the castle walls.

And then there's nothing underneath me.

Nothing but a glimpse of the city, far below.

No! I grab at his hand, trying to reach for my magic, but there's nothing there. Only that glacial chill stealing through my skin and crystallizing in my throat.

I can't breathe.

Wherever that ice touches, the heat and warmth of my magic dies down, like a fire being tamped.

Shadows swarm at the edge of my vision as if he's stealing even that from me.

"Send my regards to Kato," Malakhai whispers, the faintest hint of a smile touching that cruel mouth.

"*Vi!*" someone yells, the sound cutting through the dull ringing in my ears.

And then Malakhai lets me go.

* * *

The wind grabs at me as I plummet past the castle walls.

A scream tears its way from my throat, right through that ice.

"Vi!"

I swear I'm dreaming it.

"Vi!"

And then a shadow plunges toward me from the right.

Thiago.

The impact of his body drives the breath from my lungs. Hard arms lock around me, those familiar black eyes meeting mine. Wings block the sky, and suddenly I'm no longer falling. I grab him desperately, fingers tangling in his coat. He sweeps me up in his arms, and with a powerful thrust of his wings, we swoop along the ground—barely three feet below us.

My breath catches in my chest as I realize how close I came to being smeared all across those cobblestones.

But I don't have time to worry about myself.

"Amaya!" I tug at his sleeve. "He's up there with her. Malakhai's on the top of the castle walls. He's going to kill her! Take me up there!"

Thiago's gaze cuts sharply to my face, and then he banks hard, right above the rooftop of a house built into the base of the walls. "Stay here," he says, dropping me lightly on the roof. And then he mashes a desperate kiss against my lips. "I love you."

"Thiago!" I scream as he launches himself into the air.

But he's nothing more than a black blur as he spears into the sky.

Right into Malakhai's trap.

Because it has to be a trap.

273

"He won't kill her." The words blurt from my mouth, but they're no reassurance. And the pain is almost all-consuming now. One knee goes out from under me.

Malakhai needs the last two pieces of Death's soul. And what better way to incapacitate Thiago than to put a knife to her throat. He won't kill her. Not until Thiago arrives. She has to be safe.

But the part of me that knows that little girl is mine knows that sometimes fate isn't that kind....

Shoving to my feet, I ignore the glacial creep through my veins and the way I sway. I don't have time to feel it.

My daughter is up there.

Alone.

Frightened.

Hunted by the creature that sired my husband.

And my husband is flying directly into the trap he just set.

I don't fear Death.

But as I summon my thorns, one of them circling my waist, I can't help thinking: Maybe he should fear me.

Chapter Twenty-Two

Malakhai awaits me as I land neatly on the walkway.

"Ah, true love," he mocks. "You managed to save her just in time."

Fury pulses deep within me as I draw my sword. I can't stop seeing Vi falling....

"Or did you?" he purrs.

"What does that mean?"

A sword materializes in his hand. One as black as night

275

—blacker even. It's so dark, you can barely see the blade, as if it's forged from nothing. A void of light. A void of *life*.

"She's dying, you little bastard." The smile turns into a sneer. "She just hasn't realized it yet."

And then he attacks.

I throw everything I have into parrying that blow. Muscle flexes in his shoulder, a faintest hint of his next move, and I shift to counter that too. Sparks flare off my sword every time they meet, and the impact ricochets down my arms.

This bastard raped my mother.

Every day of my life I've felt him out there, hunting for me, looking for the fragment of Death within me.

And now he's attacked both Vi and Amaya.

Malakhai grunts as I counter him again and swings so widely I barely have time to deflect the next blow.

Metal screams. There's a moment where my sword holds, but smoke curls off his blade and then—

It shears straight through my steel.

I'm left with nothing more than a foot-long length of blade in my hand as the obsidian sword swipes past my chest.

"Darkyn steel," he says with a laugh as I retreat. "Forged from Death itself. Invincible. Now you're mine."

He lunges forward.

Suddenly, I'm in the fight of my life. I dance aside, cutting in close with the razor-sharp foot of sword still in my hand. Slashing across his ribs, I roll away.

He touches the blood there, his teeth baring in rage. I won't be allowed to get that close again.

A flurry of blows comes my way. I dodge each and every

one, on the back foot. One blow swipes the stub of steel from my hand. It flips end over end, vanishing into the wind. The tower's behind me. Running out of room. A swift glance shows the town below, but there's no time to—

I grab his hand, stepping into him and forcing his next blow to strike the solid stone of the tower. The darkyn sword wedges into the thick stone, and I shove against him, body-to-body. Rank breath exhales into my face as I slam my forehead against his.

"Fuck you," I gasp as he reels back.

He won't let go of the sword, but this is the only way I even have a chance to win it.

"Your mother was ever so sweet," he gasps. "Do you know how many times I made her scream?"

Rage ignites.

A chill of pure fury shivers through me. Grabbing him by the throat, I slam his head against the tower, but all he does is laugh. And the angle finally sees the sword slip free of the stone. My fingers touch the hilt, and suddenly I *feel* it. Feel that black blade calling to me, sipping from the dark magic inside me, drinking of it—

A knee drives into my ribs, forcing me away as Malakhai draws it free of the stone, but as I reel away I can feel the residue of the sword between my fingers, feel the call of it....

"*We can do that too,*" whispers the voice in my head. The one that's haunted me every day since I was born. "*Let me show you how.*"

The second I give in to it, I'm gone.

I know that.

But there's also a hint of desperation in its voice.

"*I die too,*" it says to me. "*If he kills you, then the part of me that's you dies too, and I become nothing more than a piece of him."*

A foot slams into my chest, lifting me off my feet.

Slamming against the stone, I roll, baring my teeth as his enormous sword cuts into the stone right where my head was. It slices right through the cobbles, cracks spearing out as if decay creeps through the stone. The wings are hampering me. I've spent so long hiding my true form from the world, that I can barely adjust to the weight and mass of them.

Kicking up, I slam the heel of my boot into his elbow, and as Malakhai staggers back, I whip my feet low, taking his out from under him. The second I come up, I vanish the wings, sliding my glamor over me like a second skin.

"Fine. Show me!"

Darkness consumes me, the world becoming crystalline clear. My hand moves of its own accord, summoning shadows, plucking them from all around us and forging a blade so dark, I swear it's dredged from the well of my soul.

It's a part of me, drawing upon the rage and the anger inside me, drawing upon all those little fears.... It wants blood. It hungers for... more.

Malakhai's eyes glitter as we face each other again. "That's it," he croons. "Let yourself surface."

I am not Death; I am not.

But I can feel the difference as we circle each other.

This time, the world is silenced around me.

Everything is a little darker, a little more insulated.

Quiet.

"Yes," says the voice inside me. *"Let us become one."*

A rose vine hurtles over the ramparts like a grappling

278

hook, sinking into the stone. It captures my attention for half a second before Malakhai lunges toward me.

He punches toward me in a mess of writhing shadows, and then he's reforming into flesh, the blade materializing too.

My sword shrieks against his as I meet the blow. Forming it is instinct. I push back against him, seeing the shock on his face as he realizes that physically, I'm stronger than him.

"You're old," I grate out, shoving him back. "And maybe you were challenged once—when you hunted your brothers and sisters—but their children? They ran from you. They fled. And you cut them down as they did so. It's been a long time since someone's matched you, hasn't it?"

Anger darkens his eyes. He hammers a blow at me that I barely meet. "You think you're a challenge?"

I slam my palm against his chest and rip at one of the souls within him.

It comes to me as if it's been waiting for me, the shadowy remnants of it curling around my fingers as I yank my hand back. Fury. It's the one I once called Fury. The first Darkyn who ever tried to hunt me, and the first I consumed.

He must have somehow captured it when it was freed upon my death.

Malakhai staggers back, clutching at his chest.

"*Yes,*" Fury hisses inside me.

"*Yes,*" whispers Death.

"You've spent years trying to hunt the rest of our kin." I attack with a blow that nearly finds his throat. "You've consumed us. Hunted us. Destroyed us." Another flurry of

279

swipes, his a little more desperate than mine. "But I've spent years thinking of you. Only you. Thinking of how I would one day ruin you."

"I think I'll make it slow," he hisses, "when I rip your daughter's soul from her."

"*Never.*" Rage obliterates my vision as I attack him with a vengeance.

He's on the back foot but there is victory in his eyes as he lures me toward him.

Malakhai vanishes into a whirl of shadow. It swarms toward me, and I barely have a second to try to predict where he'll reform.

He explodes back into being, right in front of me. Shadow-merging takes a lot from you, but he only has to do it once. He only has to do it *right* once.

His sword glances off my hasty deflection and skates down my arm.

Staggering past, he turns and tosses his sword from hand to hand. "Hurts, doesn't it?"

I can't hold the sword's form.

Shadows bleed from it.

"*No! Hold it!*" screams Death.

But the blade vanishes, fragmenting into nothingness as I grip my wrist.

A sharp yowling echoes behind us, and then a creature forms at Malakhai's throat. *Grimm.* Teeth and claws sunk deep into Malakhai's jugular.

"What in the—?" Malakhai grabs the grimalkin and throws him at the ramparts.

Grimm vanishes half a second before he hits, and then

Malakhai screams as the furball materializes right in front of his face, claws raking over his eyes and mouth.

I swear I'm never going to hear the end of it if that furry little prick actually succeeds in taking down one of the Darkyn.

"*Well, you enormous overgrown bat, are you going to help me? Or just stand there gaping?*"

"Maybe if I wait long enough, he'll put you on a skewer," I snarl, lunging forward.

"Grimm! Thiago!" Vi screams behind me. "Get down!"

Vi? What the fuck is she doing up here?

I catch a glimpse of thorns lashing toward me and hit the stone cobbles.

Malakhai lifts his sword high, and this time I know I won't be able to escape that blow—

Something blurs over my head.

A meaty splat sounds, and Malakhai gasps, frozen in place as he slowly looks down at the thorny javelin that's pierced his upper chest.

Another vine stabs through him, the thorns on it almost as long as my forearm.

And then another.

"You dare walk into my kingdom and threaten my daughter?" Vi hisses, limping toward us with her black skirts and hair blowing behind her in the wind. Thunder rumbles behind her. There's a cut on her face and bruises on her arms, but she looks like a warrior queen, defiant until the end. "You dare try and kill my husband?"

Malakhai shoots her a bloodless look, then cuts the vines in half with a single swing of his sword. The wounds heal, and he bares his teeth at her in a scarlet smile. "Death falls for no mortal wound."

It's impossible.

And yet, there's not even a single mark on him.

I can't stop him.

She can't even stop him.

I eye him grimly, staring at the sky behind him. It's a long fall to the bottom of the cliff. If I pin his wings....

"Vi, get out of here," I whisper to her, staggering to my feet.

Vi doesn't dare take her eyes off him.

"Death falls for no mortal wound," Vi repeats, clenching her fist against her abdomen. There's something merciless about the look in her eyes. "Only the Erlking can face Death and walk free. Because he is fierce and full of fight and laughter. He is sex and singing and mirth. And I remembered something: He is *life*. Death cannot be killed. But I wonder.... A queen is bound to her lands. She brings the summer, and she brings the crops. She grows the forests with a whim, and she blesses her people with fertility and bountiful harvests. Maybe I don't need to kill you. Maybe I just need to consume you."

She curls her fingers into claws, and Malakhai gasps, his spine arching. The flesh on his body crawls, as if something seethes inside him.

A thorn lashes through his skin, as if the monstrous tangle grows *within* him.

Another joins it, and they tear his abdomen apart.

Malakhai screams, driven to his knees as Vi yanks her hands through the air, her thorns ripping and tearing through my father's body with each jerk of her wrist.

Flowers bloom in his hair. One punches through his eye, sprouting into a bright yellow daisy.

He screams and thorns crawl out of his throat as if he's vomiting them.

I can't help scrambling back, flipping to my feet as the enormous nest of brambles erupts from within him. I've seen a thousand different kinds of death, but I've never seen anything like this. He fights it. Ripping at the thorns, tearing them free and trying to heal himself; but Vi keeps advancing, her teeth bared and her fingers slowly curling into a fist.

The shock wears off.

I lunge forward, driving a dagger through his gut, right up to the hilt. The second I get a hand around his throat, I hear the roar of all those voices within him. Souls that splintered away from Death becoming hundreds, and yet the song they sing is a chorus. A thousand voices singing the same song, until they almost meld together.

Mine.

I close my eyes and suck the first soul from his body. A shiver of ice runs through me, and then another joins it. One after the other. Faster. Dozens at a time.

"*Yes,*" exults Death.

"Nargh!" Malakhai screams as he grabs my wrist. He goes to his knees, the tattoos bleeding off his skin and pouring toward where my hand circles his throat. His right eye sprouts a half dozen daisies.

All these years, I've imagined this moment.

Seeing the pain on his face.

Knowing this is the only vengeance I can offer my mother.

Hearing the whisper of those souls in my head and heart and feeling the Darkness within me exult as it slowly becomes whole.

Shoving my hand into his chest, I close my fingers around his heart and jerk him close to me. "For my mother," I whisper in his ear, right before I tear his heart from his chest.

Shadows bleed from him.

Hundreds of them.

All the little pieces of Death's soul, stolen from others.

I drink them in, the shadows winding through my skin, their whispers filling my ears until they echo with one voice, a single word spoken from a hundred throats.

"Finally," whispers the voice inside me.

The voice that's been there all my life.

"There's just one little piece missing."

I let the brittle mess of dried skin and bones that was once my father drop to the ground and turn.

There it is.

One last piece.

One last sliver of my soul.

With it I will be whole again.

Staring at me with wide, scared eyes—eyes so eerily familiar, it takes me a moment to realize I've seen them in the mirror every day of my life. She curls her arms around the grimalkin, her face paling as I take a step toward her.

Amaya.

"No." *I won't let you do this.*

But as the Darkness overwhelms me, all I can see is that one final piece of Death's soul deep within her.

The world becomes still and dark. Silent as the grave.

Sound rushes past my ears like a howling wind; only it's like no wind I've ever known. It streams toward the blot of shadow in front of me.

Something darts in front of me, a palm slamming against my chest.

"No," Vi whispers, and suddenly I can see her eyes as she comes into focus. Her face. The fierceness there. She's radiant in this darkness. She gleams like the captured light of a star. "No. Not her."

The world collapses back in upon me.

Blues and reds and stormy grays. The sky. Vi's roses, blooming now as her thorns bury the mess of flesh that was Malakhai. A kaleidoscope of color, as though I stepped from the shadows back into the real world.

But it's the green I notice most.

The green of my daughter's eyes.

Not a blot of shadow.

Not a sliver of Death's soul.

My daughter.

My *daughter*.

A gasp escapes me as I collapse forward into Vi's arms. The heat of her skin is a shock against the chill of mine. There are little marks inked into my arms with pure shadow, I realize as I wrap my arms around her and hold on. Absorbing the heat, the light, the... remnants of who I am.

But for the first time in my life, I don't know if I have the strength to hold on to who I am.

And as if it knows it, the Darkness within me chuckles.

I'll wait....

"Thank you." I press my forehead to Vi's, thumbs digging into the soft flesh of her cheeks. "Thank you."

"I love you." Her wan smile begins to fade. "I want you to... always know that."

Suddenly, I realize she's not just embracing me, she's leaning against me.

"Vi? What's wrong?"

She's dying, you little bastard. She just hasn't realized it yet.

Vi's eyes roll back in her head, the light in her gaze winking out as I catch her.

Chapter Twenty-Three

Footsteps echo up the spiral staircase within the tower as I swing Vi into my arms. "Go to your room," I tell Amaya bluntly. She doesn't need to see this. I lock gazes with Grimm. "Get her to her room. I'll take care of her. She'll be fine. She'll be *fine*."

Finn bursts through the door, one hand on his sword hilt as he scans the area. "What happened? What—?"

"Send for Mariana," I snarl, slamming through the

brass doors that lead into the tower. The court healer is the best of her kind. She'll fix this. I know it.

Vi moans, her fist curling in the fabric over her abdomen.

There's no blood. Not even a sign of damage, but I saw that blade strike her deep. I will never forget the feeling of hurtling out of the sky, knowing I was going to be too late—

"Come on, Vi. I've got you." I force the words through my teeth. *Not her. Anyone but her.*

Finn vanishes as I power up the staircase. Vi's head lolls against my shoulder, as if that last vestige of stubbornness that was keeping her conscious has faded.

I slam my shoulder into her bedroom door, and haul her inside.

Easing her onto our bed, I smooth the hair from her face. The worst part is that I don't know how badly she's injured, because there's nothing visible. Reaching out, my hand hovers over her abdomen, and that's when I feel it.

Death stealing through her middle, creeping with icy cold fingers through her warm skin and stealing the life from her veins.

"Stay with me," I whisper, kneeling on the bed and slapping her cheek lightly. "Vi, don't you dare do this to me. Not now." *Not after everything we've fought through to win.* "He's dead. He's gone. You saved us." I capture her face in my hands, pressing my forehead to hers. "Don't you leave me, Vi."

Because there is no Darkness for her.

If she leaves me... she'll be gone forever.

"Thiago?" Finn bellows through the door.

His voice cuts through the anguish lodged like a stone in my chest. "In here!"

He crashes into the room, hauling Mariana with him. The court healer is usually a calm woman with tidy brown hair and an apron, but she looks like he's dragged her in out of the wind.

"What happened to her?" Mariana demands as her gaze settles on Vi.

I tell her everything.

That sword. That fucking sword of Darkness.... "She was trying to protect Amaya. He was wielding an obsidian blade—some sort of Darkyn steel—and he drove it right through her. There's no blood, no injury, but... I can feel it inside her. He said she was already dead." My voice finally catches. "Even if she's still breathing, she's already dead."

It's only as she sets her hands on Vi's chest that I realize Amaya's standing in the doorway, Grimm cradled against her chest as if she doesn't dare let go.

Amaya stares at her mother, the blood draining from her face. "Mama?" she whispers, letting Grimm ease to the floor. "What's wrong with her?"

I jerk my head toward Finn. *Get her out of here.*

He sets a hand on her shoulder. "Come on. Leave the healer to do her work. We'll go and—"

"No!" Amaya tears free of his grasp and sprints toward the bed, throwing herself over Vi in a storm of weeping. "No, please! Come back. I didn't mean it. I promise I didn't mean it. I'm sorry!"

"Your Highness." Mariana gives me a stricken look. She needs to begin work now.

"Amaya." I steel myself even as Death stirs within me.

289

"Fuck off," I snarl at him. *"Just this once leave me alone. She needs me. My daughter needs me."*

Maybe it's my desperation ceding me control. Or perhaps he actually feels sympathy for her in this moment.

Because suddenly there's nothing there anymore. Gone. He's finally gone, and I want to gasp with the relief of it, but I don't have time.

"Amaya." I reach out and slowly capture her by the shoulders, my voice raw. Raw with the need to make it all go away for her. "Amaya, we have to let Mariana tend to your mother."

It's the first time I've touched her. The first time I've dared.

Her arms are thinner than they look beneath the loose cambric of her sleeves, but there's a wiry strength in them as she captures my wrists with a snarl, her eyes opaque with unshed tears. A trapped animal, desperate for escape.

"Don't touch me!" she screams.

I let her go, my heart sinking like lead within my chest as she scrambles away from the bed—from me.

"I've got it contained," I tell her as she clasps her arms to her chest, shaking with fear.

Finn immediately squats beside her, shooting me a sympathetic look. "Come on, Princess. The healer needs all her concentration right now. We'll go bandage those knuckles."

Her tearful gaze meets mine. "Please don't let her die. Not for me."

"I'll stay with her," I tell her. "I won't let anything happen to her. I promise. If there's any change, I'll send for you."

Our eyes meet.

And I hate the fact that I don't dare comfort her. That I can't be the anchor she needs right now, with this storm of emotion sweeping around us.

"Everybody please be quiet," Mariana commands, summoning her magic.

Finn hauls Amaya onto his hip, giving me a nod.

He's got this.

Now I just have to help Mariana heal my wife.

It seems like hours pass before Mariana finally announces her work is done.

I send for Amaya, and Thalia brings her, her delicate hand tucked inside my daughter's. The sight of it is an arrow through the heart—that I can't hold her like that—but at least she's got someone she can rely upon. Someone who makes her feel safe.

"She's exhausted," Thalia tells me wearily.

I'm not surprised. Midnight has come and gone.

"Climb into bed with her," I whisper to Amaya. "Let her know you're there."

My daughter eases into the sheets, wrapping those thin arms around her mother.

"How is she?" Thalia whispers.

I glance toward Mariana, but she summons me outside our bedchambers with a tilt of her chin. I stagger after her, utterly spent after hours lending her my energy to work with.

"What is it?"

Mariana dries her hands on her apron. "She's going to survive, I think. It's not so much a wound as it's a form of necrosis creeping through her. Left unchecked, it would slowly steal her life away. I can't heal it. I can't undo the damage it has caused. But I've managed to stop it and contain that damage to her womb."

I don't know what that means. There's no answer in her face, and it's like my brain refuses to add the pieces of the equation together.

"There is some residual Darkness left over from the sword." Mariana swallows and tilts her chin up slowly. "She will never bear another child, my prince."

I don't know why it shocks me.

It's what the Mother of Darkness promised, all those moons ago.

Amaya was to be our only child, and I knew that.

But it feels like losing that chance all over again, because until this moment I didn't know there *was* a chance.

"Your Highness?"

Mariana touches my sleeve, as if she's said my name several times.

Breathe through it. Just breathe through it. "She will survive?"

"That sliver of Darkness will always be inside her," Mariana says, "but I don't think it will be able to break through the wards I've set."

"Thank you."

She hesitates. "You should get some rest too, my prince."

"Perhaps."

I know she wants to say more, but she finally leaves me alone.

I return to the room and stare at my wife, her dark hair spread across her pillow, and Amaya tucked in her arms. Grimm lifts his head from where he's settled by their feet, a silent guardian watching over the pair of them.

"They're beautiful together," Thalia whispers, easing the blanket over Amaya. She's finally succumbed to sleep.

In sleep, they both share the same features, and I'm grateful for that—that she will look like her mother.

"Is Vi going to be okay?" Thalia murmurs.

Rage flares within my veins, but it's the rage of a glacier. The chill of death. "She will survive."

"Thi?" Thalia captures my fingers, her brow furrowing as if she knows I'm not saying something.

My father is gone forever now, but even in death he's still cast us a blow.

"Watch over them for me." Leaning down, I press a kiss to Vi's hair.

Amaya's eyes blink open as if she can sense me, and we share a moment. She goes so still, I can sense the pulse in her neck thundering.

She can sense the same thing I can: The threat within me.

"You are safe," I whisper, brushing the back of my fingers over her cheek. Death stirs through me hungrily. It senses the other half of itself. It *yearns* to reunite. But this is Amaya. This is the daughter I would do anything for. I would kill for her. I would die for her. I would sacrifice the entire world for her. She will never know another moment of pain if I can help it. "I will never hurt you. No matter what I must do. Guard your mother. I will return."

She swallows and nods, but she doesn't relax until I back away from the bed.

"Thiago?" Thalia makes a move toward me, but I wave her off.

Death is strangely silent within me as I close the doors to our bedchamber.

"Well?" I demand of it.

"*Do you not think I grieve too?*" comes the whisper.

"What would *you* know of grief?"

No response comes.

I want to bury this monster within me, but in that moment, I also *need* the answer. Because when all is said and done, it's as much a part of me as I am of it.

"*It is the burden I alone truly know,*" it finally answers. An image sweeps through my mind's eye. Fae villagers running from us in fear. An old woman holding up a symbol against us as she shrinks from us in fear. Village after village, it's all the same.

Until a woman forms in the quagmire of memories.

Golden as the dawn, her blue eyes as bright as the sky as she reaches a hand toward us. "Why don't you come out of the shadows?" she whispers as she sits by a stream.

"*Because you would run from me,*" he tells her.

The woman tilts her head as if trying to part the veil of gloom. Her brow crinkles. "*Then I am afraid you are wrong. I was born without fear, they tell me. It is both my curse and my strength.*" She pauses. "*Come out of the shadows.*"

The step he takes feels momentous.

Her eyes widen....

But she does not scream. She does not run. She does not form a diamond with her thumbs and fingers pressed together—a symbol of Maia's flames—in order to ward him away.

Instead, she invites him to sit with her.

"*I cannot touch you,*" he warns, though he yearns for the silk of her skin and the warmth of her mouth. She is pure golden flame, pulsing with light. And the wretched coldness within him will smother it.

"You loved her," I breathe, still caught in his memories.

"*Always.*"

The memories flash through stolen moments. Laughter, teasing eyes, and a woman who dared talk to the nightmare who stalked the night.

The abrupt cut to a woman screaming as she plunges through a night-dark forest is jarring. A pair of hunters clad in dark cloaks chase her.

"*I was not the only one of my... kind.*" Death says. "*Not then.*"

He rides behind them, desperate to save her.

Too late, too late, too late screams through our veins as one of those dark riders lifts his bow and an arrow forged of Darkness drives through her back.

It's like watching the snip of a puppet's strings.

She falls, her pale skirts gleaming in the dark.

"*No!*" he roars. Onward he urges his horse, a scythe of pure black forming in his right hand. His counterpart turns, catching a glimpse of him, and that scythe cuts right through those startled eyes.

Slamming into the other's horse, he drives them away, but it's too late.

The arrow forged of Darkness has found her.

Death leaps from his mount.

He holds her in his arms, begging for her to live, trying to extract that wretched seed of Darkness within her from where it creeps toward her heart.

"It's all right," she whispers, blood on her lips as she touches his face.

Tears gleam on her skin.

Tears of pure light.

The wound starts to smoke, and then light pours from the tear. It heals before his eyes, though it leaves a black, ugly mark.

It is only then that he realizes he is touching her. That his caress does not steal the life from her lips.

The shock of it.... That he could touch her skin without draining her life force....

That she could burn the Darkness from within herself....

"*I was forged from the Darkness itself,*" Death whispers. "*I did not know then that there were fae who held a kernel of Light within them. A drop of sunlight, if you will. One that cannot be smothered, not even by my affliction.*" He breathes a laugh. "*They were created to end our kind. But what they did not realize was that we would be drawn to them.*"

A child appears, blinking black emotionless eyes up at me. His hair is a tuft of gold so like his mother's. I reach out trembling hands as she places him in our arms, barely able to contain the lump in my chest, in my throat. Easing the swaddling back, we touch his chubby cheek, a lump in our chest the size of a kingdom.

He is perfect. So small. So helpless. Ours.

And then the child sucks in a shocked gasp.

Tiny cracks spear across his cheek like a barren desert desperate for rain. His lips turn blue, his chest heaving for air.

"*No,*" Death whispers as his touch threatens to steal the life from his son. "*No, please.*"

"*Give him to me!*" the woman cries.

She staggers away from us, hauling her son's swaddle around him as if she cannot bear for our hand to touch him.

"*Get away from him!*" The woman curls the bundle protectively into her arms. "*Don't you hurt him!*"

"*I would never hurt him,*" Death tells her—begs her—but she is gone.

I sense him stir within me, worn thin with sorrow. "*Her curse broke,*" he whispers, "*the moment she held our son in her arms. For the first time in her life, she knew fear. Fear that I would steal him from her.*"

And then she did what all the others had done.

I catch a hundred fleeting glimpses of her as she ages. Glimpses stolen in the night, or from the shadows as Death rides by. He watches over her as she sleeps, and some nights he presses a kiss to her temples and steals away the ravages of age. They are but signs of impending death, after all. When she wakes, clear-eyed and vibrant, she calls it a miracle, but we both know she glances over her shoulder as she says it.

The boy grows into a warrior, and then one day, there's

a child in his arms too. A little girl. Two boys follow. Another little girl.

The mother's hair softens and silvers as she becomes a grandmother. Those bright blue eyes slowly film over. Each kiss he graces her with only seems to roll back the ebb of time so much. The choking knot of fear fills our throat. This shouldn't be happening. Death can conquer all, can he not?

But this one time—when it counts the most—

"*Set me free,*" she whispers, late one night, after she has seen the last of her siblings fall. The Light within her has long faded. "*Set me free. Please.*"

This last kiss is release.

A sigh escapes her, and then she is gone.

Gone into a world where we cannot follow.

The night lies silent, never again to pulse with life. The Darkness feels empty.

And his heart—which beat all for her—falls still.

"*Carolain,*" Death whispers. "*Carolain the Defiant. Carolain the Fearless. But in my heart I called her Caro.*"

And I see him walk away from her village, from their son and their grandchildren, his shoulders held rigid. A sacrifice made to protect them, for who is he but the Shadow Sinister? The Ancient Chill? The Inevitable?

"*You will be the end of your wife,*" Death whispers. "*It is the burden we all share. You yearn for her light, because a part of me is within you. But you will smother it eventually.*"

Any sense of sympathy I might feel for him vanishes. "No." I push away from the wall. "No, I will not."

"*And your daughter?*" he warns.

Between one footfall and the next, I stand frozen. I

never wanted to feel any hint of understanding for this creature, but I know its fears, just as it knows mine. "She is safe from me."

There's a brooding kind of silence within me.

"*Will your precious Iskvien still love you when you steal that seed of Darkness from within your daughter?*"

I shut him down, locking him deep inside that vault within me. We are not the same. I will *never* harm my own child.

But even as I swear it, I see his thumb stroking across the cheek of his son.

I need a target. I need to slake this fury within me.

Turning, I nearly slam right into Thalia, catching her by the upper arms. And *fuck*, I need to get my hands off her. I'm not wearing my gloves.... I'm not....

There's fabric beneath my palms. She's wearing sleeves.

And I'm not Death.

My touch won't steal the life from her lips.

Will it?

"What aren't you telling me?" Thalia asks, reaching for me.

"Nothing," I brush past. "Stay here. Keep an eye on Vi for me."

"Thiago?" Thalia's hand falls from my sleeve as I stride past. "*Thi?* Where are you going?"

Where I should have gone long ago. "I need to end this."

"What does that mean?" she calls.

"I can't just sit here any longer. It's time for Adaia to die," I throw over my shoulder, flexing my hands. "Guard my wife and daughter. I'll be back."

299

BEC MCMASTER

* * *

I make it halfway up the tower steps to the Hallow before I hear footsteps pounding after me.

Well, that didn't fucking take long. "Go back to the training yard," I throw over my shoulder. "I'll be home by nightfall."

Finn shoves past, wearing his training leathers. He should have been asleep but his shoulder-length brown hair is knotted on top of his head and sweat clings to him. Training hard, no doubt, when Thalia ran straight to him.

"Where are you going?"

"Somewhere I should have gone years ago." I take another step, until we're almost brushing against each other. "Move."

His jaw clenches. "You're going after Adaia."

This all starts and ends with her. If I'd only killed her all those years ago, then Vi wouldn't have had to suffer so much pain. Amaya wouldn't flinch when I enter a room. Evernight wouldn't be watching three fucking armies march toward it.

I wouldn't have died. I wouldn't be fighting tooth and nail against this force inside me.

And my father wouldn't have had the chance to strike Vi down.

"Get out of the way." Rage burns within me, deep as an underground river. "I won't ask again."

Finn crosses his arms over his chest. "You want to move me, then you move me. But know this.... You hurt me, and it might wrench my bond from Vi's mind. I don't know what that will do to her right now."

My fingers curl into a fist. "I'm not going to hurt you. But you swore to serve me—"

"I swore to protect you," Finn retorts, right in my face. His voice softens. "Even against yourself."

"What the fuck does that mean?"

"It means—I don't know who's talking right now. You. Or that thing inside you. You've had ample chance to go after Adaia in the past, but you've always pulled back. Because you know that if the two of you go to war—one on one—then the damage would be catastrophic. You'd tear Hawthorne Castle to pieces, obliterate the entire town around it, all of the fae within it—"

"Right now, I'm not sure I see the problem."

He sets a hand to my chest as I lean into taking another step. "Like I said, I'm not sure which one of you is talking right now. Because that's not my *friend* talking."

"You're defending *Adaia?*"

"I'm defending all the fae in Hawthorne Castle, Thiago—"

"*Asturians.*"

"You're right. *Asturians*. Vi's people. Vi's friends."

"If they were her friends, they wouldn't have let her suffer all those years."

"Or maybe," he points out, in a mocking drawl, "they weren't in a position of power to speak against their queen. You know Adaia. You think she'd have allowed it? You're a warrior, Thiago. You're a prince. You're Darkyn. You have *never* stood in the shoes of the powerless—"

Rage roars through me, obliterating all good sense. What does he know of my life? *You want to know what fucking powerless feels like? Try growing up in a hut with*

301

dozens of starving children and being forced to use your murderous gifts to hunt for them. I slam him against the wall. "And you have?"

Finn grabs my wrists, his eyes flashing warning. "You're the one that took the fucking collar off my throat, you prick. You know who I am. You know where I've come from. The ability to kill almost anything in my path doesn't mean that I held power. I've been there in the mud and the blood while you fucking kings and queens tore the world apart and crushed us commoners beneath your heels."

"I was *never* one of those rulers." That's not who I wanted to be. When I took the throne, that wasn't what I wanted to create.

His gaze darkens. "Not to me, maybe. But if you do this, then there's a little girl sitting in Hawthorne Castle who doesn't know that the roof is going to come crashing down upon her. There's a young lad in the training yards with no idea his world is about to be set on fire. There's a baker in the kitchens, a youth into her first flush of training within the Asturian guards, a fucking farmer on his way to market.... *None* of them deserve this. If you do this, Thiago, then you are no better than Adaia."

A frigid tremor runs down my spine. He's wrong. I'm nothing like that bitch. But I push away from him, breathing out a half sob. "My wife nearly *died*."

Finn cups the back of my neck, drawing me against him so our foreheads touch. "You listen to me..., you are my best friend—my brother by choice—my prince. I would die *for you*. I have always believed in you, in what you fought for. But not this. The Thiago I knew wouldn't take this step."

And there it is.

The crux of the problem.

"The Thiago you knew died back at the Black Keep."

I can end this.

I can end it all.

I have the power to obliterate Adaia and her court now.

Finn stills. "No," he says softly. "I don't believe that. I *won't* believe that. You don't harm the innocent. You don't bring ruin down upon those who don't deserve it. And if you're having a moment of crisis where you think you might go to those lengths, then I *will* stop you."

I rake my quivering hands through my hair. "I can't help thinking that if I'd killed Adaia all those years ago, then Vi wouldn't be lying in that fucking bed—"

"That's horseshit, and you know it."

"I swore I would protect her—that I'd protect this kingdom, and every fae in it—and now we're facing a war we *can't* win."

Tension slides through him. "Don't doubt your generals."

"I don't." But all I can see is Eris lying still on a bloody battlefield, and Baylor torn to pieces. They will give and give and give, and they will die because the numbers standing against us are too great. "Three armies, Finn. We both know the odds facing us. The only way...."

If I take out Adaia now, then Asturia crumbles.

"*You could unleash me,*" whispers that night-dark voice in my mind.

"*Never,*" I snarl back.

"There has to be a way," Finn says. "You taught me that."

"I spent years watching Adaia strip her memories from

her. Years watching Vi fight not to lose herself. She nearly *died*. Because of me. Because of my father, her mother, all the—"

"Because she's a queen who is stepping into her power for the first time, brother."

What?

"Don't you take that away from Vi," he growls. "She knows the risks she accepted the second she married you. She knew what it meant when your father landed on those battlements. Vi's no warrior—hell, she doesn't have a single bloodthirsty bone in her body—but she will protect those she loves with every inch of herself. You can't lock her away, Thiago. You can't name her queen and then try and wrap her in wool."

"I can't *protect* her." Not from the world. Not from her mother. Not from... not from me.

Therein lies the crux of the matter.

Not from me.

"How bad is it?" His voice drops to a roughened whisper, courtesy of the scar across his throat.

"I'm fine."

That particularly stubborn gleam I associate with Finn when he gets in one of his moods lights his blue eyes. "How bad is it?"

I push away from him. He's right. I'm not in the sort of mood to be playing to my full strengths. Adaia's a cunning enemy, and Hawthorn Castle is a trap if ever I've seen one. I'm weakened. Furious. Prone to make a mistake.

Finn doesn't let me go. "You're not alone. I want you to know that. None of us understand what you're going through—what you went through. Nobody has ever come back from death before. I get it. You don't want to talk about it. You want to bottle it all up, lock it all away. Well, it doesn't work like that, Thi. You'll explode eventually. So fucking talk to me. Let me help you through this."

Finn might play the affable rogue, but this is why he's worth his weight in gold. He doesn't pull his punches, especially when he knows you need it. The first time we met, he saved my life. Chained as he was to the will of an evil queen, he still fought past the command that demanded he take my head.

In return, I set both hands to the collar around his throat and shattered it.

Freedom.

For both of us.

Freedom and something more.... A bond that can never be broken. A friendship that will never be defied.

He will stop me. He *will* stop me.

It feels like drowning in the abyss and finally having someone throw you a rope.

But to take it, I have to tell him the truth.

"I can't fight this *thing* inside me." Every day, every step I take... it's there, breathing down the back of my neck. I spent years with it locked down deep inside me. I had every magical ward that could be summoned tattooed into my skin. Sometimes I could feel it bubbling up inside me, choking in the back of my throat, but I could swallow it down. "My wards vanished the second I died. The sorcerers who set them are long dead." It's a truth I've been staring in the face for far too long, but I've never dared look that truth in the eye. "I don't know if I can lock it away again."

Ever since Vi brought me back, it feels like razor sharp

claws have hooked deep into my soul and they're not letting go.

Death has got those claws around the edge of my shields. I can't shut the lid now. I can't lock it away.

"Then don't," Finn tells me with a growl.

"What?"

"Come on," he says, clapping a hand on the back of my neck and steering me down the stairs. "My father had a saying for this—"

"You hated your father."

Finn shrugs. "Love. Hate. Two sides of the same coin. But he always spoke sense. And he always said that if you don't face the demon inside you, then you will never win on a field of war. You spend too much time fighting yourself and by the time you hit the battleground, your shield arm is heavy."

I cut him a half savage look. "What does that mean?"

"Let's hit the training yard and figure it out. Thalia will watch over Vi."

Chapter Twenty-Four

"Alright," Finn says, draining his mug of tea as we watch dawn break over the training yard. "Let's fight it out."

I clasp both hands behind my head as he heads for the sword rack. "I don't think I'm in the mood to pull my punches today."

"Then don't."

He doesn't understand. "It's there. The edge is right there within me."

Finn picks a sword and then turns understanding eyes upon me. "Then we'll face it together."

"Finn—"

The muscle in his jaw shifts. "You won't kill me, Thi. I spar with Eris and Baylor every day. I trade punches with Xander. I get my ass kicked on a regular basis, because I can't ever let myself off the leash. You think you're the only one who rides that edge? I can't ever push back, Thi. I can't ever push too hard." A hungry light comes to life in his eyes. "I was bred for war. I was trained to kill. I am very, very good at what I do. Every day I step into this arena and face that darkness within myself. Every day I leash it. And every day I fight the urge to remove that leash, to let the hot spray of blood splash across my face and violence spill through me." He breathes in. Then out. The hunger dies, and Finn smiles. "And just in case you think this Sylvaren bastard can't hold his own against you, let me assure you of one thing: Vi gave me a fucking enormous sword that can't be defeated in battle."

He sets his hand on the hilt of the Sword of Mourning suggestively.

With it, he might actually be able to stop me. I hesitate for long moments before surrendering. *Fine.* I strip my gloves off, tossing them aside. I need to hit something.

"I've been thinking," he says.

"Good thing Grimm's not here. He might have an opinion on that statement."

"Ouch." Finn starts, and then he laughs under his breath. "Did I say I missed you? I lied. I must have lied. You're hitting me where it hurts today."

"You missed me."

Finn rolls his eyes. "That furry little fucker is tucked up in bed with Vi and Amaya. He's working his way straight to the top and he knows it."

It feels good to laugh. It doesn't last for long though. "What have you been thinking?"

"We've got three armies coming our way. Goblins. Asturia. And the unseelie. We face each battle as it comes, but we both know who the main threat is."

"The Horned One."

Vi will need Death by her side if she's going to destroy him.

An ancient god.

Suddenly, doubt traces knots in my stomach. I've always held back because of who I am and what I can do. Could I take Adaia? Maybe. She's always been strong and vicious. It's never been about being able to overwhelm her —it's about what to do if I unleash myself fully and can't come back.

The goblin threat comes in the form of numbers—they lack fae magic, but they're enormous and there are millions of them.

But the Horned One is different.

I've never had to face one of the Old Ones by myself. During the Wars of Light and Shadow I was a young commander, furiously trying to keep my queen alive. I saw them in action across a distant battlefield, but I've never stared one of them in the eyes.

"Even the Old Ones feared the Shadow Sinister," Finn says, rolling his shoulders to warm up.

"Except for the Erlking."

"And Vi's got him on a leash." He cracks his neck. "You

said Malakhai forged a sword of pure Darkness and drove it through her."

Instantly I see that blade of obsidian smoke drive itself through my wife's body, my father's vicious expression as he captured a fistful of her hair and looked me in the eye as he slid the sword home, and the fear, the desperate fear that I'd be too late as I dove toward them. My fingers flex, longing for steel. "He'll never hurt her again."

"I'm not interested in your father. I'm interested in the sword," Finn says softly. "Can you do that?"

No. I grit my teeth, shake my head. "I have no idea how to even create such a thing."

"*I could help you,*" Death whispers in my head. "*I could show you how it's done.*"

"Fuck off."

Finn's eyebrows arch.

"Not you." I gesture toward my temples. "This fucking thing."

"It's talking to you now?"

"It wants to show me how to forge that blade."

He's a long time in replying. "Why don't you let it?"

"Did you not just hear what I said in the hallway? I can't let it gain an inch."

"I'm not talking about letting it gain on you. I'm talking about facing it, finding out what it wants, letting it show you how to protect you—because make no mistake, Thi. If the Horned One kills you, then *it* dies too. Only that tiny little kernel inside Amaya will survive." He looks me dead in the eye as if he can see right through me. "You hear that, Shadow?"

There's a strange silence within me.

"*I hear him,*" he finally whispers. "*And he is correct in a way. If you die, then all that I am within you returns to the Darkness. I would be trapped there. Forever. But the Horned One won't merely kill you. He knows what I am, what I can do. He must destroy me if he's to have any hope of succeeding in his mission to shatter the Seelie Alliance. He must destroy me, and he must destroy the Mother of Night.*"

I'm surprised the Erlking isn't part of that assessment.

"*Let me help you.*" I can sense him hesitating. "*If only so that neither of us are obliterated.*"

It all sounds plausible.

If I trust him.

"Does the prince make this decision?" Finn murmurs. "Or is it Thiago? Don't let the fear win."

Fuck, we're going low today. Punching for all the vulnerable spots. I hate the fact he's only repeating something I've told him a thousand times.

I can let fear rule me. I can let hesitation cloud my judgment.

But my kingdom needs a prince to make this decision. Not Thiago. A prince must be ruthless, even when it's with himself. And Vi needs me to face those fears. A prince at half strength is a vulnerability. I can't risk Vi or Amaya's life with my stubbornness.

"Fine. Let's do this."

"Okay." Finn draws the Sword of Mourning, the whine of its blade cutting through the air. The most minute shift crosses his expression; a warrior settling into utter focus. "Let's see if you can forge Darkyn steel."

I stare at my hand. I've wielded the shadows deep within me many times. I've unleashed those souls within me—Rage, Fury, Wrath—and let them cut down my enemies. But I've never wielded this Darkness myself.

The shadows come, conjured by my will. They writhe around my hand, restless and curious.

But I don't know the next step.

"*Like this,*" Death says, a chill running down my arm.

Shadow forges into a sword-like shape. The hilt comes to life in my hand as if it's stealing the warmth from my veins, leaving me with nothing but ice, ice where—

That gaping hollow emptiness opens within me. There's no stopping the cold eating its way through my veins like acid. Vicious claws of frost sink into my lungs, and I can't breathe. I can't *breathe.* I'm falling. Alone. Slamming into nothing in a Darkness so silent and absolute I can barely hear myself breathing.

"No." *No.* I'm not going back there. I'm not going back to that Darkness, that silence. I don't want to be alone, lost in the cold and the dark.

I shove it all away, breathing hard, trying to hold in the scream that longs to break free.

It's gone. It's all gone.

Death. The Darkness. The obsidian blade.

Only my heart pounds through the sudden ringing silence, and I realize I'm crouched by the wall, my fingernails digging into my palm as if it's the only way to bring me back, the breath rasping through me. Gasping. Gasping like a landed fish.

"Thiago?" Finn asks.

"I'm fine." My voice doesn't sound fine. I can hardly fucking breathe.

Boots step into my vision. Then a hand comes to rest on my shoulder.

Heat. Pressure. I cling to the physical impression of it, clutching at his wrist.

"I'm here." He squeezes hard. "You want to talk about it?"

I want to vomit.

But that's the man talking. Not the prince.

I have to learn to control this.

"I'm fine." Thighs bunching, I push to my feet, leaning on the wall. Stone scrapes beneath my fingers, but it's like someone else's hand trails down the wall. And my feet won't work.

Finn's eyes search my face, as blue as foxfire. "You're not fucking fine. I'm sorry. I didn't realize—"

"You were right." I push past him, shaking it off, trying to still the tremor in my hands. "We don't have time for me to fall in a heap. I need to learn how to forge Darkyn steel. It's the only way I can kill him."

The only way I can protect Vi and Amaya from the Horned One....

The only way I escape that prison of nothingness.

"There's no shame in not being ready to face that." Finn stalks after me. "I don't know what happened to you. I don't know how that feels. I shouldn't have pushed you."

"If you don't push me, then we all die." I stare down at my fingers, willing myself to feel them, feel that bitter, wretched coldness I can conjure.

"Thiago."

"It's the cold." The words burst from my lips. "It's the cold I can't stand. The... nothingness. To forge Darkyn steel, I have to open myself back up to that Darkness, and it feels like... nothing."

Finn stares at me, silently taking it all in. "You're not alone. I want you to know that. And you don't have to shoulder this entire burden by yourself. If you go up against the Horned One—you and Vi—then I will be there at your side. As will Eris and Baylor. Maybe even Thalia."

Not alone, no. But maybe that's the hardest part of this. I don't want to see any of them die.

This time, the shadows come a little easier.

"You don't have to do this right now," Finn says.

I force the shadows I can conjure at will to thicken into a sword-like shape. Boiling clouds of Darkness becoming sharp-edged and vicious—

And I see Vi, curling over that sword, her knees weakening as if it cut her legs right out from under her.

"*She will never bear another child.*"

The blade vanishes, smoke dissipating into nothing.

Fuck. I turn and smash a punch into one of the training gurneys, sending the wooden knight swinging, its mace whipping through the air.

"You almost had it," Finn says encouragingly.

"Almost isn't good enough." We have days at most before Angharad's forces cross the River Nyx, and then she's right on the edges of Mistmark, a mere day's ride from Evernight's most northern borders.

The Horned One at her side.

"You don't pick up a sword and expect to master it on the first day."

"I have to."

Finn slowly sheathes the Sword of Mourning. "This

314

isn't going to work. You're too bound up. Let's work it out of you," he says, crossing to the rack and tossing me a regular steel-edged training blade.

The hilt feels like an old friend in my hand. Maybe he's right. I haven't ventured down here since I returned. I need this.

"No pulling your punches," I remind him.

Finn's cocky grin feels like old times. "You're going to regret saying that, you know?"

* * *

The following morning, there's no change to Vi's circumstances.

"She's sleeping," Mariana assures me, brushing the hair off my wife's forehead. "She will rouse when she's recovered." Then she pushes back from the bed, hands on her hips as she rakes me over with a blistering look. "And if you don't rest yourself, then you're going to collapse at her feet when she wakes, my prince."

How can I rest when every time I close my eyes, I see Vi collapsing into my arms? I spent the entire night in the chair beside her bed, sub-consciously monitoring her breathing as I went over the reports of granary hauls and recruitment that Baylor sent me. Boring, monotonous stuff that is absolutely critical in any war, practically guaranteed to put one to sleep, and yet, every time my eyes threatened to shut, I'd jolt awake with the sound of Vi's scream in my ears.

"I'll consider it," I reply.

"Which means no," Thalia says with an exasperated

cluck of her tongue as she sweeps forward to join Mariana. "Out you go, then. If you're not going to rest, then you can at least eat something and get some fresh air. We'll have the maids bathe her and change her linens, whilst you refresh yourself." As I open my mouth to argue, she arches a pointed brow. "And it will give Amaya time to visit with her mother."

Without the threat of my presence.

"Fine." I know when I'm routed. Grabbing my cloak, I retreat to the dining room where someone—Thalia, no doubt—has an enormous breakfast awaiting beneath a silver cloche.

Washing it all down with tepid tea, I head for the training yard.

Finn's there already, his stance split as he twirls his sword through the first opening stances of a Warrior Greeting the Dawn. There's something beautiful about watching him move. Despite everything I've heard about the brutal conditions of the Sylvaren war camps, the idea of seeing a hundred of them—or even a thousand—moving together like this in perfect synchronicity, must have been breathtaking.

The Sylvaren were fae who were twisted by the magic of their vicious queen, Sylvian, into vicious, war-hungry warriors that were nearly impossible to kill. Determined to destroy the southern kings and queens who had thwarted her previous attempts to expand her empire, Sylvian created an army of warsworn that broke like a tide over the south.

Every other king and queen formed an alliance against her—the first glimmerings of the Seelie Alliance—and when Maia broke Sylvian's power at Charun and ascended to godhood, the Sylvaren warbands were slaughtered by the thousands. Some of them escaped into the frozen north, but they were branded outlaws and hunted by the Unseelie queens over the last few centuries. But some of them formed mercenary warbands that made themselves indispensable to certain powerful lords.

Finn's father—the warlord of his clan—was exiled by Sylvian before the events of Charun. Finn doesn't speak of it often, but his people were cast out from the host, their clan name stripped from record, and driven into the icy north. Sylvian named them the Forbidden, and insisted that her warsworn have nothing to do with them.

They were not to be spoken to. They were not to be given sustenance, or traded with. They were pacifists who were to be spat upon in company, and sneered upon in song.

The Forbidden eked out a means of survival there, with his father giving himself over to a new way of living.

They became hunters. Trackers.

They took the brutal training regimes the Sylvaren practiced and transformed them into something beautiful and peaceful that they called the Way of the Flame.

Fire unchecked can ravage the entire countryside, Finn once told me, but the flame itself—if kept controlled—can offer shelter and warmth. And the Way of the Flame teaches a practitioner to dance like fire itself. To move with the wind, with the elements that surround it. But never to kill with.

Finn refuses to speak of it, but I know there was some sort of sundering with his father and his clan. Something to do with spilling the blood of another.

He chose a different path. A bloodier path. And that path led him to me on that fateful battlefield long ago, where he chose to spare my life.

He's the closest thing I have to a true brother.

"You checking out of my ass?" Finn asks, not breaking stride. "Or are you going to get down here and make yourself useful?"

I stalk down the stairs with a scowl. Definitely a pain-in-my-ass if nothing else. "I've seen you move. You could put me, Eris and Baylor into the dirt any time you choose, and yet you've rarely beaten one of us in the ring."

Finn stills, one leg stretched out behind him, and the line of his sword echoing the stance over his head. Cursing under his breath, he straightens and shakes himself off. "What you don't understand is that anytime I face one of you and don't hurt you, I win," he says softly. "I master the rage inside me. I prove to myself I'm in control. That I'm not some savage creature let off its leash."

I toss him the water flask sitting by his shirt. It's disturbing how much I empathize with him. Every day that I look in the mirror and see my own eyes looking back at me, and not the Shadow Sinister, is a victory.

"You make Lysander eat dirt every time."

Finn grins, taking a hefty swallow of his water. "That asshole is too arrogant to allow him a single victory. I'd never hear the end of it."

The pair of them have been arguing with each other and getting into trouble together for centuries.

Surveying the armory rack, I trace my fingers over the training swords.

It's been a long night.

I don't know if I have strength to attempt to forge Darkyn steel right now.

"Vi's fine, Thiago," Finn says gruffly, clapping a hand on my shoulder. "She's beginning to surface."

The bond.

Some part of what I feel must flash over my face. Vi told me of it, of course, and I would never begrudge her the safety and protection of another, but I can't help wishing... wishing it was me.

"Don't look at me like that," he says roughly.

I breathe out. "I'm not. Logic dictates that if Vi's ever in trouble, having you bonded to her is an enormous advantage. You'd be able to find her, no matter where she was."

"That's the prince speaking," he points out. "And how do you feel?"

"Does it matter?"

Finn scrapes his long hair back into a fistful at the back of his head and binds it afresh with his leather thong. "It matters. My father always said that burying your truths in your heart only makes them fester. You need to be calm and focused when you face Adaia."

Fine. I face him starkly. "I wish it was me. I wish I'd been the one she claimed."

Every time Adaia would send Vi back to me, and my wife would look at me with that blank lack of recognition.... Adaia stole years from us. Our daughter. Our time together. It feels like I've lost so much over the years, and now this....

"I wish it was you too."

What?

Finn sees my startled expression. "You think I enjoy having Vi's thoughts catch me off guard at times? Do you know how many times I've nearly choked on my tea, thanks to a sudden, very-visceral image of your ass? Without clothing? It's a cursed good thing I've spent five hundred years centering my mind. I've managed to block most of it, and keep my own thoughts retained." With a rough sigh, he looks away. "At the same time, I'm grateful that I could be here for her. She was drowning when she bonded me, Thiago. She thinks everything is her burden to shoulder, every fight hers to face. She lost you and it came close to destroying her. I've been trying to center her too. If I had time, I'd have her down here training with me and clearing her mind. But we don't have time."

"I understand all of that." Rolling my sleeves up, I tuck them at my elbows. "Nobody ever said that what I feel is rational."

Finn grins at me. "Prickly, territorial prince."

"Ha, ha."

He spreads his arms wide. "Want to hit me?"

"No."

"Bullshit."

Since he's asking for it....

I kick his feet out from under him.

Or at least, I try.

Finn launches over the kick, grinning like a grimalkin in the night. "Too slow," he mocks. "You practically nailed the choreography for your forthcoming move to my forehead."

Rolling my shoulders, I dance on my feet. "What makes you think that wasn't meant to be the warning?"

"Warning for what?"

"This."

I lunge forward, slamming against him. The impact

drives him back three feet. Finn's white teeth flash at me in good humor, then he hooks an arm around my neck, flips his legs up and brings me crashing to the dirt.

We wrestle together, grinding each other's face into the dirt, changing holds, turning the tides of battle more than half a dozen times—

Arching his hips, he flips himself to his feet like a lithe cat, and nearly kicks my head off my shoulders.

I roll away, coming up in a fighting stance. "That was distinctly not friendly."

"That was the warm up," he says, heading for the training rack. This time, he chooses star-forged steel. Iron is anathema to the fae, but this particular alloy holds enough other metals—off-world metals—to be touchable.

It's also lethal.

"The warm-up?" I dust off my hands. "You nearly took my head off my shoulders."

"You're getting slow," he snorts. "All that rolling around in bed with your lovely wife, and those pastries Thalia keeps feeding the pair of you.... Soon you're going to be huffing around my training yard like a thirty-year-old mule."

"Well, at least one of us is rolling around in bed with a lovely wife."

"What makes you think I want a wife?"

I snort. "You keep saying such things, Finn... and then a certain ass-kicker steals your tongue. Every single time."

Finn freezes. "Vi told you?"

"If you're talking about what I think you're talking about, she didn't have to tell me. I've got eyes."

Finn's eyes narrow as if he's not sure if we're discussing the same subject.

I take pity on him. "Since we're discussing bottled up truths, maybe you should reveal your own."

Finn swings the sword low, testing its balance. "Don't know what you're talking about."

"How about this then? You and Eris duel in the yard, but you never beat her. And I don't think it's got shit all to do with leashing your violence. If you beat her, then you might have to face the uncomfortable situation that you— among all males—might be able to force her to submit in a duel. And she has made certain terms to such a thing ever happening."

"It's a stupid fucking challenge she made years ago," he snarls.

"She swore thrice, upon Maia's name," I point out. "It's not a stupid challenge, Finn. It's a promise. If Eris finds herself disarmed, then she is honor-bound to submit to marriage to the male who disarmed her."

"You've beaten her."

"I'm married." I snort. "Don't change the subject."

"Baylor has beaten her once or twice."

"Baylor's not fae. She specifically stated 'fae male.'"

"Maybe I'm not fae either."

I arch a brow. "The Sylvaren were fae. I don't think that argument stands."

"What makes you think I want such a thing?"

"The look on your face every time she walks into a room."

Finn looks away, the muscle ticking in his jaw. "I'm just her friend, Thi. I'm the charming wastrel of the court, the rogue who likes to go his own way.... That's the category she's relegated me to. And she's never given me a single hint I can convince her otherwise."

"Because you're doing such a wonderful job of convincing her there might be a chance if she did feel that way."

"She doesn't."

"You don't know that."

His teeth grind together as he squeezes out the words, "I *do*."

"You don't—"

"For fuck's sake," he snaps. "I do. I was drunk once. I made my intentions clear. She didn't just politely rescind the offer, she set those intentions on fire. And then stomped on the ashes. She was furious. Since then... we've danced around each other. We'll probably keep dancing for the next five centuries. Now, are we done with this discussion?"

I stare at him. "Nearly done."

"What more could you have to say?"

I dust off my hands slowly, thinking my way through my words. Eris was barely an adult when she was hauled before the alliance in chains. I'll never forget the look in her eyes—like all the hope in the world had bled out of her heart, until I offered her a chance to survive.

Over the centuries, she's flourished, but I still see that expression on her face sometimes. As if she knows time is her enemy. One day she'll explode. One day she'll lose the battle she faces every morning when she wakes.

She's made a family for herself here, but she still doesn't dare let down her walls.

"Out of all of you, I understand Eris the most. The monster inside her.... It's her burden to bear. She's spent her entire life knowing she will never find a man who can love her—or accept the monster inside her—and she thinks that eventually it will overwhelm her. She's rejected every single notion she ever had about love, about marriage, about children. It's not a lifestyle she yearns for, because she doesn't *dare* dream about it. She doesn't believe it can ever happen for her.

"I've known that feeling. And if I hadn't been granted Maia's vision of Vi, I don't think I'd have ever believed *I* would ever find someone to love.

"And then here *you* are, pushing your way into Eris's life. It's safer if she relegates you to being merely a handsome rogue who's slept with every fae woman in Ceres. But Vi told me what happened when she bonded you. You died, Finn. You died in Eris's arms, and Vi said she's never heard so much anguish in her friend's voice."

Finn rakes his hands through his hair, cupping his palms behind his head. "You're such a bastard."

"I am?"

He closes his eyes. "For giving me a shred of hope."

I've seen the way the two of them dance around each other for centuries. "I think it's more than a shred."

"She's been avoiding me ever since," he says quietly.

I head toward the sword rack. "It's what Eris does. She retreats when her emotions are off-kilter."

"Fuck." Finn breathes out explosively. "I think I hate you."

"No, you don't."

"No, I don't," he says. Then his eyes narrow and he

324

steps in front of me as I reach the sword rack. "But that doesn't mean you've derailed my plan of attack. You've already got a sword. You just need to use it."

Darkyn steel.

My hand flexes. "Okay, fine."

Returning to the center of the yard, I stir the shadows within my soul. A deathly chill runs down my forearm, Death rising within me.

I'm alone in the dark.

In the silence.

In the nothingness....

A thousand stars stretch through an endless sky above me, but all I can feel is the cold....

The shadows evaporate from my fingertips.

"I've got an idea." Finn takes a step toward me, his blade dipping low in a taunt. "Maybe you need to be under threat."

He launches toward me, the sword cutting through the air.

I twist out of the way, wrenching myself back again when he slashes in the other direction. Wild, ringing swings he can afford to make, since I'm unarmed.

"Concentrate," he barks.

I duck beneath a blow, slamming my shoulder into his midriff and sending him catapulting over my back. "Why don't *you* concentrate?"

Finn's answering grin as he circles me tells me everything. He wants me pissed off. Because when you want to punch someone's teeth out, you're not thinking about the reason you're afraid to summon the shadows.

He comes at me again.

I duck out of the way, using the outside of my forearm to divert the sweep of his blade.

I can almost feel my own forging to life in my hand. Almost.

"*Let me rise*," whispers Death.

"Fuck you."

Finn forces me back, back.... I catch a glimpse of the wall behind me and understand exactly what he intends.

Evaporating into shadows, I plunge through him, reforming on the other side. The second my foot is solid, I spin and slam my boot right in the center of his back. Finn slams into the very wall he was trying to trap me against.

"Asshole," he says, pushing off the stone.

I laugh.

Right as a half-muffled shriek splits the air.

Instantly, my hand goes to where my sword would usually hang, as something catapults off the roof and slams into a pile of hay near the outer edge of the stables.

Finn holds a hand up, equally as intense. "Me, first."

Together we stalk toward the pile of hay.

A head explodes out of the straw and then Amaya coughs out a strand of hay. Grimm materializes at her side, looking at her like she's an idiot.

"*Did I not tell you to watch what you were doing?*" he sounds half frantic.

"I was watching," she snaps. "It's not my fault that stone was loose."

I can't help looking up. Fifty feet to the top of the wall if I'm right.

Her mother's going to wring her neck.

"Princess." Despite the roughened edge to his voice,

Finn puts on what I like to call his court voice as he offers a hand toward the lurching figure in the straw. "Allow me."

Amaya scrambles out of the hay, desperate eyes raking over me. "I'm fine," she says, dusting her breeches off.

She was watching us. And she slipped.

Grimm reappears at my feet, his tail curling around my calf. "*Careful, now. She's been having nightmares since your father attacked her. You'll frighten her if you raise your voice.*"

I give him a long look, then focus on her. It's been so new—this relationship between us—that I don't know if I should demand to know what she was doing up there. So I try a different tact. "How's your mother?"

"Still sleeping," she admits, watching me like a wary animal. "Thalia's checking on her."

"What were you doing up there?" Finn barks. "You could have broken your neck."

She turns on him, hackles virtually raised. "But I didn't."

"But you might have," he snaps back. "You think I'm going to be the one who explains to your mother when she wakes that you broke your back on our watch?"

Amaya opens her mouth... and then shuts it. Her lower lip starts to quiver.

Finn squats in front of her with a sigh. "I'm not angry with you. You scared me. You scared the both of us." He includes me with a jerk of his thumb. "We've lost so much, and while I know you're struggling to find your place here, I'm asking you not to take such risks. Not right now. Please."

This is what I should be doing, but I can't touch her. I

don't *dare* touch her. Turning away, I grind my teeth against the pain. Maybe one day, if I get this thing out of me....

"You think I want to return to that dark emptiness either?" Death whispers. *"You will never be free of me."*

Maybe it's better this way.

If I can't be the father she needs, then Finn....

I can't even finish that thought.

"No more walking along the edge of the parapet," I tell her quietly. "Malakhai isn't the only enemy who hunts the skies."

"I did remind her of that," Grimm sniffs.

"I want to learn to do what you can do," Amaya says. "I was just... trying to watch."

"You want to learn to fight with a sword?" Finn directs the question toward me.

I nod. She may as well.

Amaya scowls as if she saw him asking for permission. "I can fight already. I'm good with a knife. But I've never held a sword. I want one."

Finn stalks along the racks, searching for the smaller wooden swords that suit the youths who've started training. "Maybe...."

"Not one of them." Amaya trails him. "I want a real one."

"Well, we don't always get what we want," he tells her. "It will take years of discipline and daily exercise before I'm putting actual steel into your hands."

"I'll ask Thalia."

"You can ask Thalia all you like," Finn retorts. "You think she's going to give you a sword? She might rule the castle, but this training yard is mine. This armory is mine."

Defiance lights in her eyes, but there's something else there.... "Why do you want a sword?"

My words cut right through the imminent argument. Amaya hesitantly strokes one of the hilts of the training sword. "I couldn't stop him."

"Who?" But I know.

This time, the tears in her eyes threaten to spill. "He hurt her. He hurt her and I couldn't stop him." She starts to tremble, her eyes bleeding of color as the Darkyn within her rouses. "I know I'm not big enough to face a Darkyn warrior, but if I knew how to wield a sword.... Maybe I could have.... Maybe she wouldn't...."

"*Oh, child.*" Grimm butts against her legs. "*Nothing you could have done would have stopped him.*"

This time a tear slips down her cheek. "He was hunting *me*. If I hadn't been up there...."

Her whisper nearly tears my heart into two.

"If you hadn't been up there, then he would have found a way inside the castle." Drawing the dagger from my belt, I flip the tip of it into my fingers. "And none of us would have known until it was too late. Your mother's safe. She's well. None of this is your fault. Here."

She's barely nine years old.

But I was seven the first time I killed a wolf.

Seven the first time I saw one of my friends die, torn to pieces by the rest of the pack.

The life she's known was one of joy and laughter, but it was also one of pain and suffering and fear. Old Mother Hibbert was a kind old soul, but she was only one aging fae woman against an entire forest of nightmares, and while she did her best to protect and feed all her charges, sometimes the forest took its own toll.

"You should have your own knife." I offer her the hilt. It's old, the leather sweat-stained and ragged, and the blade thin with years of sharpening. It's more decorative than anything else. "This is Wolf's Tooth. My foster brother, Cian, gave it to me when I was fifteen. We swore a blood oath with it. I think he'd like it if... if you could keep it safe for me."

Amaya's eyes widen and she looks up as if I just offered her the moon.

"*Excellent progress,*" Grimm assures me.

There's no hint of malevolence within my chest as I glance down at her raven-dark hair. She can barely breathe as she accepts the dagger, holding it displayed on her fingers as if she can scarce believe it's real.

"It's mine?" she whispers.

"Yours." I reach out and brush my thumb along a wisp of her fringe.

A chill runs through my veins. I blink as Death rises, stirring within me as if he's only just sensed the presence of the slither of Darkyn soul within her.

Only Finn notices when I jerk my hand back, clenching my fingers. I turn the move into something else, unhooking my belt and drawing the sheath clear so she can put it away.

"Thank you," Amaya gushes, palming the hilt and twisting the knife this way and that, as if she's imagining invisible foes standing against her.

"*How goes your training?*" Grimm asks. "*Have you forged the shadowsteel yet?*"

"What are you trying to say?"

"I don't think it's wholly corrupting you," he says slowly. "I think you're corrupting it too. There's a symbiotic relationship between you, and its feeding off aspects of your personality." He looks at me pointedly. "Death was fractured into thousands of pieces in order to suppress its power. The piece you have inside you—what if it's been warped by all your experiences, all your thoughts and hopes and dreams? Malakhai was a vicious bastard, so the slither of soul within him became warped and twisted."

Grimm makes a sudden gagging sound as if he's coughing up a hairball.

All of us look at him.

"*It must be the end of the world,*" he says, curling his lip. "*Because this hairy idiot might actually be right.*"

Finn flashes Grimm a vicious smile. "I think I might actually have to have those words etched into a piece of stone. Did you just say I'm right?"

"*Don't push me, pudding brain.*" Grimm examines his claws. "*It occasionally happens to even the veriest idiot.*"

I'm still working my way through the implications of everything. What if it's not the entirety of the creature itself within me? What if Finn's right?

Rubbing a hand over my chest, I brush my senses against the other 'souls' trapped within me. Darkyn souls. Pieces of the puzzle that makes up the entirety of the Shadow Sinister. Rage and Torment and Fury. Names I gave them as I gutted their owners and tore the snippets of soul from their bodies.

All of them vicious. All of them dangerous and hungry for vengeance.

333

All of them strangely distinct within me, as if they were once part of a whole, but imprinted upon those who once bore them.

When I hunted Rage down, I found him in a village full of slaughtered women and children. There was nothing in his expression beyond the crushing need to destroy me. An animal, a monster, a vicious bloodthirsty beast that made me terrified to ever let Death take me over. For years I woke sweating from nightmares with that bastard's face in my mind.

But the shadow inside me, that whisper.... It's fought to consume me, but it's never even given a hint that it wants to drink the blood from someone's throat.

Is Finn right? Is this... sliver of a monster inside me as much a part of me as I'm a part of it?

"What does that mean?" I breathe.

"It means, I don't think the psychic entity inside you is going to hurt Amaya. I don't think it *can* hurt her. Because at heart, it feels all your emotions as if they're its own." Finn turns to Amaya with a smile. "Want to teach your father how to kill the Horned One?"

Chapter Twenty-Five

Iskvien

Someone is reading.

"'I love you,' the duke whispered, his eyes gleaming bright gray in contrast to the soot on his cheeks. 'I have tried not to. I knew I was breaking every single promise I ever made myself when I looked at you. But I couldn't help myself. You drive me crazy, Adele. But you also give me back a piece of myself I thought I'd lost.'" The gentle words pause. "Vi? Vi, are you awake?"

Slowly my lashes flutter open. Light spills through the

curtains—an instant stabbing ache—but it's also grounding in a way.

Soup. I can smell soup. And Mother of Darkness, is that the scent of a warm, crusty bread roll lingering in the air like the promise of a mouth orgasm?

A very eager growl echoes through the room and I clap my hands over my stomach. "Thiago?"

Thiago closes the book, setting it aside. He's wearing his seelie glamor again, a handsome fae prince clad in strict black. Every inch of his hair is disheveled. It needs a trim. And if he didn't look so deliciously wicked with his dark hair all rumpled as if my hands have been through it, I might suggest it.

My gaze locks on the bruise along his cheek. "What happened to your face?"

"Hello, Vi." The bed dips as he sinks into the mattress at my side. "I'm fine. Finn and I were working through some things yesterday morning. Are you thirsty?"

I groan as I roll onto my side.

Someone's stuffed my head with wool, and my mouth is a desert.

"Here," he says.

A cup finds its way to my mouth, and then cool, blessed water spills over my lips. I drink deeply, draining the entire cup and wanting more, even as he holds me.

"Easy." It's a rough voice. The sound of granite over velvet. A hand strokes through my hair. "You're going to vomit if you drink too much so soon. How are you feeling?"

I mentally scan my body and wince. Nothing is bleeding, but the ghostly sensation of that sword driving through me still lingers. "I'm fine. I think. Is Malakhai gone?"

"Gone," he promises. "You turned him into a compost heap. Remind me never to piss you off."

I capture his hand, stroking my thumb against his. "How do you feel about that?"

"I'm fine," he says softly.

He's not fine.

"Liar." I want to crawl out of bed, but my heart comes to a bleeding, crashing halt as the scene on the battlements springs to mind. "Amaya?"

Oh, my gods. Amaya!

"Also fine." Thiago captures my shoulders as I shove upward and then eases me back onto the pillows. "Thalia is teaching her some sort of game with string. And you are under strict orders to rest."

I grind the heels of my palms against my eyes. "Thalia is almost holding this entire castle together singlehandedly." She's been the one watching over Amaya when I couldn't. *I* want those moments with my daughter. I want to play games with string and read books and steal pudding from the kitchens. I want it all. But I don't have any fucking *time*. Because if we don't stop this war, then there will *never* be a chance to find those moments of peace and get to know my daughter.

"Thalia is doing what she does best," he murmurs, sitting forward. "The role of a queen—or a prince—is never an easy one, Vi. There's always a cost. Let her support you."

"I hate being a queen."

His dark lashes stir against his cheeks as he glances down. "I always hated being a prince. When I was younger,

I craved the idea of it, but what I was truly looking for was acknowledgment from my mother."

That surprises me. He's so easy with power, so hungry for it. When he steps into a room, not once does he ever consider the fact he might not be the most important fae in it.

"Really? You were born to rule."

"Doesn't make it any less lonely," he murmurs, lifting his gaze to mine.

Those stormy green eyes, full of mysteries and shadows. I ease my head onto the pillow, half-tempted to close my eyes and rest again. "You're not lonely now."

He hesitates.

And my lashes flicker open because that wasn't an agreement.

"Sometimes...." He stalls again. "I'm not lonely anymore, Vi. Not the way I was." Pressing his fist against his chest he sighs. "But I'm dangerous—this thing inside me is dangerous. I can never relax, not fully. I can never let my guard down. Even with you, I have to hold on to myself."

And there's a certain sort of loneliness in that.

"You will never hurt me," I whisper.

"I will never hurt you," he whispers back. "But I don't know if *it* will."

"Trust yourself." I squeeze his hand, even as my stomach gives another embarrassing rumble. "You're in control, Thiago."

"How can you say that when Malakhai wielded its sword?"

His father springs to mind again, vicious and sneering. But I've seen Death ride through Thiago's eyes once

338

or twice. It's a cold, sinister look, full of emptiness. But it's not arrogant. "Malakhai may have wielded the sword. But he was the one who drove it through me. Not Death."

As if to remind me, there's a ghostly impression of... emptiness inside me. It's not pain, but it's unsettling enough. "Soup?" I ask hopefully, trying to distract him.

I need warmth. I need something wholesome and nourishing in my belly.

I need to slough off the icy prickle of goose bumps down my spine.

"Here," Thiago says, bringing the bowl of soup toward me and offering me the spoon. "Take small sips."

I do as I'm told, and it's delicious. A light chicken broth with rice that is spiced with something that reminds me of the food on the island of Stormlight. "A Stormhaven recipe?"

They like their spices there. And there's a hint of lemon underlying them.

"One of my favorites."

"I'd be delicate about this, but I think I want to drink it."

For the first time, a smile touches his mouth. "Then do so, Vi. You don't have to be polite in front of me." He sets the book in his lap aside and leans close enough to whisper, "I've heard all the unladylike sounds you make, and trust me... nothing would shock me."

I nearly choke on the soup, my eyes threatening retaliation even as I slurp it down.

Right now, hunger is more important than vengeance, but this debt will remain.

"You were reading to me?" I slowly lower the empty soup bowl.

"How did I know that a book like this would bring you back to life?" But he tilts the battered leather-bound cover toward me. "*Dukes Are Forever.*" His eyebrows shoot up. "I found it on your nightstand."

"I needed something to take my mind off things while you were gone." Heat flushes through my cheeks. "Before my mother took Imerys, she sent me several books. She knows a trader who has a Veilwalker on his crew. Someone who can pass through the Veil between worlds. She steals books and rare artefacts from the home world. When our kind fled from the advance of technology that world lost its magic, but the books are.... It's very romantic, even if I cannot fathom half the terms they use. An icy duke. The wife he was forced to marry...."

"Yes, I have been reading it to you." Thiago rifles his way through the book. "Two desks were harmed in the making of this book, Vi, I'm pretty sure it's not the romance you like."

I shrug helplessly. Out of all the gifts and kind words I received when he was gone, Imerys was the one who understood I needed that escape.

"So guilty," he says, setting the soup bowl aside. "Look at the blush on your cheeks."

Sliding his hand through my hair, he leans down and—

"No!" I squeak, turning my cheek to his lips. My mouth tastes like a bird shit in it.

I catch the faintest curve of a smile touching his lips. "Vi, I don't care."

"*I* do."

And if he's trying to kiss me, it's definitely time to get out of bed.

I wobble to my feet. Thiago sighs and captures my arm, and together we negotiate our way toward the wash chambers.

Where I firmly shut the door in his face.

Somehow, I perform my ablutions on unsteady legs and then I scrub my teeth until all I can taste is mint.

He waits for me outside, leaning back against the wall with his gaze a thousand miles away.

"What's wrong?"

"Wrong?" His head jacks toward me.

"You're standing right there, but your mind has gone wandering." I forge a smile. "Nanny Redwyne used to tell me I looked like that when I was off 'chasing down Will-o'-the-wisps.'"

"Finn has a theory. I'm trying to come to terms with it."

Sliding my arms around him, I toy with his hair. "Oh?"

It comes out in fragments. Finn's theory that Thiago might be able to use Darkyn steel to kill the Horned One. And his utter inability to wield it.

I ease my arms around him. "Maybe you're fighting so hard to keep Death at bay that innately, you're fighting yourself."

"That sounds infinitely wise." He breathes into my hair, his arms curling around me.

It feels so good to be in his arms. We've barely had a chance to catch our breath of late, and I took for granted the fact he'd always be here for me.

Until he wasn't.

341

"Maybe because I could be talking to myself." I murmur, stroking his arm.

Thiago looks down.

I shrug. "It's been a long couple of weeks." In more ways than one. "I missed you."

Fingertips press against my cheeks, and he leans down.

The kiss catches me by surprise.

Sweet.

Soft.

Gentle.

The ever-present chill deep inside me melts as his mouth caresses mine, his tongue teasing over my lower lip.

Thiago's hand slides through my hair, cupping the base of my skull, and then he hauls me toward him, claiming my mouth with firm demand. Everything in my body goes liquid. This is the heat I was missing. This is the fire. Conjured between us with the rough possessiveness of his touch until I can barely breathe, barely even remember I was injured....

"Missed you too," he breathes.

Sliding my palm down his abdomen, I reach for—

Thiago captures my wrist. "*Vi.*" The word is a warning, a scolding, a growl. "You were injured. Mariana has healed what she can, but she told me to avoid anything energetic for at least a week."

"Anything energetic?" I've barely gotten him back and now...?

Rough laughter tears from him. "You don't have to sound so disappointed."

I close my eyes and try to will the heavy, slick feeling between my thighs to go away. "I *am* disappointed."

"That's a shame." His voice dips lower. "A prince mustn't disappoint his queen." The backs of his knuckles find me through my nightgown, riding right over that sweet spot between my thighs.

I grab hold of his shirt, nearly off-balance. "But you just said—"

"No fucking. At least not with my cock. My tongue, on the other hand...."

There are no arguments here.

Grabbing a fistful of his shirt, I cry out as the back of his knuckles work me. *Fuck.* Shoving my fist against my mouth I sink my teeth into the fleshy skin on the back of my hand. If there's one thing that he's always known, it's exactly what my body needs. Or maybe, because he was my first, my only, he's somehow trained me to want what he can give.

His mouth crashes down upon mine again, hungry and urgent. Hauling me into his arms, he presses me against the wall, every hard inch of him aligning right where I need it. Palms pressed against his face, I eat at his mouth, desperate for more. There's a sense of restraint in that rock-hard body pinning me to the wallpaper. Tension quivering through him like some sort of bottled lightning. I grind against him, winning a curse from him, and then he rocks against me, fucking the hard ridge of his cock right where I want it.

"I'm trying to behave." He swears as he captures my wrists.

"I'm fine." The firm possession of his touch steals away the last of that icy pinprick deep inside me. I love the way he manacles me with his hands. I need heat in my veins. His tongue on my skin. The graze of his stubble on my thighs.

Kissing him sloppily, I grind back against him. "Make me burn."

Drawing back, a gasp escapes him. "I need my mouth on you. Now."

He takes a step back, toward the bed.

"No." I bite my lip. "Not the bed."

"Not the—?" A frown darkens his brow.

My gaze slides toward my vanity. "It's not quite a desk...."

A look of savage intensity darkens his face. "Oh," he murmurs, pushing me back toward the vanity. "So that's the way this plays out. I think you've been reading too much about this icy duke."

"He's not always icy," I whisper. "But he *is* very delicious."

"Mmm." Thiago sets both hands on my hips and lifts me onto the vanity. Resting on his knuckles he leans close enough for me to feel the rasp of his stubble against my cheeks as he breathes in my ear, "But I have something this duke doesn't have...."

"Oh?" Every inch of me goes liquid with anticipation. "What is that?"

The first faint caress whispers up my thigh as if invisible knuckles brush against me. My nightgown slides up, revealing the edge of my drawers.

"*Magic.*"

Chapter Twenty-Six

Iskvien

T hiago tells me the truth that night, as I curl up in
his arms.

There will never be another child.

Strangely, it doesn't hurt as much as it should. The
Mother of Night once told me I would only ever bear one
child, so I never expected more. But the shock of it. The
surprise. I don't know how to process it, except to know
that Thiago shares my pain.

A single tear slides down my cheek as I rest my cheek on his chest.

Because there's a restless feeling inside me, a feeling my family isn't complete.

Or maybe that's merely the impact of everything I'm dealing with in regards to Amaya.

I hate you, she'd said.

And then she spent all afternoon weeping on my shoulder, begging me for forgiveness.

"I didn't mean it. I didn't mean it."

"I know," I'd told her, kissing her forehead. Somehow, in some ways, it feels like we've taken an enormous step forward in our relationship. And I will cling to that, even as I work my way slowly through this other quiet sense of grief.

It is, quite frankly, a lot.

I'm sentenced to two days of bed rest, which would be far more onerous if Thiago didn't make good on his promise to entertain me regularly.

But I'm tired of being trapped in my rooms.

Stirring the coals, I stare into the flickering flames.

This silence from my mother is troubling. Every day the unseelie army creeps closer, with more unseelie flocking to Morwenna of Isembold and Angharad the Black's armies, according to Thalia.

Maybe that's Mother's game—to wait us out until we're either forced to make the first move, or must pre-empt an invasion of Asturia in order to take out one of the armies coming at us.

If only we knew what was happening in the north.

I've sent messages to Blaedwyn, telling her to prepare

her armies and keep an eye on her fellow queens. She's starting to feel the pinch of our deal, because her tone was quite acidic, but I know she'll bring her warriors when we need them.

She has to, or the Erlking will have free reign to renege on his promise.

So that is one problem solved.

I stir the flames with my magic, forging them into little foxes running through the woods.

"Will I be able to do that?" Amaya murmurs, lying on her stomach on the rug in front of the fire. She's barely left my side since I woke.

"Maybe." I twist the flames to represent dolphins leaping clear of the sea. It's frustrating how easily I can control these flames, but when it comes to forging a sword or a bow and arrow, I have to wield my entire concentration merely to hold it.

Thiago thinks it has something to do with my discomfort with killing.

I can wield a merciless blade when I'm backed into a corner—or when I'm fighting for someone I love—but I will always hesitate when it comes to what feels like outright murder.

"My magic came in when I was nearly twelve," I murmur. "It's usually a little later for most fae, but sometimes circumstances force us to the react. And if your magic is strong like your father's, then it may be sooner."

"Why did your magic come so early?" she asks.

It's something I've not truly discussed with her. "My mother... wasn't a very nice mother. She had banned the reading of certain books, and when she caught my nurse

347

reading one of them to me, she had her tortured. My magic simply erupted from me. Maybe I was trying to protect Nanny. Or maybe I was simply overwhelmed. But I nearly burned the castle down."

Amaya's eyes go wide. "Will I be able to control flame too?"

"Fae gifts are often hereditary. You might have your father's gifts. You might have mine. We won't know." I smile gently. "My sister and I could both wield fire, but she's better at it than I am. Or maybe more practiced."

"Your sister?" Those eyes widen even further. "The one who was married to the goblin?"

"Maybe." We've still had no word from Lysander or Edain. Baylor can sometimes communicate with his brother over such a distance, but they have to both be aligned to each other. "We don't know what's happened to Andraste yet."

"I'd like to meet her one day."

I stir the flames into a whirlpool with a lazy finger. I can't help picturing Andi. I never got the chance to thank her for saving Amaya for me. "You will. I'm sure of it. We'll get her back and—"

"*Vi!*" a voice gasps.

"What was that?" Amaya demands, sitting upright. "In the fire?"

Something definitely flickered there. I focus on the flames again, reaching for them, through them—

A face appears, carved of flame. Trying to say something.

I shove to my feet, knocking over the glass of water. "*Andraste?*"

"Vi?" Suddenly her voice echoes through my ears. "Can you hear me?"

Falling to my knees, I lean toward the flame. "*Yes!* Yes, I can hear you! Where are you? Are you safe? Are you all right?"

There's a slight discordant buzzing in my ears. "—I'm safe.... Captured by the goblin king... but... fine.... going on? Amaya?"

"She's safe. Thank you. Thank you for everything you did for us. She's safe and she's here with us. Have you heard from Lysander and Edain yet? They're coming to rescue you."

"Edain's... here." Andraste's face becomes worried. "... You need... get to Eidyn... He's coming."

"Who's coming? What's wrong?"

"Urach! Urach's coming!"

"Urach? He's coming to Eidyn?" The goblin king she was sent to marry. "Andraste, where are you?"

"We're coming... day's ride."

"Who is we? When?"

I suddenly realize I'm talking to nothing but flames.

She's gone.

And with her, that last vital snatch of information I was trying to discover.

* * *

On day three, I'm finally allowed out of my bedchambers when news of what Mother's been up to finally hits.

Thiago reclines beside me at the dining table, reading through reports on news from the border. Baylor punctuates the silences by filling us in with regards to the situation at Eidyn. He and Eris make daily visits to the staging areas, but until the battle is engaged, their job is here, talking strategy to Thiago and discussing intel with Thalia.

"So Adaia's finished staging," Thalia mutters, toying with one of the poached pears on her porridge. "I don't understand why she hasn't pushed her forces across the river. News from Evaron's scouts in the north suggest the goblins are only days away. And Eidyn is the best place for her to launch an offensive. The keep there is on a strip of land that juts into the river. Whoever controls the keep controls the Firenze and all trade along it. And this side of Eidyn is a marsh. Our forces have to camp miles away from the keep, which means a limited response time. She has all the keys to success."

"She has some other piece in play that we can't yet see yet," I mutter, because my mother always does.

Thiago laces his fingers together. "Adaia won't launch an offensive until she's certain she can win it. She can't afford to lose. The border lords in the north of Asturia are unstable—or unwilling allies—and her hold on the south of the kingdom relies upon the myth of her power. The last time she went to war against Evernight, she was soundly defeated. She assumed we were backwater unseelie monsters with little coordination or battle experience. She learned from that moment. She won't risk it again until she is certain of victory. Or else her southern lords might start questioning whether she's truly an untouchable queen."

"If they dare, then she'll simply slaughter them."

"True. But that will not help her cause in the long run. It will even erode it, perhaps. The myth of power is a valuable weapon," Baylor murmurs. "Take Eris, for example. They call her the Detroyer, and bards sing stories of her cruelty and her viciousness all through the south. She's Evernight's secret, most dangerous weapon. When she walks onto a field of battle, armies break at the mere sight of her and orderly lines shatter as their foot troops scramble to escape. For four centuries, she's barely had to fight, because everyone remembers what she did at the fields of Nevernight.

"Fae warriors come to try their hand against her, hoping to conquer her and force her into a marriage. With every defeat, the legend grows. But what happens if one of them beats her? What happens if someone on the field of battle manages to wound her? Or some male defeats her and wins her hand? The myth shatters. Suddenly, she's no longer a vengeful god to be feared. She becomes mortal in more ways than one. And the next time she walks onto the field of battle, her enemies will not flee. They may tremble, but they will know she *can* fall.

"The same is to be said of Adaia." Baylor's silvery lashes flutter down over his eyes. "She's spent centuries shoring up her reputation after her last defeat. She rules her court with an iron fist, and her courtiers bow and scrape because she breathes fear into a room merely by walking into it. But thirteen years ago, her reputation suffered another blow. You, Vi. You escaped her. You defied her. Suddenly, all her vassals mutter among themselves. Is the queen vulnerable? Could they take a tilt at her throne? Could she fall against Evernight? She has to win this war. She needs to, if she's to hold onto her power. And so she will wait until our backs are against the wall. Destroy her myth and you destroy her power."

I can't help thinking of my mother and the last time I saw her—the night we stole her crown from her. Maybe he's right, because, although the memory of her voice can still make me flinch, I have hope now.

My mother *can* be defeated.

"*We could destroy her,*" the crown whispers. "*It would be so easy to make her grovel.*"

I close my mind to its evil.

"Here's some good news," Thiago says, reading a message. "Prince Kyrian is offering as much assistance as he can afford to offer. Twenty of his ships are sitting off the Asturian coast—precisely as many as the Seelie Alliance states he may have, without crossing treatise restrictions—but he's made no other move yet. He says he'll continue to hold them there until escalation."

"What does that mean?" I lick my porridge off the spoon.

"It means that if he joins us too soon, then it will be seen as an act of aggression within the alliance," Thiago says with a sigh. "But he's got my back. It's probably the reason Adaia hasn't sent her troops across the Firenze river yet. If she does, then she's waging war on another kingdom within the alliance, which means Kyrian—through right of his alliance with Evernight—is free to attack her ports."

"He's what?" Thalia sets her own reports down. "How long have those ships been sitting there?"

"Weeks," Thiago replies, running his fingers through my hair and massaging my scalp.

Her lips press firmly together. "And he didn't deign to inform us of this before you returned?"

Thiago arches a brow and glances at his missive again. "There appears to have been some sort of miscommunication.... Something about 'I sent an envoy. He was returned post-haste.'"

"That son-of-a-selkie." Thalia's chair scrapes back as she stands. "His envoy sneered at me, called me a 'saltkissed bastard' and then told me Prince Kyrian demanded to know how we'd gotten you killed. What else does he say?"

"Not much. Though there is a pointed question about how the fuck did I come back from the dead?"

"I am going to murder him with my bare hands," she growls.

"After the war," Baylor says calmly.

A fluttering demi-fey launches through the window, sagging as it carries something heavy in its hands. It drops the letter in Thalia's lap, before collapsing beside the tiny bowl of milk she has sitting on the table beside her for precisely this reason.

Thalia's face pales as she notes the signet pressed into the seal on the letter.

"What is it?" Thiago barks.

"Trouble." She says, slitting the seal and then reading the scroll. Her face pales further, if that's possible.

"Trouble?" Thiago stops playing with my hair.

Thalia hands him the letter.

The seal on it arrests the breath in my lungs. It's the Askan seal; a golden serpent coiled on a dark green background.

"What the fuck does Maren want?" Thiago sits up,

almost dislodging me as he runs his thumb under the seal and tears it open.

The expression on his face tightens as his gaze scans the letter.

"What is it?" I ask breathlessly.

Slowly, he lowers it. "Queen Maren has called an emergency meeting of the Seelie Alliance in Aska. Your mother claims Evernight launched an assault upon her castle and stole her crown. She demands it back upon pain of death. And she insists the Seelie Alliance judge the case."

What? "That bitch!" I snatch the letter off him. "She attacked us first. She sent her fucking Deathguard into the streets and dropped a bramblethine in the dam above the city! Does she not think that everyone is aware that her armies have been massing at the border for weeks?"

"She hasn't sent them across," Thalia murmurs, dragging Grimm into her arms and rubbing his head. "If I know Adaia, she'll claim she's responding to a threat from us."

"You wanted a chance to get inside the Tower of Dreams in Aska," Thiago muses, offering me a hand to draw me to my feet. "You want your prophecy? Maren's just opened the gates to her court."

"And she'll be watching every move we make," I point out.

"Yes. Which means we can't make that move. But I think I know someone who won't be watched. Someone who pledged support provided we take all the risks." His smile turns dangerous. "If Lucere wants your mother's blade lifted from her throat, then it's about time she took a damned risk herself."

Chapter Twenty-Seven

Iskvien

"Unhand me, you enormous lummox" comes a shrill voice.

"I was merely trying to assist you over the rocks."

"Do I *look* like I need assistance, you dirty, sweaty stable boy?"

"Do you really want me to answer that?" This time, the response is a growl.

Baylor stalks out of the shadows of the cavern, wearing

the filthiest expression I've ever seen on him. His silvery-blond hair is drawn back in a half-knot, and tendrils of it fall over the tanned skin of his face. It's the only hint of his identity. The rest of him is covered in a rough wool cloak that's seen better days, a dirty white linen shirt and dark brown wool trousers. The hilt of his sword peeks through the cloak, revealing the snarling wolf head on the pommel, but apart from that, he might be any anonymous mercenary.

He gives me a long-suffering look that promises I'd better make this worth his while. We slipped through the Hallow an hour ago and sent Baylor ahead into Ravenspire with a private message for the queen. I'm not quite sure how he managed to slip inside her personal chambers unnoticed, but clearly, the altercation has roused Lucere's hackles.

I've also never seen Baylor show such frustration before.

He's a rock, his calm expression a shield wall of protection.

And he looks like he wants to haul Lucere over his shoulder and go dump her in an icy river somewhere.

"Long trip?" Thiago mutters, trying to hide his amusement behind a fake cough.

"Felt like days," Baylor replies stoically.

Someone curses as they trip over a rock. Light spills through a hole far above us, but it's difficult to see the path toward this spot, unless you have preternatural eyesight like Baylor does.

"Stubborn as a mule," Baylor grumbles, turning to offer the queen his arm—which she waves away.

"Lucere?" I lower the hood of my black cloak.

The Queen of Ravenal responds in kind, drawing the soft fur-lined cloak back from her face, revealing the silken shine of her raven-dark hair and the paleness of her features as she takes her place beside Baylor. The spear of light highlights the tips of her eyelashes, staining them silver, and the scarlet of her cloak sets off her features so prettily, I'm fairly certain her outfit was chosen with great care.

Say what she will about no longer pining for my husband, I'm not entirely certain I believe her.

"It seems the rumors of your death were greatly exaggerated," Lucere says to Thiago before her attention shifts to me. "Unless the information I offered provided some... recourse."

Thiago shifts uneasily. "Evernight extends its thanks for the part you played in my return. You weren't seen?"

Lucere settles a frosty expression upon Baylor. "We weren't seen. This enormous monolith *rolled me in a rug* and threw me over his shoulder. I daresay even my brother's ravens didn't mark my absence."

"A rug?" No wonder she looks like a hissing cat.

Baylor shrugs. "She was taking too long and protesting too much. We were going to be seen."

Thiago pinches the bridge of his nose in a way I'm interpreting as *should have brought Finn instead*. "Evernight extends its apologies."

"Oh, it will," Lucere promises. "Now the courtesies are done, to what does Ravenal owe the unexpected pleasure of being dragged to this slime-infested cavern?" Her dark eyes glitter. "It wouldn't be a certain forthcoming meeting, would it? You're not here to extend your sympathies upon the loss of my sister, Thiago, so please, let us not mince words. What do you want?"

It's interesting how the presence of both men seems to have raised her hackles. She certainly wasn't like this in Ceres.

"We need to get our hands on a certain prophecy that is located in the heart of the Askan court," I tell her, "and this meeting of the alliance is the perfect opportunity to do so. Maren's dream thieves have filled an entire tower within the Askan court with glass-spun globes of dreams. One of them holds the words of the prophet who spoke it. It's the only existing copy of this prophecy. If we can get our hands on it, we may be able to thwart the Horned One's invasion."

Lucere's brows rise. "You've got to be kidding me. Every eye is going to be upon the two of you and your entire party. Maren won't let you out of her sight for an instant. You'll never get inside this tower."

Thiago smiles faintly. "True."

We both look at her.

"But neither Maren nor my mother is going to be watching their dear friend, the Queen of Ravenal," I point out.

"Absolutely *not*."

"You want our help with Imerys?" Thiago says. "Then you can cursed well share your allotment of the risk. We need that prophecy, and you're the only one who can get it."

"I like my head right where it is, thank you very much."

"Maybe the Horned One can appreciate your pretty face when he rolls right through the Seelie Alliance," he snarls.

"We fought him off once."

"*We?* You weren't even alive then. It took everything the Seelie Alliance had to survive that war. The only reason we won was because of the gamble we took in locking away the Old Ones. Now we're facing the entire might of Unseelie with a fractured southern alliance, two vicious queens who will stab us in the back the second we march north, and the only weapon I have right now is an untried Ravenal queen who couldn't find her courage if she searched for it with both hands—"

"Courage?" Lucere's entire face goes white as if he slapped her. "I am *trying* to keep my sister alive. I am *trying* to save my people. And I am doing it all with no fucking army, a treasury my grandmother bled dry, and an ally that dares—he *dares*—insist I take a risk when he's the fucking reason we're in this mess. If Adaia gains even the slightest hint I'm helping you, I am dead. And without me, my entire fucking kingdom burns. You think I care about the risk to *myself*? I am the *only* thing holding my court together right now. I've had two assassination attempts alone this week, not to mention the past fucking three months. You don't get to look down your nose at me. You *don't*. You wouldn't even be standing here if it wasn't for me."

"Thiago." I rest my hand on his sleeve. We share a look. I understand his frustration and his desperation, but I've also been in Lucere's shoes.

He breathes out a huff of air that says, *you deal with her.*

I go to Lucere. "It's been a trying week for all of us. We understand that. And we are grateful for the assistance you've provided us so far."

359

She cuts Thiago a look. "So grateful it's practically dripping from your tongues."

I capture her hand and squeeze it. "*I* need your help, Lucere. I need that prophecy. I need to know how to kill the Horned One." And then I release a low breath. Trust cannot be won by force. It can only be won by extending an offer of friendship. And friendship is forged from truth. "When I bound myself to the lands, I was able to access the power of the leylines that runs through the Hallows. There's a possibility I may be able to use that power against the Horned One."

"The Hallow in Ceres?" Her eyes sharpen with interest. She's only recently bound herself to Ravenal.

Another slow breath. "All the Hallows."

The remaining color drains from her face. She said once she had not Imerys's love for books, but she's clearly well-read enough to understand what I'm suggesting. "That's impossible. The only ones who could do that are—"

"The Old Ones."

"Vi," Thiago cautions.

A thousand emotions dance through her dark eyes as they dart between us. Knowledge dawns, dark and horrified. She sucks in a sharp breath. "There was always a rumor about the night your father appeared in your mother's court. My grandmother's little birds were the best in the realms. Connall of Saltmist sired you, they said, but according to Grandmother's sources, Connall never crossed the seas." Her voice drops to a whisper. "And you were conceived on Samhain, the one night of the year when the Old Ones can walk the realm."

I squeeze her fingers. "If I can learn how to access the power of the Hallows, then there's a chance I can kill him."

"Why are you telling me this?" she demands, tugging her fingers free of mine and pacing. "I could destroy you with this knowledge."

I go after her. "Because I'm not just asking you to trust me. I'm asking you to be my ally in more than mere politics. I'm asking you to be my friend."

The words make her reel. Again, she shoots my husband a look. "I don't *have* friends." It's a rare admission. "Grandmother made sure of that. Imerys and Corvin don't know how lucky they were not to be the heir. This goes against everything she taught me. Everything I believe."

"You said you wanted to escape from her when you were younger," I press. "Well, maybe, what you're looking for doesn't come in the form of a strange prince who might sweep you away from your court. Step into your power, Lucere. You're only alone if you choose to be. Become my friend and maybe, if we survive all of this, we can both help to rebuild a new world." I take a stab in the dark. "One where little girls aren't locked away from their brothers and sisters and forced to become something they don't want to be. One where they don't have to bury their hearts because they've been told it's only a weakness. One where our king-doms can find peace. That's what I want, Lucere. I want the chance to get to know my daughter. I want to know I never have to look over my shoulder for my mother's knife ever again. I want to be free of her, but most importantly, I want to be free of her ghost—the one that impacts every choice I make, the one that whispers doubt into my ear every day and every night. I want to know who I can become without her influence. Help me, Lucere, and we'll help get your sister back."

Tears gleam in her eyes. "You're going to get me killed. I know it. But there's a part of me that actually believes... that we might have a chance."

This time, when I take her hands, she squeezes back.

And then she finally nods, clenching her eyes shut as if she can't even believe herself what she's about to say. "I'll help you. Maia help me, but I'll get this fucking prophecy for you."

Turning away, she dashes her hand against her left eye. "Now, what do we need to do?"

Thank all the gods. I tug a map from inside the satchel slung over my shoulder and unroll it over a boulder. "First, I owe you this. This is a map of the layout of Hawthorne Castle." I point to the northern towers. "My mother will be keeping Imerys here. Ostensibly, she'll be serving as my mother's lady-in-waiting, but mother will house her here, where the guard can lock her down should there be even the merest hint of trouble."

Lucere splays the map wide with desperate hands. "Hawthorne Castle is a trap. If I make the slightest move toward regaining my sister, I'll lose her forever." She forces the next words past her lips. "I'm no match for Adaia."

"You don't have to be." It's a dangerous confession. "We all know I'm going to have to face my mother someday soon. Thiago and I have been thinking... maybe it would be best if the meeting occurred on our terms."

"You're going to *attack* Hawthorne Castle?"

Thiago argued against trusting Lucere with this infor-mation, but I think she's in too deep now. And if there's one thing I believe, it's that Lucere will do anything to rescue her sister.

"We can go to war against Mother," I tell her. "Our armies against hers. Our magic against hers. Thousands will die, and with two opposing armies coming at our backs, I daresay we'll lose. Or we can pick the battleground."

"A two-pronged attack," Thiago grinds out. "One party can retrieve your sister. The other party will be comprised of me and Vi. We draw her attention while you get your sister out. And we neutralize Adaia while we do it."

Which would leave us free to turn our attention toward the goblins and the unseelie. Queen Maren is the only hold-out among the Seelie Alliance who supports my mother. With Adaia gone, I cannot see why she wouldn't join with us to protect the seelie kingdoms. I may even be able to rouse what is left of Asturia to join us.

No seelie fae wants to see the southern kingdoms overrun by the northerners. And the Horned One is a figure of terror; the one we whisper about when we tell children not to stray too far at night.

A common enemy. A common cause. We may just be able to turn the tables on my mother's plotting.

"When?" A strange light comes into her eyes.

"Get us the prophecy. We'll tell you the details," Thiago replies coolly.

Lucere gnaws on her finger as she circles the map. "If it fails...."

"Your sister dies," he says.

"That is *not* inspiring."

"War is coming, Lucere." He takes a step toward her, towering over her. "If Adaia wins this bout—if she kills the pair of us—then where does that leave you and your sister? Who else will stand against her? Who else has the strength to stand against her? You will never have another chance for freedom. She will roll over you, and the next thing you know, she'll be wearing your crown too. So consider this: If you sell us out to Adaia, then you sign your own doom."

"I am *well* aware of that, thank you."She scowls at Thiago and then rolls up the map. "Now, we have seven hours before we're all due in Aska. How do I get inside this tower of dreams? Maren's offered us rooms at court. Perhaps I could slip away and leave Corvin as a decoy, but if I dare take too many guards then I risk being seen."

And without guards....

The Askan court is dangerous, after all.

"Baylor," Thiago murmurs to his friend.

Baylor steps forward, tearing off his cloak and unbuckling his sword belt. "You owe me for this."

The faintest of smiles crosses Thiago's lips. "I thought you'd enjoy a little breaking and entering. Darkness knows, you've spent the past five hundred years being the respectful member of my court. Surely it's time to have a little fun?" He turns to Lucere. "Baylor will accompany you."

Both to keep an eye on her and to prevent her from being killed.

Lucere jerks back. "Absolutely not."

"He will protect you and ensure that—"

"Are you *trying* to get me killed?" Lucere gestures to Baylor. "How am I supposed to hide... *this* in my party? Everyone knows who the Blackheart is. And who he serves. And he's not exactly... subtle in feature."

"Trust me," Thiago purrs. "Nobody will suspect a thing."

Baylor hands him his sword belt and reaches over his shoulder to grab a fistful of his shirt. "Because I won't look like this."

He tugs his shirt off, revealing the enormous swathe of muscle that runs across his ribs and down his abdomen. Baylor's a warrior, and it shows. Every inch of him is cut lean and tight, and as his shoulders flex, muscle ripples in the silvery light.

Lucere's gaze slides over *every* inch of him.

"*Enjoying the view?*" Thiago links with me, though he sounds amused.

"*Kind of enjoying the response.*"

"*We often joke that if he didn't scowl half as much, the ladies of Ceres would be flinging their undergarments at him when he rode through the city.*"

I slide my gaze toward my husband. He insisted upon bringing Baylor for this mission, and now I can't help wondering if he did it on purpose to push Lucere off-balance. Finn's gorgeous, but he's the same kind of charming wastrel who flocks to her at court.

Baylor is something else.

He looks good in court attire, even if he usually disdains it. But when you rub a bit of dirt on him, suddenly heads turn in every direction. And the most amusing part of it is that Baylor has no idea of the ruckus he causes.

"What are you *doing*?" Lucere squeaks in horror.

"Don't want to rip my clothes," Baylor tells her, tossing his shirt toward her.

She catches it with a shriek of horror and then flings it away as if he just threw a rat at her.

Baylor's hands drop to his pants, a challenging look in his golden eyes as he stares right through her.

I turn my back on him, because even though the fae aren't shy about nudity, I really don't need to see Baylor like this. He's so enormous that I'm pretty sure the rest of him will be in perfect proportion, and I will never be able to look Thalia in the face the next time she pokes him and teases him about being Evernight's secret weapon.

Lucere, apparently, has no such compunctions.

A belt hits the ground, and then the meaty sound of leather slaps as he clearly strips off his breeches.

Lucere's eyes widen and then, as if she simply can't help herself, her gaze drops and her mouth goes wide.

I was right. Judging by the way her eyes turn into saucers, he's definitely in proportion.

"She just turned an odd shade of scarlet," Thiago muses.

"You planned this, didn't you?"

"Got to keep her off-balance somehow. And I think Baylor's enjoying getting her back for the 'dirty, sweaty stable boy' comment."

A warm gush of magic washes over us.

Suddenly, a prickle of trepidation trails down my spine. It's the same feeling you get in the woods when you know something is watching you. Something dangerous.

A low growl echoes through the cavern, something that's definitely not fae anymore.

"It's done," Thiago says.

There's no longer any sign of Baylor when I turn.

Instead, an enormous silvery creature stretches before

locking his golden eyes upon Lucere as if he wants to eat her all up. He gives her a wolfish smile, and there are *teeth* everywhere.

It's not a wolf.

It makes wolves look like something that would be lovely to pat.

This thing looks like it just slid straight out of my nightmares.

She stares in horror at him. "What am I meant to do with him?"

"Here," Thiago calls, tossing her a golden leash and collar that he'd kept tucked in his pocket. "It seems you've found yourself a new pet for your trip to Aska. Follow his lead. Baylor will protect you. Just don't try and choke him with the collar, or you'll find out how sharp those teeth truly are."

Lucere fumbles with the leash, her lip curling in a half-snarl as she cuts Thiago a look. "It doesn't escape my notice that I've effectively got a spy in my party."

Thiago slings an arm around my shoulder. "We trust you, Lucere." And then he laughs under his breath. "Because I don't think you'd dare betray us."

Chapter Twenty-Eight

Iskvien

Five hours later, we land in the Hallow right in the heart of the Askan court.

Muraid of Aska awaits our party, one hand resting negligently on her sword hilt. It's not a threat. The rangy warrior simply lives and breathes the sword, and while her expression gives nothing away, she does incline her head toward us. "Welcome, Your Highnesses. Thalia. Queen Maren grants you safe passage to the Kingdom of Aska and has sent me to bring you to your chambers."

"An honor," Thiago announces, clasping her forearm.

The faintest hint of a smile touches her thin lips. "I heard the strangest story. But if you are here to greet me, then clearly, I was mistaken. It's good to see you again, Thiago." She turns to Eris. "Silvernaught. Would you care to cross swords if we are granted some spare moments to partake?"

"You're asking me to put steel in my hand?" Eris can't keep the surprise off her face.

Muraid grins; a savage smile. "We've never danced before. And I have always wondered...."

"Go on," Thiago says, clearly seeing Eris's interest. "But the question is, shall she have time? I'm afraid I'm not entirely certain of the program, considering we have been accused of a crime by the Queen of Asturia."

"If you're suggesting I betray my queen's secrets," Muraid chides him gently, "then you're sorely misguided. The Queen of Asturia arrived three hours ago. Beyond that, I do not know what the days will bring."

Mother's already here.

Thalia arches her brow just slightly.

Nothing has changed about Muraid.

Her shock of white hair is cropped at the sides and longer on top, where it's been waxed into a stylish quiff. She has the most refined features, strangely delicate for a general with the reputation she wields, and in a certain light there's an androgynous quality about her. But beneath the smile is steel, and her mismatched eyes—one brown, one green— rake over me as if she's determined to discover all my secrets.

"You look as lovely as the day you first arrived in these courts," she says to me, "though power sits well on you

369

also." She gives a brusque nod. "Be warned, Your Highness. There are those who may not greet you as kindly as myself."

Etan is at court.

It's as much of a warning as anything else she's offered.

I spent two years at the Askan court when I was younger, serving as Maren's lady-in-waiting. I know now that my mother saw it as a way to remove me from her court and a means to proffer me up to one of Maren's many male relatives as a potential bride.

But at the time, it felt like being flung at the wolves.

And the biggest wolf of all was Etan, though it took me months to see through him.

Golden and charming, his blue eyes promised me the world even as his tongue twisted lies into being. Lies that I stupidly believed. And I was so desperate for attention—for escape—that I closed my eyes and ears to any hints that aught seemed awry.

It wasn't until I caught him in bed with a blue-haired sprite that I realized the truth.

I was a game to be played, my heart simply another notch to add to his belt.

And when I defied him, his interest in me only heightened. Suddenly, I wasn't merely another summer's entertainment. I became his obsession.

At the Queensmoot where I met Thiago, he pushed Queen Maren into forming a betrothal alliance with my mother. Once promised my hand, when he couldn't win my heart with it, his smile turned vicious.

"You're mine, you frigid little bitch...."

I'll never forget those words.

And my mother is such a bitch that while she stole my

memories of Thiago, she left those ones imprinted on my soul.

I ease out a steadying breath. Etan can't hurt me anymore. He can never hurt me again. Not without causing a diplomatic catastrophe. "If anyone greets me as such, then they may find that I am not quite as defenseless as I once was."

"Queen Maren has extended her protection over this court. There is to be no blood shed in these halls. Or one will face her wrath."

It's a good thing I've learned to wield the Hallows.

Because if Etan takes a tilt at me, I'm quite happy to dump him at Charun, where I can set him on fire without being called to task for it.

Maren can't argue with that, can she?

"Who else has arrived?" Thiago asks, offering me his arm. "*What was that expression for?*" he asks privately.

Shit.

He met Etan many moons ago and knows what happened between us. If he even suspects Etan's the reason my heart kicked into a gallop, then he may just paint the walls red with his blood. He's wearing his "charming prince" smile today, but the Darkyn warrior lurks beneath the surface. I can't risk rousing him.

"*I'll tell you later.*" I pat his arm with a smile.

Which he sees right through. "*Vi—*"

"Lucere of Ravenal arrived an hour ago," Muraid interrupts—thank all the gods—leading us toward the marble arch that leads into the gardens. Some long-ago sculptor carved dozens of stars into the arch—including one that almost makes me stop in my tracks.

A six-pointed star.

The Dream Thief's symbol.

The entire court is decorated with such stars, but I've never put two and two together.

"We're still awaiting Kyrian and his retinue," Muraid snorts. "He likes to make an entrance."

"Either that," Thalia offers, "or he's struggling to get into those tight leather trousers he prefers."

Muraid almost smiles. "Could take a few more hours then. This way."

We fall into line behind her.

The Court of Nightmares is an incongruity.

The entire city is carved of alabaster. Every palace hall features a pale white dome, and scrolled columns line the walkways. There are inner gardens and courtyards opening off nearly every room, and peacocks strut through the trees, along with elegant hunting hounds.

It's the most beautiful court in the south, and yet, even as we wind our way between fountains, I can't help feeling as though danger watches us through the verdant leaves.

"We're heading to the Crystal Palace," I murmur to Thiago, sliding my arm through his. "Maren must mean business."

Inside the open hall, Queen Maren reclines on her throne, her long raven-dark hair falling in a silken waterfall down her spine. A bustier of gold feathers cups her breasts, and I'm not sure if they're carved from gold itself, or if some poor hapless firebird gave up its glory for her. The scrap of black silk around her waist could be a skirt, though the slit up her thigh reveals more leg than one would expect. They say she's the most beautiful woman in the world.

She's also the most merciless.

It makes my mother seethe when she's in private. For all my mother's chiseled blonde beauty, Maren is something else. The cold blue stare of her almond-shaped eyes is practically otherworldly, and the only hint of softness she ever reveals is when she allows Muraid, her lover, to rest her hand on her shoulder.

"His Highness, Prince Thiago of Evernight," the herald calls, before he clears his throat. "And his queen, Iskvien of... Evernight."

Maren's gaze lingers on me as I square my shoulders.

I'm no longer the hapless young woman thrown into a merciless court that threatened to eat me alive.

I'm a queen, and Thalia took great pains to ensure I look like one.

A swath of black velvet cups my breasts, though the panel of sheer mesh beneath it bares my stomach until it once again flows into midnight silk that cascades to the floor. Dozens of glittering gold beads shimmer in the fabric like a small galaxy, but it's the chains that are hooked to my bodice and drape around my waist that catch the eye. The only thing holding the bodice together is the thin gold chains that hook onto the beaten gold circlet around my neck.

A sheer mesh cape spills from my shoulders. Amaya's eyes went very wide when I walked out in the dress, and she grew a little quiet as Thalia set the golden diadem in my hair.

"Now this," Thalia told her, "is a *dress*. Every girl should know how to make an entrance at least once in her life, and in this world, sometimes the only way to survive is to look like you'd crush someone's throat beneath your heel."

Amaya's nose wrinkled. "Is it comfortable?"

"Yes." I paused to press a kiss to the top of her head. "As long as I don't breathe."

To which Thalia gave me an exasperated swat.

Thiago's appreciation for the dress was another thing entirely. He couldn't take his eyes off me from the moment I entered the Hallow to the moment we reappeared in the heart of the Askan Hallow. And that look said *I'm going to remove that dress with my teeth later.*

Sometimes, letting Thalia dress me is worth it.

"We give welcome to Evernight," Maren calls. "Let no blood be spilled in my court, nor any grievances aired beyond that which we are here for today. You are granted my offer of protection whilst beneath this roof."

"Our thanks," Thiago says.

Lucere sits stiffly beside her, arms resting upon the throne she's been given. An enormous silver wolf-like creature lies at her feet, his eyes blinking open when we appear.

Baylor very slowly gives me a wink.

But it's to my mother that my attention turns.

The red-and-gold livery of the Asturian delegation sends a shiver down my spine. A member of her gold-plated Deathguard stands on each side of her throne.

But it's the expression Mother wears that makes my heart sink.

Flawless in what looks like liquid gold, her lip curls when she beholds me.

Any warmth she might have once greeted me with is gone. Nothing remains of the woman who occasionally rocked me to sleep. I am finally dead to her, and while it's a relief in some ways, in other ways, I can't help mourning the loss.

I have no mother.

Hard footsteps follow us.

Kyrian and his coterie of red-clad warriors.

He strolls into the room like a pirate fresh off the water. His long dark hair is bound back with a leather thong, and he wears a loose white shirt rolled up at the elbows beneath an open leather vest. Compared to the four queens in the room, he's made precisely zero effort and his expression says *let's get this bullshit over with*.

"Thiago," he says, clapping hands with my husband and hauling him in for a hug. He mutters something in Thiago's ear, giving him an extra squeeze, but I can't quite hear it.

Then he turns to me.

"Your Majesty." Kyrian actually leans down to press a kiss against my cheek. He pauses. "I'm sorry. For not being there for you when you needed me. Suffice it to say I was keeping trouble off your back."

The words scrape something raw within me. Thiago's back, but that feeling of standing alone—of the nights spent poring over maps trying to figure out how I was going to keep my people safe—rises like a lump in my throat.

"Thank you." I squeeze his fingers.

Maybe it's even an offering of peace between us.

Kyrian and I have never seen eye to eye. I know it's not personal. He doesn't believe in true love, nor in loyalty between lovers. But that's his own flaw to deal with, not mine.

But he's always said I'd be the death of Thiago, and in some ways, his prediction came true.

"Lucere." He turns and gives a nod toward the young Queen of Ravenal as he prowls toward the seat set out for him. "Maren. Adaia." This time he sounds bored. "Let's get on with this... meeting."

Not the word he'd like to say.

It's a gauntlet thrown down before the three queens. He and Thiago have always held an alliance of sorts against Maren and my mother, and he's telling them nothing has changed.

Thiago escorts me to my chair, and Thalia gestures our party into place behind them.

My mother drums her fingers slowly on the throne-like chair she lurks upon. Raking her gaze over me—I know exactly what she's searching for—she turns to Maren. "Let us begin."

"As you all know, Asturia's armies have marched toward the border with Evernight," Mother begins.

"We may have heard something about that, yes," Kyrian says sarcastically. "If you cross that border, Adaia, then you break the covenant. You shatter the alliance's terms for peace. Both myself—and these two beautiful queens at my side—will be forced to come to Evernight's aid." His eyes glitter. "It will be such a regrettable turn of events."

Maren hides a small smile.

Mother leans back in her chair. "But I was not the

aggressor, Prince Kyrian. Have I not the right to hold Evernight accountable for their transgressions?"

Silence falls across the room.

"*What*?" The word bursts from my lips. "What transgressions?"

"Two weeks ago," Mother continues, ignoring my outburst, "Prince Thiago and his wife, Iskvien, entered my kingdom. They stole my crown, burned my sacred oak, and threatened my people during the midst of one of our sacred rites."

Maren leans back in her chair, her fingers steepled together. "I assume you have proof?"

Mother snaps her fingers, and one of the clerks at her side produces a box. Inside it are three enormous stacks of paper, bound together tightly. "Witness statements from dozens of my people detailing the theft."

"You want to talk about theft?" I stand abruptly. "What did you steal from *me*, Mother? From my husband?"

Thiago's hand is a gentle restraint around my wrist.

"*Don't, Vi*," he whispers in my head. "*This is what she wants. Let us hear her out. Let her lay her trap. We have to be very careful about what we say about Amaya. She may be feeling us out on the subject.*"

He's right, of course. But the fury bubbling inside me can barely be contained. *How dare she? How* dare *she?* I sink back into my seat.

"War is nasty business. None of us want war. I'm a reasonable woman. And so, I ask the alliance to sit in judgement," Mother purrs. "If the alliance finds the Prince of Evernight guilty of theft, arson and assault upon my people,

377

then he must face punishment. Asturia will back away from Evernight's borders. Justice will be served."

"Execution," Maren murmurs.

Execution.

A chill runs through my veins, and Thiago places a hand over mine as if to comfort me.

"*Don't react,*" he says.

"And if he is found innocent?" Kyrian challenges her. "What then? What price does Asturia pay for threatening war over such spurious claims?"

"Maybe we can settle this with a duel," Thiago taunts Mother.

Mother's eyes glitter. "Alas, the accords are very clear about the way these cases are to be brought to justice."

Thiago merely smiles at her, looking unconcerned. "Of course. Evernight welcomes such judgement. None of us want war. And perhaps, since this meeting brings us together in such auspicious times, we can look at other pressing matters while we are gathered."

"Other matters?" Maren asks.

Thiago doesn't take my eyes off my mother. "Like the two armies riding for Evernight's borders from the north. The Unseelie. And the goblins. And perhaps, we can assess what brings them here."

Mother merely smiles. "I know absolutely nothing about such matters. Maybe others have taken exception with Evernight's tone, of late."

"May*be*," Thiago says, the word a thrust.

They both smile.

Chapter Twenty-Nine

Iskvien

"I'm going to kill her," I seethe, my skirts rippling behind me as I pace our rooms.

"No, you're not," Thiago says, unbuttoning his coat.

"How can you be so calm?" I demand, turning on him.

"Because now we know what she's up to. Now we can counter her claims."

"How?" I retort. "They're true. We did steal her crown.

Her tree burned. You might have attacked one or two Asturians on their way out of there."

"The court case is a sham," he murmurs. "She knows that if we really want to play this game, then we can bring our own cases against her."

"Amaya." It would give us the right to have attacked Mother back. But it also opens May up to investigation. And sets up an entire outpouring of dirty little secrets, nasty little lies. It brings too many others into it. Andraste. Edain. The attack on Ceres. It would mire us here for weeks. Maybe even months. Maren would love every second of it. I turn to the mirror, ripping several jeweled pins from my hair. "What do we do?"

Thiago comes up behind me, curling his arms around my waist as our gazes meet. "This is the opening gambit. We remain patient. And we work with Lucere and Kyrian. We don't need to break her case, Vi. We just need those two to vote with us. And we're already halfway there."

I wrap my arm over his, leaning back into his embrace. "Lucere is a fragile ally."

"True. Getting Baylor into her camp gives us some leverage though."

My eyes narrow. "He's not going to bully her into voting for us. He won't do that."

"He doesn't have to." Thiago kisses the side of my neck, and then turns to pour me a glass of wine. "Lucere is a lonely woman whose grandmother isolated her. She's jealous of everything you have, but she also apparently... likes you. And you're right. Baylor is loyal and true. He has very strict moral grounds. He's protective. Kind. Good-looking...."

I stare at his back, my mind chasing itself down several alleyways. "That's what that whole meeting in the cave meant? You being the aggressor and painting me as her protector? Her friend? You wanting him to *strip* in front of her?" My eyes boggle. It's a devastatingly clever game in hindsight. "Does Baylor know you're dangling him in front of Lucere like a carrot?"

"Baylor has some idea, yes. He's not an idiot."

"And he agreed to this?"

"I'm not asking him to do anything other than guard her."

"He has the poetic qualities of a rock," I point out.

"I didn't send him there to seduce her," Thiago replies. "Especially not in his current form. I sent him there to protect her. If he saves her life once or twice, I'm fairly certain he won't need to seduce her with pretty words."

I stare at him, all of it dropping into place in my lap.

An enormous, protective, honest warrior.

One who doesn't play games.

One who doesn't lie.

One who will kill to protect her.

"You evil man," I tell him, hitting him with a pillow from the bed. "That is absolutely diabolical. And it could backfire on you spectacularly. What if he denies her? Or says something utterly Baylor-like?"

"Why do you think he's in wolf shape?" Thiago asks. "He can't speak right now. Or be seduced. And he's very furry and warm when he sleeps on the end of your bed. What woman does not want a sexy shapeshifter protecting her?"

381

I pinch the bridge of my nose. "I truly hope you've got something more than that."

Thiago captures me again, kissing my cheek. "I'm working on it."

I dream of a bloody battlefield with bodies strewn everywhere. Broken pennants snap in the wind. The flag of Asturia lies crushed and muddied next to the body of its bearer.

Golden skirts gleam beneath a blazing red sun, my mother's bloated body steaming in the heat.

"Put my throne here," I command as my warriors stack the bodies of my enemies before me.

They place the throne right on top of that pile of butchered corpses.

And then someone places a spear beside it, with my mother's head upon—

I gag and turn away, fighting against that destiny.

"*If not you,*" whispers the crown, "*then it will be her.*"

The dream twists, and this time it's my head on that spear, with my mother reigning triumphant over her new kingdoms. Thiago is bound before her, bloodied and broken, and as he screams through his gag when he beholds what is left of me, my mother smiles as if to say his death will not be so kind.

In the distance, ravens caw and pinwheel through the sky.

My heart starts racing, fear trailing clammy claws down my spine.

These can't be the only two options we have.

"Please," I beg, twisting and turning.

"Iskvien?" says a voice, one I almost recognize.

"*You will shatter Unseelie and destroy the Seelie alliance,*" the crown purrs. "*So was it spoken. So it shall be. There is no escaping your destiny. You will be a queen who conquers nations. A dark queen rising....*"

"No!"

"There you are...," whispers a voice in my head.

It's a voice I half recognize—one that's been whispering in my dreams for far too long—but as I toss and turn, I can't escape the prickling sensation that runs down my spine.

I try to move, but my limbs feel so heavy. And even as I sense something kneel on the bed and lean over me, my eyes refuse to open.

"Wake up," says the voice, and fingertips press between my brows.

My eyes jerk open. A shape leans over me.

It's like liquid shadows are woven into a fae-like form. Moonlight-gilded eyes lock upon me, and raven hair tumbles over his brow, but his expression is a mask of darkness.

"Who are you?" I reach for Thiago—

And my hand passes right through him.

It's only then that I realize my body lies asleep on the bed. My hands are mere shadows of their actual selves, and all the physical sensations of a body are muted. A single leap might carry me over a mountain.

"This is a dream." No, a nightmare. We placed webs over the bed to protect our dreams while we're here, but somehow it hasn't worked. "You're one of Maren's dream thieves." My voice rises. It's said that she uses her team of dream assassins to remove her enemies in their sleep. But some whisper that they don't merely die—they're hauled into choking nightmares that literally frighten them to death. "What do you want with me?"

"I'm not one of Maren's little poppy-addicted dreamers," the stranger sneers. "Can't you feel it, Iskvien? Can't you feel me?"

A pulse shimmers through the air.

A throb....

I lean into the Hallow's slow and steady heartbeat. It's miles away from the court, but the leyline runs right beneath us. And as I look up, I realize the crystalline shimmer of the leyline seems to trail from the stranger's forehead.

"You're the Dream Thief." Another Old One, long since locked away.

Though Maren's mirror provides access to his powers.

"I am. Maren thought she could control me, but she should have known better," the Dream Thief purrs. "The spiritual and the mindscape are my realms. The second she summoned me, she granted me access to this world again through the mirror."

I hover above the bed, a long silvery cord linking me to my body. "What are you doing here?"

"We don't have much time," the stranger says. "Maren's locked her mirror away for the night, but if she feels the urge to peek into her guests' dreams, she may seek to glimpse into the mirror."

I stare at his hand. "Where are you taking me?"

"Into the Tower of Dreams, where your friends steal inside. The prophecy is about to be woken, and the Mother of Night wants you to hear it."

I glance back.

It's a shock to see my body lying there in Thiago's arms. He curls around me as if he senses my distress even in sleep, and seeks to sooth me.

"You'll return me to my body, safe and whole? By morning?" Never bargain with an Old One without setting the terms.

The Dream Thief seems to smile. "You will be returned by morning. I will protect you, Iskvien."

"Alright," I whisper.

Though really, what choice do I have?

Maren's court is never quiet.

There's a youthful element to it—one I've not seen replicated in other kingdoms. The young nobles of the court squabble and plot; they gamble and drink and dance; and their malicious games bring about the ruin of more than one innocent.

Maren turned a blind eye to such cruel games long ago. It took me a long time to realize that she does so deliberately; Askans can be vicious and cruel, and how better to keep them from sticking a knife in her back than keeping them too busy driving their claws into another's vulnerable underbelly. She nurtures blood feuds and stirs treason. She breaks hearts and shatters alliances with her dreams and her whispers. She promises allegiance to a lord in one breath, and then instructs poison to be slipped into his cup the second he leaves her chambers. The bottle, of course, will be found upon the person of his dearest enemy.

And none of them see it.

It was only as her lady-in-waiting that I gained a powerful insight into the way her mind works.

"This is a snake pit," I whisper as we glide along the hallways.

"Yes," says the Dream Thief.

Card games fill the rooms. Fae bucks laugh and crow, casting down winning hands as lovely young ladies curl around them and coo.

It's an echo of the real world, but it's a powerful echo.

One in which I can stare right between realms.

A pair of young fae females lie dreaming in the corner, smoke curling around the chambers. Their astral selves giggle and spin in the air above them, flickering and vanishing as if they step halfway into the world of dreams before losing their grip upon it.

Next to them, a randy young satyr fucks his way into a redhead who throws her head back and screams.

And there, right in the heart of it all, sits Etan of the Goldenhills.

Thousands of rooms away, my heartbeat starts to thunder. Even in this astral form, the sudden chill I feel is real.

Shaking the die in his hands, Etan casts them across the gleaming mother-of pearl board in front of him. His shirt sits unlaced halfway to his navel, and his wheat-gold hair is somewhat more unkempt than I've ever seen it before, but as he lifts the golden reed of the dream smoke globe to his lips and breathes in its wretched smoke, his vicious blue eyes are exactly the same as I recall them.

Etan looks up and then freezes as if he can see me.

"This way," says the Dream Thief, seizing my hand and hauling me forward.

We flash through walls and doors, one chamber after the other in a dizzying rush.

"He saw me." My heart's still racing out of control somewhere in the distance.

The Dream Thief cuts me a sharp look. "Dream smoke sometimes gives one that ability."

"We have to go back." I haul against him. "He'll go to Maren. She'll know what we're up to...."

"There's no time," the Dream Thief snaps. "The prophecy will wake tonight, and you must be there to hear it."

Fuck. "Fine. Then it had best hurry up and wake."

We flash forward, the world of dreams dashing past us until we stare up at the Tower of Dreams.

Carved of obsidian, it stretches into the sky hungrily. Jagged, lightning-shaped runes glow against its dark walls— a warning on the etheric plane to stay away. There's an observation platform at the top with an enormous astro-labe, but it's the heart of the tower we're searching for.

One more leap, and we stand inside.

The heart of the tower is a storage facility for important dreams. Breathed into globes that are not quite glass, they writhe and twist like little smoke tendrils. Sitting in their velvet-padded nooks, they line the walls. I slowly lift my head, peering up and up and up.

The possibilities are endless.

The prophecy dream could be anywhere.

Iron ladders circle the room like some sort of library, except the globes are the books. There's another level above us—possibly several—and as I lean over the rail and peer down, I stare into a pit of gloom.

"How are we going to find it?"

"Prophecies are curious things," the Dream Thief says. "They're linked to the person the prophecy is about, and while they often catch the unguarded mind—the prophet who speaks them—they are only ever arrowing for one person. Long ago, this prophecy caught the mind of a dreamer. His companion took down his words, but they were lost to the test of time. Only the remnants of this one remain... the dream in which the prophet caught the prophecy."

"If Maren has it, then does that mean she knows what it says?"

The Dream Thief nods. "She knows what it says. Though whether she knows what it means is a different story."

A growl echoes through the tower.

"What was that?" I demand quietly.

The Dream Thief's head turns. Then his shoulders relax. "Your friends await. Come."

He takes my hand, and we blur again, reforming on one of the platforms high above us.

An enormous shaggy wolf-like creature prowls through the shadows, faelight gleaming off its silvery ruff. It pauses as if it hears our breathing.

Every hair along its back stands on edge, and a low warning growl vibrates in his throat.

"Baylor?" Lucere whispers harshly. "What's wrong? Is someone coming?"

I run my fingers through his fur, offering myself for him to sniff. Baylor can't see me, but I know he senses me, for his hackles slowly lower.

He stalks forward, butting his head against Lucere's thigh. She nearly topples over, but even as she grasps his fur for balance, she stares into the darkness as if she wonders what he sensed.

"You are going to give me a heart seizure," Lucere breathes.

But this time, when they move on, her fingers remain clenched in his fur.

"Prophecy, prophecy, prophecy," Lucere whispers to herself as she circles the room. "Where do you think it will be held? 'P' for prophecy?"

I give the Dream Thief a suggestive look.

"I have no idea," he replies.

As if in answer, a crystal-clear beam of light starts to glow softly in the distance. Lucere turns that way. "Is this the one?"

The closer we get to it, the more the light builds until it looks like a burning star radiating in the distance.

"Here it is," Lucere whispers, lifting it down from the shelf. She flinches as if it's hot, and the globe crashes to the floor, glass spewing everywhere as the prophecy escapes.

A voice cries out in the old tongue:

> "One queen will rise;
> One queen will fall.
> One queen will anchor;

389

Three queens in all.

One queen;
With fire in her veins,
And fury in her heart.

One queen;
With midnight in her soul,
And vengeance carved in her bones.

One queen;
With shadows whispering in her dreams,
And summer in her blood.

Three dark queens to bring him down;
Three dark queens to burn him out.
Three dark queens to shatter the shad-
    owlands.
Three dark queens to destroy the kingdoms
    of the sun.

One queen to crown herself,
With Death by her side.
One queen bleeding raw,
Her heart soon to fall.
And one queen in blooming,
The key to it all.

From darkness will she rise;
And only Darkness will stop her from
    falling.

The voice dies away, the words imprinted on my heart, on my soul.

Clapping my hands over my ears, I try to still the ringing in my head. The world spins around me like a kaleidoscope of colors. I'm losing myself in the whirlpool, circling those words as though I'm drowning in them.

Rise, dark queen, whispers the crown in my head. *Wield me to defeat the Horned One. Crown yourself. We'll make them all bleed. We'll make them all kneel. Starting with your mother....*

I can't stop its claws from digging into my soul.

"What did it say?" the Dream Thief demands, his hands gripping my shoulders.

I gasp, locking my fingers around his wrists.

Oh yes, whispers the crown, *let me get a taste of him.... All that power....*

I scramble away, trying to lock it out of my head. It's like it's been there waiting for me all this time, lurking in the dark recesses of my mind.

"Vi? Vi!" Hard hands shake me.

I gasp as the prophecy chews me up and spits me out, the words still ringing in my ears. The dream spits me out, and I slam back into my body.

Thiago's face appears, harsh with worry.

Chapter Thirty

"What the fuck was that?" Thiago demands.

I tell him everything, letting it spill from my lips as he fetches me a glass of water and eases me onto his lap.

"You're okay," he whispers, kissing the top of my head. "I've got you."

"Lucere heard everything." I rub my knuckles against his shirt. "Thiago, it said I would shatter both Seelie and Unseelie if I unleash the power of the Hallows."

His palm splays across my spine, stroking gently. "Then we'll deal with that when it comes."

Morning dawns, bringing clarity and determination.

We've got what we came for. Now we need to thwart Mother's attempt to antagonize the situation.

But since the case involves two rulers among the alliance, it means both Evernight and Asturia have been asked to step aside as the other three debate the evidence.

"Why do I get the feeling Mother is setting this all into play as a distraction for us?" I demand, summoning flames in the small garden where Thiago and I have been drilling for the last hour.

"Because you know her." He seems calm. And maybe he is.

Kyrian will vote for us. And Lucere is already working for us, but does she dare display her hand too early? Does she dare defy Mother so openly?

Will Thiago's gambit with Baylor work?

"Hold the flame, Vi."

I focus on that diamond of flame, holding it steady. Sweat drips down my spine. He's been putting me through static exercises all morning, ones designed to force me to concentrate.

"Circle," he says.

I push the diamond into a circle of flames, gritting my teeth with the effort. "Why can't I just set fire to something and save this bullshit for later?"

"Because it's all about controlling your magic, Vi. You

come up against someone who's stronger than you with their power, and surviving might come down to the fact that you can wield yours better."

"Did you ever have to do this?"

"Fire's not my forte." He shrugs, and then using his index finger, he draws a circle around him. Shadow billows out of nowhere, lurking around him.

Fire was always the one gift I owned, and while the work with Thiago is paying off, I still can't seem to push past the last of my mental barriers. I can form arrows of flame, even make a sword if I'm concentrating, but anything else—beyond those creatures in the fireplace —eludes me.

"*I'm not sorry,*" Nanny Redwyne's defiant voice plays in my memories. "*The child needs to know the truth. Vi? Vi! Don't you forget me. Don't you dare let her make you forget me! You are strong. You are brave! Remember everything I've ever told you. Hold the flame, Vi! Hold the flame!*"

Those were the last words I ever heard her spoke.

Right before Mother blinded and tortured her when she caught Nanny reading me a forbidden book that I'd begged for.

"Hold the flame," I whisper.

But they gutter and die.

I'd hoped that as my memories returned, I'd be able to push through that mental block, but something's still holding me back from fully accessing my power.

"You feeling okay?" Thiago asks, waving his shadows into oblivion. His shirt clings to him in the heat.

I twirl my finger near my ear. "My mind's wandering today."

"Understandable."

But also unaffordable.

"Want to do something active?" He holds out a water flask toward me.

Black silk does wonders for his skin. He's always been ridiculously handsome with those chiseled cheekbones and vivid green eyes, but ever since we arrived here yesterday, he's been riding the killing edge. There's something about the threat to me or the rest of his people that pushes him over that edge. I've seen that stance shift before, when he enters the ring with Finn, but not to this extent. Finn's not a threat, after all, whereas here, now, he's the Prince of Evernight. Every move he makes is self-contained, but potentially lethal.

Dangerous.

Gulping it down, I glance at him from beneath my lashes. I love curling up in his arms and simply listening to the beat of his heart, but these moments get to me in all the right ways. He's wild in bed when he's overprotective and snarly. I could make love to Thiago forever, but every now and then I need a good hard fucking from the Prince of Evernight. "What did you have in mind?"

Thiago takes the flask, putting his mouth exactly where mine just was. His pupils dilate as if he just heard my voice drop three octaves. "That sounds like an invitation, Vi. But you're still healing. And I was talking about dueling."

Dueling. Not quite where my mind was going. "I feel entirely recovered from your father."

There's a certain darkness in his eyes as he screws the lid on the flask. "That's good to hear. And when Mariana gives us her approval, we can... resume normal activities."

So controlled. I'm clearly not going to get my way. "This is bullshit."

Thiago steps closer, caging me against the wall with a dangerous curl to his smile. "Someone's on edge. Why don't we finish up here with some dueling, then head back to our rooms? The alliance isn't going to make their decision until after lunch. Maybe I can help scratch that itch that you're feeling."

"Define 'scratch'?"

"Lick it into submission."

Heat curls through me, though this time it's got nothing to do with my magic and everything to do with his words. "You know I don't do submission well."

"You will if I tie you to the bed."

Fuck. I'm so wet, and he hasn't even touched me. Every nerve in my body demands his hands on my flesh, his teeth in my skin. We've both learned I don't like to go to my knees willingly. No, I like it when he puts me there.

"Form your sword," he says, in the exact same kind of voice he'd use to tell me to strip, "and then fight me. After that, we'll go play."

The breath explodes out of me. "Seriously?"

This time, his laughter is carefree as he steps back and opens his arms wide. "Trust me, my love. The only way I'm focusing right now is by convincing myself the threat to you is greater than my need for you."

One glance down revels exactly what he means by that.

Fine. "Fight now. Then you owe me orgasms."

"By the dozen. I promise once. I promise twice. I promise thrice. Ready?"

Flames spring to life in my hands, conjuring themselves

into a sword of pure fire. It won't burn me—it can't burn me—but it's still not as spectacular as the blade Andraste can wield.

He falls into a defensive stance, shadows blurring around his fingers as he pulls them out of the air. Only the line of tension in his jaw reveals how difficult it is to forge an obsidian blade.

Maybe we both need this.

"Let's see what you've learned." He gestures for me to attack him.

He's so cocky. And I'm still utterly frustrated by his earlier tease. "What do I get if I kick your ass?"

Thiago actually raises a brow as if he thinks I can't do it. "What do you want?"

"You and me. One night. My rules."

He flashes a hot smile at me. "And what do I get if I win?"

"You and me... no rules."

Thiago's smile turns molten. It's the look he often gives me when I've surprised him. Unguarded. Intrigued. Making plans for what he's going to do when he wins this gamble. It's when he's at his most dangerous. "That's a *very* tempting proposition."

"That's because you presume you're going to win."

It's not that he won't let me be on top in bed, but it's rare that he cedes me control. I love the way he makes love to me—as if he'd like to consume me—but sometimes, just sometimes, I'd love to tie him to the bed and torture him a little.

"Either way, win-win."

He laughs under his breath. "Bring your best, my love."

Five hundred years of swordplay. I can't beat that. Finn's been working with me on what to do against opponents who are bigger than I am, stronger, and far more powerful.

Your only chance is to be a sneaky little Grimalkin. Defend, defend, defend. Pretend to be out of your depth. And wait for an opening. You'll only get one....

One is all I need.

I meet his offensive strike, countermanding with a little something Finn has had me working on. Thiago breaks off, looking impressed. "Nice. I see he's working you through the Way of the River."

"Finn had me down at the yard every day while you were gone."

Flames versus shadows. It's a different kind of dueling to steel. There's no crash of metal, no physical impact jarring up your arms. His shadows absorb, and where they meet my flames, there's a hiss and a slight resistance.

Thiago smiles at me as he ducks the sweep of my flames. "I quite enjoy my nose hairs where they are, thank you very much."

"Then move quicker."

His eyes widen in a *did you just challenge me* kind of way. And then he lunges forward, driving me back, back, back.

This. This is what we both need. It's one thing to burn off stress and unease, quite another to actually play. I flash him a smile. I missed this.

I turn aside his shadows, fully aware that he's holding back. It has something to do with that obsidian blade, I think, and how frightened he was when Malakhai skewered me with it. It's also a testament to his skill; that he can press me so hard without worrying about a mishap.

My back meets the wall. Suddenly, there's nowhere to go.

"Surrender," he says, sweeping aside my sword of flames and pressing so close I can feel his hard body locked against mine.

Vanishing the flames, I roll my eyes. "That's what you always say."

He grins at me, capturing my wrists and hauling us close, "And you love every second of it."

I twirl into his body, sweaty and dusty. "And now you've got me, what do you plan on doing with me?"

Thiago's eyes darken as he pushes against me, pinning me to the wall.

I arch my head back. No arguments here.

His lips trail down my throat, over the sensitive curve of the hollow there.

The rasp of his tongue dances over my skin as if he's tasting me, and the fist deep in my abdomen turns molten.

Grabbing a fistful of my hair, he grinds me against the wall. "I want to fuck you, Vi. So hard. But since I can't, I think I'm going to pin you to the bed instead and spend the next few hours eating you out."

"Maybe I want you to fuck my mouth instead."

Interest gleams in his green eyes. "Maybe I'll hold you to that later…. But I do like hearing you beg for mercy."

He loves using his mouth. He's always been dominant in bed, but I think he takes a particular sort of pleasure in servicing me.

Our eyes meet, and then his gaze slides lower, focusing on my lips.

His mouth follows.

It's a gentle kiss.

A tease.

Or the opening gambit to an invasive push.

Because that's the way he likes to kiss.

Thiago's tongue strokes against mine, yearning for me to soften. I melt against him, open to anything he wants to take. There is no war here. Not now. He's conquered me in all the ways that count. Pressing against me, he slides one hand over my ass and hooks it behind my thigh, hauling my knee up. The ridge of his erection brushes against my hip. It's not quite where I want it, but the threat of it, the sensation.... Gods. I moan a little, and the kiss turns hot and burning, as if he feels that moan too.

He tastes like cinnamon and apples, thanks to the small spiced honey cakes we ate after breakfast. I can't stop myself from threading my hands through his hair, gripping fistfuls of it out of desperation. It's been *days* since I've had him inside me. Days since that deliciously hard cock was rubbing against me like this.

"You were... saying something... about spending the next few... hours eating me... out," I gasp against his mouth.

Thiago stills, his hands caged on either side of my hips. Desire turns his eyes dark, but the hungry look on his expression makes me suck in a gasp. "No rules, Vi. You promised."

No rules. A thrill shoots through me like lightning. I'd never make a bargain like that—not here in Arcaedia, in

Faerie, where one is bound by one's oath—but he knows my boundaries. My trust in him is absolute.

"Why don't we—?" He breaks off, head tilting to the side as his body steps between me and whatever has caught his attention. All I can see is the wall of his back.

That tension is back.

A flash of movement out of the corner of my eye makes me turn.

Company. *Curse it.*

A furious young woman strides toward us, her scarlet skirts sweeping through the grass. There's no sign of an entourage; no sign of the wolfish guardian we specifically told her not to leave behind.

I push past Thiago, glancing around the courtyard to see who else might be watching. I can't stop myself from shaking, my body still riding that sweet, sweet edge of almost-pleasure. This might be the worst timing in the world.

"A word," Lucere demands.

Thiago reaches for his water flask, surreptitiously turning away to hide his erection. "What the fuck are you doing here?" A heated light flashes through his green eyes. "We're not supposed to be seen together."

I shoot him a look.

Is this meant to placate her?

"*She already sees me as the aggressor,*" he says calmly in my head. "*She's never going to trust me if I suddenly play coy with her. I burned that bridge when she tried to put her hand on my thigh in Ravenspire when we visited. Smile, Vi. Make friends. Do what you do best. Be empathetic.*"

"Don't worry," she retorts, her dark eyes blazing in return. "It's not going to look like we're conspiring."

Tucking her arm through mine, she leads me across the side of the courtyard. Thiago looks like he wants to follow, but I shoot him a hard look. "Stay out of it."

And then I turn my attention to her. "What's going on?"

"One could say the same to you. I saw you there last night. I *know* you were there. With that... that...."

"The Dream Thief."

Her face pales, and she turns away, rubbing her knuckles against the fabric of her skirts. "That monster."

"He's hardly a monster."

She turns on me. "He wasn't in *your* dreams, was he?" A bitter laugh escapes her. "Oh, don't worry, Iskvien. I've been warned most soundly about betraying you. I'm aware of the cost."

My stomach sinks. If she's talking about betrayal, then it's because she's been thinking about it.

She laughs again, a wretched sound. "Do you know, you almost fooled me? With this talk of friendship. But you're exactly like the rest of them. Threats and more threats—"

"I didn't threaten you."

She shakes her head as if I haven't said a thing. "I should have known better."

Oh, that's rich. "I didn't threaten you! Nor did I ask the Dream Thief to do so. It's quite telling, Lucere, that the second you feel pressure, you threaten to tuck tail and run."

"Who's running?" she retorts, folding her arms across her chest. "I could go to your mother. All I'd have to do is insist upon Imerys's freedom in exchange for telling her everything that's conspired between us. Or maybe I don't have to go that far. Maybe all I have to do is vote against you today."

I rear back.

Everything that she's done.... "You've been playing us both all along, haven't you?" On one hand I could almost admire it. "It's a bloodless means to get what you want. You'd prove yourself loyal to her. She'd no longer have to hold Imerys over your head."

"You're supposed to be talking me out of it," she snaps.

Those aren't the words of a woman trying to threaten blackmail. They're the words of a woman who's drowning, clinging to the only hint of salvation she can find.

And I feel that.

I've been there, desperately missing my husband, trying everything to think my way through the mess I was landed in. The only difference is that I had Thalia and Eris to keep my head above the water. I had Finn and Baylor, rock solid at my back.

I had Amaya to help shore up the cracks in my heart.

And while Corvin is devoted to his sister, Lucere's hinted that her grandmother alienated her from everyone within her family and court. A means to nurture Lucere's magic and power and grow her into a queen with the strength to hold her court together, but also the reason why she's now standing in her court a stranger to her people.

My voice softens. "I'm telling the truth, Lucere. I had nothing to do with last night. I was plucked from my own dreams, plucked from my bed.... The Dream Thief wanted me to hear the prophecy with my own ears. I'm sorry if you were swept up in all of it."

She wraps her arms around herself, shivering. "What do I do? Your mother's pushing me to vote against you."

"Abstain."

Lucere stares at me.

"Ravenal's always played the neutral card, Lucere. If you abstain—"

"Then it means you will have to deal with your mother's claims."

"If my mother wants her crown back, then she can fucking challenge me to a duel for it."

Lucere stares at my face, her cheeks paling. "You're serious?"

Digging my thumbs under the hollow of my eyebrows, I force myself to consider the situation strategically. If Lucere votes for us, she'll lose everything, and we both know she won't do that. If she votes against us, then we must either withdraw from the alliance—which leaves us with no allies in a war we can't win—or we have to hand over the crown.

There's only one option left.

And Mother knows it.

"This is what she wants." She's played her cards well, but then she always does. "So we'll give it to her."

Mother thinks I'm weak.

Powerless. Struggling to work my magic. Blocked.

But I've seen the strain on her face. I used to think she was undefeatable, but that was fear speaking. That was the little girl inside me who was forced to cower before her. She's lost her oak, her bond to the lands. She's lost her crown. Her daughters have both turned against her.

In a fucked-up way, that last one is probably the thing that cuts her deepest.

It's never been love, but she always saw us as hers.

Her possessions. Her belongings. Her pawns.

Betrayal is the one thing that affects her the most, and in some way she probably sees our defiance as betrayal.

"True bravery isn't always about fighting with the weapons you have. Sometimes it's about facing the doubt and fear within yourself and refusing to give them voice," I whisper. I don't know if I'm ready to face her. I don't know if I ever will be. But I'm no longer that little girl. Nobody ever fought for her, but maybe it's time she needs to step up and fight for herself. "Vote to abstain, Lucere, and let me handle her." I force a smile. "If she challenges me, I have the right to set the time and date. And she knows it."

Lucere breathes out slowly. "I'm glad I'm not standing in your shoes right now."

"What were you thinking?" Thiago growls, the second Lucere is out of sight. "Abstain? *Abstain*?"

"Be empathetic, you said." I growl the words. "You're right. We need her as an ally. In the *war*. And you're pushing her too hard. She won't vote against Mother. Not with Imerys in Mother's hands. This gives us an option."

He scrubs a hand over his mouth, and then visibly calms down. "Sorry. I'm on edge. I don't want to see you hurt."

All that violence, tightly coiled within him.... I could ask him to deal with this for me. I could hide myself behind him, use him as my shield, as my savior, as my protector. It's what I dreamed of as a little girl, and perhaps, when he first stole a kiss from me, the idea that he could rescue me from my mother was part of the attraction.

But I'm not a little girl anymore.

I don't need to be rescued.

I need to fight.

I need to stare that bitch in the face and let her know that despite all her abuse, she can't hurt me anymore.

"I was thinking that it's always been circling toward this." Ever since I discovered the truth—that Mother once heard a prophecy predicting her daughter would overthrow her. "You could kill her for me. I know you could kill her for me." And in so doing, set the entire Alliance against us. I lift my gaze to his. "But I have to do it, Thiago. I have to face her. Myself. Or I'll never truly set myself free of the shackles she bound me with."

I can see the moment he understands.

"Vi." His hands capture my forearms, his eyes deadly serious. "Vi, are you sure you're ready for this? You have the strength, you have the power, but do you have the belief? I've never doubted you can do it. I've never doubted *you*. But if your Mother demands a duel, then you will have to kill her."

And I've never owned that instinct.

"She hurt you," I whisper. "And she hurt Amaya. And May. And so many others." I can't help thinking of my people—both the Asturians I was raised among, and the people of Evernight who now belong to me. My voice hardens. "She is a blight that needs to be removed."

Thiago captures my face in his hands, kissing me hard. His thumbs stroke my cheeks as he draws back. "Then don't hesitate. And don't listen to a word she says to you. She'll seek to weaken you with her words, and throw you off-balance. You can't afford that."

I slowly lift on my toes and kiss his cheek. *I know.* "I will harden my heart against her." She can't hurt me. Not anymore. I won't let her. "Thank you. For everything. For always standing at my side."

Thiago steps back, his face hard and dangerous again. "Always, Vi. Always."

"The kingdom of Aska rules in favor of the Queen of Asturia," the herald intones as he reads from the small scroll of parchment Maren set in his hands.

Mother smirks.

It's difficult to stop myself from setting her throne on fire.

The herald opens Kyrian's vote. "The kingdom of Stormlight rules in favor of the Queen of Evernight."

As expected.

Our stares connect as the herald unfolds the final piece of paper. I can't stop myself from feeling nervous. This all comes down to Lucere and her courage, and the slow steps I've taken toward nurturing an alliance with her.

Is it enough? Will it be enough? Can we trust her?

"The kingdom of Ravenal...." The herald pauses,

glancing toward Mother. "The kingdom of Ravenal abstains."

Mother's head whips toward Lucere.

Relief explodes through me.

Lucere returns an icy glare toward Mother, her shoulders square and her expression undeniable. For all her nervousness, there's no sign of it as she holds Mother's stare. Her face says: *You may take my sister. But Ravenal will not yield. Give her back to me, and I* might *consider it.*

Whispers roar like wildfire through the gallery. Maren cuts Lucere a certain look, the faintest hints of a smile touching the sides of her mouth as if *oh, this game suddenly grew interesting.*

"The council has spoken," Maren says, enjoying the moment. "This issue will be resolved between the kingdoms of Asturia and Evernight, if either party wishes to offer a formal duel. We have no part in this."

Mother's eyes blaze, but she looks down, her fingers curling around the edges of the throne as if she's fighting to keep her mouth shut.

And that nervous pit in my stomach grows.

"She's not reacting as she should be."

Mother should be frothing at the mouth, making threats. I *know* her.

"Lucere's given her quite the public slap across the face," Thiago murmurs as the fae behind us suck in sharp gasps and whisper loudly. "And the loss of the crown did hurt her. She's lost weight, Vi. There are hollows beneath her eyes. Maybe she recognizes when she needs to bow her head."

"Mother doesn't know the meaning of the words."

408

When she's backed into a corner, she's twice as vicious. She should be on her feet screaming by now. She should be challenging me. I was prepared for it.

She has something planned.

Something we can't see.

And that's the thing I fear the most.

Anxiety twists my stomach in knots. This should be our victory, but I know it's not. I *know*.

Thiago slides a gloved hand over mine, squeezing tight.

"I have one final request of the council," Mother calls, her voice cutting through all the noise in the room.

Everyone falls silent.

Maren arches a brow. "What would you have of us, Adaia?"

"I wish for the council to formally recognize my heir." She gestures behind her and the Asturian delegation opens up, leaving a small hooded figure right in the middle. "Come forward, my dear."

I don't know why my stomach drops as the little girl takes a tentative step toward us, her hood sliding back from her face. She's wearing a gown of cornflower blue with little pink flowers stitched around the neckline, her silky black hair falling to her waist and her big blue eyes so wide, it's like staring into the depths of a lake. She searches the room, looking like she's trying not to run, trying to swallow down the knot of fear in her throat.

And my breath catches, because it's like looking at Amaya. Not by feature—though the two are startlingly similar—but by the sensation in my chest.

I'm halfway to my feet before I can even think the move through, Thiago's hand locking over mine in warning.

Mother smirks, guiding the child toward the table. "May I present my heir—my granddaughter, May."

The little girl freezes, caught in the sudden intake of breath from everyone in the room.

Even Maren straightens as if she cannot believe Mother would throw down this gauntlet right in front of me.

She's not my daughter.

But I feel it as our eyes meet, May's wide and frightened.

Because *she* thinks she is.

And the look on her face slays me. *Why did you abandon me? Did you not love me? Why did you leave me with* her?

I have been in those shoes. Pushed and guided by Mother. Punished by her. I see mother's touch all over the straight line of those shoulders as May dares to stare right at me—or no, right at the hollow of my throat, as if she's taught herself to leash the terror within her by focusing on something else.

As if she doesn't dare see my response written large over my face.

It's a trick I learned when I was seven.

"Greet your mother, May," Adaia purrs.

Smoke smolders on her throne.

"*Vi,*" Thiago whispers in my mind. "*Vi, control yourself.*"

"You want your crown back?" I lean toward her, seething with a fury so blinding that I'm almost trembling. "Then I challenge you for it. Set your time and date, *Mother*. I will meet you in the field. You and me. Winner takes the crown *and* May."

Chapter Thirty-One

Thiago waits until we're safely through the Hallow in Ceres before he captures my wrist. "Are you okay?"

I still feel like I can't make sense of the world. Everything is a rush of gray stone and the unrelenting black of his leather tunic. He hastened me out of the court room and straight to the Hallow before I could set Mother's throne on fire.

Fae rush around us. I catch a glimpse of Thalia's

worried face, but it's too much. All I can see is May. All I can hear is my mother's voice.

"Leave us," Thiago commands.

The rest of our party clears the room, and none too soon. I tear at the buttons at my throat, ripping the fabric in my haste. His hands push mine out of the way, but he's too gentle, too slow.... I push him away, unable to *breathe*.

"You're safe," he says, pacing after me. "You're here with me now, Vi. She can't touch you."

She already has.

And I can't even describe why seeing May impacted me so much.

"I'm so sorry." I swallow down the emotions fisting in my throat. "Goddess. I couldn't stop myself. I walked right into her trap. The second I saw May it was like... like looking into a *mirror*." The word comes on a gasp. "I know what she's doing to her, because she did it to me. I know... how much it hurts. How much it ruins some piece of yourself. I sent Theron to rescue May because I wanted to protect her, but it wasn't until today that I realized that some part of me was trying to protect *myself*. If I could fight for her, then in a way I'm fighting for myself—for the little girl who *deserved* better."

My expression crumples. "She hurt me. She hurt me *every* day of my life. I spent my entire youth wondering what I'd done wrong, trying to make amends for some imagined slight, trying to preemptively fix all my mannerisms, my words, my actions... just so I wouldn't set her off. I thought I lost my memories, my voice, my... my sister. But she took them from me." I can't breathe through the thumping of my heart. "She took it all. And she did it deliberately."

It was her.

It was always her.

None of my actions would have ever made a difference. I could only keep the storm from spilling over for so long, because she doesn't have it in herself to change, or to apologize, or to even understand that her own actions are the cause.

Thiago opens his arms, and I walk into them.

The squeeze of his body settles me, deep inside. I press my ear against his chest as he soothes my hair, listening to his heartbeat. It's calm and steady; it always is. He brings such stillness into my life.

Home.

This is home.

This is safety.

And I've just brought ruin down upon us.

Drawing back, I dash the wet heat from my eyes. "Are you angry with me?"

"*Angry?*" A frown furrows his brow, his mouth opening and shutting, and then he shakes his head. "Vi, of course I'm not angry."

"I just challenged my mother to a duel." The tremor lights through me. After all this dancing around, it's coming at me faster than I'd ever have imagined. "This was supposed to be... planned. I just ruined everything."

"You ruined nothing. Do you remember the first time we met?"

I dash the tears from my eyes with a wry smile. "Of course."

Thiago rubs my upper arms. "The moment I saw you, I knew it was you—the love of my life that Maia had promised me all those years ago. You were perfect. But you were an ideal. You weren't real to me. Not at first. You were just a promise made flesh; a dream woven to life right before me. I didn't even know you."

Every inch of me goes still.

"Do you know the first moment that I realized I could love you?"

I shake my head.

"You rescued Finn from your mother's torture. You risked everything for an enemy, and I realized you were brave and courageous, and... there was this light in your eyes, as though you would fight the entire world just to defy her. For me. For Finn. You saw his pain, and you couldn't bear it, and so you rescued him.

"You are rash, Vi. It's the one thing that puts my heart in my throat, because I can never predict what you'll do when you get that gleam in your eye." He cups my face, his thumbs caressing my cheeks. "It scares me, because you take dangerous risks in those moments. You struggle to fight for yourself—and I know where that comes from, I do know—but when you see someone else suffering, you become... a warrior. You were magnificent today. You owned your power and you stared her down, and everyone in that room saw Adaia back down. She knows it too.

"So no, I'm not angry with you, because that's the woman I fell in love with. The one who will risk everything for a little girl who has never known love. A stranger."

I can't help whispering, "She doesn't feel like a stranger."

"We'll rescue her, Vi." He kisses me softly, lips brushing against mine as he cups his face. "We'll set her free."

The tremors fade away, replaced by a different sort of shiver as his mouth opens over mine. He's kissed me a thousand different ways, and this is his protective kiss. The one that wants to shield me from anything that might break my heart. It's a little rough. A little demanding. But also filled with gentle longing. My body wilts against his, soft against the hard planes of his chest.

It's so easy to lose myself in his kiss.

Sliding my arms around his neck, I toy with his hair, moaning a little as his tongue lashes against me.

Thiago breaks the kiss first, breathing hard as he rests his forehead against mine. I can *feel* his smile. "You always distract me."

"*I* distract *you*?" I draw back and punch him in the arm.

Capturing my wrist, he laughs. "Yes. You do. What was I saying?"

"I don't know. What were you saying?"

Something to do with mother, and May, and how he loves me—even the rash side of me.

"You can beat her, Vi." Drawing back, he presses one last kiss to my forehead. "But this time, you can't simply hold the flame. You have to become the flame."

* * *

The challenge against my mother doesn't go unanswered for long.

The courtier steps forward the next morning, setting a small golden box on the table in front of me.

"A gift," says the courtier with a sneer as he backs away, "from Her Majesty, your mother."

"Don't open that box," Thalia warns, but I can't look away from it.

I've seen Mother send these boxes before.

Moving as if in a dream, I unlatch the clasp and open it.

It takes a moment to realize what I'm staring at. I'd expected a finger, but this looks like a piece of fine leather, painted with—

It's the mark of the blood moon.

I suddenly realize what I'm staring at, my hand capturing my gasp as I turn away.

"What is it?" Thiago demands, looking for himself.

Swallowing down my gorge, I force myself to think through the horror I feel. "I've been wondering what became of Theron." I tug the letter from the box and snap the lid shut, forcing myself to breathe through it. "I warned him not take a shot at my mother. I *warned* him."

"What does the message say?" Thalia murmurs, unrolling the letter.

I already know what it's going to say, but I let her tell the tale.

"You have until tonight," she reads. "I will see you at my sacred oak, or the next piece I send will be his head. Bring the crown."

* * *

"It's not your fault." Thiago runs his hands up and down my upper arms the second we're in our rooms. "Theron is an assassin, Vi. He knew what he was walking into."

416

"I know!" I turn away from him, pacing. "I *know*. I just hate the way she always wins. I hate the way... that I feel like I've finally thrown free of her shackles, and yet, the second she storms back into my life, my brain stops working. It's like some piece of my heart shuts down. I can't breathe. I can't *think*. I can tell myself a thousand times that I am healing. That I am stepping into my own power. That I'm free of her—winning back everything that she stole for me—but the truth is: I don't know if I will ever be free of her in here." I slam my curled fist against my chest, the anguish burning through me. "I don't know if I will ever be able to feel like I'm... like I'm enough."

Thiago presses a hard kiss to the top of my head. "You will always be enough, Vi. It's not your fault."

Not my fault, not my fault, not my fault.... I have to hang on to that.

You should kill her, whispers something in my head. I don't think it's my conscience.

"If it was that easy," I snap, "then it would have been done years ago."

Thiago blinks at me.

I twirl a finger near my head. "I was talking to the crown." Which sounds absolutely ridiculous. "And I know how that sounds."

"What does *it* think you should do?"

A vision of two armies rolls through my head. Thousands of fae warriors clash and die. I see myself clad in gilded armor as I step onto Asturian soil. The ground shudders beneath my footstep as I reach for the leylines and claim her kingdom too.

My mother screams as I crush her with the power of the Hallows.

I can almost smell the blood as I blink out of the moment. "It thinks it would look lovely with both the Asturian and Evernight banners hanging in my throne room." And then I add, "It also thinks the throne room would look better if your throne was removed and only mine remained."

Thiago cuts me a look.

"Never," I swear to him. "I would never do that to you."

"I know." He can't help smiling. "I just hadn't realized that when it was planning on conquering the world through you, it saw me as a weapon to be wielded and thrown away."

I can't help thinking of my mother. The saithe oracle showed me the origin of her power: The moment where she vanquished the Briar King with Angharad's help and claimed his throne. I will never forget the look on her face as she stared into her mirror and set the crown on her head. "I sometimes wonder if that's what drove her mad."

His face hardens. "Some fae are born hungry. Nothing will ever fulfill them. I think the crown takes what is at your core and emphasizes it."

I arch a brow. "You think I want to rule alone?"

"Sometimes what we think we want is a mask for the thing we need." A thumb brushes against my cheek. "I think... you have spent your entire life striving to please your mother. You wanted to be named her heir, you wanted power of your own in order to please her.... The throne represents that. Maybe there's a hint of longing for acceptance within you. Maybe the crown took that shadow image and used it to entice you."

I capture his wrists, bowing my head and resting it against him. "I never want to rule alone again. I hated it."

He captures my face in his hands and presses a kiss to my forehead. "Never again."

What do we do?

"She's going to kill him," I whisper, "and if she has Theron, then she may know the truth about May."

I've never seen anyone hold their secrets against my mother's inquisition.

"You want to rescue both of them."

"Politically, it would be a disaster." The world keeps reminding me of that. "He's an assassin, and not even one loyal to us. And May is...." I can't even say it. She's a little girl. She could be Amaya. She could be *me*. Maybe, in some ways, that's where this compulsion to rescue her comes from, because I begged the world for someone to rescue me. But no one ever came until I took matters into my own hands at that long-ago Queensmoot. Instead, I meet Thiago's eyes. "Mother always used to say my sense of compassion was my weakest point. She knows what this will do to me."

"Your compassion is precisely the reason I fell in love you with you. The world doesn't need another Adaia. Nor another Queen Maren." He captures my fingertips in his hand. "It needs a queen who knows what loyalty means. It needs a queen who sees the littlest members of her kingdom and considers their lives to be just as important as her own. Don't lose sight of that, Vi. If anything is going to hold that bloody crown at bay, it's that."

"If I don't rescue him, then Theron suffers and she'll send me his head. Who knows what she will do to May? If we come for them, then we're walking directly into a trap. Either way, she wins."

His face hardens. "Let her play her games. War is coming, Vi. She might win this skirmish, but we'll win the war."

"Unless...." I blow out a breath. "Maybe the crown... has a point."

"What does that mean?"

I think about the way the land quivered beneath my foot in that vision. It wasn't conjured from nothing. I felt Asturia reach for me the night Thiago and I tried to steal the crown from her. Mother claimed the lands using her sacred oak—the one Andraste burned down—but I *felt* that link with the lands. I just wasn't strong enough to do anything about it. Then. "Maybe it's time to give my mother a taste of her own medicine. Maybe we spring the trap. And we take back what's ours. We take back everything that is ours."

There's no time to lose.

I sit at my writing desk, biting my lip as I think of everything I mean to write.

The Duke of Thornwood is the key to ruining all of mother's plans. I *know* it. Now I just have to convince him of it.

"How are you feeling?" Thalia sits her bottom on the edge of my desk.

"Slightly murderous," I admit, sprinkling sand over the ink of the page to set it.

"That's possibly the only way to feel when it comes to your mother." Her expression darkens. "She's such a bitch. Do you want me to send a force to put poison ivy in her bed?"

Leaning over, I give her a hug. "Tempting. But I'm thinking about something more... inevitable."

"As long as you shield your own back, Vi." Thalia looks serious as she draws back. "I don't trust her. I don't trust this challenge. Your mother will stop at nothing to hurt you. Remember that."

"I know, T." I sigh. "I do know her best."

The doors to my rooms burst open, and Thiago stalks inside our chambers breathlessly. "Baylor's nearly ready. He's preparing an extraction team as we speak. But there's a problem."

"What is it?" I demand, folding the letter in half and dripping wax to seal it.

"Your mother's finished staging. Her armies are pushing across the river into Evernight."

I press my signet ring into the wax. Of course she is. It's no surprise Asturia's troops are engaging us now, right when we're supposed to be making our way toward her sacred grove in order to get Theron and May back. She wants us to make a choice. She wants it to hurt. "Typical. Either we're forced to leave Theron to her whims, or she wants to separate us. She thinks you'd never leave the front if her armies attack. Which would leave me to pursue a rescue attempt myself."

Thalia snorts as she plucks the envelope from my hands

and blows on the seal. "That's what comes of ruling in absolute. Adaia cannot fathom that Thiago has people—loyal people—who can see to the warfront without him."

"Can one of your demi-fey deliver my letter to the Duke of Thornwood?" I ask Thalia.

Thalia taps the envelope against her thigh. "Yes. Though I'll have to accompany them almost to the outskirts of the Asturian army just to make sure. Sometimes I think it would be easier to herd cats." She hesitates. "Do you think Thornwood will agree to your terms? We've made countless offers of negotiation to him in the past. He's ignored every single one of them. He is loyal to Adaia—"

"He's not loyal to my mother; he's loyal to his people," I counter as I take Thiago's hand, our eyes meeting. We mapped out this plan in the early hours of the morning. A way for both Asturia and Evernight to survive. "And we can give him something no one else can."

"Freedom," Thiago tells her. "From the leash Adaia has around his throat."

"The return of his daughter," I add. Grabbing my cloak, I swing it around my shoulders.

And for once, Thalia has nothing to say.

Chapter Thirty-Two

Iskvien

The trip through the Hallow to the Briar King's castle is uneventful. I make my offering to the ruins, slicing a knife across my palm and dripping my blood on the slate floors. The Hallow trembles, whispers of power curling through me. I hold myself on the brink there, teeth gritted against the pressure of all that magic, but I don't dare accept it. Not yet. I don't want Mother to sense what I'm doing.

"There's no one here," Thiago says, his eyes black and

endless as he peers up through the stone roof, as if he can see right through it.

The world around me comes alive in a way that it wasn't before.

The wight that protects the ruins stirs in the distance, but I brush my senses over it, telling it to subside, and it settles back into slumber.

Nothing moves as we make our way to the courtyard. In the distance, the sun sets, casting a rosy hue over the rose thorns that entrap the ruins.

"Here," Thiago says, casting off his glamors to reveal himself in all his glory.

His glorious black wings splay wide.

"Are you ready?"

I curl my arms around his neck. "For my mother?" My breath comes out shaky, but I try to smile. "Yes. And never."

Thiago's palms skate up my spine, rasping over the braided leather of my armor. "She has no power over you anymore, Vi. Remember that."

"I can remind myself a million times," I admit, "and yet the second I see her, I know my heart is going to tremble."

Too many years of flinching from her voice.

Too many years freezing into place, hoping her gaze won't fall on me when she stalks into a room.

"It's allowed to tremble," he whispers, capturing my face between his palms. "Remember that too. True bravery doesn't mean standing against your foes invincibly. It means standing against them even when you want to flee. It means fighting for yourself even when you don't feel very worthy of such protection."

"I'm not going to let my kingdom down," I protest. "Or you."

"I know." His lashes lower, shielding those dangerous eyes from view. "But today, I need you to fight for *you*, Vi."

I can't help drawing back, trying to work out what he's saying.

"I've seen you in action," he points out. "You took on my father without hesitating. You've faced Angharad. The Horned One. The Mother of Night. All of them without even flinching. All of them, because they dared to threaten someone you love. You are at your fiercest when you are protecting your friends or your family. If your mother put a knife to my throat, then I know you wouldn't hesitate. You'll obliterate her."

Thumbs stroke across my cheeks. "But today I want you to fight for *you*. I want you to protect yourself, Vi. I want you to use all that fierceness, all those protective instincts, and I want you to channel them for you. For the little girl who should have been loved. For the little girl who deserved to be protected by someone. Anyone. You need to start treating her as you treat others."

The flush of tears threatens to take me by surprise. Every time I think I have this worked out....

Somehow I nod. "For me, then."

And he's right.

Because I did deserve better.

I *do* deserve better.

"Then hold on," he whispers before he launches us into the skies.

* * *

Thiago sets me down outside the grove of oaks that serves as my mother's link to the lands. The Hawthorne Castle Hallow pulses not too far away. It calls to my blood, to the cut across my hand.

Yes, it whispers, reaching for me. Yearning for me to reach back.

To complete the loop.

The Hallows are linked by the leylines. If I close my eyes, they're a glowing, shining network of magic I could tug on if I so chose.

"Ready?" Thiago whispers as he lowers his arms from around me, his wings falling into shadow as he rouses his glamor. He vanishes behind his veil, but I'm not alone. Never alone.

I nod. I can't quite speak in this moment.

Be brave, Iskvien.

Each step I take carries its own weight.

The woods shudder.

Squirrels flee through the branches.

And even the wind whips up as if it can feel my rage.

"Contain it," Thiago murmurs to me as he ghosts along in my wake. A shadow named Death. "We don't want to give her warning."

"She knows we're coming."

Mother awaits us, standing by one of her oaks. Golden chainmail glitters over her body in the form of a dress, and the hood of it hides all her hair, so that her oval face and the vicious seven-pronged crown she wears remain the feature.

A queen gilded for war.

But it's the look on her face that grounds me.

Rage. Jealousy.

But I've never seen true hatred before.

Not directed at me. Not until now.

"Ah, Iskvien," she says, rings glittering on her fingers as she caresses the oak. "You're late."

It's the voice of my youth, chiding me for any one of a million small grievances.

"You can come forth, you vile thief." She lifts her voice mockingly. "I know you're there."

Thiago's shadows materialize at my side, and he steps forth from them, his face as cold and hard as hers is. "Then you know why we've come."

"You said you have Theron," I say. "Where is he?"

Mother turns toward us, and instantly, Thiago steps forward. The way they look at each other says that nothing exists outside the two of them, but I catch his sleeve.

This is my fight.

My ghost of resentment to bury.

"Mother?"

"You're right. I have something you want," she purrs, gesturing with her hand. "And you have something I want."

Warriors rise from the ground, tossing aside their cloaks of sewn-together leaves. Dozens of them lie camouflaged amongst the leaf mulch. They're clad in gold-plated armor, Mother's circlet of thorns etched onto the pommels of their swords. Her Deathguard. Raised from birth for one purpose and one purpose only: To destroy her enemies.

One of them has Theron bound and gagged in front of him, his clothes streaked with blood. Shoving him to his feet, he puts a knife to Theron's throat as if this was planned. I catch a glimpse of the guard's ruined face behind his helmet. Halvor. The fae I burned when he tried to kidnap me. His eyes promise vengeance.

I'd thought him dead.

An ambush.

A trap.

One I walked into willingly.

Mother snaps her fingers, and part of the nearest oak reforms itself, a broken branch shifting into a throne of sorts. She sinks onto it, her eyes burning through me like acid. "Well, aren't you going to say something, Iskvien? Why don't you start with begging me for mercy?"

Chapter Thirty-Three

Iskvien

"Mercy? Why bother begging you for something I know you don't own? I thought I'd let you play your hand first," I tell her, swallowing down the lump in my throat that appears whenever I see her. "Maybe gloat a little. I do know how you like to gloat."

Mother's eyes narrow. I'm not reacting the way she expected me to react.

"What can I say? That you caught us by surprise? Oh

no, it was a trap. What a shock." Making a great deal of easing off my gloves, finger by finger, I survey her warriors. The bandage across my palm is still bloody. "You're always so predictable."

Malice flares to life in her eyes. "Where's the crown?"

"I didn't bring it."

"You... *what?*" Her nails dig into the oak. "What do you mean you didn't bring it? What did you intend to bargain with?"

"What makes you think we came to bargain?" Thiago asks coldly. "Perhaps we came to take back what is ours."

Theron lifts his head as if he can't believe we were so stupid as to risk ourselves for him. His eyes settle on my face, fury etched between his brow, and as our gazes meet, I see the moment when his magic manages to pierce the glamor Thiago cast over me.

The one hiding the starshine singing in my blood.

Yearning fills me in that moment. Hunger. The land reaching for me, its desperate pleas begging me to take it from my mother, to set it free from her hold—

Theron's eyes go wide as thorns push through the soil behind my mother, creeping over the grass toward her, and then he abruptly looks down at the ground before anyone can see that shock.

Stop it. Sweat breaks out on my forehead as I try to hold it at bay. Goose bumps erupt over my skin. It's like being on the edge of orgasm, trying to hold it back, trying to keep that wave from crashing over me....

I need time.

Time to usurp her power.

Time to ease a shield between her and the land.

"Where is the girl?" Thiago steps forward as if he heard my silent plea. He's the perfect distraction, because she's always seen him as the larger threat.

A dozen guards set hands to the hilts of their swords.

Mother lifts her chin. "Somewhere you will never find her. Somewhere you will never get to her," she hisses. "You made a grave mistake today. I will kill May before you ever set eyes upon her."

"Boring, Mother," I tell her with a fake yawn, trying not to flinch as a vine curves its way around my calf. "We've heard all your threats a thousand times before. Do try and conjure something new."

"You little fool. I have you right where I want you. I have you *both* right where I want you." Her gaze cuts to Thiago. "Asturia attacked Evernight barely an hour ago. I needed to keep you off the field long enough.... Well, long enough for some of my allies to arrive." She laughs. "It's done. And now, you'll be too late to save your people. Your kingdom."

"I assume that means your friends among the goblin horde have advanced." Thiago smiles, truly a chilling thing. "Or are you referring to Angharad and her forces? You're right. If Asturia attacked, then it would be too late to save my people. They would be caught between the pincers of three separate forces. *If* they attack."

Mother stills, practically lashing her nonexistent tail.

"The problem with the Asturian forces is that Asturia's best general lives in the border lands between Asturia and Evernight," I tell her, slapping my gloves against my thigh. "The Duke of Thornwood holds command. He has only ever lost one battle, and of all your generals, he alone can stand against Eris or Baylor. Indeed, he's the only one who wouldn't flinch to do so. And while he doesn't care for you at all—something about you murdering his brother all those years ago—you have held his daughter at knifepoint in Hawthorne Castle for years in order to inspire his loyalty. He doesn't dare defy you."

"Perhaps you should take heed of such a lesson," she purrs. "Keep your friends close and your enemies in shackles."

"Oh, don't worry, Mother. I did take heed. You spent all those years trying to teach me how to play the game of politics. You berated me constantly because you said I had no heart for it. I wasn't ruthless enough. My compassionate nature would be my downfall. And for so many years, I believed it."

Her nostrils flare as if she's starting to sense the trap herself. "Get to the point, Iskvien."

"The point is this. I spent all those years watching. I spent all those years listening. And I know, that without the Duke of Thornwood leading them, Asturia is done." I smile now, letting her see the victory in my eyes. "Take out the duke and the Asturian army collapses."

"You don't have the heart for murder."

"You're right. I don't." It's so telling that her first instinct leads her there. "But I finally realized I don't need to be ruthless to be a good queen. I don't need to bury my heart to help my husband rule. We don't have to kill Thornwood in order to take him from the field. All we have to do" —my gaze shifts to the castle in the distance, noting the column of red smoke pouring from the northern tower— "is remove the knife from his throat."

The blood runs from her face as she whips her head around to see what I can see.

"Halvor," she snaps, her attention shifting to the scarred Deathguard warrior who swore to kill me. "Shut down the castle! Make sure—"

"You're too late." It feels *so* good to say it. "Lady Aleydis was rescued by Baylor as we walked in here. That red smoke says he just took the Hallow directly to Eidyn to deliver her to Thornwood. He will present her to the duke as a gift of good nature in order to establish our terms to him."

"Thornwood has no liking for Evernight," she snaps. "And he considers his word to be sacrosanct. He swore he would serve me. He will *never* attack his own troops—"

"That's why we sweetened the deal a little." I share a smile with Thiago. "And we didn't ask for him to betray Asturia. We only asked for him to hold them back until this is all done."

"The lands that Thornwood and his cohort of border barons hold have long been the bone of contention between Evernight and Asturia," Thiago tells her. "Maybe it's time I relinquished all claim Evernight has upon that strip of border lands to the border barons. Maybe it's time they ruled themselves."

She stares at him in horror.

Because she could never relinquish her hold over those lands the way we have done.

She would never concede her authority in such a way. Never let them rule themselves, the way they've always longed to.

And so, she would never see it coming.

"Evernight formally recognizes the right of the border-

433

BEC MCMASTER

lands to secede from our kingdom, and will welcome the
duke into the Seelie Alliance if he wishes to apply." I can tell
by the way Thiago says those words that he's enjoying this
too. "You had three armies, Adaia. Right now, only two of
them will still take the field."

"Angharad," I muse, "who is a queen in her own right,
and therefore unpredictable and uncontrollable."

"And Urach, the pretender to the goblin throne,"
Thiago says to me. "Whatever are we to do about *him*?"

"It's such a shame that we have no allies among the
goblin horde," I reply. "Someone like... my sister. Who was
sent north to marry a goblin king. I wonder, what did
happen to her? I heard she didn't make the wedding.
Urach's a little frustrated about that, is he not?"

"According to Thalia," Thiago replies in a conversa-
tional tone.

We share another smile, even though the truth is killing
me: I don't know what has happened to Andraste since that
one night we managed to connect through the flames.

"Enough!" Mother screams, and throws her arm toward
us both. "Kill them!"

The Deathguard attack.

It's what we were both waiting for.

"I'll handle them," Thiago tells me, spinning toward
the thirty or so warriors who encircle us. "Finish this, Vi."

Forging the Sword of Oblivion, he sweeps forward to
fend a pair of them off. Steel shrieks, but it's the scream
from fae throats that makes me wince.

"Your little ploy is ruined," I tell Mother, resting a hand
on the sheathed sword at my hip. "You are done. You are
brought down. And now, it's time to end this."

The ground trembles beneath our feet as she pulls on the power of the lands. Her laughter is chilling. "You little fool. You think *you're* going to be the end of me?"

"It's what you saw, isn't it?" I can't stop the emotion in those words as I reach for the lands too, all those little threads I've been laying in the past ten minutes surging to surround me. "It's what you saw in your dreams from the moment I was born. It's what the Crown of Shadows warned you about. A new queen, come to end your reign." Unwinding the bandage around my palm, I show her the barely reknit slash there. "Well, consider this prophecy fulfilled."

Bending, I slam my palm against the ground.

Power surges through me as I rip the lands from her.

My lands. Mine to claim. Mine to take.

It's time to finish what my sister started when she burned Mother's bonded oak.

One by one the oaks in her grove begin to topple as my power scythes through them, shearing right through their roots. The sound is astronomical.

Power surges up through the ground, using me as a conduit. There's no Hallow here, but I can feel it not too far away, feel the leyline I'm standing over.

The earth buckles beneath our feet. Her warriors cry out and fall.

And my mother staggers off her makeshift throne, her mouth agape in shock and horror as her connection to the lands is torn from her.

Andraste weakened Mother when she burned her oak.

It was the tree Mother made her pledge to, watering it with her own blood. The tree she used to bind herself to the

435

lands. The others in the grove have propped her up—supported her link—in those weeks since the oak burned, but now....

Now they're gone.

Flames sear toward me as she retaliates. I wave them aside, and her eyes glitter with fury as I barely flinch. "Bow to me, Mother. And I may spare your life."

"Never!"

More fire. I sweep it away, half-amazed at how easily it listens to me. Gesturing with my fingers, I twist it into a firestorm before letting it peter out. *Mine.* My fire. My magic.

I've spent the last year working my ass off trying to forge it into a bow and arrows, trying to control it. It fought me at every step, even though my memories were returning, even though I was no longer under her control.

And it makes me realize that while she planted the seeds in my head—fear of my magic, fear of my fire—I was the one who perpetrated the lie. I wanted to please her even as I feared her. I wanted to be what she wanted me to be—the perfect crown princess, much like my sister was. And so I let my flames flicker and dull, let them die down to sparks.

My magic was never gone.

I just did not believe in it.

"You took my fire once, Mother," I whisper. "But it no longer burns me. I understand now. When you first held me in your arms, you saw in me the promise of yourself. A child with magic, just like you. A child who could make roses bloom and thorns grow. A child who could make flames dance, and in so doing bring a smile to your lips.

And you loved me for that. You loved me for the parts of me that were you."

Fire flashes before my eyes. Nanny Redwyne screaming. My mother's guards tearing Andraste from my frightened arms. I remember it all now and close my eyes for a moment to ground myself. "But there were other parts of me that you could not bring yourself to love. My thorns began to tangle around your tower. My fire bloomed a little too hot. And I could hear echoes from the Hallow, whispers of voices no one else could ever hear. Instead of nurturing those darker shadows within me, you feared them.

"And so you stole my magic from me. You smothered my memories. You stole all those pieces from me until I was merely a shadow of you. And you locked me away from the world, from those who might have loved me."

I open my eyes, forcing her to look at me. "And you dared to be angry when I looked for love in other places. Thiago found me. He fell in love with the pieces of me that no one else ever could. He gave me back my magic and stood by my side all these years, even when I couldn't remember him. He swept me away to his kingdom and made me his queen—and not merely another version of you. He let me be who I was, and he loved me for it. You drove me into his arms, Mother, and then you punished me for it."

"He stole you from me!" she shrieks, wrenching a stave from one of her soldiers and whipping it toward me.

"He gave me back myself," I tell her, tearing my sword free of its sheath in order to meet her stave. Twisting, I force the razor-sharp end of the stave into the loam between our feet, coming face to face with her. "At every step of the way, you forced me down this track. You stripped me of allies, you took away every ounce of compassion and mercy I might have found hope within, and you forced me into his arms. You forged me into your doom. Your ruin."

I slam my forehead into hers, and she staggers back.

My ears ring as I follow up, riposting into another flailing strike. The tip of my sword lashes across her chain-mail and leaves a line of blood across her unguarded upper arm.

I see her as she staggers back, clutching at her arm in shock.

A queen standing alone.

A desperate woman, fueled by hate and vengeance.

Carved hollow by ambition and fear.

She's always been the monster under my bed, an enormous force of rage and power who made me feel so small.

Even the simple sound of her voice in a distant room could make me flinch.

But as she recovers her balance, I finally see her.

Not so tall anymore. Not so powerful. Not so monstrous.

And my sword lowers as it dawns on me that she's the desperate one now.

I have all the power.

I've always had the power. I just never dared claim it.

All my life I've been waiting for someone to rescue me from her. Waiting for some prince in shining armor—or in this case, a prince in black leather—to sweep me away from the ruins of my life where I could finally breathe freely.

And I had that.

Thiago gave me freedom. He gave me trust and love and he fought for me when I barely dared fight for myself.

But if there is one thing I've learned in the past month, it's that I can't keep waiting for someone to rescue me.

You are *the one you've been waiting for.*

Her lip starts to curl in a sneer, but that's when I take the reins.

Foot by foot I drive her back, my sudden attack seeming to shock her.

She should have had all the advantages, but with every step I see fear light through her eyes.

She cannot beat me.

And we both know it.

"Surrender," I whisper as she breaks away with a gasp. "It's done, Mother. It's done."

All her warriors are fallen.

Thiago slowly withdraws the Sword of Oblivion from Halvor's chest, and my tormentor falls to his knees and then lands, face-first, in the leafy loam. Theron stands at his side, his bonds cut open and his chest rising and falling. There's not a single weapon in his hands, but I know he didn't need one.

We stand alone in a circle of fallen oaks, and even the land has forsaken her.

"This doesn't have to end this way. You can spend the rest of your days within the tower at Clydain—"

Her head whips toward me. "*Never!*"

Plucking something from within her gown, she casts it on the ground between us.

Flames leap up around her, searing a rune into the air.

"I would rather die than see you defeat me," she hisses, and then a portal suddenly appears.

Grabbing her chain-mail skirts, she stalks inside it.

"Vi!" Thiago yells.

I lunge forward, trying to follow her, but the portal snaps shut.

In the distance, magic rumbles through the Hallow.

Vibrations echo out from it as though it's been activated.

I snatch for those threads of power, but they're gone. Obliterated. The Hallow powering down.

"She used the Hallow portal." Plucking up the object she cast down, I realize it's a circle of stone that's been chiseled from one of the sentinel stones of the Hallow. I never even realized that was a possibility. Maybe it was something the crown taught her.

"Curse it," Thiago swears. "Where did she go?"

I look toward the northwest.

There's only one place she *would* go.

"Eidyn." She went to Eidyn, to the battlefront. "She's going to kill Thornwood and take control of her army."

Thiago slams his fist against a tree, then turns back to me, his teeth bared. "The Hallow will take too long to repower. Here. Wrap your arms around my neck." His wings snap into being, and he flares them wide. "I'll fly us back to Briar Keep and we can use the Hallow there and—"

"Wait." I splay my palm over his chest, feeling his heartbeat kick beneath it. And then I reach for the power of the Hallow.

Wells. They are wells of power.

And this one is currently sucked dry by mother's portal. It will take an hour or two to repower.

But there are the threads of the leylines seeping out from it.

Other wells of power igniting along their gleaming web.

I pluck at their power, siphoning from them and channeling it all into the Hawthorne Castle Hallow. Using the piece of stone she used to anchor myself to the Hallow.

"I don't think I can take us all," I tell Theron.

He nods, stepping back and bowing his head. "I'll get myself home."

"You're injured."

A swift smile. "But not dead, my queen. Now go. Go and stop that bitch."

The ground rumbles beneath us.

"Vi?" Thiago places his hand over mine. "What are you doing?"

I look up and realize I'm glowing. "Be ready. I'm about to drop us at Eidyn."

Which will mean we'll arrive right on top of Mother.

"Vi?" His brow furrows.

I activate the newly replenished Hallow and it plucks us into the portal, as though it throws us into the maelstrom.

Chapter Thirty-Four

Iskvien

We land right in the heart of the Eidyn Hallow.

Right in the heart of Asturian-held territory.

"Keep them off my back," I tell Thiago as I push through the sentinel stones that guard the Hallow. "But don't kill them. Don't kill anyone."

Mother's halfway down the slope, her chainmail dress battered and bruised. She hasn't even realized I'm there yet.

Some of her troops see me, turning as one to stare.

The Duke of Thornwood comes out of his tent, a familiar letter in his hand and a grim expression upon his face as he sights us.

One by one, the entire Asturian army turns to look, muttering among themselves, sensing blood.

And my mother finally seems to realize she's not alone, coming to a halt.

"Mother," I yell, my fists clenching at my side. "I'm not done with you yet."

Her shoulders stiffen, and she turns incredulously.

Nobody should have been able to use that Hallow so soon.

I stride down the hill toward her, sword in hand. "Let us finish this."

Runnels of kohl streak down her cheeks, but they're no longer the marks of a woman stained by grief. They're painted on her face like a warrior marking themselves for war. Her slightly agape mouth becomes the sneer I've always known.

"Fine." Stalking toward one of her men, she yanks his halberd from his hand. There's an elegant striking falcon etched into the steel, and a deadly sharp blade just above it.

And the six-foot staff might cause me problems.

Curse it.

Now she has the reach advantage, versatility, and the moves she makes will be less exhaustive.

Strike for the hands, Finn whispers objectively in my head, as if we're in the training yard, discussing how best to incapacitate a weapon. *Her hands will be unprotected, whereas you have the cross guard.*

Get within range.

Get it done quickly.

Another whisper joins the chorus, this time a malevolent one: *Kill her.*

"No," I whisper, slipping free of the crown's grasp. It doesn't have to end that way. The prophecy spoke of death and destruction, but there has to be some other way I can defeat her and the Horned One.

I go in low, forcing myself beneath her weapon.

Too late, I realize there's a knife in her hand. Twisting hard, I earn the slice of it across my upper arm as she slams the staff of the halberd into my cheek.

Down.

I hit hard, rolling as the razor-sharp edge of the spear slams into the ground where my chest was.

Slam into her, Finn whispers, and I realize he's actually in my head right now, telegraphing the fight to me.

Scrambling to my feet, I drive into her, my shoulder slamming into her midriff.

With a scream, we both go down, rolling and fighting. Twisting and hitting.

She throws me off her, and I roll, my fingers unerringly finding my fallen sword hilt.

I twist, raising the sword and—

"Vi...." Mother crawls to her feet. Her trembling fingers reach toward me, her eyes softening in horror as if she can finally see clearly. A tear slips down her cheek. "Oh, my Vi.... Oh, what have I done to you?"

It's like finally seeing a glimmer of my mother buried deep inside her. The one who sang to me once. The one who would stroke my hair off my forehead as she tucked me into bed. And that has always been the hardest part of this: Because she didn't *always* hate me.

Once upon a time she loved me too.

Or maybe sometimes she loved me. Sometimes she hated me.

And you could never guess which day would reveal which mother.

This is always what I've secretly wanted. For her to look at me like this. For her to understand what she's done to me.

The apology I've never dared long for.

And I hesitate.

I *know* her.

But I fucking hesitate.

"Oh, Vi," she whispers, and then the sadness leaches from her eyes. A split second of warning comes before she lifts her hand with a snarl, the knife within it gleaming in the sunlight.

I catch her wrist as it descends, throwing her off-balance and slamming her into the ground. The dagger clatters to the stones. She's taller than I am, but it's been a long time since she's fought hand-to-hand, while I've had the benefit of Eris and Finn training me.

"Did you truly think me a fool, Mother?" The words tear from my lips, even as I curse myself for believing her, just for a second. "Did you think I would fall for your ruse? I *know* you, Mother. I know you."

I shove her away from me.

Eyes glittering with rage, she scrambles for the knife, but with a flick of my fingers, a tree root nudges up out of the ground and sends it flying.

445

My heart feels like lead.

This only ends one way.

I have to accept that.

Mother straightens. It's one thing to go for your dagger, quite another to be crawling on hands and knees for it. "I see someone's learned a few tricks since last we met."

There it is.

The burning spark of fury deep inside me.

"You took my magic from me because you were scared of what I could do with it if I ever learned to control it," I say softly. "You had no right to do so."

Her lip curls. "I had every right, Iskvien. I carried you inside me. I birthed you into this world. You were mine to do with—"

"No." I stop her there. "I shouldn't have to be grateful that you gave me life. I was your *daughter*. You were supposed to *protect* me."

She throws gravel at my eyes and lunges forward, but once again I'm ready.

With a twist of my hand I snag her boot with my thorns, and she sprawls at my feet, face first in the dirt.

All around me, the Asturian soldiers mutter. They edge closer, trying to catch a glimpse of their queen on her hands and knees.

Destroy her myth and you destroy her power. Baylor's voice whispers through my memories.

And maybe that's vengeance enough.

"I am done with you." It feels like finally casting off a mantle that's been weighing me down all my life.

I don't have to play these games.

I don't have to listen to her poison.

She's never going to be what I want her to be.

I finally have the strength and power to say I've had enough.

I have a place of my own now. A *home*. A man I love. A daughter I would do anything for. And friends. Friends who would walk into the Underworld with me if I asked them to.

She cannot hurt me anymore.

Instead, all I feel right now is... pity.

"You mean nothing to me anymore," I tell her, clenching my bloody knuckles and backing away from her. "I am no longer alone. I am no longer scared. I am no longer powerless before you. You have no power over me anymore."

The eyes of her entire army watch as she hisses at me from her knees.

She crawls toward me, kohl running down her cheeks. "You filthy little wretch! Come back here! Fight me!"

I shake my head, still backing away. "There is nothing left to fight for. I've already won. Look around you, Mother."

She looks.

And for the first time she sees her soldiers gathered around us. Men and women craning their necks to see. The Duke of Thornwood standing there with our letter held carelessly in his hands as he lifts his solid gaze to mine.

His daughter, Aleydis, standing at his side.

I remember her now. I remember her. The one true friend I ever had at Hawthorne Castle.

"The Asturian army is yours," I tell the duke. "Do with

447

it what you will." One last look at my mother. "Do with her as you will."

And then I turn.

Thiago watches from the top of the small hill, his hands crossed over the pommel of his sword. Our eyes meet, and this time, it's his turn to offer me his fingers. *Come,* that gesture says. *Let us go and finish what we started.*

"Don't you dare walk away from me!" Mother screams as she crawls through the dirt behind me.

I keep walking, my heartbeat as steady as my steps.

"You lying little slut. You'll never *win*. You'll never *beat* me. I am queen. I will rule the seven kingdoms. I will rule them *all.*"

I close my ears to her words.

"I will kill *her*!" she screams. "I will kill your daughter. I won't stop until I get what I want. You think you've won? I will *ruin* you."

My feet freeze.

Amaya.

The heat drains from my face as I turn around and confront her. A cutthroat smile etches her lips, knowing she finally has my attention.

"I will kill her," my mother whispers, pushing to her feet and raising herself to her full height, "as I should have done when I took her from your arms."

"*Stop,*" I tell her, breathing power into my words.

Mother almost falls as her feet ground themselves and won't move. Her horrified expression is easy to read: She didn't think I had the strength.

"No more." My fury vibrates in my voice as I stalk toward her and clasp her face between my hands. "You will hurt me no more. You will *never* hurt my daughter again. I reject you. Asturia rejects you."

The lands sing as I open myself up to them.

It's easier this time.

I already bound my blood to the lands—all I have to do is accept their claim over me, accept the power offered.

My mother tries to wrestle for that control, but her link to the lands is gone. "What are you doing? *Iskvien!*"

"*Stop.*"

Her skirts flow smoothly into the ground, sinking deep to establish roots. Her hands grip my forearms, but her fingers are longer now. Stiffer.

Becoming branches.

"No more." I shake my head, flooding her with my power. "No more suffering."

"Iskvien!"

"I forgive you," I gasp as power floods through me.

"You little fool!" She clutches at my arms, her branches raking down my skin. "I do not ask for your forgiveness!"

"I forgive you," I whisper, holding on to that beacon of light. "Not for yourself. But for me. So I can finally lay you to rest."

"You don't have the heart," she screams as her face elongates. "You won't kill me. You won't—"

"No. I *won't*. I will forget you instead."

"Iskvien!" Her mouth opens wide in a silent scream, becoming a whorl in the wood of her expression. Her eyes become knots and as her hair elongates—transforming into leafy branches—I can still see the horror in them.

I hold on, forcing her through her transmogrification. Shutting my ears to the sound of her screams, until it's no longer screaming—merely the wind whipping through her branches.

The enormous oak stretches into the sky, growing several feet with every breath I take.

And it's only once I'm done, gasping with breath, trying to recover, that I realize the truth.

She was right.

I don't have what it takes to kill her.

Maybe I don't have the heart, but maybe that's not a weakness.

I slowly push away from the tree, all my energy momentarily gone. "Find peace, Mother. No one can hurt you anymore. Not even you."

But there is no answer.

There is nothing but the rustle of wind through her leaves as she stretches her branches to the sky.

And the sudden jangle of metal as half the Asturian army goes to its knees before me in shock and awe.

Chapter Thirty-Five

Iskvien

Swords fall as I turn.
Knees hit the ground.
And heads bow.

Among them all, Thiago stands alone, his eyes filled with pride. He opens his arms, and I walk into them. I curl my arms up under his shoulders, digging my nails into his flesh as I sob.

She's gone. She's finally gone.

And I don't know if it's relief I feel, or grief, or some weird combination of it.

"You did it," he whispers, running his leather gloves through my hair. And then he looks up, something dark sliding through his eyes. "And even though her sentence was your choice, I must admit I'm half tempted to get an ax."

"No. No axes." Somehow, I summon a deep breath. "Let her have peace now."

I can see his answer in his eyes—she doesn't deserve peace.

But there's a part of me—the part that saw my mother chained and beaten at the Briar King's throne—that knows she's as much a victim of herself as all of us have been. Time and time again she made the wrong choices, but they were fueled from a place of desperation and pain. It doesn't justify them, but I think I finally understand my mother and who she could have been. It's the reason some part of my heart grieves for her.

The Duke of Thornwood's boots crunch over the gravel as he slowly walks toward us. There's snow in his auburn hair now, and hints of it in his beard, but his shoulders are as broad as ever and the black pit of his eyes utterly expressionless.

Slowly, he looks at the tree. "You have claimed Asturia."

"No." Evernight is enough. And even though the crown urges me to add more kingdoms to my list, I drown it out. "I am merely keeping it safe for its rightful ruler. My sister will return one day, and when she does, the Throne of Thorns is hers. I will relinquish all claim upon the kingdom of my birth to Andraste, as Evernight relinquishes all claim upon the borderlands."

Thornwood taps the letter against his thigh.

"Then you have my answer," he says slowly. "The unseelie are coming. The Horned One is coming. The Asturian army will ride with you to protect Evernight, the border lands, and the Seelie Alliance."

Not everyone is happy with the terms Thornwood agreed upon.

I push inside the dark red tent that's been set up for the Queen of Ravenal. Her small allotment of troops joined us an hour ago and have been setting up.

Reports came in: Angharad's army is an hour or two away. The goblins are perhaps the same. Eris and Thiago are in command, but everyone is waiting for Baylor to return. We need Baylor to lead his regiment of Black Wolves.

Lucere sits before a basin filled with bloodied bandages and a razor. A hooded cloak covers her from head to toe.

"Where in the Darkness have you been?" she demands, swiveling in her seat. "Did my message not say it was urgent?"

"Everything is urgent," I remind her.

Something catches my eye.

I reach for her hood, trying to peer beneath it.

"Don't look at me," Lucere hisses, yanking the hood of her cloak over her face.

I catch her wrist, shaking my head gently.

And maybe she senses that I don't seek to mock her, for she lets me slowly slide her hood back.

Tears gleam in her eyes. The skin on her right cheek has grayed and puckered. It almost looks like stone—or the roughened skin of a plucked bird. Creeping down her throat, it runs into soft down.

Black feathers.

"What happened?"

"If you had killed your mother," Lucere spits, tugging the fabric from my hands, "then this blight wouldn't have spread. It hit me three hours ago. I heard her voice in my head, calling me a traitor and telling me I would pay for this. This... this down started to spread across my skin." A sob escapes her. "I can't get it off."

That's what the razor is for.

That's why the bandages are bloody.

"If I'd killed her," I murmur, "then nothing would have changed. She cursed you, Lucere. And if her rage toward you was great enough when she spat the curse, then nothing would have swayed it. Not even death itself." I go to my knees, taking her hands in mine. "But it *can* be broken. Every curse can be broken."

"How?" Her laughter is bitter. "True love's kiss? Look at me, Iskvien. Who could ever love *me*?"

"Lucere," I tell her, taking her hands in mine. "Love —true love—has nothing to do with what one looks like. There's someone out there for you. Someone who will see past the feathers, see your true heart. But if there is one thing I have learned in the past thirteen years it is that true love is all well and good, but the greatest thing of all is to know acceptance and love for yourself. You deserve to be happy. You deserve to break this curse."

She looks away sharply, her lip trembling.

I take a deep breath, because we *need* her and the soldiers Ravenal has brought. "But this game is not over yet. Thiago's scouts have said there are two forces of goblins moving toward us and an enormous host of unseelie arrowing at us from the west." We don't have time to worry about curses. Not now. "If we don't stand together, then you won't need to worry about this curse."

An expression somewhat akin to steel crosses her face. "Have we heard back from Maren?"

I shake my head.

The Queen of Aska's silence is answer itself.

The Askans aren't coming.

"And Kyrian?"

"He just joined Thiago in the war tent. He's brought every warrior he can."

Slowly she pushes to her feet, tugging her hood up over her hair again. "Very well. I will prepare my generals and—" Her head tracks sharply toward the door. The color drains from her cheeks. "What's that?"

Clearly her hearing is better than mine, because I can only just make out the jangle of spurs.

The tent flaps part, and Baylor ducks through, carrying something in his arms.

I barely notice who follows him.

All I can see is Imerys, her head tucked gently against his shoulder and her lashes painting a fan across her cheeks. There's no sign of injury, but she's—

"What happened to her?" Lucere demands, pushing

past me in a swirl of red. Her hood tumbles back, revealing all the feathers down her throat, but she's so focused on her sister that she doesn't seem to notice. "You were supposed to get her out safely. What *happened*?"

"I don't know," Baylor replies, laying Imerys gently on the bedroll. There's something tender about the way he brushes her hair back off her face with his battle-scarred knuckles and the image of them strikes me through the heart: an enormous fae warrior with silvery hair half-knotted on his head, and a raven-haired princess asleep on the trundle. "We were fleeing Hawthorne Castle and she suddenly collapsed. I cannot wake her."

His voice is so gentle.

His touch so reverent.

It's like a fairy tale spinning to life right in front of my eyes.

I see it.

Lucere sees it.

The color absolutely drains from her face.

And I want to take her hand and squeeze it in sympathy, because I think Thiago's arrow struck true. I think his gambit in sending Baylor to protect her paid off.

Mess with a heart, and you risk breaking it.

I just hope the fallout isn't going to be catastrophic.

For anyone.

Lucere closes her eyes as if she's silently walling away the pain in her heart, and when she opens them again, her face is smooth. Blank. Focused entirely on her sister.

"No. *No.*" Lucere hurries to the bed and clasps her sister's face in both hands. She may think herself incapable of love, but it's there in every line of her body. "Mery, wake up. Please wake up."

"I've tried that," Baylor says.

"This is my fault. This is *all* my fault." Lucere clenches her fists together, shaking in every part of her soul. "Adaia said I would pay for my treachery, and I have. I have lost everything. But not this. Please not this. Please not Imerys." Tears stream down her face as she looks at me. "Fix her. *Do* something. You have the power now."

I try.

Leaning down, I cup my hands over Imerys's face, trying to weave strands of healing through her.

There's nothing to heal.

"She's not injured," I whisper. "She's merely... asleep. I'm so sorry."

Lucere pales. "Cursed."

Cursed.

One last parting gift from my mother.

"There's still time," I suggest. "She may wake tomorrow. Or the next day."

But my heart knows the lie.

There's an old tale about the sleeping princess of Somnus—cursed to never wake. The bards' tales speak of a dashing prince breaking through an entire maze of thorns, and pressing true love's kiss upon her lips.

In the tales, it breaks the spell and she wakes, but in truth, the kingdom of Somnus fell long ago, overgrown and choked with thorns and brambles. The entire kingdom is overwhelmed by them.

And the princess's tower lies right in the heart of that maze.

Walled up, in order to stop the curse from spreading.

With the princess inside.

"Once this war is over," I offer, "I will set the servants to searching for any sign of a cure or means to break the curse. Evernight's libraries are at your service."

"This war. This stupid fucking war." Lucere dashes the tears from her eyes. "How I wish I'd never set eyes upon you or your mother."

"Vi had nothing to do with this," Baylor growls.

She bares her teeth at him as she shoves to her feet. "And you…. You swore you would bring Imerys back to me safely. You *swore*. And I trusted you. You're nothing but an oath-breaker."

"I swore I would protect her with my own life if necessary." Baylor steps right up into her face, towering over her. "And I *did*. But not even I can sway the effect of one of Adaia's curses."

"I should never have trusted you with my sister, you filthy, wretched *beast*."

"That's *enough*." I catch her wrist. For as much empathy as I have for her situation, Baylor has done nothing wrong. "Did you expect this fight to be easy? Did you truly think you could sit in Ravenal and wait for either my mother or me to emerge the victor? War is dirty, Lucere. And there are always casualties."

I squeeze her hand, fighting the urge to protect Baylor, but also fully aware of her grief.

I know what it feels like to lose a sister.

"My offer stands," I tell her as I back away. "Evernight's resources are yours to use once you've worked your way through your grief. I know of a hexbreaker who may be

458

able to break both curses. It helped with Lysander somewhat."

"Both curses?" Baylor's head whips toward me.

Lucere's cheeks heat. "It's none of your business."

Baylor stares at her intently.

But she's right. It isn't his business.

"Baylor, with me. Take a moment to compose yourself, Lucere. Take the time you require, but do remember that you're needed in the command tent."

"Imerys." Lucere sits on the edge of her sister's trundle again, shaking her by the shoulders. "Imerys, please. *Wake up.* Don't leave me here alone. Please don't leave me all alone."

Tears stream down her face, and I gesture Baylor outside the tent in order to give the Queen of Ravenal some privacy.

The harsh line of his shoulders looks like it's taken a blow.

"She didn't mean it. You're not a beast. Nor an oath-breaker. You did your best." My voice softens. "And... Imerys's curse can be broken."

Baylor stares into the distance, his face like stone.

And then his golden eyes shift to mine, blazing in their intensity.

"I need to wash this blood off," he growls. "Then I'll report to the war tent."

* * *

Thiago and Eris are surveying the field, but the others wait for me in the command tent.

"Vi." It's a quiet word.

I look up as Thalia advances upon me, clad in a gorgeous red gown that sits off her rounded shoulders. Everyone else is wearing leather and armor, but she merely sniffed and said that if Evernight was going to end, she was going to go down looking as glamorous as usual. Her only concession to the occasion is a pair of magnificent, knee-high boots, the likes of which I still don't have a pair myself.

"What is it?"

She takes my hands in hers, far more solemn than I've ever seen her.

"You have to set them free," she says quietly.

Everyone in the tent stills as her statement drops into the room.

"Thalia, no." I know how much she fears this. The Old Ones were once gods, and while they may fight the Horned One, there's no telling what they will do once they're free. I've been trying to keep that option at the back of my mind. "I can link the powers of the Hallows. I can—"

"Die," she says simply. "You can die. And you will, you know." Tears suddenly gleam in her green eyes. "I know you, Vi. You will throw yourself at the Horned One with all your strength, and you will die because it will not be enough." She suddenly dashes away a falling tear with a laugh. "You make decisions so swiftly, and they're not all good decisions, but this one time you're holding back—"

"If I release them, then the Father of Storms will come for you." Can she not see what I'm trying to do?

Only as a last resort, I promised myself.

The Mother of Night can do what needs to be done. I

trust her. I'll free her. And the Erlking still owes me a boon, since he didn't kill Malakhai. But the others?

Thalia swallows. "I know. I'll never be able to set foot on the seas again. I'll hear him singing to me every night and with my magic gone, I won't be able to sing back. He'll invade my dreams. He'll never let me escape him." She suddenly straightens. "But it is a small cost to save the life of my friend."

Tears wet my eyes. "And Baylor and Lysander? Because they'll be affected too and—"

"Do it," Baylor growls, pushing away from the tentpole he's been leaning against. He offers me a sad smile. "We're stronger than you think, Vi. And this time, we're not alone. If the Grimm One howls for us to join him, then maybe we'll howl back this time. Maybe we'll hunt *him*. We'll have you on our side, after all."

"And Death," Finn says, leaning back in his chair.

"I will break apart the Seelie Alliance. I will break apart Unseelie. Don't you see? It's not just me! I will bring ruin down upon the fae and the lives of everyone I love!" I shake my head. "There has to be some other way."

"From ruin comes a seed of hope," Baylor suddenly rumbles. "The fae are already broken, Vi. And the prophecy doesn't state you'll destroy us all. It states that you'll break apart Seelie and Unseelie. What are those terms? Two courts of people? The pure seelie? The monstrous unseelie? Look around, Vi. Evernight is a seelie court. But we're all monsters here. We've spent years hiding our true selves so Adaia would have no ammunition to hurt our prince. Maybe we're not the only court who's hiding monsters within their midst? Maybe our old constructs need to be broken. Break us, Vi. And then let's build something better."

Everyone stares at him.

My heart starts to tick a little faster.

Because maybe he's right.

"I'm impressed," Finn says. "That's the longest speech I've ever heard you speak."

Baylor scowls. "You do enough talking for the both of us. I only bother to speak when the words need to be said."

Lifting onto my toes, I kiss Baylor's forehead. "Thank you."

He smiles at me and it's like watching the sun break over his countenance.

"Merciless Dark," I whisper. "You'd better put that smile away, Baylor, or you're going to break hearts all across the southern kingdoms."

The scowl returns.

Finn laughs, clapping a hand on his friend's shoulder. "Are we ready?"

"Ready," Thalia says with a shaky voice. I can see her endless lists spread all over the table. She's been getting the healers set up in their tents, but she'll be leaving as soon as we say our goodbyes.

Someone has to survive in order to protect Amaya.

"Ready," I tell them, exhaling the breath I've been holding.

Baylor looks toward the north, an arrested look on his face. "I swear I can sense Lysander."

"He's coming back?" I ask quickly. "Is my sister with him?"

Baylor scowls and shakes his head. "Lost him. He's busy

doing whatever he's doing. But he's definitely getting closer."

Hope bleeds through me, mingled with fear. There are two armies of goblins, after all. If Lysander and Edain rescued Andraste, then maybe they're riding ahead of those two columns. Maybe they can make it to us in time.

"Then let's go and find my husband," I tell them. "One army has been neutralized. It's time to end the others."

* * *

Dark clouds roil over the battlefields of Eidyn. Two armies pour toward us from the north, lightning flickering in their depths.

Unnatural clouds.

I swear I see a hint of horns within them, and my stomach drops toward my feet as though it's full of lead. He's coming. The Horned One is coming.

Within that gloom travels the full might of the unseelie armies. Morwenna of Isenbold's riders and Angharad's fierce warriors. They're a dark tide that stretches across the entire horizon.

Even with the Asturian, Ravenal and Stormlight forces at our backs, we'll never hold them off. We desperately needed Aska to join us.

I turn toward my husband. "No word from Muraid?"

"No. And there's no time for the Askan army to stage. If they were going to be here, then they'd already be here."

"Thi—"

"We always knew the numbers were against us," Thiago says in his Prince of Evernight voice, staring at the approaching storm. Then the coldness sloughs away. He's once again my Thiago, the prince who captured my heart. His voice becomes soft as he looks at me. "You know what you need to do."

"I need to get to the Hallow." My voice comes out as a whisper as I stare across the field to where our armies clash. It's always been the plan. Set the Mother of Night free and use the Eidyn Hallow to ascend. If I add the other Old Ones into the bargain.... "I just need time."

They've spent weeks plotting our moves. This isn't going to be a protracted battle. The numbers against us are simply too great, despite the trenches and earthworks that have been dug to slow the approaching armies down. We have to hit them hard and fast. There will be no sitting back and watching. All of us must engage on the field as soon as it starts.

But the true war will be one when we engage the Horned One.

Together, Thiago and I might be able to destroy him.

"Are you ready?" I ask him.

He's not complete. There's one final piece of Death's soul still missing, but he made himself very clear.

He will not risk hurting Amaya. Not even for this.

She is safely locked away in Ceres, and Thalia will join her as soon as she says her goodbyes, ready to defend the castle if need be.

Maybe it will be enough.

He clasps my hand, bringing it to his lips. "I will wait for you in the Darkness."

There's no emotion in his voice, but the words slay me.

He will give his everything for this moment. Even if it costs us. Even if it means he must face his greatest fear.

"And I will always come for you. Together, you and I will do wondrous things."

Capturing my face, he presses the sweetest kiss to my temples.

Before he breaks away from me. "Baylor, you're with me. We ride with Vi. We'll get her to the Hallow. The second the Horned One senses what we're doing, he'll probably come for us, but we need time. We need those armies to slow him the fuck down."

"We're essentially sending the Evernight armies to be obliterated," Finn says quietly.

"It's our only hope." There's no emotion on Thiago's face, but I know he feels it.

This will be the end of all those he swore to protect.

"No, it's not." Eris's face is calm as she checks the buckles on her armor, then her sword. "I will give you time." Her gaze cuts toward Baylor. "Recall them. Recall them all." An unsteady breath skates out of her. "Tell them to blow the silver horn. Only one of us needs die."

Chapter Thirty-Six

A stunned silence falls over the group. I've expected it for days, ever since I made the decision to do this.

"What does the silver horn mean?" Vi asks.

The silver horn hasn't been blown in nearly five hundred years, but the sound of it has been drilled into

Evernight's troops from the day they first enter the military camps.

"If you hear this sound: Run."

"Get off the field, no matter how you must do it."

"We're about to unleash Evernight's most powerful weapon. And you do not *want to stick around to see what she can do."*

"Eris." Baylor slowly shakes his head. "Eris, we can—"

"There's no time." I pause in front of Thiago. My heart feels hollow. I've known this was where it was all going to end ever since he returned from the dead. "You have given me more than I have ever had the right to ask." I take a deep breath. "Thank you. I was honored to serve for so long."

"*No.*" A harsh denial from Finn as he shoves closer. "No. This is bullshit. You're not doing this. You're not simply going to... throw yourself away."

I start plaiting my multitude of braids together and winding them into a knot at the base of my neck so they're out of the way. "Did you mistake me? Did you think you had any part in my decision?" Anger knots tightly within me. *Don't do this. Please. Don't make this harder than it already is.* "Vi needs time. And I can give her time."

"There has to be another way," Finn snarls. His focus locks on our prince. "Thiago. Tell her. There has to be another way."

And I feel it as my prince's attention shifts toward me.

He *knows* the truth.

Me. Or an entire army of our people.

"The only other way this happens is if I walk out there," Thiago says in a quiet voice that sounds more like the prince I've served—the prince I've loved as a brother—

467

than any words he's uttered since he returned. "And I would. I would spare you that if I dared."

I finish Thiago's truth for him. "We don't dare display our hand too early. You and Vi are the only ones who can end the Horned One. If he knows you're out there...." I shake my head. "He'll come straight for you. It has to be me."

Utter silence falls.

Thalia's shoulders sink. "Okay," she says as if she's trying to convince herself. "What do you need?"

"My sword. My armor." I force a shrug. "That's all."

"How about a hug?" There's a gleam in her green eyes as she yanks me toward her and crushes me tight. There's a strength to her smaller frame that I've always underestimated. "You come back to me, Eris. Do you hear me?" Her voice roughens. "We'll let you do this on one condition. You fight that bitch. You let her out of her box and slaughter our enemies, and then you fight her like you've never fought before. You shove her back down in her cage and you come back to us, do you hear me?"

"Loud and clear." I squeeze her back, fighting the urge to cling to her.

The second I step back, Baylor drags me into another hug. "You can do it," he says in a gruff voice, then gives me a clipped nod as he steps back. "I'll alert our captains."

He vanishes toward the command tent.

There's only one person standing between me and the army.

I stare at Finn, tipping my chin up.

Hot anger lies thick on his shoulders. There's a hint of challenge in his eyes as he looks at me.

"I'm doing this," I tell him.

"Fine. You want to risk your soul? Then I'm coming with you." He strips off his cloak and buckles his sword belt around his waist.

The world drops out from beneath my feet. "What?"

"I'm coming with you."

"No, you are not." I shove forward and slam a hand over the hilt of his sword. "Nobody is going to be on that field except for me."

Finn pushes forward until we're face-to-face, breath-to-breath. "Did you mistake me?" His whisper is rough with fury. "Did you think you had any part in *my* decision? You go out there and I go too."

My words. Thrown back in my face.

All I can see is the field of blood before me—what remained of the Battle of Nevernight after I came to on the ground, naked and covered with blood. The blood of friends. The blood of foes. All slain by my hand. I walked that field and I committed their names and faces to my memory so I would never forget that moment.

And then I used it as fuel whenever the daemon within me rattled its cage.

I won't add his face to my memories. I *won't*.

"Don't do this," I whisper. "*Please.*"

Finn merely shrugs. "Someone has to bring you back."

The breath skates out of me through clenched teeth. *You can't bring me back if you're fucking dead.* "I won't *stop*, Finn. Not even for you."

He merely shrugs. "I know." He flashes a swift, dangerous smile in my direction. "But first you've got to catch me."

Chapter Thirty-Seven

Finn

The horn blows, its crystalline notes ringing across the valley like the sound of a Sorrow calling for Death.

Instantly, the Evernight forces grind to a halt. There's a moment of confusion. Troops milling. Daring to ask themselves: Is that what I think it is?

And then the horn sings out again.

"Retreat!" someone bellows.

The flags wave.

And suddenly the waves of black and silver—
Evernight's colors—turn on themselves in a retreat that
lacks its usual orderly manner. You can practice something
a thousand times, but when you know what's about to stalk
out onto the field, it doesn't matter how many times you've
coordinated it. Warriors break ranks and start sprinting.
Bottlenecks occur. Fae scream and shout and shove at each
other as they fight to get *off* the field.

I don't even have the heart to chastise them for it.

Instead I slide my gauntlets on, breathing in the scent
of war.

A thrill runs through me. I was born for this. Forged for
battle and raised to spill blood. Hardened by years of
training as my mother kicked my feet out from under me
and then demanded I get up. Again. And again. And again.
Until finally, she was the one in the dirt, my sword at her
throat as she gave me a gruff nod of approval.

Today there will be no checking myself. It's been years
since I let the reins slip through my fingers, and something
inside me hungers for it.

No more leashes. Not today.

"Are you ready?" Eris asks.

"Are you?" I look at her.

Tall and lean, every inch of her is sculpted of muscle.
Her hair is braided back in neat rows, giving an enemy
little chance to grab hold of anything. When she's serving
on the front, she wears the crisp gold armor Thiago
presented her with years ago, but right now, she's garbed in
her usual braided leather. It leaves her dark arms bare and
protects her chest just enough without hampering her
movement.

471

Eris cuts me a cool look. All her emotions locked down tight until there's hardly anything left.

Maybe I'm the only one who sees the tiny glint of fear in her eyes—not fear of battle, but fear of herself.

"I'm ready." She rolls her shoulders.

Instinct urges me forward. I reach behind my neck and undo the clasp on the leather thong that hangs around my neck. It's never left my throat before, and she won't know the significance. The flame pendant that hangs at the end of the leather thong was cast by my grandfather. It was gifted to me by my mother on the day I finally stood a man.

It's the Flame of my people.

The warrior-born.

The shield against the enemy.

The last spark in the Darkness.

And the only time the Sylvaren ever give their flame away is when they gift it to the one who holds their heart.

She won't know.

She'll never know.

But I don't want her to be alone out there, and if I fall today, then she will have this one last thing of me. The most precious thing I own.

"Here." Drawing the flame pendant free, I ease it around her throat and clasp it behind her neck. "It will bring you luck. And when you feel it hanging around your throat, I want you to remember who you are and who you belong to. I want you to know that you won't be alone out there, E. I'll be there with you. Watching your back and preparing to bring you home."

Eris stills. This close to her, I can see glints of gold in her dark eyes as she glances at me from beneath her lashes.

I can't stop my gaze from sliding to her full mouth; it's the only hint of softness on her face. The rest of her is all angles—cheekbones like cliffs, and a jaw that beckons a man to kiss it at his own risk.

"Thanks," she whispers.

Tell her, Thalia and Vi urged.

But the one thing I fear most is her rejection.

And this is not the moment to send a fireball crashing through her emotions. She needs calm and focus. She needs me to be there as her friend.

I step back, the moment lost. "You'd do the same for me."

As always, being with Eris reduces me to this ridiculous state where I have a thousand things to say to her and none of them come out right.

The goblins howl down through the valley toward our retreating forces, screaming with perceived victory. The unseelie armies falter, as if questioning this sudden change of tactics, but then horns ring out and they push toward us.

Eris squares her shoulders as she looks up.

The sun starts to set in the distance, perfectly highlighting her lone form as our warriors retreat from the field. She waits until every last one of them streams past us, the goblins threatening to break over us like a wave.

One last straggler puffs past, shooting her a wary glance.

"Alright." I draw the Sword of Mourning, the hiss as it cuts through the air setting my nerves on fire. "Let's go make these goblins piss their pants."

Drums echo behind us, the Evernight bannermen sending out a warning to our enemies. Eris starts to stalk forward, her hips swaying with an unnatural effect. It's the predatory glide of a monster scenting prey.

The Monster of Evernight has been unleashed.

"Darkness swallow us all," I whisper before I start after her.

I have to bring her back.

I have to.

* * *

The screams of the dying fill the air as the leading unit of goblins attempts to turn back on itself and finds itself crushed by its rear units. I don't know who's hammering at them from behind, but between us we've got them trapped.

I laugh and howl, cutting and slashing my way through their ranks even as I keep an eye on Eris.

It took precisely two minutes before the first rank of our enemies started to realize what they were facing.

Eris mowed through them like a scythe through wheat, though it's clear she's been holding back.

I've heard the tales.

When she walked onto the northern field of Nevernight all those years ago, she left nothing standing. Friend. Foe. Fauna.

She's still holding on, trying to rein in her counterpart.

As I watch, she vanishes into thin air and then blood sprays as invisible claws strike through the jugular of a howling goblin who turned to desperately fight her off. He goes down like a puppet with his strings cut, and there she is again, dripping in blood and gore as she turns on me.

"Hello, beautiful."

For a moment I can see Eris again, superimposed over that monstrous form.

But it's an Eris I've never seen before.

Sweat slicks her dark skin, highlighting the muscular gleam of her bare shoulders. Golden eyes gleam from within her gorgeous face, though they're not *her* eyes. A knot winds tight within me. Her eyes are as black as night with flecks of gold, and as familiar to me as my own.

I've seen them in my dreams.

I've spent fucking centuries trying *not* to think of them.

And now they're gone. These are pure gold. Cat-slit. Not fae. Nothing I've ever seen before.

All I can see is the daemon within her, a smile curling over its lips as if it just found a new toy to play with.

"Don't you look... delicious," she purrs as she saunters toward me. For a moment, I see an enormous shadow following her. Despite the form she's currently in, I don't think I should fully trust my eyes.

"Battle is that way." I point toward the enemy howling in retreat.

"Mmm. This won't take a moment."

"I don't know." I squat on the balls of my feet as I hold my swords low. The second is mere steel, but it's handy as a shield breaker. "They're running pretty fast. If you take too long, you'll lose them."

That gives her pause.

A horn bellows behind us.

Just loudly enough to catch her attention.

"Not that way!" She's turning, those chaos-blighted eyes locking upon the Evernight forces settling into formation. "They're our forces, E!"

It doesn't matter to her.

Eris is buried deep within.

All that remains is the daemon.

"Why don't you stop me?" she purrs as she starts back toward our warriors.

I slam into her, carrying her to the ground. Claws lash up, but I've been watching her for the past hour, memorizing her moves. It's what my mother taught me as a child. I've spent years trying to turn away from my heritage, but in the end it may just be what saves my life.

We both flip to our feet, eyeing each other. Evernight's forgotten, but now her focus is completely on me.

She attacks hard.

Driving my shoulder low, I hit her at mid-waist, and she catapults over my shoulder.

The second I spin, I realize my error. She's on her feet, landing like a cat, her claws lashing through the thick muscle of my thigh.

Darkness's hairy balls. I grit my teeth against the pain. "My, my, grandmother.... What sharp claws you have."

"All the better to pluck your innards out."

Our swords clash, and I shove forward, using brute strength to force Eris back a step. Maybe there's a hint of surprise in her eyes, because she's always beaten me in the training yard.

But then, I was never fighting for my life.

"Don't, E. Don't force this fight."

"Maybe I want it," she hisses at me.

All around us, the sounds of battle rage on, but I tune them out. The second I take my eyes off her, I'm dead, and we both know it.

We break apart, and then she's coming at me, sword flashing like lightning.

And my sword rises to meet it.

Steel shrieks on steel. Hammer blow after hammer blow.

The call of battle rouses within me, the call of the warsworn flooding my body with aggression. Heat and fury merge in my abdomen, and suddenly an opening appears. I'm moving before I can think it through, driving beneath her sword and slashing hard. Eris leaps back, the tip of my sword skating past her abdomen, close enough to slice through her body armor.

The sight of it does what nothing else could do.

I skid to a halt, reigning my battle instincts in hard. *No. No, I won't do this. Not to *her*.* "Eris—"

Rage gleams in her eyes.

A boot drives toward my face. Windmilling back, I take it in the chest and the force lifts me off my feet.

The second I hit the ground, I roll, the tip of her sword sparking off rock. Right where my fucking chest was.

"That would have hurt," I point out as Eris comes for me like a wild, battle sworn goddess of fury.

Her eyes are completely gold now. No sign of the woman I.... The woman I call friend. "You want it to hurt, little fae?"

I force a smile, shooting a quick glance over her shoulder at the retreating armies. It's working. I just have to keep her distracted long enough to let our people escape. "Depends on precisely what you mean by that."

The daemon in Eris's body stills. Her head cocks.

I shift the sword between hands. "I don't mind a little

pain, E. Teeth. Nails. Maybe a bit of light bondage. I'm probably drawing the line at knife play though."

"What about these?" She holds up her claws and smirks at me.

"Claws... can be discussed."

"Oh, you are interesting, little fae." The daemon's sword lowers, and she tilts her ecstatic smile toward the sky. "You should feel how hard she's fighting me right now."

"Put the sword down and I'll think about it."

She saunters toward me. "Make me."

Grabbing a fistful of her leather body armor, I haul her toward me.

And I kiss her.

Hot. Hard. Furious. Tasting the blood on her lips. Hoping she doesn't rip out my tongue.

For a second, all I can taste is her heat. She stills against me, fingers curling into my chest plate as if she's not sure whether to haul me closer or shove me away.

And then she's kissing me back. Throwing herself into the action as if the walls to some dam finally broke. I sense Eris in the challenging way she claims my mouth. The heat. The fury. Maybe the daemon reigns ascendant, but she's still there, deep inside, clinging to me as though I'm the lifeline she needs.

There you are.

Thank fuck.

She tastes like everything I've ever hoped for. I stab my swords into the ground. Capturing her face between my hands, I deepen the kiss, claiming her mouth with both intent and fury. Need drives up within me. Want. The rest of the world vanishes. The war, the battle, the fact that the woman in my arms just might rip my throat out if given the chance. None of it matters. I've wanted her for so fucking long, it feels like every nerve within me is scraped raw at the mere sensation of her lips beneath mine.

And if this is the only way to get her back, then so be it. I'll pay whatever penalty needs to be paid if I can just bring her back to me.

To us.

Daemon or not, she's no longer focusing on our allies. I step back, breathing hard, prepared to run the second she comes for me.

But there's a look in her eyes that I hadn't expected.

For a second, Eris stares back at me, looking like I've slapped her. She touches her lips, her eyes round with surprise.

And then gold steals through those gorgeous dark eyes.

"Oh, you want to play?" The daemon laughs, waving her sword back and forth. "Then let's play, little fae...."

I pluck my swords free of the ground and take several steps back.

I got through to her.

Even just for a moment.

I can do it again.

I can bring her back.

I just need to stay alive long enough to do so.

"Come on, E," I croon, stepping back, foot-by-foot. "I know you like a good chase. If you can catch me, I'll let you pay me back for that kiss."

Eris hisses and launches toward me.

It's on. Now I just have to stay out of reach.

Chapter Thirty-Eight

Iskvien

"**H**old the line!" someone bellows in the distance as our forces retreat.

Eris starts walking slowly toward the enemy, the air around her body shimmering. A shiver runs through me. I hate the fact she has to embrace the creature within her in order for us to do this. I'd spare her if I could. I'd spare them all.

But right now, we need everything that everyone has got to give.

"It's time." Thiago wheels his mount around mine, our knees pressing close. "Are you ready, Vi?"

"Can anyone ever be ready to face a god?" I try for a smile and fail spectacularly.

But there's an answering flare of warmth in his eyes. "I thought *I* was dealing with him?"

And there it is. The question we're all wondering. "Are *you* ready?"

Thiago glances across the field, eyeing the enormous storm clouds that seem to contain some maleficent shape within them. His voice is quiet when he answers, "All my life I've fought it. I've buried it down deep, crushed it up as small as I could within me. I wanted to be free of it. Of... Death. But maybe, just maybe, I've been fighting myself." His lips form a thin, hard line. "Because while I've always heard its voice in my head as if it belonged to another entity, right now, that voice has merged with mine." He looks at me. "And maybe the Darkness wasn't in me all along. Maybe I *was* Darkness. Maybe it's time I accepted that."

His glance shifts to Eris.

And I want to steal the shadows from his eyes.

Leaning across from the saddle, I kiss him on the cheek. "Just remember: If this all goes wrong, I will wait for *you* in the Darkness."

His fingers catch mine. Just the fingertips. "You're not bound for the Darkness, Vi. You're bound for the Bright Lands."

I squeeze his hand. "No. I am bound to *you*. No matter where the winds blow us. No matter where the leylines pull us. You are my heart, my soul, my other half. You are *mine,*

Thiago. So if you don't want to see us both consigned to the Darkness, then try not to die."

His teeth flash in a smile. "Rousing speech, Vi. Fine." Using my fingers and his reins, he draws me close enough to touch me again. "No dying. For either of us." Then his expression darkens. "I will kill anything that tries to take you from me."

Capturing my chin with one hand, he claims my mouth for a heated kiss.

I grab hold of his braided armor for balance as Thiago slides his other hand through my hair, tipping my mouth toward his. Our horses dance nervously together, our thighs sliding alongside each other.

It's an awkward, reckless kiss, but it sears me down to my bones. *Mine*. This prince is *mine*. And I don't care what I have to do on the battlefield today, but I won't let anyone take this from us. We've spent too many years torn apart by my mother's petty games, by this curse, by the Darkness within him.

I want a chance to breathe.

I want to walk through Ceres with his hand in mine. I want to tuck Amaya into bed every night and kiss her forehead. I want a chance to see the shadows in both their eyes vanish.

Drawing back, we breathe the same air. His eyes are dark flames fueled by the promise we share.

Foreheads pressed together, we sit in that moment.

"Mine," he whispers, and his obsidian eyes glitter so fiercely, I know he's given himself over to the Darkness within him.

"Mine," I promise, pressing one last gentle kiss to his swollen mouth.

And then I draw back, trying to ignore the way our honor guard—those who've volunteered to ride right into the teeth of the Horned One—are all fiddling with their reins or making sure their feet are in their stirrups.

The only one who grins at us unrepentantly is Baylor.

The Thiago who gathers his reins is the Thiago we need right now. Dark eyes glitter with promise, a predator who fully intends to drive back those who seek to take what is his.

"Are we ready?" he bellows, raising his hand and calling his deathblade into being. Shadows slip and glide into the length of steel, until they're a void of life. One that can cut through anything living.

"Ready!" Baylor bellows, banging his sword on his shield.

"For the prince!" another cries.

"For the prince!" The sound is taken up.

"For my queen," Thiago says, tipping his head toward me as he wheels his horse. "Let's get her to the Hallow so she can drive the Horned One back."

"For the queen!" The roar is shattering.

Gwydion settles in beside me, looking relaxed and at ease. He's been the warlord in charge of holding the borders so far, and though I've never met him before, there's a flash of insouciance around his smile that reminds me of Finn. "I'll be your shield, Your Highness. Stay with me, and we'll get you to that Hallow."

As if he's a wraith, Baylor glides his horse next to Thiago's. We share a look, and he nods. He'll protect him.

"Thank you," I tell them all as I gather my reins. A dozen emotions threaten to choke me: Fear. Anger. Nervousness. It thrums through my veins and makes my fingers tingle.

And then Thiago wheels his horse. "With me!"

Nervousness flees. Fear vanishes. There's only the Hallow now, plucking at the threads of my consciousness as though it knows I'm coming for it.

The mare leaps forward as I give her rein. She's been battle trained, a gift from Eris long ago.

The entire company launches after Thiago.

He and Baylor lead the charge, pouring down the hill toward the flanks of an entire cohort of goblins. It's like watching quicksilver and shadow ride together.

Hard faces turn toward us. Shields go up. And an enormous goblin strides forward, lifting his sword to gesture his warriors on. They're cheering.

"With me!" Thiago yells, forcing his mount forward through the throng of goblins. The scythe of his deathblade cuts through them as though he's felling wheat. He's the point of our vanguard, an arrow head of Evernight warriors slicing through the horde.

I wheel my mount, urging her through the slim gap Thiago and the Evernight retinue have made. Gwydion rides at my side, protecting me with his body. He drives his horse right into a pair of goblins, forcing them away from us.

But it creates a small pocket of space.

I draw my sword as a goblin comes at me and deflect his blow, slicing under it and right through the weak spot of his armor beneath his armpit. The stink of him is an assault, and even as arterial blood gushes, his fist slams into me.

Another comes at me as the mare valiantly leaps over a fallen warrior. Ears ringing, I blink away the blow and parry hard as an enormous broadsword cuts toward me.

I cut and hack, grateful that Gwydion is keeping them off my back.

They're everywhere.

Howling as they run toward us. Screaming for our blood.

We're not going to get there. We're not going to make the Hallow....

"Thiago!" I scream.

"Ride!" he yells back at me, not daring to slow his assault. Momentum is its own weapon.

The breath chokes in my lungs as I kick one of Angharad's warriors in the face and then shove my horse through the gap that opens in his wake.

But everywhere I look, warriors clad in Angharad's black throng toward us.

They're pouring through the gap, trying to cut us off from the Hallow.

We're not going to make it.

No. No, I won't fail. Not like this.

"I'm here," Gwydion yells, cutting in from the right to guard me.

"Stay close," I yell, closing my eyes and reaching toward the Hallow.

Touching it feels like running my fingers over a smooth pool of water.

Silence envelopes me. The stink and sound of battle

evaporates, leaving my senses humming with the power of the Hallow. I drink it in, reaching for—

"Vi!" someone shouts. "Ward! *Ward!*"

My eyes blink open just in time to see an enormous ball of flame hurling toward us.

And then it smashes to the ground in front of me, enveloping the score of warriors protecting me.

The explosion slams through us.

My mare goes down with a scream. The ground flashes toward me.

Just before I hit, a silvery ward springs into being around me.

I land hard, the mare rolling right over the top of me.

Ground. Horse. Sky. Flame.

By the time it all stops, I can barely breathe.

All I can do is lie there, staring at the flames that leap and lick.

My ears ring.

Shadows flash before my eyes. Hands groping for me.

"Are you hurt?" someone demands, their voice a tinny echo.

I feel like I'm drowning. Slowly sinking below dark water, my limbs weightless and my chest aching.

I can't breathe.

I can't *breathe*.

Every inch of me aches.

And then suddenly, my lungs expand.

"Vi!" Thiago yells, finally coming into focus on his knees in front of me. Hands flip me upright. "Vi!"

I surface with a gasp, sound imploding in upon me as if

the shock of falling has finally sloughed away. Somewhere nearby, a horse screams.

Panting and gasping, I cling to Thiago as he checks me over. Steel rings on steel nearby, but the smoke is so thick I can barely see what's happening. Another enormous fireball launches into our flanks, and fae scream.

"Are you okay?" Thiago asks desperately, stroking his thumbs across my cheeks.

"Depends on if we're still... alive," I gasp, and then nod when his face pales. "I'm fine. I think. What happened?"

"Catapult." He shoots a dark look toward Angharad's forces.

My ribs ache. The ward stopped my horse from crushing me when she—

My horse.

Suddenly, the sound of equine screaming has an identity.

Snowbell kicks on her side, her back legs thrashing endlessly as if she's trying to escape the pain. Her hair is charred on one side, and the blood on her chest—

Pushing Thiago aside, I scramble toward her.

"Here, girl." She stops thrashing as I kneel by her neck, resting one hand on her heaving flank. "I'm here."

But the look she gives me—the one that says that even through the pain she knows she's safe with me—almost slays me.

"Vi." Thiago's hand closes over mine. "Vi, we have to get moving if we're to have any chance."

Tears blur my eyes. "I'm not leaving her here. Not like this."

"Vi." His voice comes softly. "Vi, she's—"

"*No.*" I bare my teeth at him. "No. I will not leave her here."

It's such a little thing. One soul in an entire battle of them, but she never hesitated to carry me into this fight. I can do no less for her.

I send threads of healing through the mare, but it's not enough. There's so *much* damage. It's power I don't have the resources to waste, and yet I can't leave her like this. If I can do this, if I can save her, then I can save them all....

"Here," Thiago murmurs, sliding his fingers through mine.

Instantly, Snowbell subsides with a gasp. Mangled flesh reknits before my eyes. I can feel that shiver through me as our powers meld.

Our eyes meet.

Together, we can do wondrous things.

Snowbell shudders, then pushes to her feet. There's blood on her coat, but no sign of those gaping wounds. She bolts through the ring of warriors, galloping after Thiago's stallion. And something in my heart soars at the sight of it.

"We're going to win," I tell him fiercely.

The words take him aback. I can see him trying to work out how to answer them as he offers me his hand to draw me to my feet. "Vi—"

"We're going to win."

There is no other option.

I'm not fighting to destroy my mother or her allies. Thirteen years ago, Thiago rescued me from a life without love or hope. He showed me a world I could live in. A world I could thrive in. A world for those of us who never fit— perhaps our bloodlines were the wrong sort, perhaps we hid demons deep inside us, perhaps we were a threat to those who considered themselves the gatekeepers of power—and now I can see it, shining brightly in my heart.

Hope.

A better world.

For all of us.

I want that world for Amaya. I want that world for *us*.

And there's nothing I won't do to fight for it.

"Thirteen years ago you saw something in me," I whisper, reaching out to accept his hand. "Something worth fighting for. Well, now I see something in *us*. In you and me. In Amaya. In Finn and Eris and Baylor and Lysander. In Thalia. Even in Grimm."

That last name chases a laugh from him. Thiago's hand clasps mine and he draws me to my feet. "Oh, Vi."

"Once upon a time you said you'd burn the world to ashes to keep me safe." I rest my palm against his chest, right over his heart. "Well, now I want you to burn the world to ashes to keep us all safe and to keep this dream alive. Step into yourself, Thiago. Be who you're meant to be. There's no fear anymore. Not in this moment. Because I know you can do this. I know you will come back to me. And I know you have the strength to face our enemies and ruin them. I love you, but right now, I need the Prince of Evernight."

He kisses me hard. Fierce and claiming. One last hint of defiance against those who've sought to tear us apart.

And I lean into that moment. *Mine.* My dark prince. My forever. My rock.

All these years he's been the one to anchor me.

Now it's my turn to be his.

"Go," I whisper, pushing him away from me as our lips

break their seal. "Get me to that Hallow."

"As you wish." Thiago shoots me one last fierce look, kisses my knuckles, and then turns, assessing the battle.

Half the Evernight cohort are on their feet. Others fight to keep the goblins off us, but they're being torn from their horses. I flinch as a sword rises and then drives through the throat of one of our guards.

Everywhere I look, we're being overwhelmed.

Thiago stalks through the line of soldiers, his cloak stirring behind him like wings. "Protect her," he says grimly to Baylor and Gwydion. "I'll get us to the Hallow."

"Fall back to the queen!" Baylor bellows.

I'm suddenly surrounded by the backs of a dozen fae.

Thiago stalks toward the ring of goblins surrounding us.

And with every step, the air around him seems to thicken and darken, until I swear there are dozens of shadows trailing in his wake.

He wasn't supposed to reveal himself to the Horned One. Not yet.

But if we don't make the Hallow, then none of this matters.

"Prepare yourself," Baylor mutters. "Shit's about to get real interesting."

"You're such a master of understatement," Gwydion says, rolling his eyes as he backs toward me.

Stillness settles over Thiago.

Goblins pause. Hesitate. You can practically see what they're thinking: One man. What is he doing?

And then Thiago's hands flick toward them.

Shadows lash through the goblin horde. Dark clouds

drive toward a dozen foot soldiers, and I can hear the screams as they're consumed by the Darkyn wraiths that Thiago's unleashed.

Everywhere I look, there's mayhem.

Thiago's power cuts through entire files of goblins, and yet, more of them keep pouring down the hill toward us. It's like the enemy knows our plans and doesn't care how many goblins we cut down. They just keep throwing them at us.

And Thiago can't leave us.

Goblins throng us on all sides.

Gwydion slams into me as he's shoved back. Evernight's warriors strive madly, feeling their leader's desperation.

I summon my thorns, and they tear through the first line of warriors descending upon us, but the others merely leap over their fallen brethren. Over my thorns.

An arrow arcs toward me. Gwydion shoves his shield between us, and I scream as the head of it punches through it, pausing an inch from my nose. Far too close for comfort.

Despite everything—Eris walking out onto the field of battle and Thiago unleashing himself—there are simply so many of them.

"Follow the prince!" Baylor bellows, surging forward after Thiago. The enormous broadsword in his hand swings, and three heads go rolling. Loyal to the last breath.

Thiago glances over his shoulder toward his warlord, his dark eyes smoky.

"We have to fall back," Baylor yells at him, turning and cleaving a goblin from chest to groin. He spins again, going down on one knee, and entrails spill as his sword completes its arc.

And Thiago looks toward me.

I see it in his eyes. I see all of it.

If we turn back, we fall.

If we turn back, they'll come for us.

Everything we've fought for will fall. They'll raze Ceres. Topple the Seelie Alliance. Kill us both. And Amaya....

Thiago's lips move. Even from this distance, I can make out his words: "*I will wait for you in the Darkness.*"

And then he's gone.

Enormous shadowy wings lash out from his back. Darkness consumes him. It plunges over the entire battle, leaving only a thin circle of light that surrounds us.

I can't see a cursed thing, but I can hear the screams.

Suddenly, the goblins breaking through that wall of shadow aren't trying to attack us. They're trying to escape.

Thiago cuts a channel right through Urach's horde.

A single path, with firelight winking off fallen swords and armor.

It's like the seas have parted, but they're a sea of darkness, and something tells me not to enter it.

"Vi?" Baylor cuts me a desperate look.

"Stick to the light. Get me to the Hallow," I say, my voice not daring to tremble. It's so close I can see the sentinel stones. I can feel it humming through my blood, tempting me to use its stored power. But I have to wait. I only have one shot at this. "We have to follow him. We have to make it. We have to—"

Light blazes. Punching through the sky like an arrow that has been launched at the moon. A fireball so bright and hissing that it lights up the encroaching darkness as it sizzles into the sky.

"What is *that*?" Gwydion demands.

I step forward, breathless with incredulousness.

My heart fluttering with hope.

"It's the First Flame of Asturia." I've never seen the flames in action outside of the training center, but I *know* it. It's a spell taught only to the royal line of Asturia. Exhilaration floods through me. *Hope*. "It's *Andraste*."

The beacon of light explodes in the sky above us, but instead of burning down to ashes, it's as though the explosion empowers it. It burns like a sun, a supernova. Light hisses, revealing an entire line of shadows appearing on the horizon.

A silver horn rings out.

And then they begin pouring down the embankment.

Goblins. Thousands of goblins.

And my sister rides at their head, the sword in her hand blazing with light.

"What is she doing?" Gwydion breathes, his face smudged with ash as he drags me forward.

I don't know how Andraste's done it. I don't even know what she's done.

But those goblins aren't *chasing* her. They're riding *with* her. And there's an enormous brute of a warrior mounted beside her on a black horse that bleeds into the darkness.

The heat drains from my face. "She's giving me time."

Urach wasn't the only goblin king to try and claim their crown.

I don't even know how she's done it, but... those goblins are allies.

Urach's horde turns to face the newcomers, their

mocking howls of victory turning to desperate screams. They're caught between Thiago's wall of shadows and the opposing force.

The newcomers smash through their lines like a knife cutting through a cake. I can barely make out the blur of light as Andraste's sword cuts both right and left, but I swear I see Edain at her back, and on the other side of him.... Lysander.

But beyond them....

Beyond them.

My breath catches as I see the enormous towering column of smoke rising over the unseelie army with spreading, bat-like wings.

The last time I saw that horned figure was in the middle of the Black Keep, when the Horned One was resurrected.

"Move!" Baylor bellows, turning his back to me and holding his sword low. "Move, Vi. I've got your back!"

"*Don't kill my sister,*" I throw out into the void, hoping Thiago can hear me as I sprint toward the Hallow. "*The second army are our allies.*"

The sentinel stones tremble as if they can sense me coming.

I scramble for the Hallow, drawing my knife.

The second I hit the stone portal, I slide to my knees and slam my palms against it. "*Are you there?*"

She has to be here....

She has to help me....

"I'm here, Daughter of Darkness," the Mother of Night whispers.

I can almost feel her hand in mine as I stare at the enormous shadowy figure approaching us.

Chapter Thirty-Nine

Iskvien

A beast of smoke wades through the battle toward us, his eyes gleaming like hot golden sparks. Every inch of him is conjured directly from my nightmares.

The clouds above us roil, an enormous malevolence of cumulus. Lightning flickers within it, but it's not the sort of lightning I'm used to. This is red. Violent. Savage. It's almost an entity in its own right.

As if the smoke parts, a male steps forth from the monster, and it wisps into insubstantial lines.

The Horned One.

Wearing a cloak of black feathers, he could almost be fae —if not for the horns that peer through his raven-dark hair. His face is horrifically beautiful, his eyes like the void between stars, and his mouth so full and lush and fucking familiar that my heart plummets to my feet.

I stare the truth in his face as our eyes meet.

"*Daughter of Darkness,*" the Mother of Night called me. Those words have been whispering in my dreams ever since, as if my subconscious knew the truth I wouldn't let myself admit.

I remember the Black Keep.

I remember Thiago's death.

And the Horned One's rebirth.

But I was so focused on rescuing Amaya and trying not to let that raw bloody scream that was trapped in my throat escape that I didn't get a chance to work my way through the truth that was standing right in front of me.

"Vi." Thiago appears at my side, his voice rough with shock.

"Samhain is the one night of the year when the veil between worlds thins and the Old Ones walk free," I whisper, forcing myself not to quake, forcing my throat to swallow its lump of gorge. "It is the night I was conceived. I always thought...."

I'd almost suspected the Dream Thief, to be honest, because the images of him in my books are quite similar to the Horned One before me.

Just not similar enough.

I squeeze his hand, desperate for the anchoring weight of his touch.

My mother is an evil queen. My father an ancient, violent god.

I searched all the books for the name of my father —Arion.

And it was never there.

There were only torn pages where the Horned One should have stood. And when I did stumble across a story containing him, he was always "the Horned One."

They wrote him from history.

They stole his name, thinking it would steal his power.

My heart skips a beat. The Mother of Night said she conjured my birth, whispering in the ear of my mother. But did she whisper in his ear too? Did she drive him toward my mother, dreaming of the child they could create?

"*Did you do this?*" I send to her. He was her enemy. There was no way he would fall in line with her plots, would he? "*Did you trick this evil monster into siring me?*"

Every inch of me feels filthy.

I sense her touch; a feather-light stroke through my hair. "*What is evil, Vi? It is nothing more than a choice, and we all face that choice each and every day. Once upon a time Arion was the hope of our people—the shining king who was going to rescue us from the invaders. There was a prophecy— from his line would come redemption. We worshiped him. We fought for him. We let him lead us against the fae. But he forgot the rules. So deep was his desire for vengeance against the fae that he drank of* ala, *the sacred power of the lands. He drained the Hallows and forgot what he was. War twisted him. The power went to his head. I argued against him—this war was destroying us, I said. We stood against each other, but it was clear that to fight each other would only bring about the destruction I was so desperate to prevent. I had to use other means.*

"*By then it was too late. The fae struck us a blow. I was so angry at first, so furious. But as I lay trapped in my prison world, I began to dream. 'From his line,' all the prophets said. They never said Arion himself would be the key to peace. I plucked the strings of destiny, I read every star in the night sky, sometimes a thousand times over. And then I saw it. A monstrous fae queen, hungry for power. And a child in her arms, a child who shone like a star. A child who shone like Arion once had. A child who could sing to the Hallows.*

"*So yes, I began to plot. I could never confront him, not without tearing the world apart, but every Samhain when we walked the world again, I could whisper in the night. I appealed to his pride, to his arrogance. I worked with the Dream Thief to plant dreams in his head. Dreams of a beautiful young fae queen, and what a jest it would be to steal into her masquerade and seduce her. And then we waited for that long-ago Samhain.*"

I'd spent years wondering what Connall of Saltmist—the mysterious fae nobleman who'd lain with my mother once—looked like.

I built a warrior in my head who owned the same almond-shaped dark eyes that I did, the same olive skin, the same dark hair.... And I would yearn for the day he would come for me, steal me away from court, and love me the way my mother didn't.

He didn't know of my birth.

He couldn't have known.

But one day he would hear those rumors and he would save me.

"Evil is a choice," I whisper, squeezing Thiago's hand desperately.

"You're not evil," he tells me, his hair whipping back in the wind that stirs toward us. "You are the light in my heart, the light of the stars conjured in the Darkness. You can do this, Vi. You can defeat him. With me."

The Horned One stalks toward us, his gaze locked on my face, then on our hands. "I wondered," he says, in a melodious voice so beautiful that I can almost hear the song of the Hallows within it, "when I saw you last. It was a shock to emerge into this world and see you try and wrench that Hallow from me." He shakes his head, his lip curling. "If this is the Mother of Night's last gambit, then it is a poor one. Step aside, child, and I'll let you live. I need that Hallow."

"You're lying." Because in all the books, that's what he does. "And even if you let me live, then you would kill all those I hold dear."

Dark lashes blink slowly over his soulless eyes.

And then he smiles.

"Very well." Raising a fist, he brings it down with a jerk.

Lightning flashes, striking the ground between us.

The earth erupts, power ripping through it like some kind of subterranean leviathan angling directly for us. For the Hallow.

There's barely time to react.

Thiago shoves me out of the way, both of us sprawling aside as a chasm opens right through the center of the

499

Hallow. His hard body comes over mine, protecting me instinctively.

Hot, golden light spills forth from the Hallow's center, streaming toward the darkening sky. It's raw power hammering along the ley lines and spilling free into the world.

"Move!" Thiago roars, glancing up as scarlet lightning writhes overhead.

We roll apart as it strikes the very spot where we were standing. The acrid scent of burned slate fills the air.

Thiago cuts me one last desperate look, his dark hair whipping forward over his face as wisps of shadow and smoke stream toward his right hand. "Get out of here."

"*What?*" I came here for the Hallow. Without it, all is lost.

"Get out of here!" His gaze rakes over the gaping crevice. "The Hallow's unstable. He's torn it open. You can't use it. Not like this." His voice drops low, an inescapable truth in his eyes. "I can slow him down."

"No. You don't get to sacrifice yourself again," I retort, my wind whipping past my face. "You promised me. This time we would do it together."

He cuts a vicious look toward the Horned One, and I know what he's thinking.

Without the Hallow, we don't stand a chance.

The Horned One laughs. "Ah, true love. I wonder.... Does he make such an offer because he cannot stand to see his lover wounded? Or does he make it because it's easier? Because this was always to be his fate... to die in the dirt like the sniveling, bastard-born wretch he is."

"Don't listen to him." I bend low, pressing my palm to

the slate surface, trying to feel how stable the Hallow is. Tornadoes of power sweep around me, wild and off-balance. It's bleeding raw magic, on the verge of implosion. But there has to be a way. "The Horned One was always a liar."

Balance, the Mother said.

There's no point trying to force the Hallow's whirlwind of power to my command. I stroke the stone, easing it, siphoning some of it off, sending it streaming toward connecting Hallows.

"He'll kill you, you know," the Horned One sneers. "It's what his kind does." He focuses all his hatred upon Thiago. "And he knows it. It's why he doesn't dare leave himself alone in the room with your daughter. Why he barely dares touch her. Will you still love him when he brings about her ruin? Because he won't be able to help himself."

Thiago freezes.

"That's not true." I slide my hand up the back of his calf. "My love for him is unquenchable. And if he suffers such moments—if he finds himself lost in the Darkness—then I will always be there for him, to help guide him back. I will be his light in the Darkness. I will stand by him through every storm. And I will help him fight, even if he faces Death himself. Because I believe in him. I know he can fight this battle. I know he will never hurt our daughter. Because he *loves* her."

Thiago's gaze jerks to mine, and for a second his eyes bleed black. I'm not staring into his face anymore, but into the cold, emotionless mask of Death itself.

Or no, not emotionless....

There's a look there, a certain shift to his eyes.

As if I've struck Death a blow.

"Thiago told me of Carolain. You loved her, but in the end, her love for you died. But mine never will." I whisper to Death. "I am not afraid of him. I am not afraid of you. I will never be afraid of you. Because fear is the void that sucks our will to fight. And I will fight for him until my dying breath."

Death vanishes, but not before I see the troubled look in his eyes.

And Thiago resurfaces.

"How touching," the Horned One mocks. "But can he say the same when he must look at his wife every day and see my kind written all over her face?"

"Always," Thiago cuts in.

The Horned One takes a step toward us, but his focus is upon me now. "You were afraid to tell him the truth of your heritage, weren't you, Iskvien? Because you knew he'd be disgusted."

"Never," Thiago spits.

"And what of the others? Your dearest friend, Prince Kyrian, who has sworn to hunt the saltkissed from the oceans. Or Queen Lucere, who has every inch of her castle warded against the Dream Thief. Or Queen Maren, who despises our kind. Your people in Ceres—the ones who spit when they speak your husband's name...." He shakes his head. "They don't know the truth about you yet, Iskvien. What will they do when they find out? Will they try to burn you on the bonfires? Will they march against you? Maybe you will have your husband, but what will you cost him? More war? You will always be the outsider in the fae courts. You will never be one of them."

The Horned One's lashes lower over his eyes as he offers me his hand. "You are a child of the Old Ones. Join me. Fight for our people. Fight for our peace." His gaze lifts, all the savagery momentarily gone. "You belong nowhere, but if you join me, you could become who you were always meant to be. You will be my right hand. An Old One who none will dare defy." His voice roughens. "And my daughter."

His words breathe life into the concept.

It's no longer Connall of Saltmist smiling down at me as he shows me how to wield a dagger. It's the Horned One leading me through the forest, only not as he stands before me. Not as the monster. This is a powerful male in his prime, barefoot in the grass, his long black robes dragging behind him. Thousands of otherkin fill the forests, banging drums and singing. He holds his arms up, a smile on his face, and they cheer and dance and scream his name. Everywhere I look, strands of berries hang from the trees, and feathers adorn them. This is celebration. This is love. And freedom. And joy.

"Come and dance," the Horned One says, taking my hand and trying to pass me off to a handsome faun with goats' legs and small horns set in his curly hair. "Rejoice. For we are free. This is where you belong. This is where you will be loved by all."

Something crunches beneath my bare feet as I am twirled.

Bones stick out of the forest floor, the roots of enormous trees slowly vanquishing them. An ancient banner yields to moss, but the edge of its herald gleams in the sphere of sunlight streaming through the canopy above.

It's the Asturian coat of arms.

Somehow, I'm on the edge of the dancing, my breath catching in my lungs.

Everywhere I look, I can see the signs of battle. Skulls tucked in the nests of owls. The snarling wolfs head pommel that once decorated the swords of every member of the Black Wolves—Baylor's fiercest command unit. A straw doll dressed up in a raggedy gown patched of scarlet silk and velvet, wearing a long black wig.

The hair looks real.

I've seen that flawless mane before.

And the sight jars me—that in this vision, someone shaved Lucere bald and made a wig to mock her with.

The Horned One might speak of peace, but what he means is genocide.

"*Yes,*" whispers a voice in my head, the one that's been whispering in my dreams for years. "*He cannot fathom a world in which the two races can coexist. But when I conjured you into being, Iskvien, I never meant for you to be a weapon. I intended for you to be a bridge between two worlds, the same way that Queen Apollonia of Mistmark was. The old social constructs need to die, my child. Seelie. Unseelie. The otherkin. Break it all. Shatter it. And create something new.*"

And as the vision fades, I realize something else.

The Horned One wouldn't be showing me this if he thought I was no threat to him.

He would have merely crushed us.

"You say I belong nowhere?" Once it was my deepest fear. "They're all lies I've told myself a thousand times over.

And I *know* them to be lies. I've confronted them at each and every turn. I know who I am. I know what I am." Finally, finally I lift my chin. "I will create peace in these lands, even if I have to break you to do so. I dream of a world where seelie and unseelie and otherkin can live side by side. I dream of a world where all the old wounds are healed. And you can't take that away from me."

The kindness bleeds from his expression, leaving it empty. The ground trembles again, like some sort of ancient monster stirring beneath the earth. "What a disappointment you are, Iskvien."

And then he smiles, as if he knows how many times my mother has said those words.

"If you cannot see her greatness, then it is you who is the disappointment," Thiago replies.

And he squeezes my hand. "*Are you ready?*"

With him by my side? "*Always.*"

Thiago gives my fingers one last squeeze, before he steps between us, his feet planted in a defensive position. "You have no power over us. You want to fight?" Darkyn steel smolders to life in his hand. "Then let us fight."

Lightning flashes, forging into a flickering blade of static in the Horned One's hand. "You poor, pathetic fool. I will kill you, and flay the skin from your body with my lightning." A hideous smile appears. "Perhaps as a gift for your wife."

Lightning crackles as he brings his sword down. Thiago meets it, and a shattering shower of sparks flashes over us.

He's the best bladesman I've ever seen, but it takes three seconds to realize he's barely holding his own against that furious attack.

"*Bring me forth, Iskvien. Summon me,*" the Mother's voice is urgent in my head. "*You must set me free, right now!*"

Every Hallow is connected.

I reach for the Mistmere Hallow, channeling the power of Eidyn beneath my feet. *There.* Mistmere lights up in a beacon in my mind, pulsing with the power that the Mother has been siphoning into that Hallow for months, waiting for this moment.

Drawing my knife across my palm, I slam it down on the Hallow stones. "I release you!"

My blood reacts with the stone, the Eidyn Hallow shuddering beneath us. Claiming the power of the Hallow, I send it spearing toward Mistmere.

The Horned One glances down at his feet as if realizing I'm not raising the Hallow against him.

And then he looks up, violence dancing through those storm-dark eyes. "You dare bring that bitch to this world?"

"Where were you when I needed help?" I retort, pushing slowly to my feet. "Because she's been there for me all along."

Thiago vanishes into a cloud of darkness, then reappears at my side, hauling me out of the way as the Horned One sends a lash of lightning streaking right toward me.

The ground shudders as if it's tearing itself apart.

"What the fuck?" he snarls.

I don't know if it's the Mother of Night being set free or the Horned One who is causing this. I grip his arms, trying to ride the flow of power.

The entire split down the middle of the Hallow wrenches wider.

506

The crevice deepens, and I go down, cracking my knees on the stone. "Thiago!" I yell as our hands are wrenched apart.

"FOOLS!" the Horned One bellows, lightning lashing the Hallow again and again.

The stone breaks away beneath me as if it's crumbling into that gaping slash full of raw power. I scream and reach out desperately, snatching for the edge, trying not to plummet inside the Hallow's molten core—

A hand catches mine.

A body materializes.

And the Mother of Night appears, her face pale and wan within her hood. "Thank you," she whispers.

Thiago slides next to her, reaching over the edge and grabbing hold of my forearm. "I've got her!"

Behind him, the Horned One laughs, reaching for the skies and summoning an astronomical amount of lightning.

"Watch out!"

Lifting her hand, the Mother of Night cups my cheek, and the faintest hint of a smile touches her lips. The Horned One seems to freeze. Thiago goes still. Or maybe it's time itself, as silence cocoons the pair of us.

"When I first dreamed of you, Iskvien, you were nothing more than a pawn. The child I conjured into being with my magic and my plotting. The child who could one day destroy the Horned One and set us free. I sang to you at night when you were a babe because I wanted you to know our songs, our legends, our stories. But what I did not understand is that my heart—long-since turned to stone—would soften when you looked at me with such trust."

Her features blur, her figure becoming hunched and

stooped over. Nanny Redwyne appears, but she's the nanny of my youth, the one who brushed my knees off and bandaged my cuts. The one who taught me games and told me forbidden stories.

Not the one my mother tortured.

"I sent her to you," the Mother admits as her features blur back to her own, "and sometimes she would let me look through her eyes while you slept in our arms. She was a hobgoblin with the blood of the otherkin in her veins, and she worshipped me many years ago. She was my eyes, my ears.... And she was my hand when we brushed the hair from your face."

"Why are you telling me this?"

"Because you were never alone. Because you were never unloved." She meets my eyes. "Before I sacrificed myself to the Hallow, my name was Imrhien. It means 'bringer of night' in the old tongue. My daughter—the child I lost— was named Iskvien." Tears blur her dark gaze. "It means 'bringer of light.'"

I can't look away from her as our eyes meet.

And then she smiles. "I whispered in your mother's head too, all those nights she lay asleep. I wanted to give you some part of me. I wanted to give you some part of my daughter, so she would live on in some way. But I never realized you would change me too. That you would remind me of what it felt like to know a mother's love. Now go and save the world, Vi. *My* Vi. My precious Vi." Her gaze drops, just briefly, to my own mouth. "The child I couldn't help loving."

A crack sounds, and one of the standing stones guarding the Hallow crumbles into dust.

The Mother looks around. "We're running out of time. I can only hold this for so long."

She's wasting her power, her energy, merely for this....

"Do something," I beg, trying to sink my toes into the cliff-face. It feels like my boots are made of lead, fighting against the intent to move. "You can stop him."

"My time is gone, Vi. I have little strength left. All I have is this.... This one last chance to tell you that I loved you. That you were never alone. And that you have the strength to stop him. I didn't come here to fight. I came here to give you the push you need to defeat him." She leans down and whispers in my ear, her thumb brushing my cheek one last time.

Then she kneels back and smiles, donning the hood of her cloak as I try and decipher what she meant.

"One last chance, Vi. One last chance to save them all. Goodbye, Daughter of Light."

Chapter Forty

Iskvien

Time catapults back into being, gravity suddenly catching at me with vicious, gnawing fingers. A lash of raw power snakes out from the Hallow, latching around my boot and hauling me toward it as if it yearns to consume me.

"Vi!" Thiago screams, my fingers slipping in his.

The Mother pushes slowly to her feet, her smile still soft as she straightens. She holds a handful of dirt in her hand, as if she longed to touch the soil again and feel the wind on her face. The enormous horned figure rises over her shoulder, a sword of pure darkness lifting high. Lightning crackles in the clouds that form around him.

"Watch out!" I scream, throwing a handful of flame at him.

The Horned One laughs as he sweeps them aside, the sound echoing through the world. "Ah, Iskvien. Your pathetic fae magics don't have the power to stand against me."

I try to summon the land's power, my thorns spearing through the surface toward him.

"*Stop,*" the Mother says in my head. In my heart. "*Save your strength. This is not your battle. This is where I have always seen my path ending. Trust me, Vi. Let go.*"

"Vi!" The muscles in Thiago's arm strains as he tries to haul me out of the crevice.

The golden lash around my foot strains to pull me under.

"*You have one chance, Vi. First you must fall,*" she whispers, all her attention locked upon me. A vicious smile crosses her lips, as if she knows her death is nigh. "*And then you will rise. Rise and use your power to light the world on fire, Vi. Ascend, my daughter. Become what you were always meant to become. Break them free. Break them all free.*" Her voice falls to a whisper, the howling wind that accompanies the Horned One's sword tearing the words from her lips, even though I swear I hear them imprinting themselves in my mind.

The sword descends.

Lightning flickers.

And in that moment, it's difficult to see if the sword

obliterates her, or if the magic eating her alive implodes within her.

I scream, on and on. Fingers digging into Thiago's as the explosion of power threatens to tear me from his grasp.

And then it's gone.

Silence falls as if even the winds have snuffed themselves in a moment of mourning. Ash rains down upon us like snowflakes.

A hooded cloak made of midnight silk flutters to the stone floor of the Hallow, and the world falls still. Empty of something beautiful. Something brave.

She's gone.

Our greatest weapon against the Horned One is gone.

Chapter Forty-One

Iskvien

"I've got you," Thiago snarls, throwing a desperate look over his shoulder as the Horned One advances. That sword lifts again, the Horned One's midnight dark eyes locking upon me.

A searing trail of heat drips down my cheek.

The sword starts to fall again, lightning burning from its tip. I gather everything within myself, desperate to stop it, desperate to save him—

"Don't you dare hurt my sister," says a voice fierce with protectiveness. A voice I know so well.

Light flashes overhead. A burning arrow of flame.

It drives right through the Horned One's chest, staggering him back.

And the breath explodes through me.

There's only one other being here who can wield those flames. The last time I saw her it was halfway across a battlefield, but the magic doesn't lie.

"Andi." I scramble for purchase on the edge of the chasm.

Another arrow of bright flame punches through the Horned One's chest. And another. And another.

The Horned One staggers back, smoldering clouds of smoke writhing from him as he consumes those brands of light. And while they flicker and die, the hiss of smoke from where they struck him lingers.

"Get her out of there!" Andraste screams, boots sliding across the Hallow's smooth floors as she appears out of nowhere. She extinguishes her burning bow, a hilt forming in her hands. Pure flame surging into a white-hot blade.

I recognize the grim determination on her face as she shoots me one last look, her mind reaching toward me. "*I'm sorry. That I never dared fight for you all those years ago.*"

"*You did your best.*" Neither of us had the strength to stand against Mother back then.

Andraste squares herself, turning all her focus back to the Horned One. "*You were my sister. And I let her extinguish the flames of my love for you, because I was a fucking coward.*" The link between us evaporates as she prepares for this one last final battle. "*I love you, Vi. Now get the fuck out of here.*"

"Come on, Vi." Thiago hauls me toward him.

I dig my toes into the cliff face, gritting my teeth as that lash of power hauls against my ankle, trying to drag me into the well. "I'm trying!"

The Horned One whips his blade around, his sword slamming against Andraste's blade of flame.

The impact slams her flat on her back.

"Andi!"

Thiago flings a handful of shadows toward him, the roar within them deafening.

The Horned One's sword slices right through those howling faces, barely pausing in its descent.

Andraste screams as she tries to scramble across the floor toward her smoldering blade.

An enormous goblin warrior slides to his knees between them, the ring of steel echoing in my ears as his sword meets the Horned One's. The blow staggers him off-balance, and he collapses back over her, thighs straining as he bends, the force of the Horned One's strike driving his own sword back toward his chest.

Blood wells across his chest, a bellow of utter pain breaking from his lips.

And then Edain appears out of the shadows, both daggers whirling.

He buries one in the Horned One's vulnerable armpit, but the bastard barely flinches. Pure iron is a weapon against the fae, but this is a god.

The Horned One backhands him out of the way, and

Edain twists through the air like a cat, landing flat on his face right in front of us.

Our eyes meet.

I see his gaze slide to Thiago's desperate grip on me, but then the Horned One roars and lightning crashes down, hammering at the Hallow's stone floors. Little pockmarks mar the slate.

Edain pushes himself to his feet, flinging his dagger at the ancient god.

"Get Andraste out of here!" he screams to the goblin king.

And then he attacks.

They're not going to make it.

Nothing can stop him.

He's a god, drinking at the power of the lands, invulnerable to mortal weapons.

And even as my sister forges another sword of flame, attacking the Horned One from the left in order to give Edain enough room to break away, I know it doesn't matter.

They're all dead.

It's just a matter of time.

"Vi, come on," Thiago snarls at me. "Fight. Push against it!"

I look at him; the face I know so well. The warrior prince who saw in me a glimpse of hope. The wicked charmer who stole my heart. The husband who spent thirteen years winning me again and again, because he knew our love was worth every second of pain.

He's been there at my side from the beginning. He believed in me when I barely dared believe in myself.

And he's fought for me.

They all have.

Andraste. Thalia. Eris. Finn. Baylor. Lysander.

Amaya.

But this time it's my turn to fight.

"*From darkness will she rise; And only Darkness will stop her from falling.*"

I finally understand it all now.

I am a child of darkness, but he saved me.

He stopped me from falling all those years ago.

But now....

"You have to let me go," I tell him, mind racing with everything the Mother of Night whispered to me. "It's the only chance. You have to let me fall."

"Vi," he growls. "Never."

"I can stop this. I can stop him."

Desperation darkens his eyes as he shakes his head. *No. Please no,* that shake says.

The Mother of Night's last words echo through my veins. "*The crown has no power over you. Not if you don't let it. But you will need it if you hope to defeat him. No more fear, Vi. The crown cannot force you to become something you're not—it needs a seed of ambition, rage, or viciousness to nurture. And you have none of that. Gird yourself with your kindness and shield your heart with your empathy, and there will be nothing with which it may fuel itself with. You proved yourself true when you faced your mother. If there was even a hint of what the crown needs to twist you, then you would have killed her. Rise up, Vi. Rise up and become what you were always meant to become.*"

And I make my decision.

"Let go, Thiago."

His startled gaze shoots toward me, then a flicker of absolute fury crosses his brow. "We promised we'd do this together. Forever. You and me."

"You're the only one who can stop him right now. You're the only one who can save them."

"Vi!" He swivels his other arm over the edge, grabbing for my slippery hand. "Climb up! Use your legs. Climb up!"

"Thiago." My boots find purchase on the rocky edge of the crevice. "I love you. I want you to know that. I will always love you." I squeeze his hand hard, trying to force him to understand. The power of the Hallow swims through me as I gather all those threads—all those leylines —and pluck at their strings. Light begins to shine through me. "I need you to hold him off. Give me time to rise."

"Rise?" His confused gaze searches mine.

"Rise," I confirm, the Hallow's power throbbing through me. Gravel skitters over the edge of the crevice. The world behind him vanishes as my skin lights up like a super-nova. All I can see are his green eyes and dark brows. "I'm coming back for you, Thiago. I promise. But you need to let me go so I can go save the world."

And then I shove against his hold, my sweat-slick skin slipping through his grasp.

Arching back into space, I reach along the leyline, feeling the Hallow in Ceres answer my call.

"*Come to me,*" I whisper, summoning the Crown of Shadows.

Heat blisters my skin.

Light blinds my eyes.

Raw power swims through my veins.

I slam into that well of power, feeling it sear right through me, even as my hands curl around the crown that suddenly appears. It blazes with heat, crumbling to ash in my fingers. All of that hatred, gone. All of the vicious relentless drive to destroy.... Nothing but ruin. A powerful offering for the Hallow.

A sacrifice.

It's the last thing I know before the power burns through me.

Chapter Forty-Two

"Vi!" I scream as she plunges into that golden aurora of pure power.

Her body slams into it, then vanishes.

Silence.

An eerie fucking throb echoes, as if time and space slows down, every single rasp of my breath through my lungs feeling like I'm choking on gravel.

The light pulses, and then it explodes outwards.

I roll away just in time.

It gushes through the crevice, soaring into the sky as if the Hallow vomits raw and bloody power.

The Horned One turns, and for a split second I see fear on his face.

Then his lip curls in a snarl as he sweeps Andraste out of the way with a lash of lightning, striding toward the crevice as if he's going to tear Vi right out of the well.

I have to trust that she knows what she's doing.

I have to trust that she's not gone.

Darkyn steel forges to life in my hand like the beating heart of a black hole. I step between them, bringing it up in a defensive stance.

"*Are you ready?*" I whisper to Death.

It's like the world ices over.

Cold shivers through my veins, the world plunging into darkness.

But it's a darkness I understand.

One I know.

A world where I see the Horned One as he truly is: a dark figure standing two inches taller than me, with gray skin and a thick mane of wild dark hair. Strands of gold stream through his veins as if his heart beats with the power of the Hallows. *Ala*, Vi called it. I can see it in him. See it surging thick through his body, his heart a beating pump of pure gold light.

His heart is his weakness.

And my sword is his doom.

"You will not take her." I step toward him, sword held low and my eyes locked upon him, searching for an opening.

He sneers at me. "Such a child. I remember dancing

with your ancestor, all those years ago. And you have not half the viciousness he had."

"I don't need it," I tell him firmly. "These are my lands. These are my people. And this is my *wife*. I *will* stop you from harming them."

His sword lashes out; a feint.

Because a fistful of lightning blurs toward me.

Heat and pain scores across my cheek in three razor-thin gouges as I duck out of the way.

"*Hold the sword!*" Death screams.

Somehow, I keep it formed. Our blades meet, the shock of it ricocheting, shearing right through the Hallow stones. An enormous groan tears through the earth as they fall outward, dust rising in plumes.

He comes at me again, smoke rippling from his amorphous form, making it hard to see where his body exists. Feinting to the left, I duck below the blade, whipping mine across his chest.

And then he bellows, his knee going out beneath him.

Edain bares his teeth at me as he staggers out of the way, barely escaping the whiplash of lightning the Horned One flings in retaliation. The hilt of one of his daggers sticks out of the back of the Horned One's knee.

"Together," he yells at me. "We can take him if we work together."

Andraste appears at my side, her golden hair whipping behind her in the wind, her ash-covered face grim with determination. Her sword is pure fire, pure heat. And while I once thought her the enemy, I nod at her, even as the towering goblin king who hovers over her like a shadow stalks the Horned One from the other side.

"We've got to give her time," I tell them.

Andraste's gaze jerks toward the Hallow as it shudders. "How much time?"

"Enough," I grate out.

"As one," she says.

"As one," I repeat.

Andraste lunges forward, forcing the Horned One to focus on her. I dart in, but he dances aside, wary of my blade.

It's the first true vulnerability he's shown. For all his talk, he fears the Sword of Oblivion.

Edain's eyes meet mine as if he realizes the exact same truth, and then he's moving, covering the goblin king, shielding Andraste.

"Pathetic," the Horned One says, flinging a cloud of shadow at Edain's face. Miniature lashes of lightning writhe within it, and Edain goes down, screaming as he clutches his face.

"Got him!" the goblin king bellows, lunging over Edain's fallen form and driving his enormous shield up to deflect that vicious magic.

He slams the shield into the Horned One's shoulder, pushing him back with brute force.

The Horned One's heels slide across the Hallow.

Fury lights through his dark eyes, but it gives Edain time to fling the lightning off his face, the skin around his eyes red and burned.

And then the Horned One vanishes in a cloud of shadow, reappearing three feet back, so that when the goblin king staggers forward at the sudden lack of resistance, he slams right into the Horned One's sword.

"Raith!" Andraste screams as the goblin king goes down.

She flings herself at the Horned One, driving him back with unrelenting sweeps of her sword. While he's not as afraid of her flames as he is of my sword, he's wary of them.

I dart in from the other side, forcing him to lay about him with desperate strikes. He bares his teeth in a dangerous smile, turning and slamming his elbow into Andraste's face. Her flames might sear him, but he moves so fast, we can barely keep up.

We're not going to be enough. No matter how many times we hit him, his wounds simply heal. We're just buying time, falling one by one.

I have to make my move.

I have to take out his heart.

It pulses like a magnet, sending an injection of pure power through his veins.

"Cover me!" I yell at Edain, lunging forward in a blistering attack.

Our swords clash again and again, even as a dark truth surfaces in my heart. I've never faced anything like this before. He's faster than Eris. Stronger than Baylor. More devious than Finn. He meets everything I can throw at him and then he hammers me back, lashing out with a fistful of lightning.

I take it to the chest, a shock of heat slamming through me.

Another.

My heart skips a beat. I'm down on one knee, desperately trying to hold onto my Darkyn steel.

And he smiles as if he senses the same truth I just have: He's got me.

"It was a good fight," he says, "It reminds me of your ancestor. But you are not whole. And without that one last missing piece, you cannot stand against me."

"Not yet," says a very quiet voice from the right.

Amaya steps out of the shadows as if she's just stepped through the Hallow, Grimm in her arms. Her black hair is braided back from her face, and though her green eyes are wide and frightened as she stares at the monster before us, there's a steely look upon her face.

The same look her mother gets sometimes.

"Brother D says he'll surrender," she whispers to me. "He said he loved me. That he'll give himself up for me. And then he showed me how to do it. How to make you whole."

Holding out her palm, she conjures a flame of pure darkness. A flame of oblivion.

It floats toward me, flickering and wavering.

"*Yes,*" Death breathes, reaching for it greedily.

"No." The Horned One bellows, hurling lightning at her.

"Amaya!" I scream, flinging a shield of pure Darkness between them.

Amaya staggers back, but his lightning is contained, flickering within the void of my power. Grimm hisses and then vanishes, and while I don't dare tear my eyes off her, I suspect the Horned One is suddenly dealing with fifty pounds of pure fury and fur.

Andraste slides across the Hallow toward her, hauling her into her arms. She gives me a nod.

She'll protect her.

"*Get up,*" Grimm says, appearing right beside me, his eyes locked on the Horned One. "*Get up and take her offering.*"

I crawl to my feet, reaching for that dark flame without hesitation.

It's like finally coming home to myself.

The frost running through my veins no longer sets me on fire. The world darkens, but there's clarity in the darkness. Strength.

I forge my sword again, but this time, there's a sense of weight to it. An edge that wasn't there before.

And then the Horned One pauses, his head jerking toward the south.

Where a shining beacon of light spears toward the heavens.

"Ceres," Edain pants.

Another one joins it, this time further south. "The Briar King's Hallow," Andraste whispers, her arms wrapped around Amaya.

A punctuation of light obliterates the north.

"Charun," says the goblin in a guttural voice.

One by one, light punctuates the north and south, as if the cataclysm has set off all the Hallows on Arcaedia.

"What are they doing?" Andraste's face pales as she drags Amaya to safety.

I turn back to the Horned One. "Vi's breaking the Hallows open. She's setting the Old Ones free. Come on! We have to give her time! We have to distract him!"

It's time to finish this.

Chapter Forty-Three

L ight races along the leylines, taking me with it. It burns through my veins, burns me whole until I can barely scream. The crown burned away to nothing, leaving a coronet of pure flame in my hands, and it emphasizes my power, leaving me limitless.

"*Rise up, Vi.*"

The Mother of Night's voice.

I smash through the Hallow in the Briar King's keep, and suddenly I'm in an ancient forest. An enormous craggy stranger turns to stare at me in surprise, deer antlers poking through his hair. Moss clings to them.

The Green Man.

"And thus I set you free," I whisper, driving all that heat —all that light—through the heart of the Hallow that imprisons him. "Come to me and fight, for the Horned One has risen."

He vanishes, and I'm nothing more than light again, hitting a nexus point in the leylines—a Hallow, though not one of the origin Hallows—and racing down each thread.

Right through another origin Hallow.

Seas surge as the Father of Storms bursts free of the gilded net that saw him bound to the sea floor, his enormous trident gleaming bone-white under a distant sun.

Mrog the Warmonger smashes through the slate of his Hallow with his enormous battleaxe, the feathers in his woven hair a brilliant red.

West toward Maren's court and the Dream Thief.

I catch a glimpse of his face in an ancient mirror—dark eyes so similar to mine—and then my power smashes through the glass.

"Come to me," I call, fingers digging right through the stone of my Hallow as I drink that magic down. I can feel my body again, feel myself rising. It's like thunder in my veins, a pure volcano about to explode.

North into Unseelie. Smashing through Hallow after Hallow. Waking them all. Freeing them.

Red Mag.

The Raven King.

Bloody Mara.

A howl echoes through the night as the Grimm One breaks free.

The Wraithenwold screams into existence.

The Frost Giant tears the ice apart and climbs through his Hallow.

All of them....

"Come to me," I whisper, burning into being once more.

Spreading wings made of pure fire, I launch into the air, hovering over the Hallow at Eidyn. I am both a phoenix reborn, and a woman made of flame. All of the fire within me is finally free, and the crown of flames on my head threatens to obliterate all in its path.

With a whirl of power, the Warmonger steps into being in the center of my Hallow.

A cloak of ravens swirls into a tall, handsome male with claws.

One by one, they appear out of nowhere—those that were once vanquished and have now been set free.

The last to arrive is the Erlking, prowling right into the center of the Hallow as if he heard my call.

Thiago drives the Horned One back. Andraste jerks Amaya out of the way, protecting her with her own body. Edain and the goblin king stand between them and the Horned One, waiting for a chance to attack.

"Where is the Mother?" Red Mag rasps, a red line of blood painted right down the center of her face. "Where is Imrhien?"

I look down toward the stone at my feet, where her cloak once lay.

"Gone," says the Erlking, slamming his fist to his chest in a sign of respect for her. "Gone to join her husband and children."

The rest of them slam fists to chest.

And then they look at me.

"What would you have of us?" the Erlking demands, his eyes twinkling.

He knows full well his debt to me is not paid.

I turn toward the enormous warrior at my side, remembering what the Mother told me. "The Horned One seeks to vanquish the world—"

"Let him," sneers Red Mag. "Let him wipe this fae scum from our lands."

It's the Dream Thief that steps forward, wearing a face so familiar that I dare not look too long upon it for fear I'll distract myself from battle. He has to be related to the Horned One. "The problem is, Magwyddon, that he will not stop there. You know my brother. You know his hunger." He turns those night-dark eyes upon me, the faintest smile playing about his lips. "What would you have of us, my child?"

"Destroy him," I whisper, conjuring sparks of magic on the wind.

It tears me into a pillar of flame.

"As you wish, Daughter of Light." The Erlking turns. "Prepare the Hallow. And open the void."

"No!" screams the Horned One as their combined magic grabs him.

Thiago drives his sword right through his heart, and the Horned One gasps as the wound turns black. It spreads out from where that sword is buried in him, consuming him by inches.

Setting my hands to his temples, I let my flames burn.

He can't fight us both.

"I will take you with me," he snarls, grabbing my wrists.

But I'm no longer whole. Merely flame.

He screams as his hands burn.

Screams until Thiago twists the blade.

And then he's finally silent.

My flames flicker out, leaving me back in my mortal body.

Every inch of me feels wrung out and empty, my bones like lead. "Oh gods," I groan.

We're not finished yet, whispers the crown. *We can crush Unseelie. Claim the crowns of all those queens.*

I can feel it on my head, and pluck it from my temples, surprised to find a wreath of golden flames. Tiny diamond shards glitter among those flames so that it catches the light and gleams. It's morphed shapes.

But not desires.

"Thanks," I tell it, summoning one last thread of the Hallow's power. "But I'm quite content to go crownless. I have everything I want, right here. Back into the box with you."

No! it screams as I use the Hallow to send it back to its lead-lined box, locked high in Ceres tower.

I'll deal with it later.

The light starts to dim, all of it centering in upon me. It should feel like there's nothing left, but I can feel it within me, shivering beneath my skin. In the wake of its loss, I finally notice the slate floors beneath me, sealed shut with a thin line of gold as if my reemergence healed the Hallow.

It's song rages through the world in perfect counter-point to those Hallows around it.

It's beautiful.

Clean. Pure. Reenergized.

In perfect balance.

And as the Old Ones lay the Horned One's body on the slate floors of the Hallow with a quiet, sad reverence, my knees go out from under me.

Chapter Forty-Four

Iskvien

"Vi!" Thiago slides to his knees beside me, drawing me into his arms. His enormous hug envelops me, drowning out the world. This is my refuge, my safe haven in any storm.

"You're alive," I whisper, splaying my palm over his heart. The beat of it is strong and firm. There's no sign of the blackness in his eyes, no hint of the chill in his skin.

"He's gone," he whispers, as if he knows what I'm searching for. "For the moment."

Drawing me to my feet, he tucks me under his arm.

The sounds of battle have fallen silent.

Dawn blazes in the sky to the east.

I stare at it, at that faint rosy hue. It had been evening as we made that mad, rushing dash toward the Hallow. Surely the ordeal with the Horned One hadn't taken—

"You made the sun rise early," Thiago says. "When you rose from the Hallow, it began to rise too."

"That's impossible."

"Not impossible," says a quiet male voice beside us. The Dream Thief smiles wryly at my shocked glance. "You ascended, Iskvien, and the ripples of the Hallow's implosion affected everything. Time. Space. Night and Day. An ascendancy—a true ascendancy—affects every Hallow in the world. We all felt it. It was the only thing that could have freed us all simultaneously. Every warrior out there on that field will have gone to their knees as time streamed past them in an instant. Fae on far-off continents will have felt the earth tremble beneath their feet as the skies flashed dark, before light exploded across the entire world. And the otherkin...." His face softens with a strange sense of peace. "They will know what it means. They will know that we are back. That they are free now."

Tension slides through the arm draped over my shoulder, but I press my fingers to Thiago's side. "And what do you intend to do now you are free?"

The Dream Thief stares at the Hallow and the lightning-jagged seam of gold painted into the floor. I don't quite know what to name the look on his face: an ancient kind of sadness? Grief, perhaps? "I will do what I have always done. I will protect my people. I will steal the nightmares from their dreams and twist them to haunt their enemies. I will guard them from those who seek to harm them, and usher them back to the forests." His mouth presses into a thin, slightly evil smile. "But first, I'm going to go and pay the Queen of Aska a visit and remind her that fae queens should never summon powerful gods from their dreams and seek to trap them in the heart of a mirror."

"While I would love to see Maren's face if you strolled into her court, I can't help thinking this would start a war."

The Dream Thief's ancient eyes lock upon me. "How does one start a war that's been running for thousands of years?"

"It doesn't have to be that way."

"You are the Daughter of Light," the Erlking says as he joins us. "You're no longer fae, Iskvien. You ascended. All the otherkin will know of it. They will worship you and—"

"No." A shudder runs through me as I seek out Thiago's hand. "I don't want that."

I want to just be me.

I want... breakfast in bed, with our daughter cuddled between us.

I want boring state dinners. Argumentative council gatherings, where Finn and Eris scowl at each other over the table. I want Thalia to lob a blueberry at me when she's exasperated. And Baylor to pinch the bridge of his nose at the mayhem, even as Lysander stirs it to greater heights.

And I want time.

Time with Thiago. I want to wake every morning in his arms and kiss him every night. I want to tell him all the boring details of my day. And shiver as he presses me down into the mattress, his tongue tracing slick circles down my abdomen.

The Erlking stares at my hand. At the final set of golden antlers imprinted onto the inside of my wrist. And then he smiles. "Why not let us try this new thing? This... thing called peace."

"Peace?" I blurt. The Erlking—the leader of the Wild Hunt—wants peace?

He shrugs, his gaze sliding toward the edge of the Hallows where our armies await. Even from here I can pick out Blaedwyn's banners in the forefront, and the warrior queen staring at us as if awaiting what is coming. "Peace," he replies again thoughtfully. "A true peace, the likes of which we've never had. Unseelie is shattered. One queen is dead, another fled, and the final queen...." His smile turns dangerous. "Well, let us just say that in ten months' time, the last Unseelie queen will be at my mercy." He glances toward the Dream Thief as if they're communing on some level I can't understand. "Let the Old Ones claim Unseelie. They are the descendants of our people, and they will worship us again. If the fae do not want them for the otherkin blood in their veins, then let us have them. Let us protect them."

I can't help thinking this is going to be a mistake.

But I can see Mrog the Warmonger staring at our armies as if he barely had a taste of the fight.

And at his side, Red Mag runs a thumb along the edge of her knife.

"That is not our pledge to make," Thiago says softly, as if he can sense the same undercurrents I can. "It would require the entire Seelie Alliance to strike such accords."

The Erlking arches a brow. "Then call your alliance together, and we will treat. Or what is left of it. Tomorrow at dawn." He nods over my shoulder. "It will give you a chance to reunite with your family."

I follow his gaze to where Amaya is standing next to my sister, a battered grimalkin in her arms.

"Maya," I whisper. I saw her earlier, when I rose, but what in the name of Darkness is she doing here? In a war zone?

Thiago's hand in the middle of my back gestures me toward her. "I believe Grimm brought her. Something about how she needed to be here."

* * *

"Amaya." I stride toward her, and she lunges into my arms, wrapping her legs around my hips. Grimm vanishes at the last minute, reappearing on the ground with a dismissive sniff.

I don't care.

My daughter smells like the soap we use. And she's warm in my arms, warm and safe and *mine*.

And crying. Her entire body shakes with it.

"Grimm said you were going to die...." She gasps. "If I didn't come, then you were going to fall."

I kiss her hair, breathing in her scent. Grimm's been right too many times about the future for me to argue against him. And he loves her. He wouldn't have brought her here if he thought she'd be in any danger. "You were so brave. And we're safe. He's gone. We're all safe."

Amaya squeezes me tight.

537

And then she slowly lifts her tearstained face as Thiago approaches.

"It helped you?" she whispers.

"It did." He holds out his hand, staring at his skin. "You did exactly what you needed to do."

Amaya bolts into his arms.

He staggers back, not expecting it. But then he lifts her into his arms, pressing his face against her neck. Every inch of him curves into her, his arms gripping tight as if he's afraid to let go—as if he's been waiting for this moment for so long, that he just needs to absorb it.

"*Did I miss something?*" I ask.

He smiles at me over her shoulder. "*She managed to give me the seed of Darkness within herself. The essence of the creature inside her gave itself up in order to save us all—and ultimately her.*"

"*Does that mean*—?"

He looks troubled. "*I think you were right. What is within me was shaped by me.*" He hesitates. "*Absorbing the others has only strengthened the psychic entity I know. It has not changed, only grown whole.*" His gaze shifts over my shoulder and he tilts his head. "I think your sister wants a word with you. I'll have a moment with Amaya."

I spin around.

"Vi." Andraste stops three paces from me, her smoke-stained pink cloak swirling in the breeze. Tall and lean with muscle, she looks every inch the warrior. Every inch a conquering queen.

It's what I always aspired to be. She was my idol, my older sister, my inspiration. And when she shut me out—when Mother insisted we were no longer to share the same tutors or the same wing of the castle—it felt like I lost everything that mattered to me.

I didn't fit in.

Once upon a time, I resented her for that. For not caring. For walking away. For letting me believe I was... nothing.

I look at her, and all I can see are two little girls giggling in the forest as they clasp hands together and swing in circles. My heart breaks for those two little girls, soon to feel the shadow of their mother's jealousy sweep over them.

We never had a chance to be allies.

We never had a chance to be sisters.

"Andi." My voice is raw.

There's a flash of black and pink and gold, and then she slams against me, staggering me back. Warm arms lock around me, and I throw myself into the hug, squeezing her tight.

"I'm so sorry," she whispers. "For everything. I have tried to make amends. I have tried and tried and tried, but if you never forgive me...."

"There is nothing to forgive. You saved Amaya for me." Tears heat my eyes. "I never got the chance to say thank you."

"You don't have to say thank you," she whispers. "I'm sorry I never dared do more. I'm so sorry if any of my actions contributed to the hurt you bore."

"I understand why you did what you had to do. And she's gone," I tell her, wanting her to understand. "Mother's gone."

Andraste clasps my face between her hands. "I know. I don't know how but I felt it happen. Edain and Lysander found us, and I begged Raith to ride south and then... suddenly I knew I had to get to you. I knew you needed me. We've been pushing day and night. What happened?"

"I turned her into a tree."

"*What?*" Andraste draws back so she can see my face. "A tree?"

"A tree?" Edain barks, reminding me we're not alone.

He stands nearby, trying to clean his knives.

"I... couldn't kill her." I can see it all over again and the story rushes out. "I didn't want to become her."

"Oh, Vi." Another hug from my sister. "Vi, you're nothing like Mother. She was cruel and manipulative and—"

"She wasn't always like that." I swallow the lump in my throat. "I've seen the past. I saw how she took her throne. It was the crown, Andi. It gave her the power to save herself all those years ago, but it slowly warped her into the queen she became. It stripped away every facet of who she truly was, until only ambition was left."

There's pain in my sister's eyes. "What did you do with the crown?"

I'm not entirely sure I want to reveal the truth. Not with so many ears listening. It's still there. Lurking at the edges of my conscious. "I locked it away where no one could get to it. And then I forgave her."

A certain hardness flashes across her face. "Maybe you're a better woman than I am, because I hope that bitch rots."

"I didn't do it for her sake."

I did it for me. I did it for Thiago. For Amaya.

I did it so we can all move on and embrace happiness.

Maybe she understands, because she releases a slow breath. "Okay. So Mother is a tree. The Horned One is gone. And my little sister is all grown up."

"Enough about me. Where have you been? What happened to you?" I grab her sleeve and draw her away from the rest of them.

The faintest of smiles playing over her lips. "Now *that* is a long story."

"It seems we have time," I remind her. "Can you imagine how horrified Mother would be to know the queens of Evernight and Asturia will sit down over wine and reminisce?" A laugh breaks loose. "If nothing else, that's the vengeance I seek. I want her to know she couldn't destroy us. Or our countries."

For the first time, I sense Andraste withdrawing. She throws a glance over her shoulder to where the enormous goblin that was riding at her side sits on a broken section of hallow stone, trying to wind a bandage around a shallow wound on his left arm. He bites the linen, forced to use his teeth thanks to the stump that is all that remains of his right hand, but I know his attention is upon us.

"No," she whispers, staring back at him. There's something on her face I've never seen before. Then she lets out a breath and straightens. "I'm not going to become Queen of Asturia. I'm not taking the throne. I'm not coming back, Vi."

"What?" I squeeze her hands. "What do you mean?"

Andraste was practically groomed from birth for the crown. She's spent her entire life with it in her sights.

"I made a promise." She won't meet my eyes. "If Raith fought for you—if he fought for me—then...." Another

541

slow exhale. "I would fight for him. I owe him a debt, Vi. And this one time, I have to pay it myself."

"Who is he?"

Suddenly, there's a hint of a mischievous smile on her face. "My husband."

"*What?*"

"It's complicated." Her smile turns into a full-fledged laugh. "Not the husband Mother promised me to, obviously." She screws up her nose. "Raith killed Urach barely two hours ago. But the one who kidnapped me on the way to my wedding."

"Kidnapped you?" *On the way to your wedding?* I link arms with her. "I think the two of us definitely need to sit down and have that glass of wine."

"I think I'm going to need more than a glass," she mutters, her gaze shifting past me.

I turn and catch a glimpse of Edain slipping his daggers into their sheaths.

Despite the battle, he barely looks touched. A vicious wolf stalking through a field of mud. But the way he's looking at my sister, as though they're the only two who exist in this world—

"This way," Andraste blurts, hauling me in the opposite direction, toward where Baylor and Lysander are embracing. "Why don't you introduce me to your daughter? I haven't seen her since she was a baby."

I throw one last glance over my shoulder toward Edain.

He's still. Motionless. His face iced over.

But I know he saw her change direction.

And as Edain stalks away, I catch a glimpse of Lysander watching him go.

Chapter Forty-Five

I circle the tree, ignoring the servant who came with me to light the way. Setting hands to the bark does nothing to still the glacial creep of rage inside me. *Adaia's gone. Gone.*

"You should be relieved," someone said to me in passing. "The wicked queen is vanquished."

It's not relief I feel. I don't quite have the words to describe the feeling clawing its way up my throat and threatening to choke me. *Cheated* might come close.

I wanted Adaia to die.

I wanted to be the one to drive a knife through her murderous heart and watch as she gasped and choked, knowing I was her ruin.

Nothing has changed. *Nothing.* The curse she cast upon me is still wound tight through my soul.

Adaia took everything from me. And I wanted the chance to take it back.

"You fucking bitch." Somehow, my knife is in my hand. I drive it into the tree, again and again, but it's a tree. It doesn't bleed. It doesn't tremble. A hint of sap pours forth from where my knife gouged it, but the wind shivers through its leaves as if nothing is amiss—

Fuck you. Casting about, my gaze alights on a nearby warrior, fallen with his sword.

Yanking it from his grip—he won't need it anymore—I turn and hammer my first blow at the trunk of the tree. The impact shivers through me, but it feels good. It feels *too* good. Fury pours through me as I lay about me with the sword. Fierce swings that blunt the edge of my anger. I strip my gloves off in order to get a better grip, and then I try and cut that bitch down.

It's only once my shoulders are heaving and my breath coming in sobs that I step back to take a look at my handiwork.

Nothing.

Her trunk is marred with blade strokes, but I've barely cut an inch deep.

The sword is no match for the oak.

"You fucking bitch," I whisper, pressing one hand

against the tree and bowing my head. She's beyond my reach now.

And I will never be the same.

"My lord...?" The servant sounds hesitant. "My lord, do you want—"

"Go," I tell him. "Go back to camp. You've done enough for the night."

"My lord—"

Growling under my breath, I turn and heave the sword into the night, and that's when I finally notice I'm not alone.

The beast watches.

He stares at me, his eyes glimmering every shade of gold. They're not fae eyes in that moment. They're not even the eyes of the bane who threatened to tear my throat apart. No, they belong to something else. Something wild and angry. Something that howls at the moon and hunts the dangerous night.

"I promised you a reckoning," Lysander says, lifting his eyes toward the tree's leafy canopy. "Once this was all said and done."

He's the perfect target to ease this anger within me. "Then let's dance." I stalk toward him, summoning two knives into my hands.

The fucker laughs at me.

And the servant scrambles to get out of the way, though he doesn't flee.

"Dance, little princeling?" Lysander doesn't even bother to draw his own knife. "I'd like to oblige, but where I'm from, we don't dance. We hunt. We kill. We fuck. None of this dueling bullshit." Those eyes gleam at me like polished gold coins as his voice drops to a growl. "I've spent thousands of years hunting your kind. You want me off the leash, pet? I don't think you can handle me off the leash."

The smile that touches my lips feels lethal. "Don't worry. I wasn't planning on pulling any punches. Dueling's not my forte."

"You prefer a male shackled on his knees," he sneers.

Oh, yes. We're finally doing this.

I circle him slowly as he does the same. "Don't pretend you wouldn't like me in the same position."

It seems I've surprised him. "True. But I wouldn't put you there in order to cut your throat."

Blood sprays across my hand as I slice my blade across his throat from behind, meeting my queen's eyes. I can see how much Adaia enjoys this moment—even as she wears her daughter's face. There's nothing she likes more than seeing me kill one of her enemy's favorite warriors, and not even the nothingness within me—that barren black hole I seek comfort in—can escape the flare of disgust that tremors through me when I see the lust ignite in her eyes.

The bane gasps and chokes as he drowns on his own blood, his lungs heaving as she steps toward me, her eyes no longer on him. Night after night, death after death, it's always the same. He'll rise at some stage in the early morning, his fingers slowly twitching as whatever magic curse is wrapped around him brings him back from death. And tomorrow night we'll play this game again until I can barely escape the sensation of his blood wetting my fingers.

Barely escape the bite of her nails in my back as she demands I fuck her. Here. Now. Still covered with blood.

I blink my way out of the memories.

And just in time, for an enormous fist swings my way.

Finally. A real match.

I duck beneath the swing, my knife kissing the air an inch from Lysander's abdomen as he leaps back. He's on the back foot, and I press my advantage, swiping low and hard, one after the after, so he doesn't get a chance to breathe.

He avoids every swing, baring his teeth in what's almost a grin before he captures my wrist—extended just a half inch too far—and then drives his knee into my ribs.

Pain explodes in starbursts behind my eyes.

But pain is the thing I know best.

We break apart and I swallow it down, ignoring the waves of heat radiating in my side, considering him as we both stalk in slow circles around each other.

"You like knives, pet?" He holds up his hands, and the fingers crack and extend, transforming into enormous claws. For a second, his pupils elongate and then he shivers and restrains the curse still riding him. "Want to play with these?"

In answer, I twirl the pair of knives in my hands.

I've spent the past few weeks as we searched for Andraste cataloguing every move he made in battle, knowing that this moment was going to come. Eventually.

And my threat assessment is: Uncertain.

Lysander moves with flawless precision, muscles bunching and flowing from one move to the next. I've always had the gift of being able to predict which move will come next—to see the shift in weight and glimpse the exact blow the bastard will hammer at me, but Lysander's like no one else I've ever encountered.

He's shockingly fast.

Far stronger than expected. Ambidextrous.

And he doesn't fight in set patterns.

All my intelligence upon the White Wolf tells me that he's a dangerous adversary. He's centuries older than me. I don't even know where he was birthed—or even *if* he was birthed. He and his brother bowed knee to Thiago sometime during the Wars of Light and Shadow, and he's served that prick ever since.

I'm forced to meet him one-on-one. Body against body. One of my knives is gone with a shocking chop of his hand to my wrist. I make him earn it, spinning beneath the lock of his arm and driving my elbow back into his throat.

It's a mistake.

And I don't make mistakes. Ever.

But he barely even grunts, his forearm hauling me back against him and cutting off my air. I knew he had two inches on me, but there's a difference to knowing it... and feeling it.

I twist my grip and throw him over my shoulder. He slams into the leaf mulch. "The bigger they are...."

Curling his abdomen up, he flips onto his feet, lashing out behind him with his claws. "The harder they can fuck."

There's that smile again as I leap over the swing of his claws.

I crouch low, my knife held backward along my forearm. "Is that what you tell yourself?"

"It's what I know."

Claws rake along my arm. My knife kisses his thigh. It's a blur of movement, so fast it almost seems like dancing.

We slam together, and I force my body in tight, too close for him to do anything more than curl his arms around me and dig those claws in. They penetrate my shoulders, and I hiss as he throws me down. I have two seconds of grace, and then he's on me again.

It feels good to give myself over to the rage.

It feels good to throw a punch and not have to pull it.

Yanking me back against him, he pins me again, his thighs grinding against the back of mine, and the crook of his arm locked beneath my chin.

The claws find my throat, tips digging deep into the suprasternal notch there.

I freeze. Breathing hard. My knife sheathed between his thighs, close enough to make him sing soprano if I twist my wrist.

And for a second I think about it.... Think about just letting him rip those claws across my artery.

But I don't want to die.

I want to kill.

Lysander grabs me by the throat, fae fingers pressing firmly enough to yield a threat, even as he slides the claws of his right hand down my chest, digging the tip of them right into the point of my sternum. He's been practicing, if he can shift one hand and not the other....

"Do it," I whisper, setting my knife against the artery in his groin. "And it shall be the last thing you do."

Turning my face, I stare into his eyes. Hot breath rasps over my face. We're both heaving for breath.

BEC MCMASTER

He considers me.

And then he shoves me forward, onto my knees.

"No," Lysander whispers, pushing to his feet. "Nothing I can do will ever punish you as much as what you're doing to yourself right now."

Maybe it's the trace of mockery in that curl of a smile. The hint of satisfaction. The world vanishes in a haze of red.

A chasm splinters through my chest.

Sheer, blind rage.

I slam into him, but he's already waiting.

It's ridiculously easy the way he throws me.

My knees hit the ground and then one arm is yanked behind my back and he shoves me down, face into the loam, the back of his thighs grinding into mine.

Twisting and wrestling, I manage to get the upper hand. I don't want to kill him. I want to *destroy* him.

I shove my hand under his jaw, forcing him to bare his throat.

Our eyes meet.

The mocking glint in his gaze makes me bare my teeth. *Fuck this.* I reach for him with my ungloved right hand.

His smile dies as if he senses my sudden determination. "Oh, no. Gloves are off." Running his tongue over his teeth, he beckons me toward him. "I prefer a firm grip, if you want to know."

He doesn't know what I can actually do with my touch. "I wasn't planning on fist-fucking you."

"Shame. You're almost pretty enough to tempt me."

I grab him by the throat, bare fingers wrapping around his windpipe. Lysander merely laughs, hammering his elbow toward my face. Ducking away from the blow, I come up defensively but he's merely dancing to his feet, waiting for me to attack.

There's no sign of my white handprint burning into his skin.

No hint of decay streaking away from where I touched him.

Whole. Untouched.

"What?" He touches his throat as if to chase away the sensation of my gaze.

I stare at my hands. It's impossible.

And then I grab him by the throat again, shoving him back against the oak, clenching my fingers tight and digging them into the smooth column of his esophagus, daring them to destroy him.

Nothing. Happens.

Lysander grabs my wrist, laughing at me. "Not to be indelicate, but it wouldn't work, pet. We both clearly prefer to be on top."

What the fuck...? My hands tremble.

I'd touched three fae before I realized what Adaia had truly cursed me with.

I've watched those black lines streak through their veins as if they're being consumed from within. I've seen their faces crumble to dust, until they collapse in upon themselves. I've tried to capture those ashes in my hands as the wind blows them away, knowing there was a fae there once. Knowing that I caused this.

Live a thousand years, Edain, and never know another's touch again....

I didn't understand what she meant until it was too late.

The day I pulled those gloves on was the day I consigned my heart to the silence within me.

But now.... "I could touch her," I whisper.

"If you're talking about Andraste, then tell yourself the truth, Edain." Lysander captures my face in one hand, leaning close enough to taste my breath. "Your princess doesn't want you. She never wanted you the way you wanted her, did she? And now she's sleeping in the same tent with the goblin king. Sharing his meals. Bathing right in front of him. You can deny it all you want, but he's treated her with nothing but kindness, and you? You're her mother's whore. Her assassin. The reason she's in this predicament. Maybe you're prettier than he is, but everything you've ever touched turns to rot, doesn't it? Why would she choose you?"

I grab his wrist and shove him off me, breathing hard. Lysander laughs as he pretends to brush dust off his shirt. "Touched a nerve?"

I reel away from him.

But it doesn't deny the truth tingling through me, the way the imprint of his touch echoes in my skin.

He touched me.

And I touched him.

Curling my fingers into a fist, I try to ignore the sensation of his skin imprinted against mine. I haven't felt another's skin in months. It's not the sort of thing I ever thought I'd miss until I wasn't able to feel it.

"You will never touch another fae for as long as you live.

Your touch will burn, your soul will wither, and your flesh will beg for relief, but there shall be none to be found."

Adaia's words echo through me.

He shouldn't be standing right now.

What if it's not impossible?

What if the curse is broken somehow?

The heat bleeds from my extremities.

I could have Andraste.

Regardless of his words, there has to be a chance.

"What?" The arrogant prick arches a brow as he brushes imaginary dust off his braided leather tunic. "Did that bitch steal your tongue too?"

"Fuck you."

He stares at me. And then he laughs. "Too easy," he mutters under his breath. "Go back to camp, Edain. Get some sleep. You look like shit." He throws a glance at the tree. "And she's not worth destroying yourself over."

"I thought that's what you'd want?"

Lysander sighs as he backs away. "Don't let her drag you down. She's gone, Edain. Gone. And she was never going to give you what you want from her."

"I don't want anything from her."

"No? Not even an apology?"

The breath catches in my lungs. The idea's ludicrous. I don't want an apology. Adaia would never dream of even issuing one. I wanted her dead. I wanted her....

I want her to admit what she did to me was wrong.

I want her to understand that she fucking took *everything* from me.

"You can spend forever waiting for someone to acknowledge what they did to you," Lysander says, meeting my gaze. For once, that fucking smile I hate so much is nowhere to be seen. "Or you can push that burden back upon them. It's not your responsibility to force them to accept what they did to you. Chances are, you'll never get it, and if you're waiting for someone else to let you move on, then you put the power of your emancipation back in their hands. You owe yourself nothing more than to give yourself space to heal. Their route to forgiveness is not your burden."

The blood drains from my face.

Because for the first time, I realize I'm not the only victim here.

Adaia gave the order to kill him, but I didn't fight that hard.

I gave up fighting years ago.

And he sees it.

Maybe that's acknowledgement enough.

Lysander nods once. "I'm not going to kill you," he says quietly. "This is enough for me."

And then he turns and walks away.

Just that easily.

If only.... I turn and stare at the tree.

"Give me the fucking torch," I say to the servant in a dead voice, even as I watch Lysander stalk away.

The stammering servant presses it into my hand.

And then I turn to the tree.

"Fuck you, you bitch," I tell her, hoping she can hear me even as I set the flame to her roots. "You think you've won? I will take everything you ever denied me. I will take your throne. I will take your daughter. And I will burn everything you ever touched to the ground."

Flames sparks, catching against the dry grass around the base of the tree.

Maybe it's my imagination, but I swear it tries to rear away from the smoldering flames.

"Burn, Adaia," I whisper as I toss the torch at her base and tug my gloves on. "I hope you feel it."

Chapter Forty-Six

Iskvien

There are a thousand things to do in the wake of the war.

But the first thing, the most pressing thing, is to work on the accords.

Unseelie is broken. The Seelie Alliance shattered.

And the Old Ones returned.

The Duke of Thornwood hastily assembled a tent in the middle of the field for the alliance to meet beneath. I kissed Amaya on the forehead as Grimm escorted her back to Ceres and then made my way toward it.

We've spent three hours arguing about whether to accept the Old Ones' treaty, and the talk seems to be going in circles again. Thiago sends for food and wine, hoping to clear the air for the moment.

"What do we do about Asturia?" Prince Kyrian finally asks, as the platters arrive.

I pause with a grape halfway to my mouth. "What about Asturia?"

"There's an empty throne sitting there," he says, arching one of those dark brows. "Who's going to rule now? You? Your sister? Precisely where does the succession sit? Who's going to cast Asturia's vote?"

"Not me. It's not my home anymore." It was never my home—

Andraste captures my hand in hers. "It belongs to someone who gave up far too much for it," she whispers, and glances to her right, where Edain sits stony-faced and silent.

"No," he says, rousing for the first time, his eyes flashing fire. "No. I don't want it."

Andraste tips her chin up. "And maybe that's the one reason you should have it. When mother claimed the kingdom, she changed the laws so the throne is not given hereditarily. Most likely because she was no heir to the previous king. She never changed them back. She insisted that as crown princess, I spend hours training in order to be able to fight off any challenges.

"So why not you? You have the ability to hold your own

against all who might see a throne in their future. And you played Mother like a fiddle. What the others do not understand is that you have always steered her policies, pushing her toward leniency, toward peace, when her first instinct was mayhem. You've had a great deal of practice in ruling already."

"Everyone in Asturia considers me an extension of your mother's will. There will be blood for this."

"There will be blood anyway," she retorts. "You think the baron of Harewood is not going to take a tilt at the throne if it's unclaimed? Or Essington? Or even the Duke of the Southern Reaches? Every aristocrat in the kingdom with even a hint of the royal lineage in their veins will be calling their bannermen to them."

"Then maybe their crown princess should return?" he bites out.

Andraste gathers herself primly, strangely calm. Something happened between them last night, I'm sure of it. But she seems at peace with it. "I have relinquished all right upon the crown of Asturia. I promised it thrice before Maia. There's no coming back from that, Edain."

"And does your sister agree with such assessment?" Edain turns to me, his words hissing between his teeth.

"I have nothing to add. I relinquished any claim I had upon Asturia long ago. Thornwood?" The duke has been surprisingly silent throughout these earlier exchanges.

Steepling his fingers together, he considers us all. He's here to represent the autonomous colony of the Borderlands, and while he hasn't spoken very much, when he does, he wastes little time on flamboyancy. "Your mother always said that whoever takes the throne, holds the throne." He tips his head toward Edain. "But he's right. There shall be issues with this if Edain claims it."

"Someone has to." Right now it feels like poison.

Edain pushes to his feet, pacing. "You want to play these games? Then fine, let's play." He turns to me. "I will hold the Asturian throne for your daughter then. Until she reaches her majority."

"*What?*" I push upright, but Thiago lays a hand on my arm.

"Adaia named Amaya as her heir before her court," Edain challenges. "It was the last act she signed into law before she started this war. The entire court of Asturia believes your daughter is their rightful heir, and I can stand against any who seek to challenge her. You want peace in Asturia? Then name me regent if you fucking must. But the crown will pass to Amaya."

It wasn't Amaya my mother claimed, but her changeling replacement, May.

But I can't say that.

Not in front of the rest of the alliance.

Thiago gently strokes his fingers down my spine. "*It will have to do for now. We may revisit this idea later. When we've had a chance to think.*"

He's right.

It still doesn't make me feel any better. I can't escape the instinct that such a move will tear her from my arms. Every inch of me wants to protect her and shield her from the world.

And there's the issue with a monarch claiming both Evernight and Asturia. The other kingdoms can only see such a move as a threat. We'd be a powerhouse; a juggernaut.

But I force a nod instead, because nothing Edain has said is untrue. Without a clear ruler, Asturia will descend into blood and chaos, and I love the kingdom of my birth too much to allow that. "Amaya will come of age when she is twenty-five. Not a day sooner. Not a day later. You have sixteen years of a regency ahead of you, Edain. I hope we can remain allies throughout that time."

His eyes narrow thoughtfully. "Sixteen years then."

"Will the alliance vote upon it?" I ask, casting a look around the table.

Lucere strokes the velvet edge of her hood. Her face is barely visible. "I will allow it. Evernight owes Ravenal a blood debt. With the queen as our friend, we feel confident Asturia will not seek to expand its borders south."

In other words: If Edain grows bored with sitting on his throne and starts to become ambitious, she expects me to deal with it.

Or else she'll call in that debt.

Kyrian rests his chin on his hand, his entire expression unreadable. A smirk appears. "If nothing else, it will make Adaia twist in her grave to see her former pet—a male prince—sitting on her throne. Stormlight will allow it."

"I object."

The tent flaps draw open, and a pair of raven-cloaked fae guards stalk inside.

My heart drops when I see Muraid's stern expression, and the hand she rests on the hilt of her sword.

But it's the raven-haired queen stalking behind her, glossy lips painted red, who steals my attention.

"Maren," Thiago says coldly, trying not to sound as if he'd like to say, *what the fuck?* "How kind of you to finally join us."

"You missed the main event," Kyrian says, leaning back in his chair and watching her like a hawk.

Queen Maren strides toward the final seat at the table, a flawless cloak of black swan feathers cascading from her shoulders and a black crown formed of seven sharp spikes erupting from her hair.

A servant stumbles over himself to jerk the chair back for her.

"What are you talking about?" she retorts, letting her cloak slide to the floor. Her gown appears—a glittering black that clings to every line of her body. "Am I not in time for the accords? I hear you're contemplating allowing that filth to conquer Unseelie."

"Do you have a better idea?" Kyrian gives a flourish.

Her smile is dangerous.

"We're not returning to the discussion of Unseelie. Not yet." Thiago sits up straight. "We have just granted Prince Edain the right to the regency of Asturia until our daughter, Amaya, comes of age."

"As I said," Maren purrs. "I object."

"Three votes to one," Kyrian bites out. "Your objection is noted." He hammers his palm flat on the table. "Let Prince Edain inherit the regency of Asturia. Strike it into the accords," he throws toward the scribe.

This is going to be a long day.

* * *

After three days of arguing with Maren, the treaty is struck with her voice the only one of dissent.

Unseelie will be given to the Old Ones, with Blaedwyn as the only recognized fae queen. Though the challenging way the Erlking looked at her as this statement was read into law makes me wonder if he's going to allow it.

She still owes me ten months of service. Ten months in which she'll play nice.

Ten months of relative fucking peace.

It will be interesting to see what comes of our alliance once that time is up. Morwenna fled the battlefield with what was left of her armies; Prince Corvin of Ravenal said he'd keep an eye on the old witch. She's not the kind to fade into obscurity quietly.

And Angharad is dead, brought down by Baylor's sword.

"Here we are," Thiago says, tugging me out of the Hallow when we arrive back in Ceres.

Baylor's in charge of dismantling the armies and clearing the fields surrounding Eidyn. Thornwood is going to assist. There's a friendship brewing there; two battle-hardened warlords who could hardly care what the monarchy was up to, as long as they're not causing wars. Considering they've faced each other over a battlefield several times, I'd expected them to each wield a grudge, but as Thornwood said with a shrug, "War is war. Peace is peace. And besides, I want to find out how that prick routed me at Devlin Gorge thirty years ago."

"You might have to get him drunk," Thiago warned.

"Consider it done," Thornwood had replied.

"Home," I say now, feeling the quiver of the leylines.

They're alive now in a way they weren't before. One pluck, and I can send the entire network singing, though the Dream Thief suggested I avoid doing that.

"It's impolite," he'd said with a twinkle in his eyes. "It will sound like you're hammering on my Hallow."

And then he'd offered to help me learn to control this vast new power inside me.

"Home." Thiago slides his arms around my waist, breathing in the scent of my hair. "I sometimes wondered if I'd see it again."

I lean into him, reveling in the sensation of peace and soaking up the strength inherent in his body.

It's been months since I could relax. Months of fighting, riding the edge of stress, barely sleeping, worrying.

And now this.

A hot tear slides down my cheeks. I don't know why. I have nothing to cry over.

"Come on," Thiago says, swinging me up into my arms and heading toward our rooms. "You're exhausted."

"I'm fine."

"You've barely slept in three days, Vi," he growls. "You're going to crash very soon."

"I'm not tired." There's too much power coursing through my veins.

"Do you ever not argue with me?"

I open my mouth and then shut it, because it's the only way to win.

A servant catches a glimpse of us and nearly drops her platter.

"You never saw us," Thiago tells her with a wink. "And if Thalia asks, we haven't returned from Eidyn yet."

BEC MCMASTER

"Yes, your Highness," the young fae girl says breathily, her eyes as large as saucers as Thiago nudges the door to our bedchambers open with his shoulder and then kicks it shut behind us.

"So commanding," I tease. "You know she's going to run straight to Thalia though."

He heads for the bathing chamber set off our rooms. "And Thalia will understand I want a few hours of peace."

Ah, it was a message for her then.

Conjuring magic into the fae lights that light the bathing chambers, he slowly sets me down. My skirts slide up between us, leaving my lower legs bare. From the glint in his eyes, the move was entirely deliberate.

"Are you going to join me?"

"Thought you might need some help washing your hair."

I snort, pushing against his chest. "Of course you did. I want to get clean before you... wash my hair. I've scrubbed three times and I can still smell the stink of the battlefield upon my skin."

Someone long ago built an enormous bath of white marble, big enough for three or four fae to fit inside it. Thiago once gruffly admitted that when he's tired of wearing his glamorized seelie form, sometimes it's nice to simply shed the glamor inside the safety of his bedchambers. Hence the enormous bed and bath and doorways wide enough to fit his wings.

"Strip," he commands, bending down to turn the faucets on.

"I love the way that sounds"—a shiver runs through me —"but I think I'd fall flat on my face if I tried."

564

"I'll catch you."

I pluck the crown from my head—a seven-pointed spiked diadem that pinches the sides of my head—and cast it on the bench. Relief floods through my temples as I massage them, and the sound that comes from my mouth might be embarrassing if Thiago hadn't heard worse.

The devilish twinkle in his eyes tells me he's thinking the exact same thing as he pours scented bubble wash in the enormous bath.

"Turn around."

I comply, shivering as he brushes the heavy weight of my bunched hair forward over my bare shoulder. Thalia sent supplies as soon as the war was won, and while it had been nice to slip into clean clothes, today was a formal situation.

There's a peacock blue leather corset underneath an embroidered tabard that cuts in from my shoulders and drapes all the way to the floor. Silver embroidered moons and stars wink in the darker blue of the tabard, and a complicated belt system ties it all together.

Sleek midnight blue skirts drape to the floor, gathering just above the knee before they flare around my calves.

It's gorgeous. Stunning. A warrior queen's outfit.

But I just want to strip it all off and lounge in my bed for a week.

Thiago unknots the buckles, stripping the belts off. He curses under his breath. "I swear Thalia does this to me deliberately. How many fucking buckles does this thing need?"

"I have no idea. I'm trapped in it until someone else

frees me. One must look gorgeous and powerful. One doesn't need to be comfortable doing so."

He finally works it out. "Lift your arms."

The belt is flung to the floor, and then the tabard vanishes too.

Inch by inch, he tugs at the strings on my corset, the material suddenly gaping. I capture it against my breasts, tension knotting through my lower abdomen. Suddenly, I'm no longer tired.

And getting undressed is no longer merely frustrating.

We haven't been intimate since before Eidyn.

There hasn't been a chance.

The night I ascended, I vaguely recall slamming face-first onto the stretcher in our tent, while Thiago left to deal with the army and command tent, and we've been putting out small summer forest fires ever since.

Maybe he senses it too, this need within me.

The rasp of his stubble brushes against the slope of my neck, sending a shiver all the way through me. "I missed you," he whispers, capturing my upper arms with those callused hands. "I missed this. Belt and all."

A hot openmouthed kiss paints itself against the side of my throat. "Gods."

His roughened laugh whispers over my skin as the corset falls around my hips. "Which gods? Or were you referring to yourself?"

This time the shudder isn't one of pleasure. "Don't. Please."

"You don't like the thought?"

"I hate it." Maybe this was why Maia disappeared after

her ascension, allowing herself to be conjured into a myth and a legend.

Maybe she's still out there, hiding in obscurity.

"Curse it. I was interested in worshiping at your altar."

I swat him on the shoulder, my cheeks flushing with heat. I haven't had time to come to terms with the consequences of my ascension. And there's no running away, no fading into obscurity, not for me. I can't leave my family behind, and while Thiago would always consider my preferences, to leave means leaving everything we've built and fought for.

"Into the bath with you," he says, swinging me into his arms and then lowering me into the hot water. "I can still worship you as my wife."

I sink into the bubbles, groaning again as the warm water soothes away all those niggling aches and pains.

Reaching over his shoulder, he eyes me with those insolent green eyes, as if he knows exactly what I'm thinking, and then hauls his shirt off. I can never get my fill of the chiseled cut of his body and the ripple of black shadows tattooed across his chest.

"Vi," he says roughly as our eyes connect again, "Stop looking at me like that or I'm not going to be able to get my trousers off."

I laugh and splash water in his direction, sinking my head back against the rim of the bath and unabashedly settling back to watch the show.

"Fuck," he swears under his breath, wincing as he tries to unleash the buttons keeping his cock trapped. "I'm going to make you pay for this."

Stripping them down his legs, he hops inelegantly, the ripples in his abdomen doing wonderful things.

"So powerful," I tease. "So much grace. So sophisticated."

There's a dangerous edge to his smile as he hurls the trousers at the wall and then steps into the bath, his cock curving up against his stomach. It's monstrously beautiful.

Suddenly, I want it in my mouth.

Shifting onto my hands and knees, I crawl toward him.

"Vi," he warns, kneeling in the bath as I prowl closer. Cupping a handful of water, he lets it trickle over his shoulder as if he knows exactly what it does to his body. Bubbles slide their way over the thatch of hair surrounding his cock, and he uses them to make every inch of his erection glisten.

I kiss one of the rivulets, tasting salt and skin. My lips brush against the hair beneath his navel, just as he twists a fist into my hair.

"Behave," he admonishes, though his green eyes gleam.

"I am behaving," I whisper, blinking up through wet lashes. Trailing my nails up his thighs, I let them break the water, digging them into the soft skin covering the groove of his hip.

His cock's a bare inch from my face, but that fist won't let me near it.

"You look like you're intent on claiming something more than Evernight," he whispers, curling his other fist around his cock. His knuckles flex, working the viciously swollen head of his erection. Salt gleams there, begging for my mouth, and he rubs his thumb over it, smearing it.

"And you look like you enjoy seeing a queen on her knees."

"I do." His voice roughens. "Are you going to let me kiss you? Or do you want this first?"

The head of his cock brushes against my lips.

I lick it eagerly, mouth opening around the swollen head of him. He gives me just a taste. Just enough. And then he rubs it over my lips.

"Please."

Thiago fists his erection, another salty bead forming at its tip. "It should be me begging."

Maybe that says everything about him: He's always been the powerful prince, the protector, the one who spends every moment of his life making sure I'm happy. He doesn't ask for such things in return. I'm sure a part of him will always be that lonely young man who stared up at these castle walls, wondering about his mother.

He didn't even hesitate to throw himself at the Horned One in the Black Keep when he learned that one of us would die.

And he would have done it again at Eidyn, I know. It was tangled in all the things we left unspoken, in every inch of the encounter. He left his fucking back unprotected against the Horned One because there was no part of him that could have let me fall.

So now it's my turn to return the favor.

"Never," I whisper, curling one hand around the base of him and trying to close my fingers. "I love pleasing you."

Closing his eyes, he tilts his head back, his throat bare and vulnerable as I swallow him whole, working my lips and tongue over him, and watching his face the entire time.

A twitch jerks through him, his fingers clenching slowly in my hair. A movement of such restraint that it speaks volumes. He wants to take control; I can feel it.

Just as he's forcing himself to let me pleasure him the way I want to.

This is power.

It makes me wet, makes me want to grind against nothing.

"I love you," I whisper, kissing and licking the swollen head of him. *"I'll take care of you."*

Startled eyes meet mine as he hears my psychic voice. This time, his touch gentles, his fingers combing through my hair. "I love you too," he breathes, biting his lower lip.

Time to destroy that rock-hard control.

Drawing back with a long sucking pop, I alternate between flicking my tongue over the head of him and then working my hot mouth over him. The mood shifts, and we both feel it.

I'm rewarded with a harsh snarl. *"Vi."*

"Do something about it," I whisper, biting his hip.

He starts, and then he laughs under his breath, clasping my face in both hands. "Oh, I will, you little minx."

Sensation trails down my spine; there's nothing there, of course, but I can feel his touch, feel his magic whispering over my skin. *"Who will break first, do you think?"*

"Definitely you," I shoot back.

"I'm going to come all over your pretty breasts, Vi. But first you're going to beg me...."

"I'm going to drink every last drop of you down," I counter. *"And then maybe I'll come for you."*

The caress of his magic slides between my thighs from

behind, spearing inside me. Two invisible fingers stretch me until I groan. His touch works me over until I can hardly breathe, gasping around his cock.

I clasp the back of his thigh, desperate for more, struggling to breathe as he drives his cock so far down my throat, I almost choke.

"Sorry," he gasps. "Sorry. Goddess burn me. *Vi.*"

I'm not fragile. Nor am I to be denied right this moment.

I take him deep, encouraging him. Grabbing his ass, I dig my nails in, desperate for more, desperate for this connection between us.

The soft caress of his touch is a whiplash right where I need it. A moan escapes me, and Thiago throws his head back, revealing the strong column of his throat as he gasps.

"*Fuck.*" It's a word raw with destruction. A sign of how far gone he is.

He never begs. He's always in control.

I love watching his undoing flash across his face as he bucks against me. Suckling hard, I let my throat work against his depth, and he rewards me with the hot splash of his seed.

His magic is gone, his touch lost in the moment.

But as I slowly withdraw, swallowing every last drop, his green eyes flick open, locking on me with the intensity I know lingers beneath the surface. His thumb caresses my cheek, his expression hot with sudden determination.

"Oh, now you're in trouble," he whispers.

Turning to escape, I make it half a splash away from him before a strong arm goes around my waist and he tugs me back into his arms.

Capturing my face, he hauls me into his lap, his mouth claiming mine in a bruising kiss. It's a hot, hungry kiss, one to make up for the lack before I drank of his cock. Sometimes I think he loves kissing me even more than he desires oral sex. It's like all of this has been pent up inside him. A demand to claim me. Own me. Bruise. Tongues slick against each other, my breasts pressing against his chest.

"Fuck," I breathe, drawing back for air.

He laughs as if he knows exactly what's going through my head. "Come here."

My knees settle on either side of his hips, and firm fingers dig into my ass as he drives me against the rigid line of his erection.

I'm wet and swollen, aching with the need to claim him.

"I want you inside me," I breathe against the wet skin of his throat, planting little kisses against his jaw. "I need you. Now."

"As you wish, my love," he purrs, sinking inside me with slow, aching precision.

Chapter Forty-Seven

Iskvien

I can barely move in the aftermath, but Thiago refills the bath and hauls me into his arms, where my head rests on his chest.

One of the servants discreetly brought us a pitcher of wine and two goblets before vanishing. It's not the sort of thing I'm used to, but I know it's Thalia's way of saying, *I know you're in there, you have a couple more hours to enjoy it, and then I am going to haul you out to deal with this mess.*

In hindsight, I think I'd rather stay here with the wine and my husband.

"You're quiet," Thiago murmurs, stroking my arm.

"Maybe you've worn me out."

A soft chuckle escapes him as he sips his wine. "I'd believe that if I didn't know how insatiable you could be at times."

It's an opening if I want to talk.

Or a means to laugh it off if I don't.

"I broke Unseelie." The weight of the prophecy's been sitting heavily on my shoulders ever since I heard it, but I never realized this was what it meant.

"And then you took a fucking sledgehammer to the southern alliance too," Thiago says with some amusement, resting his head back against the rim of the bath. "I will never forget the expression on Maren's face. It's the best thing that's happened to me in days."

"You helped."

He bumps his knee against mine, kissing the slope of my shoulder. "Partners in crime."

"Mmm."

Thiago's laughter fades. "Tell me what you're thinking."

"It's nothing." I want to sink under the water.

"It is something, or you wouldn't be trying to slink away. How do you feel?"

"Fine."

"You keep using that phrase," he murmurs, and the rub of his fingers indicate he doesn't believe it.

It's hard to put into words the way I feel. "There's too much to think about. I keep pushing it aside, sitting it in that silent box in my head that I forged years ago, until I'm ready to take it out and process it."

"Talking it out helps."

It does. I sip my wine. "I refuse to be a god. It sounds horrible. And I don't feel any different—I feel the same way I always did, just... finally in control of myself and my magic."

Thiago's a long time replying. "Then don't be."

He doesn't understand. "It wasn't as though we can hide what happened at Eidyn, Thiago. There were thousands of warriors there. Three entire armies worth of them. Everybody saw the implosion. Word spreads. The queens and princes of the Queensmoot said nothing, but Corvin will have had his ravens in the field. Lucere will discover it soon enough. I can't *hide* from it. I've seen them all at Maia's temple—casting their coins into her fountain and begging for her luck, for her mercy...." My breath feels like ice. "I don't want that. And I don't want more war."

"There's no saying it has to come to war."

"You've *met* Maren," I say acidly. "If she discovers I can wield the Hallows, then she'll stop at nothing to destroy me. Before I can become a threat to her."

"*If* she discovers it."

"What?" Water splashes as I jerk. His glamor is good, but not even Thiago can make an entire field of armies forget what they saw.

"I've been gathering reports from the battle site. Every warrior says the same thing. The grounds shook, the sky spat lightning, and then this enormous firebird rose into the air, flames lashing the Hallow. They're calling her the Daughter of Flame and Fury, and rumor has it that she rose to fight the Horned One before her flames finally burned themselves out. She was a creature of myth and magic. A legend in the making. Nobody saw you, Vi. They saw... a goddess. A firebird. And that's what they'll believe."

The words capture me for a moment. "Did it really look like that?"

"You had wings, Vi. Wings of pure flame. And the look in your eyes.... For a moment I couldn't breathe. You were so fucking beautiful. You were vengeance, fury, power. You were incredible." He kisses my knuckles. "And then you and the Old Ones tore the Horned One's power from him and cast him down."

I remember how it felt to fly on those wings of fire. Maybe there'd be something good to come of it.

If I can summon the creature again.

As if she knows I'm thinking of her, those fiery wings unfurl inside my chest.

"You're reheating the bath water, Vi."

"Sorry." I snap those metaphorical wings shut.

"Don't be sorry. Now I know I'll never have to spend another night shivering in some wet, rainy hut ever again. I knew I married you for a reason. You can warm my blankets."

"I can also set them on fire."

"I thought we agreed that wasn't going to happen again."

"It's a good thing I didn't want to be worshiped." I poke his arm. Then the weight of that legacy begins to press down again, making it hard to breathe. It's not something we can deny. Too many fae were there.

Thiago stirs, shifting me in his arms. "And it was a good thing that the firebird saved us."

I jerk my head toward him.

Thiago sips his wine, his eyes locking on me over the rim of the goblet. "Andraste and Raith aren't going to say a thing, Vi. And Edain can be convinced to remain silent. It's against his own vested interests for rumors to spread that the Queen of Evernight is the Daughter of Flame and Fury. Maybe we can learn from the best? Maybe it's our turn to twist the story? Thalia can plant rumors that the Daughter of Flame and Fury resides near Eidyn and can only be roused by a desperate heart to fight against the forces of true darkness."

I blink. "Did you just create a fairy tale?"

"Do you want to help me flesh out the details?"

It could work. Stories twist, after all. And what better way to cast attention elsewhere than to create a mythical being? Nobody's going to look at me and believe there's a smoldering heart of fire deep in my chest.

"And if you ever want to test out your powers," Thiago says, "I know a private little hunting cabin deep in the heart of the forests surrounding Mistmere. We could sneak away in the winter, when there's enough snow to protect the forests, and I could teach you how to fly."

"Fly?" My heart skips a beat.

"I did see the look in your eyes when I mentioned your wings, Vi." He smiles. A soft, beautiful smile full of shared joy. "I'd love to go flying with you. You're not the only one who's hidden their wings for far too long."

It sounds perfect.

Everything I've ever wanted is right in front of me. A

home. A family. A daughter. A husband who adores me. And now this....

My magic.

Fully and wholly mine.

"I'd like that," I whisper, sinking back into his embrace.

* * *

"Knock, knock!" someone calls through the door. "Are you out of the bath yet? You're going to get all pruney!"

I giggle as Thiago tries to button me into his shirt. "I'm surprised you lasted this long."

An impatient growl echoes through the door. "Are the pair of you decent?"

"No," Thiago calls, just as I yell out, "Yes."

There's a moment of hesitation.

"You're such a liar," Thalia says, shoving the door open and entering with her hand over her eyes. "But just in case you are actually not decent, Thiago, I'm prepared to protect my poor eyes."

"He's wearing his trousers," I tell her.

Thiago scowls and swats me on the backside. "Traitor."

Thalia lowers her hand, rakes the room with a practiced eye—her eyebrow lifting when she sees the bubbles and towels everywhere—and then she turns back to us with a grin.

"You're back!"

I have a second's grace before she throws herself at me.

"Safe, Thalia. Safe." I close my eyes and lean into the embrace. "Thank you. For looking after Amaya."

"Yes, well," she growls. "I had some choice words for a

certain walking carpetbag who simply plucked her out of my lap while I was reading a book to her. They both fucking vanished right before my eyes, and I had half the bloody castle out looking for them before they returned."

"It's a long story."

"Oh, I've heard half of it." She takes my hands, her eyes suspiciously shiny. "Furious battles. Goblins coming to our aid. The Horned One. And this mysterious firebird thing that destroyed him. Did you have something to do with that?"

"Me?" I protest, though I know my face pales.

"Burning half the Hallow?" Thiago laughs under his breath. "Whilst it does sound like something Vi would do, I think it had something to do with the Mother of Night's sacrifice. Perhaps she was reborn into a new body?"

Our eyes meet.

"Mmm. I need to know more about her." Thalia taps her lips. "If there's something with that power flying around our kingdom, then we need to know if it's friendly."

"The last we saw her, she was flapping north." Thiago shrugs.

"North." Thalia sighs. "I'll look into it later. I wish I could tell you to lock the doors to your chambers and enjoy the next couple of days, but I can't. It's why I'm here. You have guests awaiting you both. One set in the audience chambers for Vi. They've been waiting for you to return."

"Guests?" Who would be calling so soon after we returned? And why me?

"And Finn's back," Thalia says, looking Thiago in the eye. "Alone."

579

His face turns grim. "Is she—?"

"Gone, Finn said. Eris came back to herself somewhere to the north of Eidyn and told him she wanted to be alone. She gave him the slip, and took the Hallow somewhere."

Thiago sighs. "I'll go talk to him."

"This way, Vi," Thalia says, clapping her hands and turning toward our bedchambers. "I've had the maids lay out a gown for you."

I groan. Not another torture contraption.

"If I have to rip her out of it later," Thiago calls, "I will do so."

"You tear the buttons off this dress, and I'll stitch them to your ass," she throws over her shoulder. "It took seventy hours to have them all sewn on!"

"For fuck's sake, Thalia." He stalks after her.

"Fashion!" Thalia retorts. And then she winks at me. "Though I must admit, there might be a certain pair of boots awaiting Her Highness as my little gift."

"Really?" I squeal. "You got me the boots?"

Thalia rolls her eyes. "You were practically planning to mug me for mine. What else could I do?"

And everything is right with the world again.

Chapter Forty-Eight

Iskvien

It's not an enemy.

Nor is it, precisely, a friend.

"Your Highness," Theron says with a rasp, a red handkerchief knotted around his throat where my mother cut his tattoo from his skin. He goes to one knee. "I owe you a boon."

"A boon?"

The assassin tilts his face toward me. "You came for me. You sent your men to rescue me. I've never—" He breaks off then with a curse. "I wasn't expecting that."

He was in bad condition when we arrived at the Hallow. Somehow, when Baylor's elite group stormed Hawthorne Castle and rescued Imerys, they managed to stumble across each other, and Baylor dumped him here in Ceres, before meeting us at Eidyn. Thalia sent him immediately to the infirmary, and with everything that was happening, I'll admit I hadn't managed to spare him a thought until this moment.

"I sent you into that," I whisper, hating the fact he was injured on my behalf. "I knew better. I knew it would be a trap. And I still sent you into that."

"You were right," he admits wryly. "Your mother left an opening. I saw a chance and it was too good to resist. It was a trap."

I wince as I examine the bandage around his throat. "I'm sorry."

"I'm not." This time, he turns around, gesturing to someone near the door. "Because I succeeded in my task. I managed to rescue the girl before I took a swing at your mother. I had her hidden beneath the castle when you arrived. It's why I had to go back."

I recognize the fae woman by the door as Lithia, one of Healer Mariana's acolytes. She tugs on the hand of the small hooded figure at her side, and my breath catches as I realize who it is.

"May," Theron says in the gentlest voice I've ever heard him speak with. "May, come here and meet the Queen of Evernight."

"Hi," I whisper, kneeling down so I'm level with her. "You must be May. We met at Aska, remember? I'm Vi."

May takes a step to the side, almost letting go of Theron as she whispers, "You're *not* my mother?"

It's a question, and I suddenly realize that this little girl may have spent her entire life thinking I was until a few days ago.

Only to have that knowledge torn out from under her.

And I feel that.

All those years wishing for someone to come and rescue her. All those years wondering who I was, why I wasn't there for her. Mouthing my mother's vile platitudes. Living in fear within Clydain's walls, and yearning for someone to protect her.

She may as well have been Amaya.

And it occurs to me that while I may never carry another child myself, it doesn't mean we won't have more children.

You will never bear another child, the Mother of Night once said to me.

But I feel it—I feel that click of destiny—as if she knew this moment awaited me. And her choice of words was clearly deliberate.

"No, I am not the mother who gave birth to you." The breathless sensation stretches inside me. It's too soon to spring this upon her, and perhaps I need to discuss this with Thiago first, but I *know* this child will be mine too. "But if you'd like to, then you can stay here with me and Thiago. You'll be safe here."

Her lip trembles, her eyes darting.

And Theron—of all fae—goes to his knee before her,

583

taking her hands. "Remember what I said back in Hawthorne Castle? The woman who raised you was evil. Adaia was a wicked queen, right out of the fairy tales. And she lied. A lot. Prince Thiago is not the monster she told you he was. And Iskvien begged me to save you, because she is kind and she worried about your safety. Adaia was the monster. But now you're free. Now you're safe."

May gives me a wary look.

But she nods.

"Why don't you come and we'll see if we can find you something to eat?" I whisper, holding out my hand to her. "I'd like to introduce you to my other daughter, Amaya. I think the two of you could become very good friends."

"Okay," May whispers, curling her fingers in mine.

And as our eyes meet, I know I've never felt more right about a decision in my life.

* * *

The sound of two little girls squealing with laughter echoes through the castle.

Thiago rests on the parapet beside me, his mouth soft with an almost-smile. "Thalia's having the time of her life."

Indeed, Thalia's blowing bubbles of magic into the air while the girls try and catch them. They run through the gardens, giggling and squealing as they try to pop the bubbles. Every time they do, a fragment of song escapes—all that's left of Thalia's voice.

"And you?" I wrap my arms around his waist.

"It feels strange...." He pulls a face. "Strange to hear laughter through these gardens."

The whole castle feels like it's changed in the space of a day. I've caught the servants laughing more, and cook's already bustling honey cakes out of her kitchen as if there's a renewed demand for them.

This has been my home ever since the curse broke and my memories returned, but I know what he's saying: It is strange to realize that barely a month ago, neither of us even knew Amaya existed, and now we couldn't imagine a life without the sound of that laughter.

This was always home, but now it feels like *home*.

"I'm also wondering what my wife is up to," he muses, cutting me a look with that eyebrow. "Because you have a certain look in your eye."

I can't help focusing on the girls. "May has no one, Thiago. Andraste said she was an orphan she exchanged for Amaya at birth. She's spent her entire life thinking I was her mother—that we were her parents. Maybe she grew up fearing us, listening to the lies my mother told her about us. But there's a little part of her that has to have wondered about us. About whether we truly were as my mother painted us. This has to be hard for her." I finally confront the truth I've been avoiding for far too long. "And I cannot give you another child."

He draws back, examining my face. "You know I don't care about that. We have already been gifted with one daughter."

"I know...." I just... hoped. I never got the chance to hold Amaya in my arms when she was a baby. I missed out on so much. "I wanted more. And it would be nice for Amaya to have a sister. She's been through a lot—they've both been through a lot."

He strokes his thumbs up my arms, glancing once more at the girls.

"Are you trying to say—?"

"I want to formally adopt May," I blurt out. "I want her and Amaya to be sisters. And I want her to be safe. She's been cruelly used in this entire game. She deserves happiness. She's such a sweet girl, Thiago."

I want to protect that sweetness.

And maybe it's a means of healing the wounds deep inside me.

Because this time, the little girl was rescued.

And she was whisked away to a beautiful palace, where a family awaited her. A family who would love her. A sister who would adore her. And those sisters will never know what it felt like to have their bond broken.

I will protect them with all the power I can forge.

A moment of surprise flashes over his expression before he turns to me. He sees the single tear sliding down my face, and I know he understands everything I cannot put into words. "Then let's do it. Let's make our family whole."

Flinging my arms around his neck, I kiss him.

Right as a bubble floats up and pops right beside us, the crashing crescendo of waves breaking against a foreign shore echoing in my ear.

We break apart breathlessly.

"None of that, you two!" Thalia calls, hands on her hips as she looks up. Her eyes narrow upon Thiago. "Come down here and play, Your Highness!"

Two mischievous faces peer up at us from the gardens.

Thiago's fingers drop slowly from mine. "I believe I'm being summoned," he drawls.

"I sense a trap."

"So do I."

But the smile he flashes me as he hurries for the stairs is strangely boyish.

Maybe I'm not the only one whose inner wounds are healing.

* * *

Dinner is a boisterous affair as Baylor finally returns.

"Ah, the mighty warlord graces us with his presence," Lysander drawls as he slices turkey from the bone and deftly eases it onto his plate. There's a certain calmness to him again, as if the weeks away from me have done wonders to ease the fracturing of my mother's curse.

He even managed a smile at me earlier, though I daresay it will take a while to rebuild the shattered relationship between us, but at least he's willing to try.

"You look good, Baylor," Finn says, leaning back in the chair next to Lysander. "All that killing seems to have done wonders for the soul."

Finn looks terrible. He's lost weight, and Thiago said he's been hitting the training yard at all hours of the night and day. The two of them have been practically inseparable, though Thiago said Finn won't breathe a word about what happened on the battlefield between he and Eris. Instead, they hit each other and duel every morning. Apparently, it helps.

I can't even feel a hint of his emotions through the bond any more, as if he's locked it down tight.

The only thing we can do is be here for him when he's ready for us.

"Didn't see either of you cleaning up after the battle," Baylor says gruffly, taking a seat at the table.

Thalia claps her hands, and a swarm of demi-fey set about filling a plate for him. The girls crashed into bed half an hour ago, so the wine is flowing, and the language around the table has grown bawdier.

"Does this face look like it does cleanup?" Lysander looks horrified as he points at himself. "I kill, Baylor. I hunt. I am very good at doing both those things." He shudders. "But my organizational skills end with picking a good wine to pair with a meal."

Baylor breaks apart a bread roll, arching a brow. "Thought you must have picked a fight with His Royal Iciness, considering how quickly you both vanished once the fire burned down."

Thalia leans over the table. "Who is His Royal Iciness?"

It has to be Edain. I glance up too, chewing thoughtfully. "What fire?"

Baylor and Lysander share a look. One that says, *oh fuck, we weren't supposed to mention that.*

When no answer arrives, I set my knife and fork down. "*What.* Fire?" I turn toward Lysander. "You were supposed to keep an eye on Edain."

Lysander sighs. "I did. He had a little... frustration to work out."

It's Baylor who says it. "Edain burned your mother's tree down."

Thiago's hand settles over mine in comfort. He was there. He knew why I made the choice I made.

"The tree's... gone?"

Baylor scrubs at his mouth and nods.

Oh.

Just like that, she's gone from my life forever. I don't know how to feel about that. Except... "And did it make him feel better?"

Lysander, for once, cannot find a smile. "I don't think anything's going to make him feel better right now. Your sister returned to the north with Raith, and while your mother's gone, her curse still lingers."

"What curse?" Thalia asks.

Lysander swirls the wine in his glass. "Look, I'll share that information with my prince"—he glances toward Thiago—"if he insists upon it. But I'd prefer not to discuss it with all and sundry. The prick and I still have a reckoning to come, but airing his affliction is a little underhanded, even for me."

Thiago steeples his fingers together. "We'll discuss it later. In private."

Lysander gives him a grateful nod.

"So you've forgiven him?" Thalia demands. "Just like that?"

More wounds. The entire table is full of them.

"It's complicated." Lysander grimaces. "No, I haven't forgiven him. But I can still feel empathy for his situation."

"Oh, goddess." Finn pinches the bridge of his nose. "Tell me you did not fall for those pretty eyes?"

Lysander looks horrified. "The prince does some wicked things to tight leather, but fuck no." He scrubs at his mouth. "*No.*"

Finn narrows his eyes. "There is color creeping up your throat."

Lysander throws a bread roll at him. "He's poison."

"That's never stopped you in the past."

Lysander searches the room, then stops upon his brother. "Why are we focusing on my sex life when my dearest brother finally noticed a female existed?"

Baylor freezes with a spoonful of soup halfway to his lips. I could swear his hackles just rose. "What?"

Lysander points his fork at his twin. "Don't think I didn't happen to notice how much time you were spending in the Ravenal tents after Eidyn." He bats his eyelashes. "The Queen of Ravenal was practically hissing at you to stay away from her sister."

"Her sister?" both I and Thalia echo.

"Imerys?" Finn lowers his wineglass. "The sleeping princess?"

"She's not sleeping," Baylor growls. "She's been cursed."

Lysander snorts. "Only you could find the one female who absolutely cannot return any interest in you. I swear you do this to yourself deliberately. You're going to have the world's bluest balls."

"I am *not* interested in Princess Imerys." Baylor's face looks like thunder. "I was only seeing as to her welfare."

"Baylor," Finn says pointedly, "I can count on one hand how many times you've even remembered someone else's welfare. You are disturbingly single-minded, my friend. Eat, fuck, fight, sleep. Repeat."

"The Queen of Ravenal is not someone we want to irritate right now," Thiago warns.

Baylor closes his eyes, as if he's picturing punching a hole in the wall and then kicking all of us through it.

"Leave him alone," Thalia protests, circling the table toward Baylor and wrapping her arms around him from behind. "Maybe he'll break the curse? True love's kiss does wonders, after all...."

"For fuck's sake," he growls.

"That's not what truly happened," I can't help saying. "The Sleeping Princess of Somnus never woke. The thorns surrounding her tower crept across the entire kingdom, and a dark forest overtook the plains. Nobody has ever managed to get in to see if she's even still breathing. And it's been a thousand years."

"She's still there," Grimm says in my head, licking a paw at the end of the table where Thalia set a plate of milk on the placemat in front of him. *"Though is she still breathing? I guess the true question is... does she still require breath?"*

Everyone pauses.

"That's incredibly creepy, Grimm," Thalia says with a shudder, returning to her seat. She glances toward Baylor. "And perhaps a little inconsiderate. We'll break the curse, Baylor. I'll set my demi-fey to trying to discover anything they know about sleeping curses."

"Blaedwyn might know something. She owes me a favor. Or three." Since curses originated in Unseelie, she'd have to know more than we do. "And if not, then the Erlking might recall something."

"So we're just going to nip on up to the Erlking's castle and have a pot of tea with him now, are we?" Finn asks.

Baylor moves his soup out of the way and slowly rests his forehead on the table.

591

"Oh look." Finn rubs his comrade's back. "I think we broke him."

Slowly Baylor lifts his head. "Where's Eris?"

Finn's laughter vanishes as if it never existed. "Didn't anyone tell you?"

Thalia makes a throat cutting motion behind Finn's back.

"Tell me what?"

"Eris finally resumed her fae form after the battle," Finn murmurs. "She wanted some space, so she managed to activate the Hallow and vanished. North. Into Unseelie."

"And you didn't go after her?"

Finn's face blanches. "She didn't want me to go after her. She made that quite clear. And I don't know where, exactly, she went. But I'm pretty sure she's able to kill anything that might come her way in the mood she's in."

A moment of silence falls.

Lysander sighs, casting his napkin at his brother. "Good one, B. You just ruined dinner."

"He didn't ruin dinner," Thalia protests. "He has a right to ask. She's his friend too."

Thiago laces his fingers through mine. "Eris will return when she's ready to return. This is her home, and she knows she's always welcome here."

"Does she?" I want to believe it, but Eris had her own nightmares. "Grimm." I kneel down in front of him. "I wish to ask of you a favor."

"*A favor?*" The grimalkin stops licking his paw and turns those golden eyes upon me. "*You do realize I do not do favors. I expect payment for my services when they're offered.*"

My eyes narrow. "Do you really want me to run up a tally of who is ahead in this game of debts between us?"

His eyes narrow too.

But perhaps he's counting them out, for he merely stretches. "*Fine. I'll indulge you. Maybe I'm curious enough to grant you leeway. Do tell me.... What favor would you wish of me?*"

"Can you find Eris?"

His lip curls and his gaze slides toward Finn. "*What do you take me for? That sack of suet over there who could barely find his ass with his hands? Of course I can find her.*"

"What did he just say to you?" Finn demands, because even though he's not privy to our conversation—or Grimm's part of it anyway—there's a definitive sneer on the grimalkin's furry face.

"He said he will find her," I reply, meeting that implacable unblinking stare. "And he will keep her safe and provide company for her if she's alone. Until she's ready to return to us."

"Night's cold breath, Vi. I thought you liked Eris," Finn protests. "You want to send this furry carpetbag to drive her to frustration?"

"He's not going to irritate her." My words are entirely for Grimm. "That would mean he reneges on his part of the bargain. He is going to be the soul of courtesy. Polite. Protective. And even a friend for her if need be."

Grimm rolls his eyes. "*I think I'm going to cough up a fur ball. Or no... maybe I'm just gagging.*"

"Please, Grimsby." This time, it's Thalia who says the words. "I don't want Eris to be cold and alone."

Grimm freezes. "*Thalia,*" he warns. "*Don't you dare squeeze out a tear.*"

"Please?" It's a whisper.

For all his arrogance, he's claimed Thalia as one of his own.

Grimm looks at me. Then back at her. Then his shoulders deflate. "*You wretch. Fine. You win.*"

Thalia grins and drags him into a hug. She winks at me over his shoulder as Grimm miaows in protest and pushes at her chest.

"*You're rumpling my fur.*" He sighs as he looks at her. "*I will find Eris, and I will treat her as if she was a kit of my own. And I will bring her back—when she is ready—whole and unharmed.*"

With one last sniff, he bumps his head against Thalia's calves and vanishes into a shadow.

"I'll bet four hundred crowns that Eris is going to roast him alive," Finn says, clapping his hands with glee.

Baylor laughs gruffly. "I'll meet that bet—but I think she's going to come back scratching his belly, and then you're going to have to survive the insufferable little bastard's smug purring for the next five hundred years."

Finn pales.

Then he looks at me.

"Vi," he groans.

I give him a kiss on the cheek. "If anyone can find her, it will be Grimm. Besides"—I tear a fragment off my own bread roll—"maybe he'll keep your feet warm when you finally get her into bed."

"Did I miss something?" Baylor does a doubletake.

"Did *I* miss something?" Lysander demands, leaning forward and looking at Finn.

Finn gives me a very rude gesture.

"Seriously, are all the males in this room blind?" Thalia throws her hands in the air.

And for the first time in a long time, my laughter feels free and easy.

This is home.

This is family.

And even if Thalia howls with laughter as a bread roll is lobbed in her direction and one of her demi-fey tries to tackle it—with disastrous results—I know this chaos is my happy ever after.

Chapter Forty-Nine

Iskvien

There's just one last task to see to.

"Are you ready?" I ask Thiago as we stand before the entrance to Kato's throne room. Only the two of us were allowed to come, and I'm desperately missing the presence of Finn or Baylor.

My husband stares ahead, his gaze distance. "I am. I don't know if he is."

The two of them have worked out some sort of wary peace between them in the past week, but Thiago said Death's been strangely quiet within him ever since we started planning the logistics of this.

"Do you think he'll agree to our terms?" I blurt.

This all fails if Death refuses to leave.

"He said he wants to see Kato," Thiago replies. "He wants to talk with him. And then we shall see."

It's a start.

"Let them in," Kato calls, and his guards stand aside.

The negotiations for this were intense. There are precisely fifty guards in the halls, all of them brandishing spears as if they expect Thiago to suddenly forge his obsidian blade and go for Kato. They have the numbers. They're prepared for any eventuality.

Orlagh even stands at his side, one hand on her knife and the vial of light hanging around her throat. There's no hint of friendliness this time. Only focus and duty and a certain sense of grimness as she tracks Thiago's every move.

This could go so very badly.

Though I did pointedly remind Kato there's a Hallow here, though one unlike anything I've ever seen.

I think I finally know what it is.

It's a portal, like the others, but this time, it's a portal to another world.

The Underworld.

And if he dares go back on his bargain and attacks us, then I'm quite happy to show him what an Old One can do with the power of a Hallow.

"Don't burn anything." Thiago gives me an amused glance, as if he knows exactly what I'm thinking.

"No promises," I tell him. "Though I will *try* not to. It all depends on Kato."

We march toward the throne.

"As promised, I will speak with the creature," Kato says arrogantly, sitting on his throne. "And then he will give himself over to the Darkness."

Thiago glances toward me. This is the moment where it could all go wrong. We don't know how Death will react if he's given free reign to rise within Thiago. Kato was one of the warriors who tried to destroy him, after all, and even though the entity within Thiago has changed over the years, there's still some part of it that was once the Shadow Sinister.

But we have no other choice.

If we don't do this, then Kato has promised us no relief. It will not be war. It will be assassins when we least expect it, treachery at every turn.

And Death has agreed to... consider giving himself up.

"Be ready," Thiago tells me.

"Always," I promise him fiercely, because he knows I will fight for him in this moment.

Turning his face to the ceiling, he stills.

A ripple shivers over his expression. A change. And when he opens his eyes and locks that stark gaze upon the Lord of the Underworld, I know my husband is gone.

"Hello, old friend," Death mocks.

Kato stiffens. "What do you want?"

Death takes a threatening step toward the dais. "You know what I want," it croons, shadows rippling toward it.

Kato actually pales, but it's Orlagh who steps between them, drawing the sword at her side.

"Get you back, you dark fiend," she spits. "You promised not to harm my husband."

"Did I?" Death smiles, turning all his focus upon her. "I said I would talk to...."

And then he freezes as the drop of sunlight within the vial around her throat starts to glow.

"I'm not afraid of you," she snaps. "My kind was born to hunt yours." A line of light springs down the edge of her sword, as if she's dipped it in sunlight too. "Bring your blade of Darkness, you wretched thief. And it shall dance with mine."

"Orlagh." Kato shoves himself between them, flashing her a look.

But Death doesn't move.

It anything, he actually looks like he's paled too.

"Where did you get that?" he whispers, his gaze locked upon the vial around her throat.

Orlagh's hand curls around it. "It was gifted to me by my mother."

"Where did she get it?" he snarls, shadows rising high behind him as if they're prepared to strike.

"Thiago." I grab his arm, but Death cuts me a dangerous glare.

"*Do not meddle here*," it whispers in my head, somehow using the bond between me and Thiago, which is disturbing enough in itself.

Orlagh and Kato share a look, as if this conversation is going awry of their expectations.

"*What is going on*?" I hesitantly ask it.

And then Orlagh speaks again. "It has been gifted down through my line for centuries. My mother received it from

599

her grandmother, and so on. All the way back to my many times removed great-grandmother."

"Carolain," he says, his voice so rough I can't quite pick the emotion that charges it. "Was her name Carolain?"

Orlagh stares at him. "Yes. How did you know that?"

All the threat and menace seem to deflate from Death's figure. His shadows fray until he looks like my husband again, albeit with those haunting black eyes that can't seem to tear themselves from Orlagh's face.

"How did you know that?" Orlagh demands, angry now. "What is going on here? What does the vial have to do with anything?"

Kato grabs her arm as if in warning.

But Death has subsided, staring down at his hands as if he sees something else when he looks at them.

"I will give myself up," he says in a voice stained with grief. "I will give myself over to the Darkness, and willingly. On one condition."

What? I gape at him, barely daring to breathe, to hope....

"What condition?" Kato demands.

Death locks eyes with Orlagh. "You will visit me once a month. You and the daughter you are carrying."

Orlagh blinks, her hands clapping over her lower abdomen. "My what?"

"Daughter?" Kato barks, looking between them.

Orlagh shakes her head at him in denial. She didn't know either.

Kato's face is absolutely white with shock, but fury forms there. "Absolutely not," he hisses, shoving Orlagh behind him. "What do you want with my wife? And my child?"

Death gives a faint, bitter smile. "It seems you and I must come to some sort of terms for peace." His gaze seeks out Orlagh. "Carolain was my wife. And Orlagh, and the child she carries, are of my line. I only wish for what any great-grandfather wishes. To know them. To watch them grow and flourish." He pauses. "And to help soothe the ache that will come when the child reaches her teenage years and must face the seed of Darkness within her. For there is only one vial of sunlight, is there not? Only enough to allow Orlagh to hide from that kernel of Darkness deep within her. So she must make the choice to give her child the vial and accept her own dark nature, or to allow her daughter to give herself to the Darkness within her."

Orlagh's face absolutely blanches. "I am a Lightbringer."

"And a Child of Death," Death says, not unkindly.

For the first time since I've met him, Kato has absolutely nothing to say.

"Can you learn to love the Darkness within your wife?" Death asks him.

Kato sinks onto the dais. "Of course I love her."

Death hesitates. "My kind were not all monsters. I can help them... learn to overcome the urge to reap. I can help them control it."

Kato stares at him.

Just stares.

And so Death takes the first step.

He reaches a hand out for the Lord of the Underworld, drawing him to his feet. "I forgive you for what was done to me. I will endure Darkness, for them. But I must have your promise. I cannot.... I cannot face the Darkness alone without some sense of hope. Allow me this.... The chance to learn to know them."

Kato finally rallies. "That is not my choice to make."

They both glance toward Orlagh, who looks like she wants to throw up. But she nods. Closes her eyes and nods, as if she can't quite bear to face the consequences of her choices.

"Your word upon it," Death insists.

"I promise once," she whispers. "I promise twice. I promise thrice. I will visit you once a month with... my child." Her voice hardens. "But not in the Darkness. I will not take my child into that place."

Kato frowns.

"Dinner, once a month," she tells her husband. "Here. At home. You will fetch him for me."

"I promise thrice," Kato finally agrees.

And Death looks at me. "Goodbye, Queen of Evernight. I wish you both well. Tell him.... It has been an honor to know him."

And then he conjures a dark flame between his fingers.

"Quickly," Kato says, and his guard's step forward with a soul-trap.

They capture the flame within the trap, and Thiago sucks in a sharp breath, as if he hasn't drawn one for minutes.

Kato stares at the soul-trap the guard places in his palm for long seconds.

"You promised him," Orlagh whispers.

Nostrils flaring, he hands it to one of his guards. "Return this to the Darkness. And then... release him."

Orlagh gives his hand a squeeze. The look they share is intimate, shocked, still processing everything that has just happened, but his palm comes to rest upon her lower abdomen and their eyes meet as if they simply cannot believe this turn of fortune.

I push past them, hurrying to Thiago's side.

Green eyes meet mine. He stares at his hands in shock. "He's gone?"

I throw myself into his arms and he squeezes me tight, holding me as if he never truly dared believe this could happen. "I can't feel the cold anymore. I can't feel the Darkness."

I draw back, kissing his mouth.

When I finally come up for air, his smile is absolutely radiant.

"Please tell me the other gifts remain?"

An invisible touch tickles my side. "That one was mine alone."

I slip my hand inside Thiago's, still struggling to come to terms with the truth of what just happened. But my heart feels fit enough to burst. "Let's go home, my love." Unable to keep the grin off my face, I kiss his cheek. "Let's go home and celebrate."

THE END

WHAT'S NEXT?

Thank you so much for reading **Curse of Darkness**. This world has been a story that's been bursting out of me for years, desperate to be told and I'm so grateful to have had the opportunity to give Thiago and Vi the HEA they deserve.

What's up next?

As Andraste says, it's complicated.

One princess. A goblin husband she owes a debt to. And the fae prince who sold his soul for her....

If you want to know what really happened when Andraste was sent north as a bride to a goblin king (or one of them, anyway), then keep an eye out for **The Uncrowned King,** coming in 2023.

* * *

Want to know when my next book is released? Want behind-the-scenes exclusives? All the McMasterverse news?

Sign up to my mailing list at:
https://becmcmaster.com/gift/

Or follow me on:

TikTok: @becmcmasterauthor
Instagram: @becmcmasterauthor
Facebook: facebook.com/BecMcMaster/

Want to chat with other reader?
Join my Facebook group:
The Company Of Rogues
facebook.com/groups/860001327471449

Also by Bec McMaster

DARK COURT RISING

Promise of Darkness

Crown of Darkness

Curse of Darkness

The Uncrowned King

Novellas in same series:

Seduced By Darkness

LEGENDS OF THE STORM SERIES

Heart Of Fire

Storm of Desire

Clash of Storms

Storm of Fury

Master of Storms

Queen of Lightning

Legends of the Storm Boxset 1-3

COURT OF DREAMS SAGA

Thief of Dreams

Thief of Souls

Thief of Hearts

CLAIMED BY THE DEMON

Prince of Ruin

LONDON STEAMPUNK SERIES

Kiss Of Steel

Heart Of Iron

My Lady Quicksilver

Forged By Desire

Of Silk And Steam

Novellas in same series:

Tarnished Knight

The Clockwork Menace

LONDON STEAMPUNK: THE BLUE BLOOD CONSPIRACY

Mission: Improper

The Mech Who Loved Me

You Only Love Twice

To Catch A Rogue

Dukes Are Forever

From London, With Love

London Steampunk: The Blue Blood Conspiracy Boxset 1-3

London Steampunk: The Blue Blood Conspiracy Boxset 4-6

DARK ARTS SERIES

Shadowbound

Hexbound

Soulbound

Dark Arts Box set 1-3

BURNED LANDS SERIES

Nobody's Hero

The Last True Hero

The Hero Within

The Burned Lands Complete Trilogy Boxset

SHORT STORIES

The Many Lives Of Hadley Monroe

Burn Bright

About the Author

Kidnapped by a dread pirate when she was a child, USA Today Bestselling Author, **BEC MCMASTER**, was raised on myth and legend, and offered her younger siblings to the goblin king many a time. Unfortunately, he did not accept.

Now she writes epic fantasy romance with a dark and sexy twist, which is almost as much fun. She has a secret weakness for villainous heroes, wicked fae princes and dangerous vampires, though in all her daydreams she's the one rescuing them.

Bec lives happily-ever-after with her very own hero and princess-in-training in the wilds of Australia, where she can often be found drinking tea or plotting her next travel adventure.

Escape the ordinary at
www.becmcmaster.com